ROCK STAR

A Literary Guild Dual Main Selection

(more...)

"Nobody does it like Jackie Collins.... *ROCK STAR* is Collins at her unmatched best. From the instant *ROCK STAR* opens, you're caught.... Collins' pacing has never been tighter, carrying the action and reader along higher and higher until her usual climax of suspense, danger and trial by fire.... *ROCK STAR* stands head and shoulders above the rest of popular fiction today."

—*Daily Nebraskan* (Lincoln)

"Collins' devotees will...relish the snappy dialogue, whirlwind pacing, irreverent humor and opulent locales that are her trademarks."

—*Publishers Weekly*

"*ROCK STAR* is engrossing.... The world of rock and roll is brought vividly to life.... Jackie Collins... displays a knowledge of what goes on behind the scenes ...and let's not forget the rock stars' sexual interplay. I was compelled to read every page to find out just what happens to this unlikely, but fascinating, trio of rock stars, and I know you will be, too."

—Kathryn Falk, *Rave Reviews*

"Jackie Collins pulls out all the stops with a strong vein of suspense.... You'll have a marvelous time."

—*Washington Post*

"Jackie Collins' act is polished to a diamond gloss."

—*Detroit News*

Jackie Collins

Rock Star

POCKET BOOKS

New York London Toronto Sydney Tokyo Singapore

POCKET BOOKS, a division of Simon & Schuster Inc.
1230 Avenue of the Americas, New York, NY 10020

Library of Congress Catalog Card Number: 88-3264

ISBN: 0-671-70880-5

First Pocket Books printing January 1989

10 9 8 7 6 5 4

POCKET and colophon are registered trademarks of Simon & Schuster Inc.

Printed in the U.S.A.

FOR MY BROTHER,
BILL COLLINS,
WHO HAS ALWAYS
BEEN THERE FOR ME

LOS ANGELES 1987
Saturday, July 11th

★ ☆ ★ ☆ ★

It was a perfect cloudless Los Angeles day. The Santa Ana winds had driven off the smog, and Saturday, July 11th, dawned crisp and clean, settling into a seductively lazy heat.

Kris Phoenix awoke early. Unusual for him, but he had flown in from London the previous afternoon and gone straight to bed. Fourteen hours later he surfaced in his oversize California King bed, in his oversize palatial Bel Air mansion, and rolled over to find that his Los Angeles girlfriend, Cybil Wilde, had joined him sometime during the night. Fortunately for her, she had not tried to wake him. Sex was great, but woe betide anyone who came between Kris and his jet lag.

Cybil slept on, her nineteen-year-old body smooth and naked, long, honey-blond hair fanning out around her wholesomely pretty face.

Cybil Wilde was a highly paid, extremely visible commercial model. Not quite Christie Brinkley, but on her way. Recently she had appeared on the cover of *Sports Illustrated* in a revealing one-piece swimsuit. Now the offers were pouring in, but Cybil never accepted anything without deferring to Kris's superior judgment. And he preferred having her at home—whether he was there or not.

He debated waking her; after all, it was several weeks since they'd seen each other. Then he remembered the concert tonight, and decided he could wait. Astrid, his London live-in, had not exactly let his motor idle. In fact, Astrid was a maniac in the sack, she never left him alone.

Astrid, the clothes designer. They'd met four years ago in Paris, when his manager hired her to design some leather pants for him, and she'd ended up feeling a lot more than the material. At twenty-eight, Astrid was nine years older than Cybil, but she had the requisite long blond hair and knockout body, plus she was Danish, and everyone knew about Scandinavian women. He liked his women blond and long-legged, with a big bosom and an amiable disposition. What more could any man ask?

Silently Kris stepped from bed, making his way into his black, mirrored, high tech bathroom.

Fortunately he'd managed to stay sober on the flight from London. It was amazing the difference it made—he actually felt like a human being. And on close inspection in the mirror above his black marble sink, he actually looked like one.

Kris Phoenix was thirty-eight years old. He had intense ice-blue eyes, longish dirty-blond hair subtly streaked by the sun (and if the sun wasn't around, an English hairdresser called Spud took care of it), and rakish good looks. Neither tall nor short, he hit a comfortable five feet ten inches—and since taking up weight training he was all dynamic body power and rippling muscles. Hardly Arnold Schwarzenegger—more Bruce Springsteen fused with Mick Jagger.

Kris Phoenix was a rock star. A very famous rock star indeed.

In fact, some said, Kris Phoenix was a rock legend.

All that talk never bothered him. As far as he was concerned he made music, sang songs, and played a mean guitar. So did a lot of other guys. Kris reckoned he had a hold on reality. Just because he divided his life between two fantastic mansions, made millions of dollars a year, owned seven cars, and kept two beautiful live-in females, that didn't make him any different inside. He would always, deep down, be plain Chris Pierce from Maida Vale, London. There was no getting away from the fact that his mother once scrubbed other people's floors, and his stepfather drove a bus.

"Ohh . . . my . . . God! You . . . are . . . *sooo* . . . sexy!" Cybil barefooted her way into the bathroom, and it wasn't only her feet that lacked coverage. "I've really missed you, Kris!" she sighed, throwing her arms around him.

Suddenly Astrid the maniac began to fade from his thoughts.

"You too, kiddo," he replied, kissing her warm, inviting lips.

She rubbed her full breasts against his bare chest, knowing full well what that would do to him.

One snag. Sex was out on the day of a performance. Only somebody should tell the massive hard-on growing in his pajama pants.

Regretfully he pushed her away. "Leave it out, Cyb. Y'know the rules, and tonight's that goddamn private gig for Marcus Citroen."

Snaking her arms around his waist, she rocked him back toward her. "How about a private gig just for me?" she whispered in her best sexy voice. "After all, I *am* asking nicely. And I promise I'll be good." A meaningful pause. "Very good."

There was no way Kris would break his rule. And no-body—not even the gorgeous Cybil Wilde—could make him. On the day of a performance he was like a fighter entering the ring, he needed every ounce of his precious sexual energy. Not one drop got spilled until it was all over.

"Later," he promised, disengaging himself and moving purposefully toward the shower.

Cybil pulled a disappointed face.

"I said later, luv," he repeated, flashing his famous crooked grin as he stepped under the icy needles of water and grabbed a bar of lemon soap.

Lathering his chest, he decided the shower felt good. Freezing water. Freezing out the old sexual urges. Making him feel alive and alert, ready for anything.

Anything except a private performance for Marcus son-ofabitch Citroen.

Coldly Kris reflected on how much he loathed the powerful record magnate.

And with dull resignation he realized there was nothing he could do about it.

Not yet anyway.

Rafealla alighted from Marcus Citroen's private jet and entered Marcus Citroen's personal Mercedes stretch limousine waiting on the tarmac. She nodded curtly at the driver, and was relieved to see upon entering the limo there was no welcoming committee to greet her.

Great, she thought, *no one to bother me until I reach the hotel.*

She was wrong. As soon as she settled back, the driver requested that she pick up the car phone. "Mr. Citroen on the line," he said reverently.

"Thanks." Her voice was flat. Marcus Citroen followed her every move. She couldn't go to the bathroom without his knowing about it.

"Hi, Marcus," she said listlessly.

"Mr. Citroen will be with you in a moment," replied the velvet-toned voice of his ever-so-efficient secretary, Phoebe.

Rafealla waited. Marcus liked to keep people waiting; she had seen him do it countless times. "Builds character," he would say dryly, with just a hint of the European accent he had never quite managed to get rid of.

Nervously she leaned forward and asked the driver if he had a cigarette.

"I gave it up," the man said with an apologetic shrug. "Would you like me to stop and get you a pack?"

"No," she said, shaking her head vigorously. She too had given up the dreaded habit, although right now she was prepared to kill for the chance of one long deep drag on *anything*.

"Rafealla?" Marcus's voice. The slight accent. The oily thickness.

"Yes, Marcus."

"You're here."

Of course I am, you summoned me, didn't you? "Yes."

"Was your flight comfortable?"

"Very."

"Good, good." He cleared his throat. "I have booked you into a suite at L'Ermitage. I'll call you as soon as you get there."

Yes. Probably the moment I walk through the door. "Fine," she said coolly.

"Rafealla?"

"Yes."

"You won't regret your decision."

Ah, but I will, Marcus. I will.

He had given her no option, she thought, running a hand despairingly through her long, dark hair. With a deep sigh she slumped back against the plush leather seat.

Rafealla. She was known by just one name.

Rafealla.

When she sang, her voice evoked magic. Sultry nights and smoky nightclubs, for she did not sing of virgins and fresh young love, she ventured back to Billie Holiday territory and the blues. At twenty-seven years of age she knew plenty about the blues. More than she ever should have known.

Rafealla was an exotic beauty. Green-eyed, with sharply etched cheekbones, a wide, luscious mouth, and a deep olive complexion. Her dark hair, straight and shining, swept in a curtain to her waist. She was slight of build, not voluptuous—but her body was still quite something in the oversized man's suit and thin silk top she wore.

Rafealla had risen to the heights from nowhere, it seemed. Eighteen months ago she had been unheard of. Now she was a star. Burning bright. A meteor streaking her way to the top of every record chart in the world. And whereas she had imagined stardom would bring her freedom, exactly the opposite had happened. Stardom had brought her Marcus Citroen. And she hated him with a deep and burning passion.

"Bobby Mondella, do you have any idea how much you are loved?" the pretty black woman crooned affectionately as she perched on the edge of a large circular desk. Her name was Sara.

Bobby, sitting in a comfortable leather chair next to the desk, reached out to touch. "Tell me, girl, tell me good."

Bobby Mondella gave new meaning to the word "handsome." In his thirties, he was tall, well over six feet, with dark-chocolate skin, curly jet-black hair, and a great body.

"I'll do better than tellin' you, honey," Sara said enthusiastically, grabbing a random pile of press clippings from the desk. "I'm gonna read you some of the reviews comin' in on *Mondella Alive*. We are talkin' *dy . . . na . . . mite!*"

Bobby reached for the dark glasses covering his unseeing eyes, took them off, put them on again. He made the same gesture about a hundred times a day. It was impossible for him to accept the fact he would never see again.

"Yeahhh. *Dy . . . na . . . mite!*" Sara repeated excitedly.

"I know 'bout the reviews," Bobby said patiently. "The album's been number one on the soul charts for five weeks now."

"Six," Sara corrected matter-of-factly. "Six straight weeks, an' *still* goin' strong." She paused for breath. "Oh, sure, Mister Mondella. I know you've heard all about the *Billboard* rave, an' *Rollin' Stone*, not to mention the *L.A. Times, Blues an' Soul,* an'—"

"What's happenin'?" Bobby interrupted. "Whyn't you just get to the train station an' save me the trip?"

"What's happening," Sara said importantly, "is that all across the country, in this great land we call America—"

"Cut it, babe."

Ignoring him, she continued her speech. "In every little hick town—they are lovin' you, honey, but I mean *lovin'* you." She paused triumphantly, shuffling the stack of press clippings. "Want me to read you some of this stuff?"

"Sure," he said casually, not wishing to appear too eager, although hiding anything from Sara was almost impossible; she knew him too well.

"Ridgway, PA," she read crisply. "Bobby Mondella *is* King Soul. Buy *Mondella Alive* an' *really* get down, for Bobby Mondella puts more meaning into a lyric than anyone out there." She paused, then said, "You like?"

"Not bad."

"Hey—listen to Mister Conceited!"

"Bring your cute ass over here, I wanna play basketball."

"Will you stop?" she scolded. "Here's another one. The *Duluth Herald*. The return of Bobby M. makes for the finest soul album of the last decade. Since his unfortunate tragedy the Mondella magic is hotter than ever."

Sara's sweet voice droned on, heaping praise upon praise, superlative after superlative.

Listening carefully, Bobby couldn't help being delighted by all the extravagant praise. It was good to be number one again. Real good. Especially since everyone had counted him out, said he was finished, written him off as a has-been.

Everyone.

Except Sara.

And Marcus Citroen. Damn him.

Bobby felt the hate envelop him like a noxious cloud. He loathed the man, and for good reason. But he had to admit that Marcus Citroen was the only one who had given him a chance to come back—and back he was, with a vengeance.

"Enough, Sara," he interrupted quietly. "I want to get some rest before tonight."

"I don't know why you agreed to do this dumb fund-raiser," she grumbled. "Marcus Citroen and his rich friends don't deserve to be entertained by the likes of you. Especially your first live appearance since the accident."

How come everyone—including Sara—referred to his loss of sight as an accident? It was no accident, goddam-mit. It was a crime. And one day he would find out who was responsible.

"It's for an interesting event," he said shortly.

"Her event," Sara sneered, taking his arm and guiding him toward the door of his bedroom.

Her event. Bobby hadn't seen *her* since it happened. Nor had he heard one word from the coldhearted bitch.

Nova Citroen. Marcus Citroen's wife. The thought of being in her company excited and disgusted him. He wondered what she would do . . . say. . . .

Oh, Christ. Don't tell me I'm still hung up, he thought. *I can't be. I mustn't be. . . .*

As if sensing his thoughts of another woman, Sara withdrew. Her voice became cool and businesslike. "The limo will be here at three o'clock. What time shall I wake you?"

"Make it one-thirty." His hand reached for her smooth cheek. "An' I'll have a bacon sandwich with all the trimmings. Okay?"

"I'm not your resident cook," she said stiffly.

"I know, baby. But nobody—like I mean *nobody*—makes a better bacon sandwich than you."

Letting out a deep sigh of resignation, she realized she would do anything for Bobby Mondella, and he knew it. Whether he appreciated it or not was another matter.

Left alone, Bobby made his way over to the bed, took off his shirt, unzipped his pants, and lay down.

Nova Citroen. Now that he had started, he couldn't stop thinking about her.

Removing his dark glasses, he realized with a dull feeling of hopelessness he would never be able to set eyes on her again.

Nova Citroen could not decide which important piece of jewelry to wear that night. The Harry Winston emeralds were inviting, so green and rich-looking. A single huge stone surrounded with diamonds for her neck, matching earrings, outrageous ring, and a magnificent bracelet. But she had worn that set in February to the great annual Niven-Cohen-Moss Valentine party, and again to Irving and Mary's Oscar event. Twice in one year was enough, so she discarded the emeralds, moving on to the Cartier rubies.

Ah, such nice bright baubles, but a touch too jazzy for her requirements tonight.

Without hesitation she turned to the deep burgundy box that housed her new diamond necklace, bracelet, and earrings. No contest. She had known all along the evening cried out for nothing less than dazzling diamonds to complement her upswept white-blond hair and the stylish Galanos dress she planned to wear. So appropriate for a simple summer evening by the sea.

Nova Citroen's idea of a simple summer evening by the sea and the rest of the world's might possibly differ. Nova and her husband, Marcus, lived part of the year on Nova-roen, a magnificent twenty-five-acre estate perched on the top of a high bluff overlooking the Pacific Ocean a few miles past Malibu. The estate boasted two separate mansions—one especially for guests, an Olympic-size swimming pool, three north-south tennis courts, a recording studio, a fully equipped gym, a luxurious movie theater, stables for their expensive Arabian horses, and garage space for Marcus's collection of immaculately restored antique cars.

They called it their weekend hangout. Only this particular weekend a little more than hanging out was taking place. Nova and Marcus Citroen were hosting a fund-raiser for Governor Jack Highland—*the* fund-raiser of the year. An exclusive black-tie affair for fifty couples, each of whom had paid a hundred thousand dollars per couple for the privilege of being there. It was called protecting their future. And a very select group they were too. Nova had been ruthless in her choice of whom she would allow to attend. Once word got out that it was an impossible ticket, everyone clamored to part with his money. After all, those in the know felt that Governor Highland was a sure thing for the next President.

Nova was suitably pleased with her final guest list. Only the crème de la crème. The richest, the most powerful, the most talented, and the most famous. She had not wanted too much Hollywood—her desire was to attract the *real* power, with just a scattering of rare stardust. And she had succeeded. They were flying in from all over the world.

The evening she had planned for her guests was spectacular. A five-course open-air dinner catered by the ultrachic Lilliane's restaurant. Followed by a surprise concert, where three of the biggest recording stars in the world would appear. The legend—Kris Phoenix. The comeback—Bobby Mondella. And the rising star—Rafealla.

One night. Five million dollars raised for Governor Highland's forthcoming campaign, and that was *before* the silent auction and raffle, where anyone, for a thousand dollars a ticket, could win prizes ranging from a case of Cristal champagne to a Mercedes coupe.

Clasping the magnificent diamond necklace to her throat, she decided it would be perfect for later, and carefully replaced it in its velvet-lined box. After all, she had a certain reputation to live up to. She was known for her fabulous jewelry collection.

Nova Citroen was an elegant-looking woman in her early forties, with lightly tanned skin, fine aquiline features, and mesmerizing violet eyes. Men got lost in Nova's eyes. They were her greatest asset. She was not beautiful, but seductively attractive, with a body slim to the point of anorexia. It suited her, enabling her to look wonderful in clothes.

"Excuse me, Mrs. Citroen." Discreetly, Norton St. John, her personal assistant, entered the room. "Mr. Citroen would like to speak to you. He's on your private line."

"Is he?" For a moment she considered telling Norton to inform Marcus he could go to hell. It was a pleasurable idea, but one she thought better of. Marcus Citroen was her continuing ride to the top, and much as she detested him, she was aboard for the entire trip.

Speed liked money. Only one snag. Money didn't seem to like him. Every time he made a bundle—something happened. He'd win at the track and some big-boobed bimbo would take it all from him. He'd score in Vegas. Whammo! A showgirl or two would step into the picture and it was all over. When he worked legitimately, which wasn't a steady activity, his ex-wife's lawyer was on his case within hours of his first paycheck. What was it with him and his freakin' luck? He just couldn't figure it out.

And then, one day, a meeting came to pass with a dude named George Smith, and Speed finally knew his fortunes were about to make a drastic U-turn. There was a big job going down, and George Smith wanted him in, because goddammit, Speed was the best freakin' driver in the whole of Southern California, and let nobody forget it.

There had been several meetings since the first one, and now today was D-Day, and Speed knew exactly what he had to do.

Dressing carefully in the gray chauffeur's uniform he had hired from a Hollywood costumer, he admired his reflection in the long hall mirror of his one-room apartment.

So he wasn't very tall. Big freakin' deal. Nor was Dustin Hoffman.

So the hairline was receding. Big freakin' deal. Mr. Burt Reynolds had the same problem.

So he had the features of an inquisitive ferret. Was Al Pacino a matinee idol?

Speed creamed over the way he looked. As far as he was concerned he was a real lady-killer. And when he had the money to back up his imagined charm, he was a hotshot with women. All women except his ex-wife—a platinum-blond stripper with bazoombas to break a man's heart, and nagging to break a man's balls.

Speed thought the uniform looked pretty ritzy on him. He admired himself for quite a few minutes before turning to other matters at hand. There were things to do before the evening's big caper.

He nodded to himself knowingly. This was the big score he had been waiting for all his life, and there was no way he was going to blow it.

Vicki Foxe had a strong urge to kick the grinning jackass security chief in the balls. Men. Sex. That's all they ever thought about. Most of them, anyway. There *were* exceptions—few and far between, and those always turned out to be the ones who played hard to get.

For a moment Vicki allowed herself to think about Maxwell Sicily—now *he* was an exception. Of course he'd crap in his pants if he ever thought she knew his true identity—but who the hell did he think he was dealing with anyway? Some dumb dingbat with big tits? Oh, no. When Vicki Foxe got involved in a business caper, she knew what it was all about.

George Smith my ass, she'd thought, when he first contacted her. And it didn't take her long to find out his real name. It never took Vicki long to find out anything.

"Are y'all wearin' a bra, sweetie?" The beefy man leered, staring bug-eyed at her greatest assets.

Up yours, dickhead, she thought. *What a cretin!*

If he ever saw her at her best he would go into cardiac arrest without pausing to make a will. Right now, skillfully disguised as a maid, she looked her worst. Her bright-red hair was scraped back in a bun. She wore little makeup on her face. And her truly sensational body (39 D cup, small waist and accommodating hips) was mostly concealed beneath a drab maid's uniform.

"Don't be so nosy, Tom," she scolded, flirtatiously batting her eyes at him, forgetting that she was not wearing the sweeping false lashes she usually favored. "It's none of your business, big boy."

Tom was chief of security on the Citroens' vast oceanside estate, and already, after Vicki had worked there for only six weeks, he was hot to do anything she might ask in exchange for a sexual favor or two.

"I'd sure like ta find out," he drooled.

"Well . . ." Suggestively licking her lips, she gave him a little body brush. "Whatcha doin' later?"

They both had a good laugh at that one. Later was the

big concert—the giant event. Tom would be up to his eyebrows handling massive security arrangements.

"If only we could watch the concert together," Vicki sighed, deliberately popping a button on her uniform, and then another, and then—very slowly, another.

Tom almost choked on his coffee. "You've got great ti—" he began.

Somebody walked into the service kitchen and he shut up.

Vicki quickly turned away, doing up her buttons. She could hear Tom's heavy breathing all the way out the door. And when the time came to take care of him, it would be no problem. Absolutely no problem at all.

Across town, Maxwell Sicily reported for work at Lilliane's, the exclusive Beverly Hills restaurant. Maxwell Sicily was twenty-nine years old, five feet eleven, one hundred and forty pounds, and of Sicilian origin. His hair was patent-leather black and greased back, his eyes brooding and close-set. His nose was too long, and his mouth too thin. But the overall effect was of a certain cold handsomeness. He looked like the son of a mob boss.

He was, in fact, the son of the infamous Carmine Sicily —one of the top drug kingpins in Miami.

Father and son did not speak. Maxwell had come to California to make it on his own. He'd certainly had the right training.

"Hiya, George," greeted Chloe, the pudgy supervisor who sat behind the desk at Lilliane's, answering the phones and keeping a sharp eye on the waiters as they punched in.

Maxwell nodded. At work they knew him only as George Smith—a suitable pseudonym.

"Hot today, isn't it?" Chloe said, coquettishly fanning her drooping bosom with a copy of *People* magazine.

Maxwell ignored her, thought better of it, and nodded a curt yes.

"I never got to ask you before," she said quickly, glad of an opportunity to chat with the handsome waiter whom she'd had her eye on ever since he started work there. "You're an actor, aren't you?" She gazed at him hopefully. "I'm right, huh? I can always spot 'em."

Maxwell repeated his nod. Thank God this was the last day he had to put up with this. Tomorrow he would be on a plane to Brazil with a king's ransom supplied courtesy of Mr. and Mrs. Marcus Citroen.

Maxwell Sicily couldn't wait.

KRIS PHOENIX
London 1965
★ ☆ ★ ☆ ★

Chris Pierce celebrated his sixteenth birthday three weeks after being expelled from school. He hit the streets with a vengeance, changing his name to Kris Phoenix, because he wanted—more than anything else in the world—to be a rock star.

His entire family thought it was the dumbest thing they'd ever heard. Out of school and out of work, he was not the most popular member of the household. Both his older sisters called him a lazy layabout. His stepfather said he should get himself a job and throw away the third-hand guitar he'd been strumming since he was thirteen. And his brother, Brian—considered the prince of the family because he'd landed a job as a bank clerk the moment he'd left school four years earlier—said, "Come off it, deadbeat. You're never goin' to get anywhere with your lousy voice and stupid guitar. Pack it in, make Mum happy for once."

Mum. Kris wondered why it always had to come back to Mum? Everyone knew she ruled the family with her loud voice and sarcastic tongue, but she hardly ever gave him a hard time, and it pissed them all off. Especially Brian, who liked to think of himself as her favorite.

16

The truth was, Avis Pierce was secretly pleased her youngest son showed signs of wanting to do something different. She had worked as a cleaner in other people's homes since she was fourteen, and was proud of the fact she'd done that *and* raised a family. Shortly after Kris was born his father was killed in an industrial accident, and for six years Avis had got by on her own. It was tough with four hungry kids to feed, but she'd managed, until eventually she met and married Horace Pierce, a bus driver, and a brave man to take on the responsibilities of a woman with four children.

Kris had no memories of his real father. Just a faded snapshot of himself balanced on his dad's knee when he was a few months old. His father appeared to be quite a lad with his spiky hair and crooked grin.

"Ah, yes," Avis would often say, a faraway gleam in her eyes. "'E was a real caution, your old man. Give 'im a beer an' a smoke an' 'e was 'appy as a pig in muck. 'E was a wicked bugger!"

Avis had a way with words.

Kris wished he'd known the father he looked just like. He never seemed to be able to communicate with Horace, who spent most of his waking hours glued to the front of the television.

While he was growing up, Kris had spent a lot of time with his mum. When he was a kid she used to take him with her on her rounds. Mondays, Wednesdays, and Fridays she cleaned the Edwards house on smart Hamilton Terrace. And Tuesdays and Thursdays, around the corner on Carlton Hill, she "did" for Mr. Terry Terence, a show-business agent.

The Edwardses lived in a five-story luxury house, with a permanent maid and butler. Avis was brought in to do the hard work, such as polishing floors, cleaning windows, and taking care of the laundry. Kris liked it best when the Edwardses had one of their frequent dinner parties, and early the next morning he was sent around the living room and the library to empty all the ashtrays. At eight years of age, pocketing the cigarette butts and producing them at school made him quite popular with the other lads.

The Edwardses had two daughters, snobbish little fair-haired girls. Kris developed a crush on both of them, but they never gave him the time of day.

Mr. Terry Terence was his favorite. Avis liked him too. "A real gent," she was fond of saying.

"He's a pansy!" Horace used to sneer, whenever his name came up.

It wasn't until Kris reached the ripe old age of ten that he found out what a pansy was.

Mr. Terence was an interesting man. He had an autographed picture of Little Richard in a pewter frame on his desk, and a large poster of Johnnie Ray in his hallway.

"Who's Johnnie Ray?" Kris asked one day.

"Johnnie Ray is the best bloody singer in the whole bloody world!" Avis replied with gusto. "I saw 'im at the Palladium once. Nearly wet me pants, din't I."

Mr. Terence thought that was most amusing. He gave Kris two Johnnie Ray singles, and threw in an Elvis Presley for good measure.

Kris listened to them on his sister's record player. He hated Johnnie Ray, was crazy for Elvis, and decided then and there—he was eleven years old—he would be a singer and learn to play the guitar.

Now, five years later, he was trying to do just that. Only it wasn't easy. In 1965, teenage boys with aspirations to rock & roll were everywhere. Ever since the giant success of the Beatles and the Rolling Stones every Young Turk in England fancied himself a future international rock star. The only difference was that Kris was dedicated; he thought of nothing else. Not even girls.

"Ain't it about time yer got a leg over?" his best friend,

Buzz Darke, asked one day. "I got two little darlin's lined up fer later. Whyn't yer come with?"

Buzz was always trying to drag him along on his girl-finding missions. Kris preferred to practice his guitar in the dank and dusty back garage attached to the old house Buzz lived in with his divorced mother.

"I thought we were goin' to play tonight," Kris said accusingly. "You promised me."

"Not *every* night we can't," Buzz replied in exasperation. "Cor! I don't believe it! Ain't yer interested in crumpet?"

"It's more important getting our group together," Kris said stubbornly. "If all you want to do is chase scrubbers instead of practicin'—fat chance we got of ever gettin' anywhere."

"Balls! I need t'get me leg over!"

"I'll practice with you then."

"Good. An' *I'll* tell yer wotcha missed."

"I'm pantin' t'hear," Kris replied sarcastically.

At seventeen, a year older than Kris, Buzz Darke had developed a look all his own. He never wore anything that wasn't black. He never smiled. He was thin and agile as a snake, and had a bruised, satanic look. Girls loved him.

Kris loved him too because they were soul mates when it came to music. They could spend hours on end discussing the merits of the Rolling Stones as opposed to the Yardbirds. Or was Bob Dylan's latest album better than the Beatles'? And who was the greatest soul singer in the world—Sam Cooke or Otis Redding? Also, Buzz could play a mean guitar—not quite up to Kris's standard, but pretty impressive all the same.

Kris had decided long ago he couldn't be bothered with girls. He had his guitar, his singing, and his treasured import record collection. That was his life. Besides, he always came off like dunce of the year whenever he got anywhere near a female. At school he'd never been able to understand any of them, and once he'd even caught two of them discussing him. "That Chris Pierce is a weirdo," one had said. "Yeah," the other replied. "He's got 'orrible starey eyes. Wouldn't like to come across '*im* on a dark night!"

That overheard conversation, plus the sneering giggles of the two little Edwards girls over the years, put him off the female sex altogether. Anyway, what did they know about music? Exactly nothing.

Buzz had set up a rehearsal room in the garage of his house. There was a third-hand drum set he had cadged off an uncle, a large tape recorder Kris had found on a garbage dump and promptly repaired, their joint collection of records, and a great-sounding stereo with giant speakers, a gift from Buzz's mum, Daphne—an emaciated-looking woman who wore too much makeup, constantly chain-smoked, and worked as a hostess in a Soho nightclub.

Kris liked Mrs. Darke, although she didn't seem at all mumsy with her stiletto heels and all-black outfits. In a funny sort of way she looked exactly like an older, female version of her son.

Sometimes, when Kris and Buzz were locked into their music, playing guitar riffs along with Chuck Berry—the great Chuck, who had taught them more than any music academy ever could—she would enter the garage and stand silently by the peeling paint of the old double doors. "Hmmm . . . not bad," she would say when they'd finished. "You boys are going to get somewhere one of these days."

Yeah, Kris thought, if only Buzz would give up on stupid girls and concentrate.

It annoyed him that his own mother hadn't heard him play in years—ever since he palled up with Buzz and moved all his stuff over to the garage. His family were relieved. "Thank God we don't have to put up with your bloody racket night after night," Brian had said. "You sound worse than the bloody cats around the dustbins."

Kris made up his mind then and there that if he ever made it, his brother would be the last person he'd invite to one of his concerts.

"Well, mate, see yer," Buzz said, throwing a tatty black scarf around his neck. "Sure yer don't want t'change yer mind?"

"Give 'em one from me," Kris said with as much enthusiasm as he could muster—and wondered exactly what he was missing, and why Buzz pursued it so relentlessly.

He didn't have to wonder for long. Soon he was lost in the magic of the music, playing along with his precious record collection, fighting Chuck Berry for a solo, shouting out the lyrics on a Little Richard track, marveling at the Ray Charles mastery on "What'd I Say."

Kris had taught himself everything he knew just by listening to the greats—starting off at eleven on an old acoustic guitar kept in the music room at school and graduating to his own third-hand electric model bought at thirteen with his savings from a paper route and a little help from his mum. Avis hadn't exactly encouraged him, although, to be fair, she hadn't discouraged him either. It was the rest of his family who were a pain in the neck, always bitching and complaining about the noise.

Getting together with Buzz—two likely lads with the same dream—saved him. They shared the rock star vision and were prepared to work hard to achieve it.

He was deep into a guitar lead on Buddy Holly's "That'll Be the Day," when he realized Mrs. Darke was leaning against the garage door quietly watching him. "Don't stop," she said, smoke curling from her nostrils.

So he didn't, allowing the music to envelop him, feeling the beat, the heat, letting his instrument become a welcome part of him.

When he was finished, along with the record, she

clapped, scattering cigarette ash on the floor. "You're not half bad," she said, walking toward him.

"Thanks," he mumbled.

"And not bad-looking either, for a kid."

Was he hearing right? Nobody had ever told him *that* before. Oh, sure, he knew he wasn't ugly—just sort of ordinary looking—maybe weird, if he listened to the girls at school.

"Tell me something—how come you're not out cattin' around with my Buzz?" she asked, squatting down on her haunches and flipping through some of the albums stacked against the wall.

"I'd sooner practice," he replied, trying not to stare at the thin line of flesh showing between her tight black skirt and form-fitting sweater.

She turned to look up at him, and to his embarrassment he felt a solid hard-on begin to grow in his pants.

"Don't you like girls?" she asked, staring at him intently.

"Uh . . . n . . . no . . . I mean . . . y . . . yeah," he stammered, wishing only for a locked loo and a *Playboy* magazine—for that was the only way he could deal with the urgent feeling in his pants.

"No?" she said, with an amused glint. "Or yes?"

He struggled to regain his composure. "Er, I like 'em okay," he managed, and repeated weakly, "I'd just sooner —y'know, like, practice."

"Hmmm." She licked her lips. They were thin, like the rest of her. And then, as if it was the most natural move in the world, she raised her arms and took off her sweater, revealing small hard breasts, with large purple nipples.

Kris actually heard himself gulp. The sound echoed across the dusty garage.

"You're sixteen," Mrs. Darke said matter-of-factly. "And I'm thirty-two, luv. It'll be better for you to do it with me than some messy little teenager who'll get herself knocked up before you can turn around."

Reaching for the zipper on his jeans, she pulled it down slowly. Then she touched his cock, which he knew was just about ready to burst. Springing it loose from his y-fronts, she deftly rubbed the tip, and to his embarrassment he came all over her hand.

A blush suffused him from head to toe, but Mrs. Darke didn't seem at all put out. "First time?" she asked sympathetically.

He nodded dumbly, too humiliated to speak.

"Don't worry," she continued. "You learned how to play the guitar pretty good. Now you'll learn how to make love to the ladies. Just lie back an' enjoy lesson number one. I'm the best teacher *you'll* ever have."

Having a secret thing with Buzz's mum was not exactly easy. Whereas before, Kris was always badgering his friend to practice, now he couldn't wait to get him out of the way.

"What's the *matter* with you?" Buzz asked irritably one day, after a long and not very good practice session. "This used t'be all yer wanted t'do, an' now 'alf the time yer screwin' up. We'll never get anybody innerested in us if yer carry on like this."

Kris shrugged. It was true. He *was* screwing up, but not on purpose. Somehow, for the time being, playing had lost its edge, and being with Daphne was a greater thrill.

"It's my bloody job," he muttered. "I hate it."

His mother had insisted he do something rather than just pick up unemployment checks. "It's about time, lad," she'd announced grimly. So he'd found work as a window cleaner, and it frightened the shit out of him every day when he had to ride on the precarious little platform hanging from the side of a multi-story giant office tower.

"Do somethin' else then," suggested Buzz. He'd got himself a job as an attendant at an amusement park for the summer, and was enjoying every minute. "I can pull twenty birds a day if I want," he boasted. "An' right little darlin's, too."

The truth was, Kris was undergoing a massive guilt trip. He'd discovered the joys of sex along with the culpability of sticking it to his best friend's mother. Plus his brother was getting married, which meant the atmosphere at home was chaotic, with Avis acting as if a royal wedding was about to take place.

Brian's bride-to-be, Jennifer, was the daughter of an accountant. Brian was marrying up, and Avis let no one forget it as she nagged them all about how they were to dress and behave in front of Jennifer's family.

Kris was elected best man. His mother made him hire a suit. It was too tight and smelled faintly of stale sweat. One day, he thought to himself as he stood behind his brother in the church, he was going to buy suits that he wore only once and then gave away—maybe to Brian if the bugger was lucky.

The summer progressed.

Kris's affair with Mrs. Darke progressed.

Buzz announced he was fed up with England and wanted to go abroad for a while, suggesting Spain. "It'll be a right giggle," he said. "Plenty of cheap booze, lotsa crumpet, an' I've 'eard we can get jobs playin' our guitars in the local restaurants an' bars. It beats stayin' here through the winter freezin' our balls off. Besides," he added with a knowing wink, "if yer don't get laid soon, yer balls are gonna *fall* off—without any help from the bleedin' winter, thankyouverymuch."

Buzz still had no idea of the steamy affair going on in his own house.

Weighing up the possibilities, Kris decided it wasn't such a bad idea. He had just turned seventeen, and nothing was happening. He hated his job. He hated the duplicity involved in seeing Daphne. He hated watching his mother arrive home every day, worn out, her hands red and chapped from cleaning other people's dirt. He hated listening to his sisters fight all the time. He hated the weekly Sunday visits from Brian and his uptight wife. And, worst of all, he was getting nowhere with his music.

"Okay, we'll do it," he decided.

"Fanfuckin'tastic!" yelled Buzz, quite elated for once.

Avis had a fit when he told her. "You're too young to go to one of them dirty foreign countries," she informed him. "They eat dogs an' drink filthy water in them disgusting places."

"Let 'im go," said Horace, an unusual ally, rousing himself from the telly. "It's about time 'e stood on 'is own two feet. 'E's old enough an' ugly enough."

Daphne Darke took the news calmly. She even helped pay for the secondhand bikes they bought and gave them money for the ferry trip across the English Channel to Belgium.

Kris had a funny feeling he would never see her again.

BOBBY MONDELLA
New York 1966

★ ☆ ★ ☆ ★

At sixteen years of age Bobby Mondella was a handsome, if blubbery (he weighed over two hundred pounds), singing star. "Sweet Little Bobby" as he was known, had made quite a few country & western hit records between the ages of eleven, when he had started to sing professionally, and sixteen—when it was suddenly all over.

His voice broke, and before you could say, "Two flop records in a row," Sweet Little Bobby was dropped by his record company, his manager, and all his so-called friends.

Mr. Leon Rue, his guardian/manager in Nashville, relinquished both appointments, gave him a check for six thousand dollars plus twenty-five dollars in cash, and put him on a plane back to his Aunt Bertha in New York, from where he had plucked him five years previously.

Sweet Little Bobby didn't know what had happened: one day he was churning out best-selling records, the next he was on an airplane heading home—and he was so used to doing what he was told that it seemed the right thing. It wasn't until the plane landed at Kennedy airport, and there was no one to meet him and no waiting limo, that slowly realization dawned. He'd been disposed of. Cleanly. Neatly. He was on his own. And the funny thing was, he didn't mind too much. No more pressures, no more non-stop work. He was free! And he was coming home to dear old Aunt Bertha.

Managing to find a cab, he got himself and his luggage (three suitcases filled with glittery stage and television outfits) into it, and set off for Aunt Bertha's house in Queens.

There was only one problem: Aunt Bertha had expired six months earlier, leaving behind six cats and a thirty-year-old daughter named Fanni, who was even fatter than Bobby.

Fanni's greeting was not friendly. "What *you* want, boy?" she screamed, standing on the doorstep, hands on ample hips, huge bosom quivering with indignation.

"I've come home," he said simply.

"You done *what?* This ain't your home no more," she yelled, attracting the attention of several neighbors, who leaned from their windows in rapt attention. Everyone within miles knew who Sweet Little Bobby was. Hadn't Bertha kept his picture in a frame on her windowsill? Hadn't she always talked of him proudly? Boasted about how she'd brought him up ever since her sister died when he was only two years old?

Yes indeed.

"Where's Aunt Bertha?" Bobby asked plaintively. He was beginning to feel tired and hungry, not to mention depressed—for he knew it was all over, and at sixteen that was a frightening thought, even if it did mean freedom.

"Don' give me none of that where's Aunt Bertha crap." Fanni mimicked his voice with mounting fury. "She done be ten foot under six months now, an' you don' even sen' no flowers. Big star my fat ass!"

Bobby felt the tears well up in his eyes. For five years he had been away from his aunt, recording, writing songs, performing. And all that time he had known that one day he would come home. Now that day was here, and Fanni was telling him that Aunt Bertha was dead.

"Mr. Rue would have t-told me," he stuttered. "I d-don't believe it."

"You callin' me a *liar*, cousin?" Fanni roared.

"Nobody told me," he repeated dully.

"Well, ain't *that* a good excuse." Sarcasm dripped from Fanni's wide, angry mouth. "I guess when you all are a *star*, little things like a *death* in the family are sure 'nuff kept from you."

By this time the cabdriver, a gum-chewing Puerto Rican, had dumped all three of Bobby's suitcases on the doorstep and was getting impatient. He started doing knee bends and cracking his knuckles. "Ya wanna pay me?" he asked. "Or mebbe I wait around, have a meal, play some pool, huh?"

"This boy ain't stayin' here," Fanni said firmly, indicating Bobby. "You kin put his stuff right back in your cab."

The Puerto Rican grimaced. "Hey, lady—I look like a porter? Ya wanna put his bags back in my cab? Sure. *You* put 'em there, Mamma."

"Don' you call *me* Mamma," Fanni cautioned, giving him a filthy look.

"Just pay me, lady," the cabdriver said wearily.

Suddenly Bobby remembered his check. Six thousand dollars for five years' hard work. Pulling it from his pocket, he handed it to Fanni. "This is for you if I can come home."

Fanni eyed the check, devoured the amount, held it up to the light as if it were a counterfeit bill, and then finally she said, "Inside, cousin. I'll take care of the cab fare."

Fanni lived with a man called Ernest Crystal. Ernest was large in every way. Six feet five inches in height, and a solid three hundred pounds. A former pro football player, Ernie did a little bit of this and a little bit of that. He had two ex-wives and several children. Right now he was staying with Fanni and not doing much of anything.

Ernest took one look at the six-thousand-dollar check

28

Fanni brandished in front of his eyes, and his face lit up. "Woman, where you get this?"

"Sweet Little Bobby's back."

"Holy mother! Don' you be tellin' me I finally stepped in *she-it!*"

Ernest and Fanni were married two weeks later, whereupon Ernest appointed Fanni and himself as Bobby's legal guardians. The first thing he did was drag Bobby around on a relentless tour of all the record companies. But he was too late to make a killing. Nobody wanted to know about Sweet Little Bobby any more. He was yesterday's news. A fat teenager with a baby face and a cracked voice.

Aggravated, Ernest then set about hiring a lawyer to find out what had happened to the rest of Bobby's earnings from the five years he had spent with Mr. Leon Rue. Six thousand bucks didn't seem right at all. And it wasn't. But Mr. Leon Rue had covered himself with legal documents giving him most of everything Bobby earned right up until he cut him free. Plus he owned every song Bobby had ever written.

"Shyster honky bastard!" Ernest complained to Fanni. "Your mamma musta bin some dumb woman. She jest signed the kid away. Now *we* got him back worth nothin'."

"We have ourselves six thousand dollars," Fanni said tartly.

"Pig swill," Ernest spat in disgust. "That honky cheater stolen hundreds an' thousan's of big bucks shoulda bin *mine*."

"Ours," Fanni corrected, double chins quivering indignantly.

"Yeah, ours," Ernest agreed.

Bobby couldn't help overhearing their discussions. He had the little room next to the kitchen, and most of the day he just lay on the bed munching cookies and candies, thinking about how nice it was just to laze around doing nothing. The five years he'd spent with Mr. Leon Rue were all work. Weekdays, weekends, and if he wasn't performing, Mr. Rue had him sitting at a table, writing. He had lost count of the number of songs he'd composed. No time to make friends or get to know anybody. A tutor kept him up with his schoolwork three times a week. A hooker gave him his first sexual experience when he was fifteen—paid for and organized by Mr. Rue. He hated every minute of it. The woman had hair like an oven-cleaning pad, and smelled of sour milk.

There were always lots of girls in the audience when he performed. They squealed and giggled, but he never got to meet any, and now it was over. The truth was, he didn't care if he ever sang or wrote another song again. He couldn't sing anyway—puberty had struck—and his voice was now an unfamiliar croak.

Mr. Leon Rue had discovered Bobby the day after the boy's eleventh birthday. Bobby was singing and playing the piano in a local talent contest, and he was good, having learned to do both at Aunt Bertha's weekly prayer meetings. The music came naturally to him and gave him enormous pleasure. It gave Aunt Bertha pleasure too. She encouraged her nephew and boasted about his God-given talent and pure falsetto voice to all her friends. Bobby won the contest and fifteen dollars, while Mr. Leon Rue won Aunt Bertha's confidence, and within weeks he had persuaded her to let him take over Bobby's career, become his legal guardian, and build him into a big singing star.

"It's for your own good, Bobby," Aunt Bertha whispered sadly when the time came to say goodbye. "This be the only way you'll ever get yourself a real chance."

Soon he was whisked off to Mr. Rue's large house in Nashville, where he was put to work writing simple country & western ditties. He was used to gospel, but he soon learned what Mr. Rue wanted by listening to countless country records, most of them with the same familiar cheating-lovers-and-lost-loves theme.

Churning out hits was easy, even though it failed to inspire him.

Bobby's six thousand dollars did not last long. Ernest needed a new car, which took most of it. And Fanni needed new clothes, which took care of the rest of it. Aunt Bertha had left her only daughter the house and a small amount of money. However, the time soon came when everyone had to get a job, including Bobby.

Fanni resumed her old position as bookkeeper in an accounting firm, and Ernest began working as a magazine salesman.

"What *you* gonna do, boy?" Ernest demanded belligerently. "Can't sit 'round here on your fat ass livin' off your cousin all day long."

Conveniently he had forgotten Bobby's six-thousand-dollar contribution to the family's fortunes.

Bobby had no idea what he could do. The only thing he knew was music, and that part of his life was over. He was sixteen years old and finished, and yet there had to be a future for him. Scanning the job ads, he circled anything that looked remotely interesting and did not require a college degree.

Five interviews later he found he had been turned down for a variety of reasons. Too young, too inexperienced, too fat, too uneducated, and most of all—too black.

Of course, none of the people who interviewed him actually came out and gave their reasons, but he knew. Living in New York, he was wising up fast.

Finally, after several weeks of looking, he tagged three years onto his age and got a job in The Chainsaw, a vast Manhattan discotheque, as a men's room attendant.

The final humiliation. Sweet Little Bobby no longer existed.

RAFEALLA
Paris 1967

★ ☆ ★ ☆ ★

It was Rafealla Le Serre's seventh birthday, and as she skipped along the Paris street hand in hand with her best friend, Odile Ronet, she could feel her heart beating fast with excitement. Odile had celebrated her own birthday ten days earlier, and she had received a bicycle—a fantastic shiny red bicycle.

Rafealla desperately hoped she would be as lucky.

Mrs. Macdee, her Scottish nanny, walking ahead with Odile's nanny, turned to scold the two little girls, but in an affectionate way. "Come along, do come along," she said briskly. "There won't be time to change into your pretty frocks if you don't hurry."

Rafealla giggled nervously, squeezing her friend's hand. Odile giggled too, and they whispered together about bikes and dolls and dresses and chocolate cake.

Nanny Macdee led the way as they turned briskly into the Avenue Foch, where Rafealla and Odile lived in neighboring houses. The two little girls kissed each other on the cheek and ran up the stairs to their respective homes.

"All this fuss! You're going to see each other in a minute," grumbled Nanny Macdee.

The front door was opened by a uniformed manservant.

Rafealla rushed by him, racing up the grand staircase to her room, where her party dress was laid out on the bed, just waiting for her to climb into. *Oh, what a beautiful dress,* she thought, gazing at the pink organza creation with its full skirt and white satin sash. Throwing off her school uniform, she attempted to struggle into it.

"Dearie me, no," stated an out-of-breath Nanny Macdee, as she entered the room. "We'll have a wash first, missy, won't we?"

Rafealla stifled a groan. Washing was so *boring*. She obliged anyway; arguing with Nanny just wasn't worth it.

Soon she was ready. Face washed. Hands scrubbed. Long, dark hair brushed and ribboned. Pink dress in place on her young, lithe body.

"*Now* we're ready," said Nanny Macdee, finally satisfied. "Come along, dear."

In the living room, Anna and Lucien, her parents, waited. Rafealla paused in the doorway so they could both see how pretty she looked. And then with a whoop of delight she ran straight toward her father, who swooped her up in his arms, swinging her around and around as if she were a limp rag doll.

"Papa! Papa!" she shrieked happily.

"Happy birthday, my sweet little sugar cake," he said in his wonderfully deep booming voice.

Wriggling free, she ran to her mother, who enclosed her in exotic fragrances as she hugged her close.

Out of the corner of her eye Rafealla spotted a pile of colorfully wrapped presents.

"Yes, they're for you." Her mother smiled, gently releasing her. "You may open them now."

To her great consternation Rafealla couldn't see any package that looked big enough to conceal a bicycle. With grim determination she began tearing open the fancy paper wrappings, wondering if perhaps her precious bicycle was divided into pieces and scattered among the presents.

"Not so fast," admonished Nanny Macdee from the doorway.

"It's all right, she's so excited," Anna Le Serre excused, watching her daughter with warm amusement.

"Just like her mother when she gets presents," teased Lucien, putting his arm around his delicately beautiful wife, causing her to gaze up at him with open adoration.

Nanny Macdee averted her eyes. She had never worked for people who were quite so openly affectionate as the Le Serres. They acted like a honeymoon couple, always billing and cooing as if no one else existed.

Nanny Macdee had been in their employ since Rafealla was born, and she had decided long ago it was because of Mr. Le Serre's background. He was . . . different. Not only was he famous—a great tenor who performed in the most prestigious opera houses in the world. He was also black—half Ethiopian, half American—and quite the most imposingly handsome man Nanny Macdee had ever set eyes on.

Anna Le Serre was the perfect foil for her giant of a husband—he was six feet five inches, and she was a bare five feet four. Her skin was alabaster white, and her hair raven black. Fine-boned and slim, she possessed a rare and gentle beauty, combining English and French blood. Once a promising ballerina, she had given up her career to marry Lucien—a career she now hoped her daughter would follow.

Rafealla had inherited the best of both her parents with her smooth olive complexion, luxuriant thick dark hair, long legs and budding beauty.

Her mouth turned down with disappointment as she unwrapped the last of the presents and discovered no cleverly concealed bicycle.

The doorbell rang, and her school friends began to arrive for her afternoon tea party. Breathlessly, Odile, in brown velvet with a white lace collar, asked to see her gifts. Her eyes commiserated with her friend when she realized a bicycle was not among them.

Tea was delicious. Cakes and scones and tiny little English tea sandwiches filled with cream cheese and cucumber, jam and chocolate spread. All of Rafealla's favorites. And then out came the cake, a huge confection of meringue and strawberries, with seven candles.

I'm seven, Rafealla thought in wonderment. *I'm almost grown up*.

Lucien picked her up and gave her a big kiss. "I love you, sweet-cakes," he said in his big, gruff voice. "You make my life so very pleasurable. And don't you ever forget it."

He then carried her into the front hall, where there was the biggest, the best, and the shiniest red bicycle she had ever seen.

With yells of joy she fell upon it. Her day was complete.

Later, when her friends had gone home—all except Odile, who, as a special treat, was to stay the night—they sat at the feet of Anna as she prepared for an evening out. Both little girls found it fascinating to watch as she applied makeup, pinned her luxuriant tresses on top of her head, and clipped on exquisite diamond-and-turquoise earrings and a matching necklace.

Rafealla knew for sure that her mother was extremely beautiful, and it made her very proud.

Nanny Macdee soon arrived to shoo the girls away. "Give your mamma privacy, for goodness sake!" she scolded.

They fled downstairs to the library, where Lucien was entertaining Odile's father, Henri, a prominent French politician. The two men were good friends as well as neighbors, and tonight they were attending an important political dinner together. Odile's mother, Isabella, was away visiting relatives in the country.

"What naughtiness have you two been up to?" Lucien demanded with a big smile.

The girls protested their innocence, and were each rewarded with a tall glass of forbidden Coca-Cola. Nanny Macdee would have a fit. No fizzy drinks, especially just before bedtime.

Anna entered the room, a vision in pale-lilac chiffon. "I'm ready," she said apologetically. "I do hope I haven't kept you waiting."

The men told her how lovely she looked, and she accepted their compliments with grace and charm.

Rafealla felt happy inside; it had been a lovely birthday.

"We'd better get moving," Lucien announced. "We cannot be late." He stared intently at his daughter. "There's something different about you, my sweet little girl. Ah, yes, I know what it is," he added with a chuckle. "You look like you must be seven!"

Amid much laughter the three grownups moved toward the front door. Lucien flung it open, standing back to allow his wife to pass through first.

"Oh, dear!" Anna exclaimed. "I forgot something. You start the car, I won't be a minute."

"We're going in Henri's car," Lucien said with a sigh of impatience. "Hurry up."

Smiling at Odile's father, she said, "You can't take Lucien's driving either, eh, Henri? I thought it was just me!" With that she hurried upstairs.

Rafealla stood on tiptoe to kiss her father, but even then she couldn't reach. Picking her up he whispered, "Sweet dreams, my baby girl."

"Papa, I'm grown up now," she protested.

"Ah, well." He kissed her affectionately. "In that case, sweet dreams, my *big* girl."

And then he and Mr. Ronet walked down the front steps and climbed into Mr. Ronet's silver Mercedes.

The two little girls stood at the open door waving as

Nanny Macdee came bustling up behind them with a cross expression. "You'll catch your death!" she complained. "And I'll be blamed. Now come along upstairs. Right now."

Obediently Rafealla turned away, ready to do as she was told. So did Odile.

"It's about time too," sniffed Nanny, not really as cross as she made out.

Anna was on her way downstairs, lilac chiffon flowing behind her as she rushed so as not to keep Lucien and Henri waiting. She had never looked more beautiful.

All of a sudden there was a roaring explosion. It came from the street. A blast so loud it sounded as if a bomb had landed on top of the house.

And then came the effect. Windows shattered as the full force hit, and they were all thrown to the ground and showered with lethal shards of glass.

Rafealla saw her mother begin to fall down the stairs, and it was as if she were watching a slow-motion ballet.

As pieces of glass embedded themselves in her legs, causing unbearable pain, she began to whimper.

"Papa," she called out in frozen terror. "Oh, Papa! Save us! Please save us!"

KRIS PHOENIX
1968

★ ☆ ★ ☆ ★

After a late start, Kris discovered sex with an enthusiasm surpassing even his best friend's.

"Cor blimey!" Buzz exclaimed one day, as they lounged on the beach in Majorca, a popular Spanish holiday resort. "You never bleedin' stop! At least I give it a breather once in a while."

Kris laughed. Two and a half years away from home, fending for himself, including a year and a half spent hitchhiking across Europe, had given him a new sense of confidence. He was not only sure he could be independent without scrounging handouts from his mum, but he was now secure in the knowledge that he could pull the birds with the best of them. He might not be tall, dark, and traditionally handsome, but at nearly twenty he had his own style. Crooked good looks, dirty-blond hair, a wiry body, and a solid suntan.

"Best thing I ever did was draggin' yer out of England," Buzz remarked.

Kris rolled over on the hot sand. He had his eye on two giggling girls in bikinis standing by the edge of the water. "I'm not gonna argue with *that*, mate." He squinted at the girls. "Which one you want?"

Buzz looked surprised. "Am I gettin' first choice for a change?"

"Yeah, why not?" Kris said generously.

"The one with the big tits," Buzz decided.

"Aw, *c'mon*. Do me a favor. Y'know you like 'em skinny."

"I feel like a handful today."

"Screw *you*."

The two friends laughed, while the girls, who knew they were being watched, pretended not to notice.

"*You* pull 'em, then," Kris said.

Buzz groaned. "I'm still recovering from that little Swedish raver last night. I can't bleedin' move, can I?"

Buzz had lost his eerie pallor, and was now a deep gypsy brown. He wore his black hair long and unkempt, and one gold stud earring decorated his right earlobe. He was so thin his ribs stuck out.

"Bloody hell!" Kris said, with mock annoyance. "Why have I always gotta do the pulling?" Leaping up, he swaggered across the sand toward the giggling girls. "'Ello, darlin's," he said confidently. "Speaka da English?"

They spoka da English all right. They were on vacation from Liverpool.

Taking a survey one day, both Kris and Buzz had decided that the easiest girls to have it off with were the English. A quick bit of the verbals and it was up, up, and away. Second were the Scandinavians—Swedish, Danish and Finnish—easy pickings. The local Spanish señoritas were a no-no, while German and French girls were a pain in the backside. And Americans—impossible, unless you romanced them and got them pissed—which took time and money. Neither of which Buzz or Kris was inclined to do.

After a brief chat-up, Kris led the two giggling females over to meet Buzz, and before long it was Sangrías (a lethal combination of red wine, fruit, and lemonade) all around, and playful gropings on the hot sand.

By sundown things were getting serious, and a romantic stroll along the beach led the way to a quiet wooded area, where after five minutes of concentrated foreplay it was time for the great moment.

Kris got off on that first plunge into a new girl. Every time he did it he thought of the two stuck-up little Edwards girls and the other girls at school who'd called him weird and wouldn't give him the time of day. When he jammed it into a new female he was doing it to all of them, and it felt good.

"Will I see you later?" his latest conquest asked, awkwardly hitching up the bottom half of her bikini.

"What hotel are you at?" Cleverly he avoided answering her question.

She told him and he nodded knowingly. "An' how long you stayin', luv?"

"Six more days," she said obligingly, adding hopefully, "Can I see you later?"

Ah, six days to avoid that particular beach and hotel, and then it would be safe again. "I wish I could, but I can't manage tonight," he sighed regretfully. "Whyn't I see you here tomorrow?"

And that was how it usually went. In and out and on to the next. Evenings were for work. A gig at a local restaurant, playing the guitar and singing—and then usually a late-night session at a club or discotheque where they got together with other musicians and really let rip. They were getting so hot on their guitars, they'd acquired quite a reputation, and any visiting players sought out the two English kids to jam with.

They had stayed in Majorca for nearly a year, sharing a one-room apartment. The weather was sensational, the booze cheap, and a continual stream of tourists kept the place interesting, not to mention hot and cold women on tap at all times. Before that they had traveled across Belgium, Germany, France, and Italy, taking jobs along the

way and enjoying every moment of their new-found freedom.

The drag was, they hadn't been discovered, and that
bothered Kris more than it did Buzz, who seemed quite
content to live his life in the sun without any of the hassles
of England. Kris knew for sure if they were ever going to
put a group together and try to do something decent, it was
not going to be in some Spanish holiday resort getting laid
regularly. Eventually they were going to have to go home,
whether Buzz liked it or not. England was where it was all
happening, and he was anxious to be a part of it. New
groups were springing to prominence all the time—he read
the trades, a couple of weeks late, but better than nothing.
The Musical Express and *The Record Mirror* were full of
success stories: Rod Stewart, the lead vocalist from the Jeff
Beck Group, was making his mark, and groups like The
Who, Yes, and Led Zeppelin were leading the trends.

It was 1968, and ever since the advent of the Beatles and
the Rolling Stones, England was hot. The swinging sixties
all started in London with fashion, movies, style, and most
of all—music. London was definitely the place to be.

One day, after receiving a letter from his mother, Buzz
said, "I think I'm gonna ask Daphne t'come an' stay with
us fer a couple of weeks."

Buzz never called Daphne Mum; he always referred to
her by name.

"Why?" Kris blurted out, forgotten guilt creeping up on
him.

Waving her letter in the air, Buzz said, "She's given up
'er job, chucked out that new bloke she was livin' with,
an'—I dunno—she sort of sounds on edge, y'know what I
mean?"

"Where'll she sleep?" Kris asked. "There's no room
here."

"She can have my bed. I'll kip on the floor. Yer don't
mind, d'you?"

Christ! Did Buzz know? Impossible. Daphne had sworn him to secrecy; she would hardly confide in her son.

Forcing himself to sound casual, he said, "I couldn't give a monkey's."

"Okay, I'll give 'er a ring then," Buzz decided. "I guess I can just about scrape up enough readies for 'er ticket."

Kris wondered if Daphne would expect him to resume service. He had no desire to do so. After all, he was no longer the innocent virgin she had initiated on her garage floor. It wasn't that he didn't like her, it was just that the guilt of giving one to his best friend's mother was too much to take.

Buzz went off to the local bar to call her, while Kris figured out what he was going to do.

He didn't have to figure too long or too hard. When Buzz returned he was pale beneath his tan.

"What's the matter?" Kris asked quickly.

Buzz sat on the edge of his bed, his thin face a mask of shock. "She topped 'erself, din't she? Daphne's dead."

Returning to England for the funeral was the most depressing thing that had ever happened to Kris. It was October, and he had forgotten the icy cold, the early afternoons where it was dark by four o'clock, the relentless drizzling rain, and the heavy traffic. Most of all, he had forgotten what it was like to live at home with his two sisters, both unmarried, shrieking at each other all the time. His stepfather, Horace, the television zombie. And his mum, Avis—still cleaning other people's houses and ruling the home front with her loud voice and bossy manner.

"Yer too skinny," she informed Kris sternly. "Why din't yer write? I could box yer ears, y'little bastard!"

Both his sisters stared at him jealously. The younger of the two said, "It's all right for *some* people, ennit? Just laze about in the sun all day an' don't send Mum no money. I pay for *my* room an' board."

"Don't get your knickers in a twist," Kris said quickly. "I'm not stayin'."

"Shame!" exclaimed his other sister, who had inherited her mother's sarcastic tongue. "Goin' off to *America* to be a *pop star,* are we?"

He couldn't stand his sisters, but his dislike for them paled in comparison to his relationship with his brother. Brian came over for Sunday tea trailing wife Jennifer, and two snotty-nosed kids. The two-year-old was the reason Brian had been forced to get married in the first place, and the baby, Kris figured out, was just to make *him* feel bad. Brian's smug face said it all: *I've got a job, a wife, and a family. What have you got, little brother?*

"It's about time you decided what you're going to do with yourself," Brian lectured pompously. "Don't you think it's a bloody disgrace the way you're worrying Ma?"

"Fuck you," Kris muttered, a low aside destined only for Brian's ears.

Unfortunately, the two-year-old caught the rhythm and proceeded to chant, *"Fuckoo, fuckoo, fuckoo!"*

"You lowlife scum," Brian said angrily. "Teaching my boy to swear. You're just a no-good layabout. Whyn't you start behaving like a man, cut your hair, and get a job?"

"Is that what you think being a man is all about?" Kris asked with a derisive snort. "Short hair an' some lousy job?"

"I don't have to worry about it," Brian puffed self-righteously. "You're the one that looks like a bloody queer."

Kris started to laugh, which infuriated Brian even more.

Avis cracked the whip. "Will you two shut up?" she said, her loud voice booming across the table. "If yer wanter act like squabblers, go outside an' do it."

"Yes," chorused the sisters, livening up at the prospect of a possible fight.

"Another cuppa tea, luv," Horace requested, oblivious to the simmering hostilities going on around him. "I don't want ter miss the football on telly."

Kris knew he wasn't going to be able to take family life for long. He was used to his freedom now—and sleeping on the couch in the front parlor because one of his sisters had taken over his old bedroom was a real drag. He had been home only five days, and already it was time to move on. The problem was, he had no money, and Buzz was no help. Ever since Daphne's funeral Buzz had refused to leave his house. He didn't want to practice or go around to the clubs. He didn't want to do anything.

Daphne had killed herself in the traditional way—stuffed her head in the oven and turned the gas on. Nobody knew why. "Poor dear. She got depressed a lot," a relative explained at the funeral. "Depression's a terrible burden to bear."

Buzz thought differently. "It's 'cos I left her alone," he said grimly. "We was always close, an' I deserted her."

Kris didn't know what to say. He still felt guilty, maybe it was *his* fault.

"C'mon," he told Buzz. "You can't just sit around bein' miserable. We gotta get somethin' goin' for us."

"What?" Buzz said stonily. "Fuckin' what?"

"I dunno," Kris replied with desperation. "But I'm goin' to figure somethin' out. You can bet on it."

With fifty pounds borrowed from his mother and a temporary job washing windows again, Kris moved away from the family home, dragging Buzz with him. Buzz couldn't stay in his house anyway; the lease was up and he had to get out. Daphne had left a few hundred pounds. Unfortunately the funeral and other expenses soon ate that up. Buzz gave all her possessions to relatives and followed Kris to the squat he had found in nearby Kilburn. The squat, an abandoned derelict house, had been taken over by a bunch of hippies whose credo was LOVE AND PEACE. The place was a mess, but Buzz fitted right into the indolent life style. It suited him fine to do nothing all day, and then sit around at night playing his guitar by candlelight, watched by a bunch of admiring long-haired girls.

It did not suit Kris. He had far more ambitious plans. With the money he'd borrowed, he bought himself a secondhand motor scooter, enabling him to get up to the West End of London, where he began hanging out at all the rhythm & blues, rock, and all-night jazz clubs, hoping to get a chance to connect.

He soon found out he was not the only one. Before long he met a black guy called Rasta Stanley, a would-be drummer currently marking time running errands for a record company. And Ollie Stoltz, a talented bassist straight out of a scholarship year at the Royal Academy of Music.

Triumphantly Kris told Buzz he thought he'd found their group.

"It's all horseshit," Buzz said, dragging heavily on a joint—his new favorite habit. "I'm not gettin' into any of that competitive crap."

"Right," agreed Flower, Buzz's current love, a sixteen-year-old runaway from Brighton, with huge, limpid blue eyes and fair hair that hung in a straight curtain reaching below her ass.

Kris felt the anger boil up inside him. This is what they had been striving for since school. The right combination. The dynamite group. And then . . . *Pow!!* Rock stardom would be theirs, and there'd be no looking back. He could buy his mum a mink coat and tell Brian to go shove it in his left ear.

Now this little frother with the dirty hair and big, stoned eyes was telling Buzz what to do. He wasn't going to stand for it. No way.

"Flower, luv," he said calmly, "whyn't you go down to the corner shop an' buy yourself a packet of fags an' a box of Maltesers?" He fished a precious pound note from the pocket of his jeans. "My treat."

This got Flower's attention. After smoking dope and screwing, normal cigarettes and chocolate were her main passions.

"Really, Kris?" she asked unsurely, as if he might whisk the pound note away as soon as she got up.

Pressing the money into the palm of her grubby little hand, he said, "Yeah, only I want you to go right now. Okay?"

She looked at Buzz for approval. Laconically he nodded. Jumping off the old mattress where they lounged away most of the day, she smoothed down her crumpled blouse, added a miniskirt and floppy sandals, and scurried off.

Buzz drew deeply on the last of his joint, stubbed it out on the floor and, leaning back, clasped both hands behind his head. "Go on then," he said. "Start pissing me off."

Kris knew how to play it. Turning away he said, "Hey, man. You wanna stay on your back all day gettin' laid an' stoned, *I* don't care."

"It suits me," Buzz said stubbornly.

"Good, 'cos I just wanted to be sure before I take off on my own."

"Whadderya mean—on your own?" Buzz asked suspiciously.

"If you think I'm goin' to sit around here watchin' *you* get bedbugs, you're balmy. I'm settin' somethin' up with Ollie an' Rasta, an' there's another bloke—he plays guitar —does vocals. He can take your place." A meaningful pause. "I just wanted to be certain you didn't want in."

"Fuck!" Buzz grumbled. "What other bloke?"

"He's an okay guy, you'll like him. When we get our first gig you'll come an' see us."

Buzz sat up. "Like hell I will."

"'Course, he's not quite as good as you, but with practice . . ."

"Sod it!" complained Buzz, hauling himself off the bed and throwing a dirty black shirt over stovepipe black jeans. "Yer won't quit until yer got me. Let's go."

A few days later they had their group. And a name. The Wild Ones. Two lead guitars—Kris and Buzz. A bassist and sometime keyboard player—Ollie Stoltz. A dynamite drummer—Rasta Stanley. And vocals shared between Kris and Buzz.

They were all set to fly, with nowhere to go.

"Fuck!" snarled Buzz. "We'd better get our freakin' act together or die. I've had this being poor shit."

All of a sudden Buzz had ambition. Kris decided it was a good sign.

BOBBY MONDELLA
1968

★ ★ ☆ ☆ ☆

"You're a fat lazy sonofabitch, an' I don' wan' you livin' with us no more. So pack your bags an' git the hell out." So spoke Ernest Crystal, all six feet five inches of him. He had never forgiven Bobby for not laying the golden egg.

"No way this boy goin' nowhere," cried Fanni, shaking chubby fists in his direction. "He *my* flesh, *my* blood, an' the only way he done go is if 'n *I* say so."

"You arguing wit me, witch?" demanded Ernest, glowering ferociously.

"I'm just sayin' what's right," retorted Fanni, refusing to back down. "An' don' you be callin' *me* no names, Ernest Crystal. You watch your damn mouth."

"I'll call you what I pleases, woman," steamed Ernest.

Standing between them, Bobby felt as if he hardly existed. Neither of them cared about him. They merely enjoyed using him as a prop for their never-ending fights. He had lived with them for two years, and throughout that period Ernest had tried to throw him out more than a dozen times, with cousin Fanni always springing to his defense. She did not do it out of love—rather, out of a bitter desire to never let Ernest get the better of her.

"The day this'n boy goes, *you* go," she announced spitefully, glaring at Ernest.

Bobby hoped she knew what she was saying, because in one week it was his eighteenth birthday—and as soon as that day came, he was out of there.

For two years now he had been working in the men's room at The Chainsaw discotheque, and he had learned plenty. Being locked up in Nashville all those years being looked after by Mr. Leon Rue had taught him exactly nothing.

"You all are *dumb,* boy," Ernest Crystal often said, and in the beginning he was right. Sweet Little Bobby was about as dumb as they came.

Working at The Chainsaw had given him the opportunity to see life as it really was, and he soon began to get a whole lot smarter—fast. The fact was, he had to. Surviving the rigors of The Chainsaw's men's room was like treading through a mine field in lead boots. The last thing people came in for was a simple pee. They entered the men's room for many different purposes—the number one reason being to score drugs. Bobby cottoned on to that the first night he worked there, when he tried to stop a major sale and nearly got fired for his trouble.

"Listen, kid," Nichols Kline, the manager, told him. "You clean up piss, you clean up shit, you stop any fights, an' you keep your mouth tightly zipped. Don't interfere with the customers an' they won't interfere with you. Got it?"

Yes, he got it, especially when he heard about the last men's room attendant who'd had his face carved up by an irate drug dealer claiming the attendant was ripping him off by selling his own stash.

"Keep clean an' you'll stay alive," a white waiter called Rocket Fabrizzi warned him. "They're hirin' kids now 'cause it's a tough pace. The guy before the last one had a heart attack an' dropped dead over the crapper. Oh, an' you'd better watch out for your ass. Don't get caught with your pants around your ankles."

Bobby didn't figure that one out for several weeks until he had to fight off an overexcited old queen who kept on crooning, "I just *adoooore* chubbos, especially black ones. I'll give you three hundred dollars and a simply *delicious* time!"

And so he learned. They came in to—
Buy
Sell
Cruise
Talk about sex
Pop pills
Sniff cocaine
Have sex
Smoke a joint
Throw up
Shoot up
You name it, they did it.

At least once a night Bobby had to remove some drunken but willing female who was either sitting across a guy's lap in the one john with a door or giving all and sundry a blow job.

Dull it wasn't.

Sordid it was.

However, it certainly afforded him a crash course in survival. He'd lied about his age to get the job, making himself three years older than he actually was. And once he had it, he was determined to stay, because working at The Chainsaw certainly wasn't ordinary.

The Chainsaw was the first of the really large discotheques—a vast, two-story emporium of flashing strobe lights and outrageously loud music—sometimes live groups, mostly records. Hot-looking bartenders in black bell-bottom pants with skintight white vests. And equally hot-looking waitresses in leather minidresses.

The Chainsaw was what hip New Yorkers called a "happening" place. It catered to the rich, famous, and infamous, most of them notorious for never picking up a check. And to pay the bills, it also catered to whoever looked beautiful enough or bizarre enough or outlandish enough to gain entry. In other words, no polyester crowd ever broke through the heavily guarded doors of The Chainsaw. And the word "tourist" was *never* mentioned.

"I gotta go to work," Bobby announced, squeezing past his cousin Fanni, who had now launched into a loud tirade about Ernest's disgusting bathroom habits.

They both ignored him as he left.

He was sweating as he walked toward the subway, and he knew why. Anyone would sweat carrying around the extra weight he packed, and he'd finally decided to do something about it. A new waitress had started work at the club a few weeks earlier. Her name was Sharleen. She was black, about twenty-three, and she was gorgeous. Bobby was in love. The only problem was, she had no idea he existed. Every time he tried to talk to her she gave him a blank look as if she'd never set eyes on him before.

On quiet nights he studied his reflection in the ornate mirror above the line of porcelain sinks in the men's room. When he was Sweet Little Bobby the chubbiness kind of suited him—it went nicely with his white sequin stage suits and modified Afro. Now, at nearly eighteen, and growing taller every day, he looked like a huge blob. "Fat Big Bobby" could be his new title.

Living with Fanni was no help. The woman loved to cook. Grease was her middle name. Even the once muscular Ernest was getting fatter by the minute.

Bobby knew he had to move on. If he stayed with Fanni and Ernest, he'd remain fat forever, and there was *no way* Sharleen would notice him.

He had his plans. Rocket, the waiter who had given him advice on survival, had promised there might be a bed available in his basement apartment, as his roommate was leaving. Bobby said he'd take it, and had handed over a month's rent in advance. Unfortunately, every time he asked what was happening, Rocket had a ready excuse. Finally Bobby insisted he move in on his birthday or get his money back. Rocket had promised everything would be worked out.

Arriving at the club, Bobby found the usual frantic staff activity. Friday night was the hottest night of the week. It was also the night the celebrities came out to play before taking off for long, restful weekends.

Hurrying straight to his supply cupboard, he checked out boxes of Kleenex, soap, clean towels, packets of Durex, and bottles of cheap aftershave.

"Bobby," said the manager, appearing at his side.

"Yes, Mr. Kline," Bobby replied alertly. He had this lingering fear that one of these nights he would get fired and not be able to afford to move away from Fanni and Ernest.

"I'm puttin' you in charge of the private men's room tonight," Nichols Kline said. He was a tall, jumpy-looking man in his thirties, with a shock of abundant rust-colored curls and a Captain Hook nose. He had the reputation of being a formidable stud, and was often to be found behind locked office doors with any female of his choice. "Seymour's out sick. Can you handle it?"

Jumping to attention, Bobby said, "Yes, *sir*."

The private men's room. Wow! He wondered what was wrong with Seymour, the usual attendant. He hadn't missed a night since Bobby worked there.

"Just take it easy, play it cool, an' let 'em do what they want," Nichols said, lustfully eyeing a passing waitress.

Oh, God! He's checking out Sharleen, thought Bobby.

She sashayed by with a pert "Good evening, Mr. Kline," failing to notice Bobby.

"Famous people—y'know, like singers, film stars, society folk—well . . . they're different," Nichols explained.

52

"You gotta leave 'em alone, yet be right there if they want anything." He scratched inside his shirt, jangling a few gold chains. "Never stare. They don't like that. And no autographs—even if it's for your dying mother in Nebraska. Got it?"

"Yes, Mr. Kline."

"Oh, an' if they do any drugs, just ignore it." Casually he added, "Of course, if they wanna score, you can send 'em to me. No selling. One complaint, kid, an' you're out. I don't care how many years you've worked here."

"Yes, *sir!*"

For one brief second Bobby thought about telling Nichols he had once been a famous person himself. Minor league, of course, but he'd had his moments.

Common sense told him to forget it. First, Nichols would never believe him. And second, what did he have to gain by letting everyone know he was a has-been?

No. His secret was locked deeply within him. Since leaving Nashville and Mr. Rue, he had not sung one note or written one word. Music was his past.

The private men's room—or Seymour's Palace, as it was known around the club—was a deco fantasy of black granite floors, black marble washstands, shining urinals, and silver walls adorned with framed sepia photographs of Marilyn Monroe caught at every stage of her career. Nichols handed Bobby a key to Seymour's famous locked cupboard, and there he found atomizers of expensive aftershaves and colognes, the finest hairbrushes and combs, a half-filled bottle of Courvoisier, a glassine envelope containing a white illegal substance—probably cocaine—and an assortment of mixed pills.

Bobby shoved the cocaine and the pills to the back of the cupboard, took out what he needed as far as supplies were concerned, and locked up. He had never had much contact with Seymour, a short, dour black man in his fifties, who, the rest of the staff had informed him, only enjoyed talking to his famous clientele.

After setting up, Bobby made his way down to the kitchen, where the staff had an early dinner before the club opened.

Rocket waved to him, so, collecting a plate of pasta from an assistant chef, he went to sit with his waiter friend.

Rocket was an aspiring actor from the school of Method acting. He was of Italian origin, in his early twenties, with long, greasy hair and darting, inquisitive eyes. "I hear you got lucky tonight," he said in his flat, nasal voice. "Upstairs doin' big time, huh?"

"That's right."

"Shame you didn't know about it earlier. If you'd known, you could've come prepared." He dropped his tone to a low whisper. "You could've done us both a favor."

"I *am* prepared," Bobby said.

"Naw," Rocket disagreed. "You're not gettin' my drift. In the private john y'can *really* get a score goin'. They got big bucks an' they ain't got nothin' to do with 'em but buy. Why d'ya think Seymour never socializes? The creep is a fartin' king up there. Makes a fortune." He looked furtively around before continuing. "Give me an hour—if I can get someone to cover for me I'll try t' get everything you're gonna need. Then we'll split your take—fifty-fifty."

Bobby didn't want to get into selling drugs. He was smart enough to know it only led to trouble. Besides, Nichols Kline had already warned him.

"No," he said, shaking his head. "Like it's too dangerous, man. I don't wanna risk my job."

"You'll risk your fartin' job if you *don't* give 'em what they want," Rocket said knowledgeably. "Hey—old Seymour's lasted a long time up there, right? He gives those famous fuckers pronto service, an' if you don't—believe me, you're out. They're *mean* rich motherfuckers."

Bobby thought about Seymour's locked cupboard. Maybe there was something in what Rocket had to say after all.

"C'mon, Bobby, we gotta make a killin'," Rocket pleaded, sensing a weakness. "Maybe we only got tonight —so let's go for it, huh?"

Working the private men's room was a different world. Bobby was used to a crowded never-ending line of noisy sweat-soaked, hyper customers who, if he was lucky, might leave anything from a ten-cent to a dollar tip. He was not used to a thin trickle of expensively clad movie stars, rock stars, sports stars, producers, clothes designers, investment bankers, occasional politicians, directors, and a mixed bag of other success stories.

Remembering Nichols Kline's words, he tried not to stare. But it was difficult when a fair number of the faces were so very familiar. Most of them were in and out, some leaving no tip at all, while others threw down a ten or twenty as if it were nothing. Jefferson Lionacre, a famous black singing star, palmed him a hundred-dollar bill with a wink and an encouraging "Today the crapper—tomorrow the world."

Bobby wanted to shake his hand. What a title for a song! Only he wasn't writing any more.

Why not? he asked himself. He had lost his sweet, childish voice, not his songwriting abilities. Why *shouldn't* he go back to composing—if only for his own enjoyment? And not the country & western stuff Mr. Leon Rue had forced him to write—but soul, sweet *sweet* soul music. *His* kind of music.

Lately he'd been listening to a lot of James Brown and Aretha Franklin. The two of them certainly knew how to sell a song.

Hey—if he set his mind to it he could write soul. Fresh

melodies were always churning around in his head. Wasn't it about time he did something about it?

Okay—first he was going to move out. Next, he would write a song. Just for himself.

"Hey—*you*—fat boy."

His reverie was interrupted by a skinny, stoned rock & roll star wearing a tight lizardskin jacket, orange pants, high-heeled boots and a spacy leer. "Where's Seymour?"

"He's not here tonight," Bobby replied, humiliated at being called "fat boy" although he knew it was true.

"Shee-it, I kin see *that*," the rocker said, posturing in front of the full-length mirror. "Where is the old bum?"

"Uh, I think he's out sick," Bobby replied, recognizing the rock & roller as Del Delgardo, lead singer with a group called the Nightmares.

The rocker pouted his thick lips and adjusted his bulging crotch. "Did he leave you my stuff?"

"What stuff?"

Narrowing his eyes, Delgardo said, "Don't give me dumb Sambo shit or your ass'll be on the auction block. You goddamn spades always stick together." His voice developed a whiny quality. "I want my stuff. It's paid for. And I want it fast."

For a moment Bobby thought about smashing the skinny asshole's face in. But it wouldn't achieve anything, he'd only get fired.

Taking a deep breath, he thought about the glassine envelope in Seymour's locked cupboard. What should he do? Go for the hunch or wait for this maniac to start screaming?

Going for the hunch, he unlocked the cupboard, reached inside, took out the envelope, and shoved it at the jerk. "Is this it?"

The rock & roller claimed what was his with a petulant snarl. "How come ya didn't ask me to get down on my fuckin' knees and beg?" He then proceeded to lay out thin lines on the black marble and snort an inordinate amount.

Bobby turned away. He'd only sampled drugs once. Two years of seeing what dope did to people was enough to warn him off forever.

"Join me," Del commanded, suddenly becoming friendly.

"No, thanks. It's not my scene."

"Do it!" the rock star insisted.

"I can't, I'll lose my job."

Del Delgardo reverted to his true self. "You'll lose it if you *don't,* you fat fuck."

Bobby wished someone would come in before he punched this jerk out. But the private men's room remained private.

"I said, do it!" Del repeated threateningly.

Bobby wondered how the great Seymour would handle a situation like this. And then he was saved. A middle-aged man in a tuxedo walked in, attracting the rock star's attention.

"Hey, Marcus," Del greeted. "You're just in time. Come on in an' join the fuckin' feast!"

To Bobby's surprise, the affluent-looking man walked over to the stoned singer as if they were the best of friends, patted him warmly on his lizard-clad shoulder, extracted a small gold straw from his inside pocket, and elegantly snorted a line of the addictive white substance.

Bobby heaved a sigh of relief. He was no longer needed. Crisis over. Discreetly he busied himself polishing the pristine marble sinks.

"My album's walkin' out the stores—fuckin' walkin'. Right, Marcus? Right?" demanded Del.

"Yes, indeed it is," the man replied in a slight European accent.

"I'm fuckin' beatin' the *cock* out of Mick. Right?"

"We're making money. That's all that's important, isn't it?"

"Yeah," replied Del unsurely. The most important thing to him was outselling Mick Jagger and the Rolling Stones. Never mind the money.

"Shall we return to our ladies?" Marcus asked smoothly.

Greedily Del Delgardo snorted his last line of coke. "Yeah, let's do that. Why not?" He took one final look at himself in the mirror, liked what he saw, and unsteadily accompanied the older man from the room.

As soon as they were gone, Rocket darted furtively through the door. "You know who that was?" he asked excitedly.

"Del Delgardo. What a creep."

"Not him. The other guy."

"Who was he?"

"Marcus Citroen. He owns Blue Cadillac Records. He's power, man, with a capital P. Here—" Rocket emptied out his pockets. "I got joints, pills, ammis, an' some sleepers. It's the best I can do for tonight. Let's hope Seymour stays away for a while."

"How much I gotta charge?" Bobby asked, not really wanting to become involved.

"Jeez!" Rocket rolled his eyes. "Sometimes I wonder about you, Bobby. Where the hell you *bin* all your life?"

"I hear you met Marcus Citroen last night."

Sharleen was talking to him. She was actually acknowledging his existence!

"Yeah," Bobby mumbled. He didn't know how to handle it. They were standing next to each other, clocking in. It was the closest he'd ever been to her, and he hadn't realized she was so petite, like a little doll. And pretty! Oh, was she pretty!

"Listen." Sharleen leaned toward him speaking in an urgent whisper. "I can't get near any VIPs. I'm stuck downstairs with the junk skunks. So do me a big favor. If he comes in tonight give him this for me. *Please*." Pressing a cassette into his hand, she gazed at him pleadingly.

This was his golden opportunity. All he had to do was say, *Sure. Go out with me, and I'll pass him your tape*. Real flip and cool, exactly like Rocket would do. Instead he just about managed a weak "Yes."

"Thanks, sweetie." Sharleen stood on tiptoe and kissed him on the cheek. "You're a nice guy."

And then she was gone, and he'd lost his chance. Damn!

Rocket appeared, grinning with anticipation. "Have I got us the works tonight! Primo, primo! Seymour's not back, is he?"

Secretly Bobby hoped he was. Catering to the big shots was too much like hard work; he preferred the hustle and craziness of downstairs. And selling dope wasn't to his liking either, although he had to admit he could use the money. After all, it wasn't as if he were out on the street pushing to kids. As Rocket pointed out, these people had plenty of money, nobody was forcing them to buy.

"You're back upstairs again tonight, Bobby," announced Nichols Kline, looming up behind them, causing Rocket to jump guiltily. "You're doing okay up there. No complaints."

"What's the matter with Seymour?" Bobby ventured.

"Don't you worry about Seymour," Nichols replied lightly. "Just do your job and stay out of everyone's way."

"Yeah," crowed Rocket, as soon as Nichols walked off. "Do your job, an' stay *in* everyone's pocket!" He cackled hysterically.

It turned out to be another crazy night, and when people asked, Bobby supplied them with what they wanted, soon learning money was of no great concern to the rich and famous—they seemed to enjoy throwing it around.

At closing time he looked for Rocket to pay him his share, but his waiter friend was nowhere to be found, and since he was in a hurry to get home, he left. Marcus Citroen hadn't shown up, and Sharleen's tape was still in his possession. He couldn't wait to hear it.

When he got home he played it on his portable tape machine—a souvenir from Nashville—and was mortified to discover she sounded terrible, straining to be heard above a far too loud backup group, her voice small and tinny.

So ... Sharleen wanted to be a singer. Well, at least they had music in common, and Bobby knew, just by listening to her, he could help her sound a lot better.

With that comforting thought in mind, he fell asleep, only to awake several hours later with agonizing cramps in his stomach.

"Oh—Jesus!" Moaning with acute pain, he dragged himself out of bed and into the bathroom, where he promptly threw up.

Relief was not forthcoming. The unremitting pain persisted, tearing at his gut like a constant, jagged edge.

Panic overcame him. Something bad was happening, and he didn't know what to do. Gathering all the strength he could muster, he staggered into Fanni and Ernest's room, switching the light on and waking them both up.

"What you all doin', boy?" yelled Fanni, launching herself into a sitting position, her huge bosom escaping from the cheap pink nightgown she wore.

"I'm sick," he gasped. "I got this terrible pain."

"What kinda pain?" Fanni asked suspiciously.

"He's drunk," muttered Ernest, pulling the covers over his head.

"The boy don't drink," retorted Fanni, always ready for a fight.

"Tha's what *you* think, woman," replied Ernest knowingly.

Bobby clutched his stomach. This was his punishment

for selling dope. He'd known it was wrong. Why'd he let Rocket talk him into it?

He felt the sweat break out all over his body, followed by a spiraling sensation of serious pain. And then, with an enormous thud, he fell to the floor, dead to the world.

The last words he heard were Ernest saying, "*Shee . . . it!* I need my rest, woman. I don' expect these kinda goin's-on in the middle of the night. Do somethin' about it, witch. Throw him outta here! I can't stand lookin' at his fat, lazy, no-good ass one more day!"

1987
Saturday, July 11th

★ ☆ ★ ☆ ★

Emerging from the shower, Kris found the delectable Cybil arranged across his bed, completely naked except for a blooming red rose placed strategically between her thighs.

"Wanna pick a flower, ya lucky man?" she drawled in a put-on street accent. "Twenny bucks for a trip to the rose parade, an' you don't even havta go to Pasadena!"

Why was she tempting him like this? Feeling the heat rise, he was aggravated. Retreating back to the bathroom he said, "Do me a favor, luv, put your knickers on an' stop messin' about."

"Oh, boy, you'd better have some *good* things in store for me tomorrow," she threatened.

He closed the door. "I'm not coming out until you're dressed."

"You *veal* regret *zis* day," she said in a heavy foreign accent. "I *veal* 'ave my *beeg* revenge."

One thing about Cybil—there was never a dull moment. She was good-natured and fun, a natural-born joker. She was also fancied by every straight male in America, yet it was his bed she was sharing. He had exclusive rights to the gorgeous blond body, the Miss America face, and the cascade of shining hair.

So why did he need Astrid, the mistress of his English mansion?

Insurance. While Astrid was on the scene he couldn't get too involved with Cybil. And vice versa. Kris had a natural-born aversion to marriage. The very word sent chills up his spine. To him, being married equaled being trapped. He had sampled it once, and had no intention of getting caught a second time.

Dressed in jeans and a casual shirt, he peered into the bedroom. Cybil was gone; only her perfume lingered. *Eau de Horny Blonde,* he thought with a ribald laugh.

Downstairs his live-in Scottish couple busied themselves with domestic tasks, jumping to attention when they saw him.

"Welcome back, Mr. Phoenix," said the plump and motherly Mabel. "Why don't I make you a nice cup of tea?"

Nodding, he wandered outside to inspect his property. Immediately his two golden Labrador retrievers came bounding over to greet him. Bending down, he petted them for a good ten minutes.

His Bel Air mansion stood on two acres of impeccably kept grounds. Flowing lawns, sumptuous flower beds, lemon and orange trees, brilliant bougainvillea, and the obligatory Hollywood swimming pool and tennis court. Not bad for an English lad who was chucked out of school at fifteen without two pennies to rub together.

Several Mexican gardeners toiled diligently. He gave them a cheery wave. Being back in Los Angeles was a kick. The weather appealed to him. Having grown up in England with constant rain and fog, he appreciated warmth and sunshine. Besides, he enjoyed cultivating a healthy tan.

Cybil came running out of the house in a minuscule bikini. The gardeners stopped work and stared. The dogs barked. Flashing Kris a winning smile, she dived gracefully into the pool.

Was there no end to her desire to turn him on? Tomorrow she would pay for her teasing, oh, how she would pay!

"Coming?" she called innocently, surfacing with a lethal crawl.

"Naw. I'm gonna work out."

He made his way into the luxurious pool house, where there was a fully equipped gym. He'd been working with a body trainer and weights for almost two years, and the difference in his body was amazing. Whereas before he'd been wiry and naturally athletic, never a slouch when it came to moving around on stage, now he was in incredible shape—fitter than he'd ever been. Thirty-eight was the age some rock stars began to think about winding down. Not Kris—he had a new energy, a steely strength. Whatever he was doing, it worked for him—plus he was performing better than ever.

Twenty minutes of punishment and he was ready for a swim. The pool was empty; Cybil had moved on to other activities.

Churning up and down for thirty lengths, he emerged fit and refreshed.

Waiting poolside was his manager, Hawkins Lamont— an American usually known as the Hawk.

The Hawk was fashionably dressed in white duck pants, a white polo shirt, white loafers and a pale-beige crocodile Gucci belt. A tall man in his forties, with a George Hamilton tan, the Hawk radiated an air of supreme confidence. And so he should—he was one of the most successful and sought-after managers in the business, with a stable of first-class talent. Kris had been with him for three years, ever since leaving his former manager, the notorious Doktor Head.

"You seem to be in excellent shape," the Hawk said,

settling himself at a patio table under a yellow striped umbrella.

Kris nodded. "I feel great—I mean we're talkin' *really* great."

And he meant it, only too aware of the fact that he couldn't have made that claim a few years ago.

The Hawk smiled—a Hollywood smile made entirely of porcelain. "I just came over to convey a personal message. Marcus Citroen is delighted you've agreed to appear at his wife's function tonight."

Wrapping a towel around his waist, Kris sat down. "I didn't have much choice, did I?" he said dryly.

"You made the *right* choice," the Hawk replied pointedly. "Tonight is special. Marcus wanted the three hottest recording stars in the business, and he got them. I wouldn't have been pleased to see your place taken by Springsteen, would *you?*"

Kris stared at Mabel walking across the lawn bearing a tray with tea and toast for him, and a lead crystal glass of Perrier decorated with a slice of lime for his guest. "As long as I'm in an' out," he said dourly.

"We agreed on that. You're appearing last, *after* Bobby Mondella and Rafealla. That was one of my conditions to Marcus, the star spot or nothing."

"Sure," Kris said listlessly. He hated the whole deal.

"Is Cybil coming with you?" the Hawk asked smoothly.

"I dunno. Haven't asked her."

"It's going to be quite an evening."

"Yeah, but I'm not stayin', am I?"

"You might change your mind."

"Naw."

The Hawk took one sip of Perrier and rose. "I'll check with you later. The limo will be here at three-thirty. I'd like to plan on leaving at the latest by four."

After the Hawk departed, Cybil reappeared. Thankfully, she had dressed, although her ensemble left little to the imagination. A skimpy tank top under which she very obviously wore no bra. Crotch-hugging shorts, and white ankle socks worn with nifty Reeboks. She looked like an overdeveloped cheerleader.

"Where are *you* off to?" he asked.

"Didn't I tell you?" she said, wide-eyed. "I've got a shoot with a *vereee* randy photographer. He'll probably want to ravish my girlish body—what shall I do?"

"Make 'im wear a condom!"

She frowned. "Kris! That's not funny. You wouldn't like it if I *did* sleep with him, would you?"

"I'll tell you something, luv. You wouldn't be around to tell the tale."

"No?" she said challengingly.

"Nope. You'd be out, kiddo. Bags packed an' on the doorstep."

Cybil was unamused. Suddenly she was all grown up. "You're such a chauvinist. I suppose you think I don't know about that Danish hooker you keep in London."

There it was, out in the open. It was the first time in the months they'd been living together she'd ever dared to mention Astrid.

"Listen carefully," he said calmly. "I never pretended I was perfect. The only thing is—I *do* expect you to be."

"You're an asshole!" she blurted. "All my friends keep on telling me what a two-timing rat you are. Why *should* I put up with it?"

"Nobody's tying you to the bedpost, are they?"

"I hate you, Kris Phoenix. One of these days I won't be around when you get back, then you'll *really* be sorry."

She flounced off.

He sighed deeply. It wasn't going to be a good day.

George Smith, alias Maxwell Sicily, piled into the first of the special buses hired to transport the waiters and entire catering staff of Lilliane's to the rambling Novaroen estate in preparation for the most exclusive party of the year. The chefs, waiters, and busboys talked excitedly among themselves. This was one event nobody wanted to miss. The press had been headlining it for weeks, it was the hottest ticket around. Fifty couples at one hundred thousand dollars per couple was some shot.

Maxwell settled back in a window seat, staring out as the convoy of buses set off along Sunset—a winding, twisting route which would take them all the way to the Pacific Coast Highway where there would be a further twenty-five-minute drive along the scenic coastal road.

Humming softly to himself, he tried to blank out the conversations going on all around. Snatches reached him anyway, mostly about money, because everyone was anxious to get a load of the people who could afford to pay such an unbelievable price for one evening's entertainment.

"I wanna see Rafealla sing," said a young busboy to nobody in particular. "She's the greatest."

"Nah. Give me Whitney Houston any day," argued an assistant chef. "Now there's a *real* sexy broad."

"So what? They all fuck," sniffed a skinny waiter with eyeglasses and a permanent sneer.

Yes, Maxwell thought, *it's true. They all fuck, and they all lie, and they all spend your money and run out on you.*

He should know. His father had taught him at a very early age. Which is why he stuck to hookers.

Pay, and you know exactly what you are getting.

Pay, and you're the boss. No argument.

Women were inferior creatures. Keep them on their knees where they belong. Let them know who's in charge. Never take any of their garbage. Never.

He thought about Vicki Foxe for a moment. A lot was riding on her involvement. If she screwed up . . .

Stop! No negative thoughts. Vicki might be a woman, but she came highly recommended, and if he wasn't certain she could do her part, he wouldn't have hired her. The same with Speed.

Usually Maxwell preferred to work alone. Who needed the headache of depending on other people? But this job was too big. He had to have help, and Speed and Vicki were it. Already Vicki's inside information had proved invaluable. She was good. He'd had no doubts, really. She was a woman used to getting paid for her services, and therefore she knew how to deliver.

He wasn't so sure about Speed. The man was a weasel, crafty and devious. But when it came to driving he was supposed to be one of the best. And that's all he had to do. Be in the right place at the right time. And just drive. Maxwell felt sure everything was under control.

He was on his way to a fortune, and nobody was going to stop him.

The moment Rafealla entered her suite at L'Ermitage, Marcus Citroen was on the phone.

"Are you comfortable?" he asked.

"Yes, thank you."

"Do you have everything you need?""

"Yes, Marcus, I do."

"I'm going to try and come over."

"Please don't," she said quickly. "Not today. I'm tired and I have the concert to think about. I'll see you tonight."

He didn't sound too pleased. "Very well. I'll phone you in an hour."

She had an hour's grace. An hour to unpack, soak in a long hot tub, lie on the bed and chain-smoke while flicking the channels on American television.

She found herself on MTV. Rafealla doing what she did best. Looking sultry and moody, her long dark hair a lush curtain framing an exquisite face. Her smoky voice evoking erotic thoughts in all who heard it.

Rafealla.

Sophisticated.

Worldly.

Knowledgeable.

Sensual.

What a phony! She hadn't been to bed with anyone for a year.

Career first.

Life second.

Her choice.

Dear Marcus Citroen, make me a star and I will be yours.

Well, he had kept his part of the bargain, and now the day of reckoning was here.

She was surprised she'd managed to keep him waiting so long.

The girl behind the desk at the car-rental company studied the papers Speed handed her with a blank stare as her jaw rhythmically decimated a piece of chewing gum.

"The gray Cadillac limousine," Speed repeated patiently. "I took it out last Saturday, and the weekend before that."

Without saying a word, she picked up a pen, scrawled authorization on the rental form, reached for the phone and mumbled, "Dan, gray Caddy limo." Then she nodded at a side door. "Pick it up in the alley. How're you payin'?"

He fumbled for cash. She counted it out, handed him his copy of the papers, and automatically mumbled, "Have a nice day."

"I will," he replied with a quick wink, knowing she probably thought he looked pretty ritzy in his smart gray chauffeur's uniform with the jaunty peaked cap. -

Could he help it if women loved him? Even his ex-wife wanted to give him a roll every time he visited her—which, he had to admit, wasn't often, on account of her residing in Las Vegas, a town he tried to stay away from, because every time he went back there, he either got married or gambled away every last cent he possessed.

Jeez! Tits and gambling. His two passions.

A mechanic brought the Cadillac around and Speed climbed inside. He loved the smell of an expensive car. Once he'd done a stint as private chauffeur to a rich Pasadena couple. The woman used to arrange for her maid to place a dozen white roses in the car every day. What an aroma! He'd fucked the maid, enjoyed the roses, and left after three months. Legitimate work was boring.

The Cadillac handled nicely. And so it should. On the two weekends he'd taken it out he'd given it plenty of tender loving care. Under the hood throbbed an engine hot to trot. When Speed tinkered with an engine, miracles happened. It wasn't that much different from handling a woman. A little delicate finger action, some rubbing and dipping and smearing on of lubricant. Searching for just the right spot to make that sucker purr.

Speed chuckled to himself. Today was going to be easy. All he had to do was be in the right spot at the right time. And then fly.

For ten grand he could manage that.

The smell of bacon woke him before Sara did, and Bobby Mondella lay on the bed lost in his own private world of darkness. Sometimes he got panic attacks, other times he was quiet and in complete control. Sara helped. She was always there for him, and suddenly he desired her with a force that surprised him.

He heard her walk into the room with that special step he would recognize anywhere.

"One bacon sandwich, one alarm call comin' up," she said cheerfully.

"Come over here, woman," he said, his voice thick with desire.

She didn't need asking twice. Sara knew everything

Bobby wanted, sometimes before he knew it himself. Placing the tray on a table, she went to him willingly.

His arms reached up, pulling her onto the bed beside him.

She lay very still, her heart beating fast with the anticipation of what was to come, for Bobby Mondella was the greatest lover in the world.

Slowly he began to feel her body through the clothes she wore. Lightly his sensitive hands roamed across her large breasts, rounded stomach and childbearing hips. His fingertips barely touched, but soon she was longing for him to rip her clothes off.

She moaned, a stifled sound, for Bobby liked her to remain passive until he indicated otherwise.

With maddening restraint his hands leisurely found their way inside her blouse. He undid the buttons one by one, opening the garment.

Her breasts strained to escape the confines of her bra. But he teased some more, playing with her swollen nipples through the material, tracing intricate patterns of intent.

"Please, Bobby, *please*," she had to beg.

"Be patient, Mamma," he crooned. "I'm gonna get there, all in good time. Just you be quiet."

"Oh, God!" Her face was flushed, he tortured her with the waiting, and yet it was sweet torture and she was addicted to every wonderful moment of it.

At last he snapped the clasp, allowing her breasts to burst free. She almost climaxed there and then, that's how good his touch was. But he didn't allow her to do so. Ignoring her newly liberated bosom, he moved down to her thighs, feeling the inner flesh, caressing, teasing, lifting her skirt inch by inch, pulling down her panties at a snail's pace.

"Bobby, you are drivin' me *crazy*," she managed.

"Honey baby, you don' know what crazy is."

And then he proceeded to show her with slow and sure

expertise, bringing her to orgasm twice with his hands and tongue before finally consummating the sexual act.

As he thrust in and out, Sara sobbed with a mixture of relief and pleasure. She loved the man so much, and yet she still wasn't sure of his feelings for her. He needed her, oh, yes, she was confident of that. But did he love her? He had never said so, although in moments of passion she told *him* all the time. In fact she was saying it now. "I love you, Bobby Mondella. Love you, love you, love you. Oh, how I *loooove* you." And again she was climaxing, just for him, the man she loved, the man she wanted more than anything in the world.

His reply was no more than a long-drawn-out groan as he finally allowed himself release.

Immediately he withdrew, rolling across the bed, pulling a sheet over his nakedness as if he didn't want her to see him in any other state except arousal.

"Was it good for you, baby?" She couldn't stop herself from asking.

The fires were vanquished, he was back in control. "I'm hungry," he said, abruptly changing the subject. "Did I hear talk about a bacon sandwich?"

Dutifully she got off the bed, announcing, "It's cold, I'll make you another one."

"Cold is fine. Just hand it to me."

Without bothering to cover herself she padded over to the table where she had left the tray and took it to him. Normally she would have been self-conscious about displaying her body. She considered her legs too short, her ass too rounded, and her breasts too big; but with Bobby it didn't matter, he couldn't see her anyway. And if he could, he wouldn't want her, she was sure of that. Because in his time Bobby Mondella had been with the most beautiful women in the world, black and white.

Sara remembered the magazine stories, the scandals and the gossip. She also remembered the first time she saw him perform onstage back in 1980. She was eighteen years old and had just graduated from high school. Two girlfriends had dragged her to a concert he was doing in Philadelphia. "He's the sexiest man alive!" they both assured her. "Wait'll you see him! This man is pure horn!"

And she'd had to agree they were right. When he walked out on that stage in finely cut black pants and a white silk shirt, fifty thousand women began to wet their pants while screaming their lungs out. Bobby Mondella exuded sex. He was a walking, living, breathing phallic symbol. And what a voice!

Sara became an immediate convert. Although she'd never dreamed that years later, soon after his terrible accident, she would be working for him as his personal assistant, and more.

"I'm gonna take another shower," Bobby said, finishing the sandwich in a couple of hungry bites. "Are my clothes ready?"

"Everything's set," she replied. "Your favorite black pants and white silk shirt."

"Thanks, babe." Yeah, they were his favorite clothes all right. His lucky outfit. Only his clothes hadn't been so lucky for him on that fateful night two years ago.

Oh, Jesus. Soon he would be in the presence of Nova Citroen. That seductive, cold *bitch*.

He didn't know if he could take it.

Sara held his arm, assisting him to the bathroom.

He shook her hand away. "I know the layout," he said sharply. "You've got to stop takin' every step for me."

Sometimes he wanted help. Sometimes he couldn't stand it. Today he wanted to do everything on his own.

"I'll go get dressed," she said quickly in that small, hurt voice he couldn't stand.

She was such a sweet kid, so warm and helpful. She'd brought him back from the brink, and he didn't know what he'd do without her. And yet, there were times she got on his nerves.

Lightening up, he said, "You mean you're still walkin' around bare-assed, girl? Shame on you! Somebody might see you."

Bobby's idea of a joke. Sara didn't find it very funny.

Nova Citroen prowled around her luxurious estate checking the details that had made her one of America's number one hostesses and aggravating the hell out of everyone who worked for her. She had an eye for the smallest speck of dust, the slightest imperfection—everything had to be just so.

Concentrating on the guest house, she ordered a collection of silver frames be repolished. Insisted there were fresh rolls of toilet tissue in every one of the seven bathrooms. Had a manservant change every light bulb, and personally rearranged nine vases of garden-picked flowers.

Finally she returned to her bedroom with her masseuse, hairdresser, manicurist, and a top makeup artist—an English girl called Tracy—the only one allowed to touch the precious Nova Citroen skin.

"This is all so boring," she informed her diligent entourage. "However, I enjoy raising money. And the Governor is such a worthy cause, don't you think?"

Little did any of them suspect that twenty years ago Nova Citroen had been one of the highest-paid call girls in her native Germany.

Vicki Foxe had a way of moving around that enabled her to go wherever she wanted. The uniform helped—the dreary brown-and-white maid's uniform that Mrs. Citroen insisted every female employee wear.

The old broad probably doesn't want any competition, Vicki thought smugly. Man, without the uniform, and with all her makeup and shit in place, Vicki Foxe could give competition to any of those big fancy movie stars. Not that the new ones were so big and fancy any more—mere shadows of what they used to be like in the good old days. Not that Vicki had been around then, but she knew. There were no Marilyn Monroes and Lana Turners today.

Vicki Foxe had arrived in Hollywood at sixteen, a runaway from Chicago, with sixty bucks in her pocket and two great assets—her incredibly large breasts.

The sixty dollars didn't get her very far at all, but the assets got her a job as a topless waitress and go-go dancer, and from there she graduated to nude modeling. Hooking came next, and by the time she was twenty-five she was scoring fairly big bucks, until she met a small-time hood who was married, generous, and wanted her all to himself. He set her up in an apartment on Ventura Boulevard and paid all the bills. She sat at home filing her nails, eating chocolates, and watching soap operas all day. Four years passed quickly, and then her boyfriend got himself arrested down in Florida on an armed-robbery charge, and was promptly sent to jail. Vicki, a little older, a little plumper, went back to hooking, but her heart wasn't in it, and when Maxwell Sicily—who had shared a jail cell with her former lover—contacted her, she was ready for a touch of excitement. At thirty she was all set for action. She was also undeniably attracted to Maxwell Sicily, so she accepted his plan without question. Now she was playing dress-up and loving every minute. After all, what was the whole scam anyway? Just taking from the rich, and giving to Vicki and Maxwell. Nobody gave a shit when the rich got ripped off. So what? They had insurance and all that crap. Stealing from them was nothing, it wasn't like a real *bad* crime.

Entering Marcus Citroen's private study, she carried a feather duster in case she was stopped. Nobody bothered her; the rest of the staff were all too busy worrying about the evening's big event.

Vicki never worried, she just went for it, and did what she had to do.

Marcus Citroen employed three personal secretaries, each one more loyal than the next. He made it a strict rule that they were not to fraternize out of office hours. The penalty for breaking that rule was immediate dismissal.

The three women (Marcus did not believe in male secretaries) vied with each other for their boss's attention. They told him absolutely everything that went on below boardroom level at Blue Cadillac Records, and therefore, among the three of them, he knew every piece of gossip; who was sleeping with whom, and other un-business-related facts which might not have reached him through normal channels. Keeping people at each other's throats was one of Marcus's specialties. He was a master at it. And knowing everything helped.

His three secretaries were all spinster-type women in their fifties. Marcus did not wish them to be bedded by anyone who might work for him. He demanded complete loyalty, and got it. They loathed each other. It suited him fine.

"Mr. Lamont is here," Phoebe, his senior secretary, announced on the intercom.

"Send him right in," said Marcus. Certain people he kept waiting. Hawkins Lamont was not one of them.

The man in white entered Marcus's spectacular office, which looked more like an antique-filled living room than the workplace of a record magnate. He went straight to the humidor on the ornate walnut desk and selected a thick Havana cigar.

"You don't mind, do you?" the Hawk asked, confidently

sitting himself down in a plush leather chair across from the desk.

Amused, Marcus said, "Go ahead."

At fifty-nine, Marcus Citroen radiated power. Although he was forty pounds overweight for his height of just under six feet, his impeccable English tailoring covered a multitude of flaws. Mostly bald, his head was egg-shaped and olive-hued, the same color as his face. He had a thin upper lip, an obscenely thick lower one, a prominent nose, and mysteriously hooded eyes with indolent drooping lids. Originally from Beirut, he had lived in America for over forty years, and had been a citizen for thirty. He was enormously rich, extremely powerful, and, in the business he had chosen to excel in, universally feared. A somewhat different figure from the young man who had arrived in New York in 1948 aged twenty, with barely one hundred dollars to his name but a heart already as hard as steel. Marcus Citroen had seen too much of life ever to change. He'd grown up in wartime Europe, and he knew everything about the darker side of man's nature. He'd seen his wealthy father reduced to poverty, his beautiful mother become a whore, and his brother, plaything to a group of perverts.

Marcus desired money. He desired power. And he came to America to seek both out.

He'd succeeded.

"Well," the Hawk said. "Kris Phoenix is delivered. Bobby Mondella will be there. Has Rafealla arrived?"

"She's here," Marcus confirmed. "At L'Ermitage." Fixing the Hawk with an intent stare, he leaned back, placed the tips of his elegantly manicured fingers together, and said, "And so the game begins, my friend."

The Hawk puffed on his cigar. He'd known Marcus for over fifteen years, and yet, deep down, he felt he didn't really know him at all. Nobody did. The man did not encourage intimate friendships, although the Hawk considered himself as close as anyone could get. He laughed dryly, almost nervously. "What game?" he asked, his curiosity aroused, for Marcus had been obsessive about the three stars being there—especially Rafealla.

Marcus's expression was inscrutable. "Any game I wish to play," he said slowly. "Any game at all."

KRIS PHOENIX
1970–1972

★ ☆ ★ ☆ ★

For two years The Wild Ones played their collective asses off with nothing to show for it except an increasingly appreciative cult audience and as many girls as they could manage. Which wasn't bad, but it certainly didn't mean as much as getting a manager, an agent, a recording contract, money, and maybe the smallest speck of recognition from an industry that so far had chosen to totally ignore them.

Whenever they could get a booking they appeared at clubs all around the suburbs of London. Small clubs, big barns, local hops, anywhere they could get a chance to be seen. Sometimes they landed a gig at a wedding or a birthday party. It was all experience. But none of it paid the rent, so they continued with their daytime jobs. Kris packed window cleaning in, and along with Buzz got himself a stint as a lifeguard attendant at a local indoor pool. They were both strong swimmers, and the work was not unduly taxing, although the smell of chlorine and the hordes of screaming school kids drove the two of them crazy. Buzz made out with every fanciable female who ventured into the place, even though he was still living with Flower. Kris found he was becoming more choosy—just because they were under twenty-five and moved didn't mean he automatically had to get a leg over. They were never short of female company. Show a girl a guitar, and the little darling almost came on the spot.

Rasta Stanley, their black drummer, worked at a small radio station as a general gofer. It was a useful gig, enabling him to smuggle out all the new record albums, which Kris taped before Rasta smuggled them back in again.

Ollie Stoltz, bassist and keyboards, had a job in a library.

During their year together they'd become a tight-knit foursome. Kris was the driving force, Buzz, the moody one, with a bizarre, off-center black humor, Rasta, the easygoing comedian, and Ollie, serious, studious, kind to animals and old ladies.

The Wild Ones. They had their own look. Kris—so alive and sexy, with his raunchy strut, shock of dirty-blond hair, and intense ice-blue eyes.

Buzz—quite the opposite with his emaciated, satanic demeanor.

Ollie—an innocent face, John Lennon glasses, shoulder-length brown curls, and a cherub's smile.

Rasta—a ball of energy and cheeky good looks.

Girls loved them. Girls came to dance and stayed to stare.

When they were onstage playing, everything fit together nicely: Rasta on drums, Ollie handling bass and keyboards, Kris and Buzz exchanging guitar solos, swapping back and forth from lead to backup with swift practiced precision.

They covered every big hit, taking turns as vocalist, although it soon became obvious that Kris was the favorite when it came to singing. On guitar he was an original, doing anything he felt like, but on vocals he played it safe —a touch of Rod Stewart, a pinch of Mick Jagger, shades of American soul, and a rock & roll swagger.

He could do a perfect "Jumping Jack Flash," a moody

"Gasoline Alley," a hot and raunchy "Ain't Too Proud to Beg," and a touching "Your Song."

"The trouble is," Buzz announced one day as they stood idly by the side of the steamy indoor swimming pool watching a bunch of kids being taught to swim, "we're not doin' anythin' *different*. Y'know what I mean?"

Kris knew exactly what he meant—but it wasn't his fault. The audience wanted to hear familiar songs, and that's all they wanted to hear.

"We should be writin' our own stuff," Buzz said reflectively. "'Stead of churnin' out other people's hits. We gotta get Ollie t'come up with somethin'—he'd be good at it."

Kris nodded. He didn't feel like saying anything, but he'd been working on a few ideas of his own and had several songs he was anxious to try out. He'd held back because he didn't want the others putting him down.

Buzz eyed a buxom brunette emerging from the girls' changing room. "Nice pair of bristols," he remarked casually. "I bet she's a right little raver."

"When have you ever seen a pair you *didn't* like?" Kris responded.

"We gotta 'ave original material," Buzz repeated. "It's the only way we're goin' t'get bleedin' noticed."

"I know *that*," Kris replied. "As a matter of fact, I—" He didn't finish his sentence, because out of the corner of his eye he noticed a swimmer in trouble. Without hesitation he made a racing dive into the pool and headed for the struggling man, who was flailing around in the deep end in an advanced state of panic.

Maneuvering himself behind the victim, he grabbed him under the arms and began to swim to the side of the pool and safety.

But it wasn't so easy. The man really thought it was all over, and with arms and legs thrashing in every direction, he fought for survival, not realizing, in his panic, that Kris was trying to save him.

Together they sank beneath the water, whereupon the man suddenly changed tactics, clinging on to Kris for dear life, wrapping his legs around him in a death hold, dragging him to the bottom of the pool, where they hovered in a state of battle as Kris desperately tried to free himself from the man's fierce grip of unadulterated fear.

Without the intervention of Buzz, it might have been all over. Buzz didn't hesitate. He dived in like a kamikaze pilot, prying the man off Kris with lethal force, grabbing him around the neck.

With a sudden wild burst the three of them surfaced, and Buzz and Kris between them managed to drag the man to the side of the pool, where helping hands hauled him out. Kris immediately went to work pumping water out of the poor old sod.

"Fuck!" exclaimed Buzz. "This gig deserves danger money."

"Really—you're both so brave!" cooed the brunette he had observed earlier, now in a wet bathing suit with very sympathetic nipples on red alert.

The victim gasped and tried to sit up. A group of schoolchildren burst into applause.

Kris peered at the man he had rescued. He looked familiar, even in his half-drowned state. "Mr. Terence?" he asked tentatively.

"Oh . . . my . . . God. I owe you . . . my life," the man spluttered. "I had a cramp—an unimaginable pain. I couldn't move. I was—"

"Mr. Terence?" Kris repeated, definitely recognizing him as the show-business agent whose house his mother used to clean.

Terry Terence gazed up at the cocky-looking twenty-year-old with the bulging crotch and crooked grin. Maybe he'd died and gone to heaven. Ah . . . he'd always liked them young.

"Yes," he replied dreamily. "Do I know you?"

Mr. Terry Terence no longer lived in his house on Carlton Hill. He had moved to a rather grand apartment on Abbey Road, quite near the famous Abbey Road studios where the Beatles made all their records.

Later that day, when Kris and Buzz turned up for tea, they were greeted by a lanky, effeminate-looking man with watery spaniel eyes and a low cultured voice. "Do come in," he said softly. "I'm Justin, Mr. Terry's companion. He's resting right now; however, his instructions were to wake him as soon as you arrived." Justin extended a limp white hand. "My deepest thanks for your bravery. You know, Mr. Terry suffered a heart attack six months ago, and the doctor advised him to take more exercise. He started walking, soon got bored with that. Then tennis—much too strenuous. Finally he settled on swimming—the perfect answer."

"Yeah, it was nearly the answer all right," joked Buzz morbidly, peering at an Andy Warhol poster of a series of soup cans.

"How's he feeling?" Kris asked, checking out the photo frames, searching for the old signed picture of Johnnie Ray he remembered from his childhood.

"Thankful to be alive," Justin said crisply. "Usually he swims at the Grosvenor House pool, but today, for some unknown reason, he decided to venture locally." Justin made a clucking sound. "Life! How blithely we tread the path of fate!"

Buzz threw Kris a look as much as to say, *Who is this wacko?*

"Maybe we should come back another day," Kris suggested. "Y'know, if he's restin' an' all."

"Not at all," Justin said quickly. "He'd be most upset. I'll wake him now." He hurried from the room.

"Talk about light on yer feet!" Buzz said.

Kris zeroed in on the old photo of Johnnie Ray—different frame, same picture. "Look at this," he said triumphantly, picking it up.

"Who is it?" demanded Buzz.

"Johnnie Ray."

"Who's 'e when 'e's at 'ome?"

"A big singer in the fifties. My mum loved him."

"Hey—get a load of this," Buzz said, picking up a picture of the Beatles. "The fab four themselves. An' they signed it—all of 'em."

"Really?"

"Yeah. This old fart must really know people."

"I told you, didn't I?"

Mr. Terry Terence entered the room resplendent in black pajamas under a scarlet dressing gown elaborately embroidered with gold; he wore matching slippers. He was a middle-aged man, rather plump, with bland features, a ruddy complexion, and a puff of dyed brown hair. He bore a passing resemblance to Liberace.

"Well, boys," he said. "How am I ever going to repay you?"

And that was how The Wild Ones acquired their first agent and manager.

Right from the beginning, Mr. Terry Terence had eyes for Buzz. He took one look at the moody unsmiling twenty-one-year-old with the agile body, pale complexion and ragged black hair, and it was love at first sight. Although he was careful to conceal the way he felt, it soon became common knowledge and a great joke among the boys. That was what Mr. Terry Terence called them once he took them in hand—the boys—*his* boys. He was going to mold them into stars, or so he said; and after a year of trailing around the clubs getting nowhere, they were only too happy to put themselves in his experienced hands.

First he attended a couple of their local gigs, after which he sat the four of them down in his office and told them exactly what they were doing wrong.

"You're a copycat group," he told them, "bleating out other people's hits. Any bunch of musicians can get together and do that."

"I told 'em," Buzz said in his best know-it-all voice.

Kris shot him a disgusted look. "It's what the kids want to hear," he said stubbornly. "We'd love to do original stuff."

Mr. Terence sipped from a cup of strong black coffee. "Naturally. They're used to hearing familiar songs. Only you must understand, it's not going to get you anywhere. We have to have original material. Can any of you compose and write lyrics?"

Tentatively Ollie raised his hand. "I write music," he said. "Lousy on lyrics, but I'm quite into creating a melody."

Kris was surprised; it was the first *he'd* heard of it.

"Anyone else?" asked Mr. Terence, anxious eyes lingering on Buzz, as usual.

"Uh . . . yeah . . . I got some stuff," responded Buzz with an embarrassed shrug. "'Course, it probably stinks—sod it—what the hell. . . ." he trailed off.

Kris had always thought he and Buzz were pretty close—now this revelation. Shit! He'd better make his own announcement soon or he'd be left out. "I've put together quite a bit of material," he said quickly.

Now it was Buzz's turn to look surprised. He raised a cynical eyebrow. "You 'ave?"

Rasta laughed, always one to break the tension. "Seems like you've *all* bin at it in secret. Someone should've told *me*, I'd 'ave given up wankin' an' done somethin' useful with me right hand!"

"It's never too late," said Mr. Terence fussily, ignoring their ribald laughter. "The more original material the better."

"Right on," agreed Buzz.

"Next, we have to work on your image," Mr. Terence continued, adjusting the knot on his old school tie.

"Why?" Kris demanded. "There's nothin' wrong with the way we look."

"There's nothing right with it either. Onstage you resemble a raggle-taggle group of misfits. There has to be a sense of unity—a feeling you belong together."

"I'm not wearin' no stupid stage costume," Buzz warned. "I wear me black gear, an' that's that."

"You could *all* wear black," Mr. Terence suggested, diplomatically, careful not to ever say anything that might offend his favorite.

"I'm better in red, man," argued Rasta. "I got enough black on me already, thankyouverymuch."

"I have the answer," Mr. Terence said triumphantly. "All black outfits with red scarves." Naturally he had observed that Buzz usually wore a long tatty scarf wound around his neck.

"I don't want some faggot outfit," Buzz said rudely. "I think we should go with whatever we got on at the time."

"The Beatles look good," Ollie observed.

"Bunch of wankers!" Buzz sneered.

Mr. Terence inspected his nails, buffed to a pearly shine. "Next we have to talk about buying you decent equipment," he said. "And sending you out on tour, so you can acquire real experience."

"What about a recording contract?" Kris asked, getting down to the nitty-gritty.

"That's not something that just happens," Mr. Terence replied testily. "It's a goal we have to work toward. If I sent you into a studio now you'd be laughed out of the room." Pausing, he took another sip of coffee. "First you'll develop original, fresh material, and if you can't do that, we'll buy you some. Then you'll go out on the road and learn presentation and discipline. It'll all be worthwhile. When *I* say you're ready to go into a recording studio, that's when we do it."

"What about our jobs?" Ollie inquired seriously. "How can we tour and still work?"

"You can't. That's obvious." Mr. Terence was crisp and to the point. "I have decided to not only be your agent but to manage you as well. As your agent I will receive ten percent of your collective earnings. As your manager I shall require a further twenty-five percent. And for that I take it upon myself to finance your climb to the top. I will purchase new equipment, a van for you to travel around the country, clothes for you to wear onstage, and I will also advance you a reasonable living allowance."

"Wow!" exclaimed Rasta. "That's fuckin' fabulous!"

Kris shot him a warning look. "We'll have to think about it."

"Yeah, right," agreed Buzz, catching on that enthusiasm could only lead to getting screwed.

Mr. Terence was perfectly calm. "Think away," he said. "You can let me know within a week."

"You'd be gettin' thirty-five percent of us," Kris said unsurely, calculating aloud. "Isn't that a lot?"

"Thirty-five percent of nothing," Mr. Terence pointed out. "*And* risking a goodly amount of my own money, not to mention my valuable time. Take it or leave it." He sighed, as if he couldn't care less either way. "I think you have potential. Others might not."

A week later all four of them signed individual contracts tying them irrevocably to Mr. Terry Terence for the next seven years. Kris had to have his mother sign for him as he was still a few days away from his twenty-first birthday.

Avis came to Mr. Terence's office in her best yellow dress, a silly hat perched rakishly atop her graying hair. "I bought it for you, luv," she whispered to her son. "For luck. Two quid in Marks and Spencer."

Impulsively he hugged her. "Thanks, Mum."

"Mrs. Pierce! What a joy to see you after all these years," Mr. Terence said, and in a low aside everyone in the office heard, *"Nobody* polishes silver the way you used to."

"Thank you, Mr. T." Her voice was stiff and proper, unlike her usual raucous shout. She had never told anyone why she'd abruptly left Mr. Terence's employ over nine years ago. He had accused her of stealing a pair of gold cuff links, and when one of his gentleman friends turned up with them two days later, he had merely said, "Found 'em, dear," as if that was apology enough. She never went back.

Now here she was, in his office, signing important contracts on behalf of her Kris. She'd sooner have given him a black eye for his stinking mistrust.

After signing, they went to a pub to celebrate, just mother and son. Mr. Terence had wanted them to stay in the office and split a bottle of champagne, but Avis tugged on Kris's sleeve and hoarsely whispered, "I'd be more comfortable down the pub, lad." So the pub it was.

They sat there for two hours enjoying each other's company and a few beers. It was one of the best times Kris had ever spent with her. She mentioned Brian only four times.

"I'm goin' to buy you a mink stole, Mum," he promised, as they walked out into the cold night air. "You deserve it."

She laughed—her wonderfully familiar bawdy cackle. "Cor luv us! You an' who else—Prince bleedin' Philip?"

The Wild Ones toured for a full year, covering the country. They traveled across England, Wales, and Scotland. Up north, down south, across to Ireland and back again. And all the time squashed together in a cramped Volkswagen bus with their equipment piled high around them. They took turns driving, and on one-night stands they slept in the back of the bus smelling like a bunch of clapped-out camels. They even took turns having girls in the bus. One little raver in the front, and another on her knees in the back. Some of them were barely in their teens. "Baby groupies," Buzz christened them. "Straight off the bottle an' onto the rod!"

Once in a while Mr. Terence came to see them. He made full note of the enthusiastic audience reaction, listened carefully to their new material, made his criticisms and general observations, then left.

"When are we coming to London?" Kris always asked.

"As soon as you're ready. I'll let you know," was Mr. Terence's invariable reply.

They were exhausted and burnt out. Where was the recognition Mr. Terence had promised them? Where was their recording contract? Where were Fame, Fortune and the Good Life?

To say they were disillusioned and fed up would be putting it mildly.

"We have seen the asshole of England," Kris observed solemnly, late one night, as they sat in a roadside café outside Manchester sharing a greasy plate of sausages and chips. "And it bleedin' stinks."

"Write a song about it," Buzz said, yawning. "Yer manage t'write about everything else."

"Oh, yeah, very pretty—'The Asshole of England,' by Kris Phoenix. I can see it now—a big hit. It'll knock the Stones right off the charts!"

Rasta began beating drum rhythms on the table, while Ollie made fake boom-boom sounds.

"*I met a girl an' 'er name was Sally. Kissed 'er on the cheek an' fucked her in the alley,*'" sang Buzz. "'*She looked so sweet, she looked so neat. An' I din't know she lived in*'—ALL TOGETHER NOW—LET'S BLOODY HEAR IT—

"'THE ASSHOLE OF ENGLAND!'" They all screamed, hysterical with laughter.

"Enough of that," grumbled a fat counterman in a filthy apron, looming over their table. "You're makin' too much noise."

"Sod it!" sneered Buzz. "Can't even have any fun any more."

"What's fun?" Kris asked wearily.

"Gettin' your dick sucked in a bed instead of behind a bloody amplifier?" Rasta suggested.

"I dunno," Kris sighed. "I'm tired. I just wan' t'go back to London."

"Call the fag an' tell 'im," Buzz said. "It's about time 'e kept some of his bloody promises. If I 'ave to sleep with your hairy arse in me face one more night, I'm packin' it in."

"*You* call him," Kris countered. "You're his blue-eyed boy."

Adopting an exaggerated pose and mincing voice, Buzz said, "Hmmm, do you really think so, dear?"

"You'd make a horrible girl," Ollie remarked. "All white and pasty!"

"Yeah, but you'd like t'fuck me, wouldn'tcha?" Buzz joked. "You'd like ter give me one, wouldn'tcha, darlin'?"

"Not bloody likely," Ollie responded indignantly.

"Aw, c'mon, admit it," Buzz taunted. "Don't be shy. We all know what goes on in them fancy *music* academies. I bet you've slipped it up an arse or two in yer time."

Ollie leaped to his feet, red-faced. "Don't even joke about it, you fucking wanker."

Buzz narrowed his eyes. "Hit a nerve, 'ave I?"

"Shut up, you two," Kris said, flicking a greasy chip in his friend's face.

"Yeah, shut up," agreed Rasta, grabbing a handful of chips and throwing them at Ollie and Buzz.

"'Ere we go!" yelled Buzz, reaching for a sausage,

which he proceeded to tear into pieces and pelt across the table.

Kris responded with a squirt of tomato ketchup, and Ollie followed with the mustard. Within seconds they were yelling and screaming, letting out the tension, embroiled in an enthusiastic and enjoyable food fight.

"That's about enough of that, you yobbos, *enough!*" commanded the fat counterman, lumbering over.

Ignoring him, they continued their fun.

"Sling the buggers out, Bert," roared a heavyset truck driver sitting nearby. "Fuckin' bunch of pansies with their long 'air. Chuck 'em out. Me an' my mates'll help yer."

Bert had no say in the matter. The truck driver and his friends were only too happy to join the fight. The trouble was, they weren't playing with food. Fists were their weapons, and they launched into the unsuspecting boys with vicious gusto, taking them by surprise.

"Let's teach the fuckin' *girls* a lesson," shouted the heavyset driver, encouraging his troops into battle.

"Aw . . . shit," groaned Kris, as one of the bullies grabbed him by his long hair and attempted to frog-march him to the door. He twisted free, kicking the much bigger man sharply in the balls.

"Yer fuckin' scummy bastard!" roared the man, doubling over.

Kris took quick stock. Five burly truck drivers and four skinny would-be rock stars. The odds weren't good.

"Let's get the fuck outta here," he yelled.

But he was too late. The fight was on.

BOBBY MONDELLA
1972

★ ☆ ★ ☆ ★

"Happy birthday, honey," Sharleen said with a captivating smile, placing a tempting chocolate cake in front of Bobby.

"Yeah, man," agreed Rocket, hovering nearby. "How about this bein' *our* year?"

"Ain't gonna fight with those sentiments," Bobby said —a new Bobby, a slimmed-down version of the former blimp. Bobby Mondella at twenty-two was tall, good-looking, and fit. Impossible to recognize as the fat boy who had been carried from Cousin Fanni's house four years ago and rushed by ambulance to Emergency, where he nearly died.

The two ambulance attendants almost had hernias when they lifted the stretcher with Bobby on it. He had a burst appendix, and the surgeon who operated told him that another hour and there would have been no chance of saving him. As it was, he hovered on the critical list for several days.

"Cutting through your fat nearly cost you your life," the surgeon said bluntly, when he came to remove the stitches. "You'd better get rid of the blubber or be prepared to check out early."

92

"Check out of the hospital?" Bobby asked innocently.

"No. Check out of life, young man."

Fanni came to visit a week after his operation. She brought *Playboy* magazine and three Hershey bars. *Jerk off and get fat:* the story of his life.

"Did you call The Chainsaw?" he asked anxiously.

"Why? Was I s'pose to?"

Groaning, he said, "I'll lose my job. You should've called."

"They'll understand."

They didn't. When Bobby returned four weeks later, and already twenty pounds lighter, Nichols Kline was unsympathetic. "Your job's taken, Mondella. Get lost," he said.

Bobby hung around outside, waiting for either Sharleen or Rocket. She arrived first and was about to walk right past when he grabbed her arm and reminded her who he was.

Eyes flashing angrily, she said, "Where's my tape?"

"I've got it."

"Yeah? Exactly where, may I ask?"

"At home."

"Why didn't you give it to Marcus Citroen?"

"He never came in that night," Bobby explained. "And after that I was rushed to the hospital with a burst appendix. The truth is, I nearly died. I was real sick."

She couldn't have cared less. "I want my tape back," she said flatly.

Shifting uncomfortably, he said, "Y'know somethin'? I played it. I'm sure it's not the best you can do."

Indignantly she glared at him. "How would *you* know?"

"I used to be in the music business when I was younger." Hesitating, he decided he had nothing to lose, and added, "I . . . uh . . . made some records, wrote a few songs."

Sarcasm dripped. "When you was *twelve*, sonny?"

"I *was* very young, but it's true—I swear it."

She was getting bored. "Sure, honey."

"I'll write *you* a song," he volunteered.

"Oh, boy! I can't wait."

"Listen, don't fight it. I can help you sound much better on tape."

"Just bring it on back, sonny."

She was being stubborn, but he was sure that given half a chance he could convince her. "When?" he asked.

"Tomorrow."

"I won't be around. Nichols fired me. Let me drop it by your place in the morning."

Biting her lower lip, she thought for a moment, then said, "What the heck," and produced a dog-eared card with SHARLEEN—CHANTEUSE printed on it. She scribbled an address and thrust it at him. "Ten o'clock. Don't expect to stay."

"I won't," he said hastily, watching her walk swiftly through the back entrance of the club.

Another ten minutes and Rocket appeared. "Jeez, Bobby! I never expected to see *you* again. Thought you'd scrammed with all the bread—yours an' mine."

"Thanks for being so trusting."

With a nonchalant shrug, Rocket said, "Ain't the first time I bin ripped."

It was great coming across two people so thrilled to see him. Trusting they weren't. He repeated his hospital story, adding he'd been fired. "Any suggestions?"

"Clooney's," Rocket said without hesitation. "They're hirin' bouncers. Get your ass over there pronto." He flipped a cigarette from his pocket. "Do I get my money?"

"I don't have it on me." The truth was, Ernest had stolen every penny while he was in the hospital.

"Hey, man, I guess I've waited four weeks, I'll wait another day," Rocket decided. "You can bring it by in the mornin'." Scratching his head he added, "Just make sure you deduct the advance on rent you paid me—I got myself a new roommate. You're out."

Great! Before he was even in. But he couldn't blame the guy. After all, there'd been no guarantee he'd reappear. "I can't make the morning," he said, thinking of his rendezvous with Sharleen.

Rocket shrugged. "Lunchtime then. I'll buy ya a hot dog an' split a beer." Snatching Sharleen's card from Bobby's hand, he took a pencil from behind his ear and scrawled an address on the blank side. "Tomorra," Rocket said. "Try Clooney's. Ya look like a bouncer. Tell 'em you're over twenny-five. They'll buy it."

Rocket was right. They bought it, and Bobby had a new job throwing people out of one of the hottest singles bars on the West Side.

When he got home he confronted Ernest about the missing money.

Ernest was furious. "You accusin' me, boy?" he demanded belligerently.

"I sure am," Bobby retorted. As he was shedding weight, so he was gaining in courage. It was about time he stood up to Ernest.

"Well, I ain't gonna take it," Ernest steamed. "No, sirree, I ain't gonna take no more of your goddamn shee . . . it."

"It wasn't my money," Bobby tried to explain. "I was only—"

"I'm not interested in your bitchin' an' whinin'," Ernest interrupted, obese belly heaving with emotion. "You all's jest a weight 'round your good cousin's neck. That woman bin too damn good to you. Whyn't y'git out. An' do it now."

"If I had my money I would," Bobby retorted angrily. "You took the six thousand dollars I came here with. You spent it pretty good."

"*I* took it? You done got the goddamn balls to say, I,

Ernest Crystal, took somethin' wasn't his." He started to yell. "Fuck you, boy. *Fuck you*."

Fanni arrived home, causing Ernest to shut up and Bobby to go to his small room in the back. He made up his mind, if Rocket was prepared to wait for his money, he would take his first week's paycheck and get the hell out. The sooner the better.

The next morning, clad in his best pants and jacket, both now too big for him, he arrived on Sharleen's doorstep, tape in hand. She lived in a basement off Tenth Avenue. The steps down were littered with garbage, lewd graffiti were scrawled all over the door, and there was no doorbell.

He knocked tentatively. After a few minutes and no response, he knocked again. A large rat scuttled out of its corner hiding place and raced past him up the crumbling stone steps.

"Comin'," yelled a muffled voice, and eventually the door was flung open.

Standing there was Rocket, in grubby jockey shorts, with his lank hair all over the place. He had a disoriented look on his face. "Bobby," he said vaguely. "I thought you was goin' to be here later."

For a moment Bobby was startled. But then he realized he must have made the stupid mistake of going to Rocket's address instead of Sharleen's. Both were scribbled on the same card.

"I s'pose you'd better c'min an' visit the palace," Rocket mumbled, adding a loud burp.

Bobby stepped inside chaos. Peeling brown walls, a linoleum-covered floor, old furniture scarred with cigarette burns, stacks of used Chinese food take-out cartons, and piles of old newspapers and magazines.

"This is the tidy part," Rocket said with an unapologetic shrug. "You should see the bedroom, an' what passes for the bathroom."

"Hey, at least it's yours," Bobby said enviously.

"Yeah, I know, I know—it coulda bin yours too." Lazily he scratched his stomach. "That's the breaks, I guess. You'll find someplace else." Pausing, he contemplated a rusty hot plate on a table in the corner. "Wanna cuppa coffee?"

Bobby thought of Sharleen, probably impatiently waiting for him, wondering why he was late. "I can't stay," he said quickly. "I just came by to ask if y'can hold out a couple of weeks for your money."

Rocket threw him a quizzical look. "Y'know somethin'? You *really* got jumpin' balls." Lighting a match beneath a saucepan of water, he flipped a cigarette from an open packet of Lucky Strikes. "If you weren't such a fartin' babe in toyland, I'd be pissed. What's the problem?"

"It's like this—" Bobby began.

A woman entered the room. A woman wrapped in a bath towel and nothing else. She smiled sweetly. "Bobby," she greeted him in a low, singsong voice. "Are you early or am I late?"

It was Sharleen.

The shock of discovering the love of his life was living with his best friend did not exactly boost Bobby's morale. When he checked out the card she'd handed him, he saw that she and Rocket had written the same address. Obviously they hadn't tried to hide anything. It was a drag, but he faced it.

They made an incongruous couple: Sharleen, the pretty black girl who wanted to be the new Diana Ross, and Rocket Fabrizzi, a would-be actor who saw himself as a sort of seventies Marlon Brando.

Over the course of the next four years the three of them forged a solid friendship based on mutual trust and respect. They were all orphans, in one way or the other. Sharleen had no family. Rocket had long ago disowned his. And Bobby left Fanni and Ernest's with no regret on their part, and rented a room that made his friends' basement look like the Plaza.

What they had was a loyal support group. Bobby took up music again, mainly because of Sharleen's encouragement. He wrote songs for her, helped her with voice training, presentation and style, and got himself a daytime job selling sheet music, while still working nights at Clooney's.

Sharleen nagged him to diet and work out, meanwhile urging him to return to music full time. Although she was a lousy housekeeper, she made him the best meatloaf he'd ever tasted.

Rocket was just Rocket. Always there, always up, always working on schemes to make an extra buck or two, in between going out on auditions and coming home with a turndown and an undefeated grin.

A week before Bobby's twenty-second birthday he heard of a loft in Greenwich Village—a sublet. Quickly he figured out if they all shared the rent, they could move in and begin living like human beings. It didn't take much to persuade Sharleen and Rocket.

"Blow out the candles," Sharleen urged, her ebony skin glowing.

Bobby smiled at her. She was still the prettiest girl in the world, but she belonged to Rocket, and he had long ago learned to accept that sad fact of life.

"Yes, go on, Bobby, make a wish," said his current girlfriend, an adorable little blonde who looked exactly like all the other adorable little blondes he'd dated over the past few years—for when Bobby finally lost all the excess weight, the girls came running. Now Sharleen was always teasing him, calling him Mister Stud and other crazy nicknames.

Shutting his eyes, he wished for many things. When he opened them, Sharleen was staring straight at him. "Did you wish for me to become a star? Did you, Bobby?" she asked urgently, licking her luscious lips.

"Yeah, yeah, yeah," Rocket jeered. "We're *all* gonna be stars. Just hang around another ten, twenty, thirty years. We should live that long."

A week later Rocket got a small role in a movie shooting in New York. Two weeks after that Sharleen auditioned for a Broadway show and succeeded in joining the chorus. And Bobby sold his first song.

"Honey," Sharleen said to Bobby, her big brown eyes gleaming with delight, "when you make a wish—you *really* make a wish. We're on our way!"

RAFEALLA
1972

★ ☆ ★ ☆ ★

Birthdays always made Rafealla sick. She hated them. Each time another year passed, she felt the pain and hurt and loss all over again. And this year, her twelfth birthday, was especially bad, as her mother, Anna, was thinking of getting married again, and Rafealla was enraged at the very idea.

Mother and daughter had argued back and forth interminably.

"It's not fair to Papa," Rafealla had screamed.

"Your father's been dead for nearly five years," Anna tried to explain. "He wouldn't want me to continue being on my own."

"Yes, he *would*!" Rafealla shouted. "He would! He would!"

She loathed the man her mother was seeing. He was an English lord with a stupid stammer and stupid red hair and a stupid son and a stupid castle in the English countryside. His name was Lord Cyrus Egerton, and he was hateful.

"Well, young lady," Anna had finally said, a sharp edge to her normally gentle voice. "Whatever I decide to do is *my* decision. Fortunately I do not need your permission, although your approval would be nice."

100

"Never!" Rafealla screamed dramatically. "I'd sooner be dead!"

And she meant it.

Nanny Macdee had tried to calm her, but to no avail. Rafealla knew for sure if her mother remarried it was a terrible thing to do to her poor dead father. And nobody could change her mind.

Papa. Lucien. She thought of him often. The nightmare of his shocking death was forever with her.

How could she forget? She was right there when it happened, standing at the door of their house in Paris, waving, while her dear father was blown to pieces by a terrorist's bomb planted in Henri Ronet's car. They had meant to kill Henri Ronet. Lucien Le Serre's being in the car was just bad timing on his part.

The noise of the explosion had wiped out Rafealla's world. Shards of glass embedded in her legs caused temporary paralysis and put a dismal end to her hopes of a future in the ballet. She was in the hospital for several months, enduring two operations. When she was well enough to go home, her mother had already packed up, sold the Paris house, and was all set to move to England. "We'll leave the memories behind," she'd said to her daughter. "We have to. It's the only way."

Mother might think that, but Rafealla knew it wasn't possible. She would never forget her wonderful papa and all that he'd meant to her.

Right from the start she hated England. Cold, damp weather. Rainy streets. Strange food, and a language she didn't care to speak, even though she was bilingual—she had grown up speaking both French and English.

Anna sent her to a strict private school where the girls taunted her because she was "different." They nicknamed her "Gimp," as since the accident, she walked with a slight limp. And sometimes they called her "Darkie" on account of her olive-hued skin.

Nanny Macdee suggested to her mother that a private tutor might be a better idea until Rafealla became more acclimated to the English way of life. Anna agreed, and Rafealla did not return to school until she was eleven. By that time she had toughened up, and anyone who called her names paid for it.

Now it was her twelfth birthday, and the memories were flooding around her, and Anna was planning on marrying again, and it was all so unfair. . . .

Rafealla went to her mother's bathroom, opened the medicine cabinet, emptied out every bottle of pills she could find, and swallowed the lot.

Soon she would be with her father again, and that was all she really wanted.

KRIS PHOENIX
1973

★ ☆ ★ ☆ ★

While getting beaten up in a motorway café just outside of Manchester was hardly the highlight of their tour, it did enable The Wild Ones to get back to London and an anxious Mr. Terence.

Buzz had a broken nose, which upset Mr. Terence far more than any of the cuts, bruises, and black eyes of the other three. Nevertheless he had them all checked out by his own doctor, and everyone was shocked to discover Kris had two broken ribs.

"I told you I was in bloody agony," he informed anyone who would listen. "Bleedin' hell, talk about ignoring an injured person."

"Getting into fights is irresponsible and just not done," Mr. Terence tut-tutted.

"Wasn't our fault," Ollie explained.

"Yeah," agreed Rasta. "These great big bruisers came right at us outta nowhere."

Mr. Terence canceled the rest of their tour, moved them into a small house he owned near Hampstead Heath, and informed them he'd had interest from a record company, and soon they would be going into the recording studios to make their first single.

"Soon" took three months, but the great day finally came, and they were ready for it.

Mr. Terence had put them together with a young producer, Sam Rozelle, and Sam was as enthusiastic as they were. He loved their material, especially the songs Kris and Buzz had written together, and he predicted great things ahead.

Kris didn't know what to believe any more. He still felt good about the group—especially now that they were doing their own songs and not just belting out copies of other people's hits. But he was also wary. There were so many fine groups out there—so many singers, songwriters, and guitarists. And so few hit records. How could they possibly stand a chance, with all the competition?

Sam took him out for a beer the night before the recording session. They sat in a pub in Kilburn and discussed things. Sam was a quiet man in his early thirties with thinning hair and a conservative style. He was married, with two small children and a wife who looked ten years older than he. He seemed perfectly happy and content, and Kris sometimes wondered if he hadn't strayed into the music business by mistake.

"Well, Kris." Sam raised his glass in a toast, glancing around the crowded pub. "Make the most of this. Anonymity is something you'll miss."

"Huh?"

"Going about your business unrecognized."

Kris snorted with laughter. "Oh, yeah, sure."

"Don't underestimate your future," Sam said very seriously. "I *know* what's going to happen. Believe me. I've seen it before."

Kris tried to make light of Sam's prediction. "Well, mate," he said with a cheery wink, "I bloody well hope so, it's about bleedin' time. We've been at it for long enough."

* * *

Back at the house, Buzz was sitting on a sofa sharing a joint with Flower and a couple of her girlfriends. Ollie was asleep, and Rasta out.

"'Ere, sit yourself down an' join in the outrageous fun," he deadpanned, when Kris arrived home.

"Yeah, c'mon, Kris," enthused Flower, her wide blue eyes as stoned as ever. She had only just forgiven Buzz for giving her a nasty case of the crabs.

Kris checked out her girlfriends. Usually he stayed well away from Flower and her friends, but tonight he was on edge; he needed something or someone to calm him down and force him to relax.

One of the girls was out of the question—she looked no more than fourteen. The other had possibilities for a one-night stand. She was the Julie Christie type, only not as good-looking. Her name was Willow. She was nineteen years old and worked as a sales assistant in the same dress shop as Flower.

Sitting down next to her, he started with the chat. It never took long—half an hour later she was in his bed. To his amazement he soon found out she was a virgin. This was a first. He'd never encountered a virgin before.

"You shoulda told me," he said, thrusting for entry.

"Why?" she whispered, shivering. "Would it have made any difference?"

He pondered that one. Would it? When Kris Phoenix wanted to get laid, nothing stood in his way. "I dunno." Pausing, he said, "D'you want me to stop?"

"No," she answered quickly. "Get it over with."

Get it over with! Oh, that was charming, really romantic. He felt his hard-on deflate, and suddenly sleep seemed the most tempting item on the menu.

"Listen, luv," he said, disengaging himself, "I think you'd better go home."

Willow began to cry. "I've disappointed you, haven't I?" she asked tearfully.

This girl was certainly different. He was used to the

lower-echelon groupies out on the road, and the hard nuts he encountered in London—tough little cookies who had been around and around and then some. Yes, this one was definitely unusual. She had *feelings*.

"C'mon, don't cry," he said uncomfortably. "It's not your fault."

Tentatively she touched his limp penis and started a slow stroke. "Can we try again?" she asked timidly.

Who was he to say no?

Rising to the occasion, he made another attempt, and this time it was all the way home with hardly a sound from her and a loud grunt of satisfaction from him. Exploring uncharted territory was quite a kick.

After the deed was done they lay companionably in each other's arms. Usually, when it was over, he couldn't wait for them to get dressed and get out. With Willow he didn't seem to mind. She fitted into his arms nicely, and she had a lovely firm pair of bristols.

With a sigh of satisfaction he drifted off to sleep, not waking until morning, when he was quite surprised to find her still there. Lustfully eyeing her sleeping form, he quietly rolled on top, making a stealthy entry.

She awoke with a little gasp, followed by a little smile.

"Somebody forgot to go home," he teased, thrusting back and forth. In the daylight, with no makeup, she was prettier than he'd thought. He liked the fact that she wasn't a slag.

"I wanted to stay and wish you luck," she said timidly. "Buzz said today's the big day."

"Yeah." He nodded, tweaking an appealing nipple as he deftly maneuvered her above him, and really got to work.

Cheeks flushed, breathing fast, she did everything he asked.

"Spread your legs," he commanded.

She did so, and immediately began to climax.

Joining her in the dance, he realized he'd never felt so good in his entire life.

Today was going to be a winner!

"I'm fed up with the friggin' faggot makin' goo-goo eyes at me," Buzz complained. "If 'e's not bleedin' careful I'm gonna belt 'im one. I mean it."

Kris looked up from the newspaper. "What happened?"

"I went round to 'is flat today—'e said he had to talk to me."

Kris put the newspaper down. He was angry—he'd told Rasta, Ollie *and* Buzz, if there was any talking to be done *he'd* do it. They had to have a leader, and he'd thought it was understood he was it. "Why'd you do that?" he asked sharply.

"Fuck! I dunno. He said it was somethin' private."

"What was it?"

"A bunch of old cobblers 'bout the record comin' out soon, publicity crap, an' how he thinks I should dump Flower. Bad for me bleedin' image." He scowled. "What bleedin' image?"

Rubbing his chin, Kris shrugged. "Beats me."

"Then the stupid old geezer puts 'is 'and on me knee. Cor blimey! He's lucky he's still walkin'."

"What did you do?"

"What *din't* I do," Buzz ranted. "I told 'im straight. Mr. T., I says, do I look like a friggin' queen?"

"Very subtle. I bet that went down like a ton of shit."

"'E got all red in the face an' nervous. 'Dear boy,' 'e says, 'how can you even think such a thing?'" Angrily Buzz flung himself into an armchair. "Y'know somethin'? All I wan' outta life is to play great guitar an' get rich. Then I can tell 'em *all* to go get fucked."

"Not a bad idea," Kris responded mildly. "Only if you'd leave everything to me, you wouldn't have to put up with his bollocks, I'd deal with it."

"Right. You're on. Just keep the creep away from me an' Flower. She's bin my girlfriend for five years, an' I'm not gettin' rid of her for any old fairy. Okay?"

Kris decided he'd have to talk to Mr. Terence. He might be financing their rise to nowhere, but he certainly didn't own them. And when their record came out and the money started rolling in, he'd be making plenty on his initial investment. Thirty-five percent of The Wild Ones was a pretty secure bet.

Kris was excited about their record, "Lonesome Morning"—words by him, music by Ollie. He couldn't wait for it to hit an unsuspecting public. The big time had to be just around the corner, and he was ready. Oh, was he ready!

Five weeks later a conversation took place.

"I'm pregnant," Willow said, her pale face flushed.

"You're what?" Kris replied, sure he couldn't possibly have heard her correctly.

"Pregnant," she repeated, with tear-filled eyes. "And my father's going to kill me."

"Oh, *shit,*" he said.

BOBBY MONDELLA
1973

★ ☆ ★ ☆ ★

"Please, Bobby, *please*." Sharleen was pleading with him. "There's no *point* in your tellin' Rocket. He'll only get mad, and you know what he's like when he's mad. And it's not as if anything's going to *happen*. This is a business date, purely business. If Rocket were here I'd take him with me. But he's not, he's in California, and I wish I was with him, and since I'm not, there's no harm in this. Honestly! Now pass me that rhinestone earring and stop *fussing*."

Reluctantly Bobby reached for her earring and watched her clip it into place. She looked radiantly pretty, as usual, with her glowing black skin, fluff of jet curls, and large brown eyes. Tonight she was wearing a slinky dress sparkling with deep-purple sequins. It plunged in front, dipped in back, and he knew she must have blown a week's salary on it.

"I could come with you," he suggested.

"Bobby, Bobby, don't you trust me? Rocket trusts me, and he's my *boyfriend*. If anyone should be concerned, it should be him."

"He's not here, Sharleen," Bobby pointed out. "And he doesn't know."

Spraying Arpège liberally up and down her bare arms and across her cleavage, she said, "No. He's not here and he doesn't know. Maybe he's out with one of those cute-assed Hollywood starlets. A nice little *white* girl with pink skin and blue eyes."

"You know he's not."

"*How* do I know?" she sighed petulantly. "He ran off to L.A. fast enough, didn't he?"

"He's working on a movie."

Standing up, she surveyed the finished product in the mirror with a critical eye. "*I'm* working too," she said firmly, inspecting her body profile. "This is a work date, and nothing else."

He could see there was no way to argue with her. If she thought a "work date" involved going to a man's apartment at twelve o'clock at night—alone—that was her problem.

"Help me find a cab, huh?" She dazzled him with her smile.

Escorting her to the street, he hailed a taxi and saw her safely into it. "Call me if you need me," he said sternly.

"I won't need you, silly." Her silky hand touched his cheek. "This is my big chance, Bobby. There's no way I'm going to blow it. Please be happy for me."

Watching the cab skid off down the street, he couldn't help wishing Rocket would get back soon. The responsibility of baby-sitting Sharleen was starting to get to him. Two nights ago she had come home from the theater where she was still in the chorus, a triumphant expression lighting her face. "*Guess* who was in tonight," she'd breathed excitedly. "Just start guessing because I want you to *know*."

"Stevie Wonder."

"Nope."

"Billy Dee Williams."

"Would I still be alive?"

"The great Miss Diana Ross?"

"Bobby. This is important. This is my *future*."

"Who?"

"Marcus Citroen." She savored the sound of his name. "Blue Cadillac Records. *The* Mister Citroen himself. And he sat in the front row an' never took his eyes off me all night!"

"Maybe he's shortsighted."

"Bobby! Get serious. I had the stage manager deliver an envelope to his driver with my resumé and picture. Oh, Bobby! He called me from his car before I left the theater and invited me to a party at his apartment on Saturday night. *And* he said when the other guests leave, we'll talk about my career. Isn't it fabulous?"

"Are you *kidding?*"

"No. I am most certainly not. This is the break I've been wishing for all my life."

There had been no talking her out of it. When he tried, she'd merely snapped at him, changing the subject. Sharleen was ecstatic, and in a way he couldn't blame her. For eighteen months she'd stood by and watched both his and Rocket's careers begin to warm up, while nothing except the chorus had happened for her. Rocket landed small roles in two movies, and then a Hollywood agent signed him, and within weeks he was on his way to Los Angeles to play the second male lead in an important film.

As for Bobby, his songs were in demand, *and* his musical arrangements, not to mention his piano backing. He was doing very nicely, and several of his songs had been in the top twenty, recorded by various artists. He'd given up both his outside jobs, and now spent his days composing.

Twice he'd managed to get Sharleen studio time, where she recorded demos of two of his songs. The songs sold, Sharleen didn't. At least she had the tapes to console her. But she wanted much more than that.

Hey—what was *he* worrying about? She wasn't *his* girl-friend, although he had spent the last five years wishing she was.

Falling asleep with the television on, he awoke in a cold sweat at 4 A.M. He'd been having some kind of nightmare, but couldn't remember what it was about. His mouth felt like sandpaper, and he was hot and covered in perspiration. Getting out of bed, he padded silently into the kitchen and poured himself a glass of water. The loft consisted of a large living space, with two screened-off bedrooms, one at each end. Before going back to his area he decided to peek in on Sharleen, just to make sure she was safely home.

She wasn't. Her bed was undisturbed.

Goddamnit! What was he supposed to do now?

Go back to sleep and mind your own business, an inner voice warned him.

But he couldn't, and when Sharleen came in at five-thirty in the morning, he was pacing around the loft like a distraught father. "Where the hell you been?" he demanded, too angry to notice her bedraggled appearance and shaken expression.

"Leave me alone," she said wearily, pushing past him and locking herself in the bathroom.

"Just you listen to me—" he began.

"Shut up!" she screamed from behind the closed door. "I don't have to answer to you or anyone. Leave me the fuck alone!"

He did just that, and early the next morning went off to a recording session at Soul On Soul Records, a small record company run by a woman producer named Amerika Allen. She was using him quite often. Today they were recording one of his songs with Rufus T. Ram, a young soul singer.

Amerika greeted him warmly. She was a heavily built black woman of thirty-three with an enormous bosom and a taste for flowing African-style clothes. "Hiya, Bobby boy."

He kissed her on the cheek. "Hey—Amerika, my favorite lady. You are lookin' hot!"

"Charm! The man is learnin' charm." Narrowing her eyes, she peered at him closely. "Thing is, Bobby, you all look like you had a *haaard* night. One of your little blond chickies keep you up?"

"Nope."

Amerika grinned. She had the widest smile and the whitest teeth. "You can't fool me, man. I can *smeeell* a sleepless night."

He wasn't about to tell her about Sharleen. Twice he had brought Sharleen to the studio, and Amerika had not been exactly enthusiastic. "Pretty chick. Small voice," she'd said dismissively.

"I wish you'd give her a chance," Bobby had pleaded.

"Honey—not even for you. I only deal with genuine talent."

"C'mon, Sharleen's got a great personality. She'd really come across on television."

"Sure, baby, she'll come across all right, but not at *this* record company."

End of story.

"You bin holding out on me, Bobby," Amerika said accusingly, putting a friendly arm around his shoulder as they walked into the studio.

"I have?"

"Yeah, baby. I've bin findin' out things."

"Like what?"

"I'll buy you lunch, an' then I can tell you all about it."

"Hey—tell me now, you got me curious."

"Be patient. Don't you want a free tuna fish sandwich?"

Rufus T. Ram was six feet four inches tall, skinny, with wild Afro hair and a high-pitched, musical voice, reminiscent of a young Smokey Robinson. He'd already had a couple of near-hits with Soul On Soul.

The song Bobby had written and arranged was a slow, throbbing ballad, "Girl, I Want Your Body." Rufus T. Ram sang it with a cheerful beat.

"Wrong!" announced Amerika, after a couple of run-throughs. "C'mon, Rufus, baby, you gotta get *down,* get *dirty.* I wanna *hear* the hard-on in your voice."

Rufus T. Ram nodded as if he understood exactly what she was saying. The only trouble was—he didn't. The way he sang the song evoked images of a breezy walk in the park, a light musical stroll. It soon became clear that Rufus T. Ram and "Girl, I Want Your Body" did not fit.

Amerika called an early lunch break. "We gotta talk," she said to Bobby, guiding him from the studio with a firm grip on his arm.

He really wanted to call Sharleen, but Amerika was on the move, hurrying him down the street to a small Italian restaurant she favored.

"I'm gonna treat you to more than tuna," she announced with a wide smile. "I think we both need a *beeeg* plate of nourishin' spaghetti an' meatballs to survive the afternoon."

He agreed. Now that he was thin he didn't mind indulging once in a while, and he liked Amerika. She had been good to him, ever since a musician friend had taken him to the Soul On Soul studios nine months ago and introduced them.

"I gotta tell you, Bobby, your song is the greatest," she said, ordering a bottle of red wine, then reaching for a hot roll. "Only problem is—Rufus T. Ram can't sing it."

"I know," he admitted.

"So." Sitting back, she surveyed the crowded restaurant. "What we gonna do?"

"Write him another song," Bobby suggested logically.

She looked surprised. "You can do that now?"

"Huh?"

"Well, *c'mon,* Mondella, I got a studio full of musicians. I need a steady line of product. Can you have another song an' full arrangement ready to go right after lunch?"

Disbelievingly, he said, "Are you crazy?"

She selected a thin brown cigarillo from her oversized

purse, reached for the book matches on the table, and lit up. "I want *you* to record the song."

"Me?"

"You."

"Now I *know* you're crazy."

The waiter arrived with the wine and poured a small amount for Bobby to taste. He passed his glass to Amerika. She sipped and nodded a brisk okay. When the waiter left, she said, "Hmmm . . . 'Sweet Little Bobby.' Honey, don't you think it's about time you jumped back to where you belong? On vinyl, baby. Makin' hits."

Sharleen was not in when he got home later that evening. She had left for the theater. Scotch-taped to the refrigerator door was a scrawled note:

> SORRY!
> LOVE YA!
> DON'T TELL ROCKET!!!
> DON'T WAIT UP.
> S.

Quickly he figured out her shorthand. "Sorry" meant she didn't want to discuss it. "Love ya" was her salve to keep him at her feet. "Don't tell Rocket" meant exactly that. And "Don't wait up" translated into "I'll be home very late."

Thankfully *he* wasn't involved with her. This girl was out chasing ambition, and nothing was going to stop her.

Sharleen . . . Sometimes he wished he'd never set eyes on her, let alone joined up with her and Rocket to become the adventurous threesome.

Tonight even thoughts of Sharleen couldn't bring him down, he was too goddamn high on life. Today he had sung for the first time in seven years, thanks to Amerika Allen. He, Bobby Mondella, had gotten up in that studio and sung the pants off Rufus T. Ram. Yeah. He had surprised everyone—including himself. He had a voice, and it was really something! Not the plaintive high-pitched wail of Sweet Little Bobby, but a low-down, raunchy throb. And if anyone could put real meaning into his lyrics, he could.

Amerika had been thrilled "You got it, my man," she'd said, hugging and squeezing him. "You sure have got it! Some bitchin' voice!"

What a day! Amerika hitting him with his hidden past was quite a surprise. It was a secret he thought nobody would ever discover. He'd never even confided in Rocket and had only mentioned it to Sharleen once, and she hadn't believed him, so he'd let it drop.

But Amerika knew. She'd done a touch of detective work and come up with an old 1963 album of his with a fat, smirking "Sweet Little Bobby" on the record sleeve.

"First time I set eyes on you I figured I'd seen you before," she said. "An' I got to thinkin' an' *thinkin'* an' *thinkin'*. Still couldn't remember where. Then one day, 'bout a week ago, I remembered. More than ten years back I was visiting Nashville with some friends, an' I saw this cute little fat boy on a TV show. What's this black boy doin' singin' country? I remember thinkin'."

"So how come all these years later you figured out it was me?"

"Honey—you come walkin' in here claimin' no musical past. Hadda be somethin' wrong somewhere. My bones told me you'd bin in music all your life. An' then this one mornin' I just woke up an' *knew* you was once Sweet Little Bobby." She laughed triumphantly. "I got a memory like a camel stores water!"

"I don't get it. I look different. I sound different. How did you make the connection?"

"Your eyes haven't changed, baby. They just got a little older an' a whole lot wiser. An' now it's time for you to get back to work—doin' what I *know* you can do. An' a lot better than Rufus T. Ram."

Amerika was very persuasive. She talked him into giving it a try, and it was almost as if he had all this stored-up vocal energy just waiting to burst through. And when he opened his mouth, out came the voice—the *new* Bobby Mondella voice. And he was certain that finally he was on the road to where he wanted to go.

Right now he felt like celebrating. Putting Marvin Gaye and Tammi Terrell on the stereo, he went through his phone book and finally settled on a cute ball of blond fluffiness who worked behind the cosmetics counter at Bonwit's. Since Sharleen was going to be out late, he decided he might as well take advantage of the empty apartment.

The blonde arrived in a backless summer dress with four-inch stiletto heels. Soon the dress was history, but the shoes remained. He satisfied his newfound lust for living, and she squealed, "I guess it's true what they say about black men!"

Within fifteen minutes she was history. Picking up the phone, he reached Rocket in L.A.

"Everythin' all right?" Rocket asked anxiously.

No. You'd better get your ass back here. Sharleen is shacking up with Marcus Citroen. And it ain't my problem. "Sure. How's the movie goin'?"

"Couldn't be better. I'm like a piece of shit off the streets of New York, bringin' back good memories to every fat-butt exile out here."

"Sounds exciting."

"Yeah, I guess it is. There's some kinda love goddess 'round every corner, an' tits an' ass a man could kill for."

"So?"

Rocket made a disgusted sound in the back of his throat. "So nothin', man. With what I got stashed at home, there's no way I'd blow it. Let me speak to her."

Shit! If he told Rocket the truth, Sharleen and he might

break up. Which—if he could get rid of Marcus Citroen— would leave the field clear for a certain Mr. Bobby Mondella, who had been waiting patiently in the background for five long years.

No. He couldn't do that. Not to Sharleen.

"She's uh . . . getting back from the theater late," he said vaguely. "One of her girlfriends is throwing a birthday party."

"Where?"

"I don't know. Somebody's house."

"What a kid, that Sharleen," Rocket said fondly. "Y'know what I'm gonna do? I think I'll surprise her with a trip out here. Get her to meet my agent an' that kinda jazz. She'd like that, wouldn't she?"

"You said you were coming back next week."

"The film's runnin' over. Besides, I told you, they like me here—they're buildin' up my part."

"Great."

"Yeah." He jiggled the phone, reaching for a cigarette. "Hey—guess who I ran into last night?"

Bobby remembered Sharleen asking him the same question. "I'm no good at guessing games."

"This is *really* gonna blow your mind."

"Who?"

"Nichols Kline. Can y'believe it?"

"Our old boss? The manager from The Chainsaw?"

"Ya think there's *another* Nichols Kline around?"

The Chainsaw had closed down four years earlier, the result of a major drug bust.

"What's he doing in L.A.?" Bobby asked curiously.

"Pretty fine, if you ask me. I ran into him at this rock and roll party at the beach. He had a redhead on one arm, a brunette on the other, and more gold chains than a street hustler could rip off in a week. He's a concert promoter now. Not bad, huh?"

"Did he remember you?"

"Do hookers take money? Of *course* he remembered me. I'm unforgettable, man. One of a kind. When they made me, they threw away my mother!"

"All right, all right, so he remembered you," Bobby said, anxious to tell his news.

He was too late. Rocket was ready to go. "I gotta hit the sheets, man. Gotta get some sleep. We're shootin' downtown tomorra. It's just like bein' home—rats, dirt, maniacs roamin' the streets. My kinda town!"

"Hey," Bobby said quickly. "I just wanted to tell you—I'm singin'."

"So are the fartin' birds. All day long. California. It's a whole different world. Listen, tell Shar to call me tomorra. Love ya both."

After the phone call Bobby still didn't feel like sleeping. He was up and speeding. Elated, restless, full of boundless energy. Sitting down at the used piano he'd bought with the first money he'd made as a songwriter, he played a few notes. And before long the notes became a tune, blending with the lyrics he made up as he went along.

He wrote a simple, soulful ditty full of his feelings for Sharleen.

The lady herself staggered home at five in the morning, glassy-eyed and obviously stoned.

"What the hell is going on?" he asked grimly, thinking, *I'm beginning to sound like a broken record*.

She was giggly and mellow, the pupils of her brown eyes dilated and starey. "Bobby, Bobby, Bobby," she sing-songed. "Handsome, handsome, Bobby boy!"

"Sharleen." He gripped her by the shoulders. "What are you on?"

Gazing at him blankly, she said, "On?"

"What did he give you?"

She started to giggle. "Ohhh . . . Bobby doesn't wanna know *that*. Bobby's a *good* lil' black boy. He don' wanna hear no *naughty* things!" Hiccoughing and swaying, she began to fall.

He caught her in his arms, swept her up, and carried her to the bed she shared with Rocket.

She stared up at him, a goofy smile on her swollen lips.

"You look terrible," he said sternly.

"Lil' ole me's got herself a recording contract," she sang. "I'm gonna be bigger than Diana Ross. A star, baby, a star. *Ooooh,* Bobby." Reaching for him, she locked her hands behind his neck, pulling him down toward her. "Wanna celebrate? Wanna kiss me? Wanna make love t'me? I know y' do. You've always wanted to, haven't you, baby?"

The opportunity was right there. Sharleen, inviting him to do what he *had* always dreamed of.

Two things stopped him. His best friend, and the fact she was so stoned she didn't know what day it was. When he and Sharleen got together—and he knew that one day fate would arrange it—it would be after she and Rocket were through, and whatever else, the lady had to know exactly what was happening.

He wanted Sharleen.

But only on his terms.

LOS ANGELES 1987
Saturday, July 11th
★ ★ ☆ ☆ ★

Cybil arrived home early from her photo session. She was fully made up, her blond hair a thick mane of stylized curls. She seemed to have forgotten about their fight, and was full of good cheer.

"How was your *veree* randy photographer friend?" Kris asked sarcastically.

"Gay," Cybil laughed. "*Veree* randy and *veree* gay and *veree* careful. My God, Kris, with this AIDS scare, nobody's doing it anymore."

He didn't want to discuss AIDS. The very word panicked him. Somewhere he had heard that every time you got into bed with a new person you were also getting into bed with every one of their sexual partners for the past seven years. Jesus! That meant hundreds of people—maybe even thousands—all rolling around together swapping germs. Frightening! One of the reasons he stuck to Cybil in America, and Astrid in England. Playing musical beds was out.

"I'm going upstairs to change," Cybil said. "What time are we leaving?"

She obviously expected to go with him to Novaroen, although he couldn't recall inviting her. But what the hell, he wasn't in the mood for another fight. "The Hawk's comin' by in half an hour. Will you be ready?"

She grinned. "I'm a quick-change artist. Just watch me!"

The smell in the bus was stifling, and Maxwell Sicily was delighted when the vehicle turned off the Pacific Coast Highway and started up a steep incline to an open-space area, where everyone was instructed to disembark.

The air was fresh and strong, a brisk ocean breeze tempering the afternoon heat. Glancing around, he noticed security guards everywhere busily organizing the restaurant staff into groups, readying them to board the small shuttle buses that would take them up to the main estate.

As they climbed into the shuttles, eight at a time, a guard ticked their names off a lengthy list, while a uniformed woman holding a two-way radio relayed the checked-off names to some unseen person.

"This is worse than prison," joked one of the waiters.

"How would *you* know?" sneered another.

True, Maxwell thought. How would any of them know? The grim realities of prison life bore no connection to a glorious sunny day on a billionaire's estate overlooking the white-tipped waves of the Pacific.

"George!" The plaintive whine of Chloe, the plump woman who sat behind the desk at Lilliane's, wafted through the air. "Wait!"

Putting his head down, pretending not to notice the floppy cow bearing down on him, he mumbled his name to the guard as he jumped on the shuttle.

Chloe pushed her way through, managing to squeeze on beside him. "Phew!" she exclaimed. "What a journey. I'm tired before we even begin!"

Cheap perfume assailed his nostrils. Sweet and clinging. Hooker perfume. The kind the filthy whores the prison guards smuggled in for hefty compensation wore. Dirt bags, as they were known around the joint.

Chloe laid a pudgy hand over his. "You'll havta keep an eye on me today, George," she trilled coyly. "You watch out for me, an' I'll do the same for you. One thing's for sure, I'm not gonna miss the concert. I'll find us a nice place t'watch it. How would you like that?"

She shifted on her seat, leaning against him, enveloping him in her cheap stink.

He didn't say a word. Chloe was just another minor irritation to dispose of when the time came.

Two representatives from Blue Cadillac Records and an abrasive young publicity woman arrived at L'Ermitage ready to escort Rafealla to Novaroen and the evening concert.

She kept them waiting in the lobby for forty-five minutes, causing all three to break out in a nervous sweat.

At last she appeared, wearing baggy khaki pants and a loose shirt, her long dark hair tied back. A bellboy trotted behind her carrying a plastic hanging bag containing her outfit for the concert—a simple black dress.

She had requested neither a makeup artist nor hairdresser.

"This one's gotta be weird," Trudie, the publicity woman, had said. "I never heard of a female artist who didn't want the whole shebang."

The two record executives fawned all over Rafealla, while Trudie stood back and took stock. Who needed makeup and hair when they looked like this? Rafealla was startlingly beautiful, more so than in her publicity photos, which did not do her justice at all. The reverse was usually true. Glamorous photographs mostly seemed to belong to very ordinary-looking women. Rafealla was certainly the exception.

"We'll do a sound check as soon as we arrive," one of

the record executives said, helping her into the limo. "Then you'll have at least a couple of hours to relax before the show."

"Fine," she said quietly.

Not the talkative type, Trudie noted.

"You'll be on after Bobby Mondella, and before Kris Phoenix," the executive said.

Rafealla did not reply. Bobby and Kris. Two names from her past. *Kris* and *Bobby*. . . .

Sadly, only one of them would remember her.

Speed was running early. He had the uniform. He had the car. And he had several hours to kill.

No big deal. There was a new Sylvester Stallone movie just waiting for his attention. Or maybe he should catch up on *Beverly Hills Cop II*. Speed loved going to the movies. First, he always bought popcorn, candy, and Coca-Cola. And when he sat down in that darkened theater, with those larger-than-life images flickering on the screen, he *became* the character he was watching. Shoot! He was tougher than Clint, hornier than Warren, fairer than Redford, and funnier than Chevy.

Speed often thought he'd missed his vocation. He should have been an actor. No, not an actor. A movie star. Yeah. For sure.

With a snort of resignation he realized there was no way he could go to the movies today. Too much of a risk. How could he possibly leave the Caddy limo? What if it was stolen?

Reluctantly he knew that whatever he was going to do, he was going to have to do it from the car.

He headed for Westwood, where he picked up some Kentucky Fried Chicken, stopped to buy *Penthouse* and *Playboy,* and set off toward the beach.

* * *

The limousine driver was a brother. A brother with a script and a mouthful of ideas.

"Shut him up," Bobby muttered to Sara. "I don't need this."

"Driver," Sara interrupted politely, "Mr. Mondella is very tired. He'd appreciate silence."

"Silence!" the driver exclaimed excitedly. "I wrote a song called 'Silence' once. Maybe I should sing it for y'all!"

"No!" Sara said hastily, vowing never to use this limo company again. The least they could do was check out their drivers and not send out would-be screenwriter-singer-songwriters.

"I understand," the man said in a hurt voice, sounding like he didn't understand at all. "I'm cool."

"I'm sure you are," Sara said. But just to make sure, she found the button to raise the glass partition and hurriedly pressed it.

Nova Citroen's white-blond hair was swept up in an elaborately twisted chignon. Her fingernails and toenails gleamed with slick crimson polish. Her body tingled—the result of a vigorous massage—and her makeup was porcelain-perfect.

She was ready hours too early, but that was the way she liked it. Slipping on a plain blue silk shirt and matching slacks, she thought about the three superstar singers due to arrive at Novaroen shortly. A glimmer of a smile brought back the memories.

Kris Phoenix. What a randy bad boy *he* was.

Bobby Mondella. Ah . . . Bobby. . . .

And Rafealla. Her smile faded. The bitch Marcus wanted to fuck.

Nova decided to greet them all personally.

* * *

One of the things Vicki Foxe enjoyed as she play-acted at being a maid was the downstairs gossip. Boy! What scandal and rumor—it made the *Enquirer* seem positively tame!

Everyone loathed Nova Citroen. "The Iron Cunt" was her nickname. "She makes Imelda Marcus look like a pussy," was the general opinion of her loyal staff.

Marcus Citroen was regarded with a sort of grudging admiration. "At least he says please an' thank you once in a while," was the chief cook Bertha's opinion.

Talk of the Citroens' bizarre sexual practices was rife. "There's handcuffs in his bedside drawer," revealed one maid.

"And a closetful of kinky outfits," said another.

Vicki herself had found a concealed cupboard with whips and chains and all the paraphernalia of sexual perversions. She couldn't care less. Her years as a professional had taught her many things, and one of them was never to be surprised. The thought of either Nova or Marcus Citroen trussed up and ready for action amused her. Sadomasochism wasn't her kick—but each to his own. Vicki Foxe never judged anyone.

She often wondered what turned Maxwell Sicily on. He certainly hadn't given any hint. Most men, when faced with her lethal charms, started drooling on the count of three. Maxwell had stayed cold as ice. That kind of disinterest intrigued her. What were his future plans? Was there a woman in his life?

So far he'd only paid her a quarter of the money she was supposed to get. The deal was, he would contact her twenty-four hours after the caper and tell her where she could pick up the rest.

"Yeah? An' what makes you think I'm gonna trust you?" she'd asked suspiciously.

"We do it my way. Are you in or out?" he'd replied icily, without so much as a moment's pause.

She admired a man who didn't waver. "I'm in," she'd said, and set about finding out exactly who George Smith really was. Not so difficult. Vicki had her ways.

"I've been lookin' for you." Tom, the chief of security, startled her as he came up behind her in the front hall of the main house.

She held her shoulders a touch straighter, thrust her bosom forward, straining the limits of her drab uniform. "And you've found me," she answered sassily. "What's up?"

He edged close to her, his bad breath offending her nostrils. "How about you an' me watchin' the concert together like you suggested?" he asked with a knowing leer.

"Don't be silly," she said guilelessly. "You're working, and so am I. It's not possible." Softening her voice, she added, "Much as I'd love to."

His eyes dropped to her breasts, big balloons just straining for his touch. Tom knew when a tootsie wanted him, and this broad had been giving him the eye for weeks. Now he'd finally figured out a good time to get her to himself. "I got a place for us to see it," he said.

Looking surprised, she cooed, "*Oooh*, Tom, you're so smart! How exciting!"

"It will be, honey," he said, managing to brush against her. "Just keep everything hot."

With one deft movement her hand slid across the telling bulge in his pants. "It'll take a *real* man to cool *me* down," she whispered. "See ya later, big boy!"

Marcus curbed his desire to visit Rafealla at her hotel. He had to be so careful. The girl reminded him of a horse

127

he'd once owned, a magnificent Arabian filly which allowed nobody close.

Marcus had tamed the excitable, exquisite animal. It had taken him many months of discipline and extreme patience.

He planned to do the same with Rafealla. But this time he was running out of patience.

KRIS PHOENIX
1975

★ ☆ ★ ☆ ★

The baby was whining—some might say it was crying, but Kris knew a whine when he heard it.

He wasn't good with babies, couldn't quite get the hang of them. And he knew for a fact that it wasn't *his* job to be watching over some smelly little sod with a nappy full of crap, even if it was his.

Putting down his pen, he picked up a newspaper. Writing songs was a kick, but only when he could concentrate, and who could concentrate with a whimpering baby making distracting background noises?

Willow was going to have to give up her job, there was no other answer. They'd just have to manage without her salary. Screw it. He needed peace and quiet to create, and he sure as hell wasn't getting it at home.

Home was a basement flat in Kilburn—was he ever going to get out of there?—with a tiny, dark bedroom, matching bathroom, a cramped kitchen, and a dreary living room that led out to a seven-foot patch of weeds, where they kept two rusting deck chairs and the baby's pram, a rather fancy gift from Willow's uptight parents.

Kris thought grimly for a moment of Willow's formidable mummy and daddy. Mr. Wigh was a bank manager in

Esher, and his neurotic wife a raging snob with delusions of grandeur. No wonder Willow had run away from home twice before she was sixteen, finally moving out on her nineteenth birthday to attend secretarial college in Hampstead. Her parents sent her such a paltry allowance she was forced to get that part-time job where she had met Flower. Flower, of course, had introduced them, and before he could turn around, Willow was pregnant, and he, suburban schmuck that he was, married the girl.

Kris Phoenix—rock star. Forget it. Let's all give a big hand to Kris Phoenix, husband, father, jerk of the year.

He threw the newspaper down in disgust, not even bothering to study the naked Page Three girl with tits you could balance a mug of beer on.

"Shit!" he said aloud, and the baby shifted from a whine to a hearty wail.

Nothing was going right for him, not one damn thing. Eighteen months ago The Wild Ones had cut their first record, "Lonesome Morning," and everyone had been so high on it. Kris hadn't doubted that success and all that went with it was just around the corner.

"Lonesome Morning" descended on an uninterested public, and got no radio play. "How can people buy it if they've never heard it?" he'd demanded of anyone who would listen.

"You're not on any of the play lists," Sam Rozelle told him regretfully.

"So tell the fucking record company to *get* it on. That's their job, isn't it?"

"Everyone's doing their best," Sam replied, not looking him in the eye.

Kris suspected otherwise. He went into six record stores, and not only were they completely unaware of the record's existence but, after searching, found they didn't even have it in stock.

"There's somethin' funny going on," he complained to Mr. Terence, who took absolutely no notice.

"Nonsense!" Mr. Terence said. "The time isn't right for you. You all need more experience." And he promptly sent them back on the road. Back to the one-night stands, the greasy roadside cafés, groupie slags, and sleeping in the back of the clapped-out Volkswagen bus.

Back to square one. Do not pass go. Do not collect a fucking thing.

In London, Willow's pregnancy progressed. Flower relayed news bulletins when she arrived to visit Buzz.

"Her father's furious."

"Her mother's having a nervous breakdown."

"Willow moved home last week."

And finally: "Her old man's making her have an abortion."

"What?" Kris shouted, the blood draining from his face. "No fucking bank prick's gettin' rid of *my* baby." And before anyone could stop him, he was on a train.

He turned up at Willow's parents' house in the middle of the night. A frightened au pair let him in and immediately shouted for Mr. Wigh, who came downstairs and attempted to throw him out. Mrs. Wigh appeared next, and feigned a fainting fit. And then Willow, scrubbed and clean, with just the hint of a tiny belly beneath her robe.

"I'm gonna marry you," Kris blurted.

"No you're not," stormed Mr. Wigh.

"Just watch us, mate," retorted Kris. And he took her back to Leeds, where they got married in the local register office with Buzz as best man, a stoned Flower, Ollie, Rasta and an assortment of teenage groupies in attendance.

The wedding ceremony took less than ten minutes, and after it was over they all went to a local café and got well and truly pissed.

In the heat of the moment it was an exciting time. After that it was downhill on a fast sled. What was an aspiring rock star supposed to do with a wife, let alone a pregnant one?

Mr. Terence went ape-shit when he found out, ranting and raving, threatening to tear up their contract, swearing them all to secrecy. "Nobody is to know about this. Absolutely no one," he said severely. "And if anyone finds out —deny it. Do you hear me? It never happened, she's just a girlfriend."

Apparently, in their quest to become rock stars girlfriends were acceptable, wives were not.

Willow agreed she wouldn't wear a wedding ring. Not that he'd bought her one. Who had the money?

When Mr. Terence calmed down, he took the situation in hand, finding them the furnished flat in Kilburn and advancing Kris the cash to pay for it. "I'll deduct this from your songwriting royalties," he said testily.

"What royalties? I haven't *had* any bleedin' songs published yet—only 'Lonesome Morning,' an' that's dead in the fuckin' water," Kris replied.

"Didn't I tell you?" Mr. Terence said vaguely. "Del Delgardo and the Nightmares heard it, liked the song, and cut their own version. It'll be out in America next week."

"No, you didn't tell me." Kris was furious. He felt betrayed.

"Lonesome Morning," the Del Delgardo and the Nightmares cover, was a smash, reaching number three in the States, and a healthy number two in England.

Proud as he was of the song, Kris would sooner the hit belonged to The Wild Ones. Still, after he got over his initial anger, it was a satisfying feeling for him and for Ollie, who had written the music to his lyrics. It would have been nice if Mr. Terence had asked their permission before handing their song over to someone else. At least it was a hit.

The most annoying thing of all was, when they performed the song onstage, everyone thought they were covering Del Delgardo and the Nightmares' smash single, even though Kris announced they could go out and buy The Wild Ones' original recording. Big deal. Nobody did. Or maybe they just couldn't find it.

With Willow installed in the flat, Kris at least had somewhere to go on the one weekend a month he managed to get back to London. It made a pleasant change from being constantly on the road. Willow could cook, and she cared about him. She was pretty, clean, and loving. What more could any man ask?

She was also getting bigger every day, her stomach swelling like a large ripe watermelon preparing to burst.

Naturally he had to introduce her to his family. Mum acted okay, but his two sisters carried on alarmingly, telling her every embarrassing story they could think of about him. Brother Brian sneered derisively. "How did *you* get to marry the daughter of a bank manager?" He was impressed, in spite of himself.

"Just a big cock, I guess," Kris replied nonchalantly. "Shame it doesn't run in the family."

"You're no good at anything you do," Brian snarled, glaring balefully. "Why don't you pack this stupid singing lark in and get yourself a proper job with a future?"

"Why don't *you* shove it up your arse?" Family. He tried to stay away from them.

When Willow gave birth he was onstage in Glasgow playing to an audience of appreciative, squealing girls. The Wild Ones had quite a following in spite of no record deal, no publicity agent, and no-hope venues.

Avis took Willow to the hospital in a taxi. She phoned the uptight Wighs, who drove down from Esher the following morning. By the time Kris arrived from Scotland he was the father of a seven-pound six-ounce baby boy. Willow sat in her hospital bed surrounded by a loudmouthed Avis, a stoned Flower, and a tight-lipped Mr. and Mrs.

Wigh. The perfect group. From that moment on, Kris felt completely trapped.

They named the baby Peter (after Willow's grandfather) John (after Kris's father) Buddy (a respectful gesture to the late Buddy Holly—one of Kris's personal heroes). Somehow Peter John Buddy never got called any of those names. Bo was his nickname. Baby Bo.

He'd been with them for fourteen months, and in that time The Wild Ones split up—temporarily. Rasta went on a tour of Europe with a German rock & roll band, which made him an offer he didn't want to refuse. Buzz took off with Flower to Ibiza, a tiny island near Spain, where he got a job as a waiter and resident guitarist in a local restaurant. And Ollie concentrated on composing new songs, while Kris settled down to supplying the lyrics.

They sold a few of their songs, causing Mr. Terence to grab a hefty percent. But their best compositions they saved for the re-forming of The Wild Ones.

Mr. Terence was furious with the group for splitting up, but as they straggled off the road he could see they were all burnt out and needed to do other things for a while, so he didn't put up too hard a fight.

"When we get back together," Kris informed him, "we're goin' to do it properly. No more screwin' around. An' if you can't do it for us, we'll find someone who can."

"Let us not forget that we have a contract," Mr. Terence said waspishly. "A *legal* contract."

"Fuck the contract an' fuck you," Kris steamed. "You sold us down the river with 'Lonesome Morning,' an' it ain't happenin' again."

"How dare you! I've supported you boys through thick and thin. Given you money, a roof over your heads, looked after your personal problems. I've—"

Kris held up a commanding hand, stopping the fussy Mr. Terence in his tracks. "I know all that," he said. "An' believe me, we're grateful. But we're not goin' to waste any more days bustin' our arses in deadbeat cities performin' to crummy audiences who don't know shit from chocolate. We want the big time."

Kris had made that little speech three months ago, and he meant every word of it. He was twenty-six years old, getting up there. The dreaded thirty was only four years away, and he was determined to make it before then. The Wild Ones were good and he knew it. God! He wanted success so much he could taste it in the back of his throat every morning when he got up, and every evening when he went to sleep.

The baby's crying increased. Gingerly he picked the infant up, cradling it awkwardly. Holding the baby reminded him that since giving birth, Willow did not like to make love. She lay there, a stone slab, with all the enthusiasm of a deceased fish.

Miraculously Bo stopped crying and gurgled happily. Kris carried his son over to the table, placing him on a clean towel. Removing the baby's nappy, he stared down at the Phoenix crown jewels. It certainly looked as if Baby Bo had a major inheritance coming his way.

Kris grinned, just as a steady stream of pee hit him straight in the left eye.

"I don't know," Willow said, a worried frown creasing her brow. "What about germs, and the water, and all that heat?"

Kris had just suggested what should have been a welcome family holiday in Ibiza with Buzz and Flower, and she was moaning about germs and heat. She was lucky he was even considering taking her and the baby. The smart thing would be to leave them behind while he talked Buzz into rejoining the group. The time had come for The Wild Ones to get back together. He'd already contacted Rasta, who was raring to go. And Ollie waited impatiently on red alert. They had a stash of dynamite songs, and Kris had no doubts that this time around it was going to happen for them. All he needed was Buzz.

He had not as yet given the good news to Mr. Terence. He wanted to be sure of Buzz first, and he knew the best way to hook the lazy layabout was to tell him face to face.

The holiday idea seemed perfect. There were cheap flights to Ibiza, and Buzz had said they could stay with him and Flower any time they wanted. Kris had thought Willow would be delighted. No such luck.

"C'mon, luv," he wheedled. "It'll be fun."

"For *you*," she said with a toss of her head. "I'll be looking after the baby the whole time."

"We'll share."

"You say that now, but I know you."

"No, you don't." He grabbed her playfully around the waist. Lately he was feeling randy all the time. Maybe it was because Willow tried to limit their sexual adventures to once a week, which was about six times too little for him. Before he was married he'd had sex every day. Wasn't marriage supposed to improve things?

Sliding his hand up, he cupped her right breast.

She tried to wriggle free, but his grip on her waist was firm.

"Stop it, Kris," she scolded.

"Why? We're a respectable old married couple," he said, hand diving beneath her blouse, burrowing under her bra like a mole.

"I said, Stop it," she repeated, her voice developing an annoying whiny quality. "It's the middle of the afternoon."

He was on a mission and had no intention of coming back to earth until mission accomplished. Pulling her reluctant hand down to his hard-on he said, "Feel this. I don't care what the fucking time is."

"Don't swear."

"Why?"

"It's coarse."

"So am I. You didn't marry the bleedin' Prince of Wales, y'know."

Roughly he pulled her blouse open and unhooked her bra, as she stood motionless in the center of the room like a martyr about to be sacrificed.

He didn't care. He was beyond caring. He was too busy deciding whether to suck on one of her deliciously inviting tits or go for the goal in one.

The boobs triumphed. It was more fun for him if she enjoyed it too, and he'd noticed she was never averse to a certain amount of stroking and caressing in that area.

And so they both stood there, Kris carefully working her up to the great moment.

Finally she gave in, sinking to the floor with a small moan of acceptance.

Pulling her panties down he zeroed in for the home run. It was quick, but ultimately satisfying.

"We're going to Ibiza," he said firmly. "Pack your bags an' count on it. Okay, luv?"

RAFEALLA
1975

★ ☆ ★ ☆ ★

"Remember when you tried to kill yourself?" Odile Ronet said matter-of-factly. Like Rafealla, she was bilingual; she spoke perfect English without a trace of a French accent.

"Remember when *you* tried to do *your*self in?" Rafealla retorted sharply.

"Hmmm . . ." Odile replied with a reflective shrug. "Neither of us did much of a job, did we?"

"Thank goodness!" exclaimed Rafealla.

"It certainly would have been a waste," Odile stated, admiring her slim figure in the full-length mirror.

Odile was visiting from Paris. Since she and Rafealla now lived in separate countries they had spent nearly every summer together, usually dividing their time between their two families. Odile's mother, Isabella, had also remarried.

"Yes," agreed Rafealla, standing beside her best friend so they could compare reflections.

Two fifteen-year-old girls on the threshold of adventure. Both long-legged and coltish. Both attractive promises of things to come. But there the resemblance ended. Rafealla was dark, Odile fair. Rafealla's looks were strikingly unusual, Odile had a simple prettiness.

Best friends and not a secret between them. They shared more than friendship—they shared a tragedy that would never go away.

"My breasts are bigger than yours," Odile announced, sticking her chest out to get the best effect.

"No, they're not," objected Rafealla strenuously.

"They certainly are."

"Certainly not!"

"See." Odile raised her sweater, exposing firm, small breasts without the hindrance of a bra.

"Ha!" exclaimed Rafealla, opening her shirt. "Look at these."

"Fabulous!" exclaimed a male voice from the doorway. "Utterly fabulous!"

"Rupert—you little shit," she screamed, pulling her shirt closed, while just as quickly Odile dragged her sweater down. "I've told you never to come into my room without knocking. *Never!*"

"The door was ajar," Rupert Egerton, son and heir of Cyrus, Lord Egerton, newspaper magnate, pointed out.

"So what?" yclled Rafealla furiously. "So bloody what?"

"Hmmm . . . and what are you two doing anyway, comparing each other's thingies? Couple of lesbos, I bet."

"Fuck off, Egerton."

"I will not." Rupert sat himself down on the edge of the bed. "I'm bored."

At nineteen, Rupert was an amiable, younger mirror image of his father, and his grandfather, and his great-grandfather before him. Ancient portraits decorated the halls of Egerton Castle. There was no mistaking Rupert's heritage. He was tall and gangly, with a shock of bright-red hair, hundreds of freckles on parchment-white skin, and sharp patrician features. The only thing he hadn't inherited was the Egerton family stammer.

When Rafealla's mother, Anna, had married Rupert's father, Cyrus, Rafealla had thought she would die. And for one whole year she refused to acknowledge Rupert's existence—until one day, while out riding in the grounds of Egerton Castle, Rupert had sneaked up behind her on his horse, startled her, and made her mount rear into the air, causing her to be thrown to the muddy ground. "I hate you!" she'd yelled. "You stupid, freckly dumb *boy!*"

"And the same goes for me, missy," he'd yelled back. "You're a stuck-up, conceited wog brat. I wish you'd never come here."

Rafealla had burst into tears. She was thirteen and he was a big bully of seventeen. It had never occurred to her he didn't want her around either.

After that little incident they began to talk to each other, grudgingly at first, but soon they found they had certain things in common, like riding and jazz records and a hatred of cook's potpies. One night they sat together in the empty grand ballroom and began to speak about their outrage and hurt at losing a parent. Rupert's mother had drowned in a boating accident when he was seven—exactly the same age as Rafealla when she'd lost her father to a terrorist's bomb.

Suddenly they were close, and from that moment on Rafealla loved her stepbrother as if he were the real thing. Of course, like the real thing, he could be an absolute pain, and today was one of those days.

"Rupert," Rafealla said briskly, "I don't care if you're bored, I really don't. Odile and I hardly ever see each other, so will you kindly go and be bored elsewhere?"

"Yes," Odile agreed. "Why don't you run away and read the *National Geographic?*"

"Nobody reads that any more. Not when you can see human, white—well, almost white—bosoms at home."

"Fuck off, Egerton," Rafealla repeated, with a finger gesture to match the phrase.

"Hmm . . . just when I thought I might treat you two young ladies to a night on the town in London," he said casually, getting up and wandering toward the door. "Of course, if you want me to leave . . ." He trailed off, waiting for their response.

"Really?" asked Rafealla suspiciously. She wouldn't put it past him to dangle the carrot and then withdraw it at the last moment.

"I don't offer idle invitations," he said, affronted.

"Yes, you do," argued Rafealla.

"I most certainly do not."

"Children!" interrupted Odile. "Let us not waste precious time arguing. A night in London sounds divine. The answer is yes, Rupert. Yes. Yes. *Yes.*"

Rafealla loved going to London, although usually she went there only during the day with her mother. They always lunched at Harrods, shopped around the busy Knightsbridge streets, and then devoured a delicious tea at Fortnum and Mason. Sometimes Lord Egerton drove in to meet them, and they dined at his favorite restaurant, Wheelers, in Old Compton Street, where Rafealla always ordered the crab salad.

Once or twice she had played truant from school, taken the train and visited London with a girlfriend. They'd walked up and down the Kings Road admiring the fashion parade of punks with their purple and green spiked hair, bizarre makeup, and outlandish dress—and the Sloane Rangers, the properly brought up daughters of well-bred and affluent parents, clad in twin-sets, pearls, and sensible Gucci shoes.

After watching the fashion parade they'd spend hours looking through the record albums in W. H. Smith before going home.

Rupert's London was different altogether. He took them to San Lorenzo, an Italian restaurant on fashionable Beauchamp Place, where he seemed to know almost everyone.

Mara, the warm proprietress, chucked him lovingly

under the chin. "You like 'em young, Rupert, huh?" she asked with a wicked twinkle.

"This is my *sister*, Mara," he said reproachfully. "Rafealla, say hello to the great Mara. She runs this place with an iron fist. We're all terrified of her."

Shyly Rafealla shook hands.

"Your *sister*, Egerton?" said a tall young man with a sly smile. "Since when did you have a sister?"

"Since my father remarried," Rupert replied. "Rafealla, meet Eddie Mafair—he's a pain in the backside and rolling in filthy lucre. And Eddie—this is Odile Ronet. Hands off. One day I'm going to marry this girl."

Rafealla and Odile exchanged amazed glances.

"Didn't I tell you?" Rupert said casually, winking at Odile. "Must have slipped my mind—thought I did."

They dined on mushroom salad and fresh pasta with shrimp, followed by a wonderful creamy dessert concoction called zabaglione. Rafealla spotted two Hollywood movie stars, a world-renowned tennis player, several English actors, and Del Delgardo, lead singer with the Nightmares.

"I think I'm dreaming!" she whispered to Odile. "Isn't Del Delgardo *gorgeous?*"

"Ugly," replied Odile with a pantomimed shudder. "Those teeth!"

"Who cares about his teeth? Everything else is perfect!"

"How do *you* know?"

"I can dream, can't I?"

Pulling a face, Odile said, "He's old. He must be at least thirty."

"That's not old."

"One foot in the grave, my dear."

Sometimes even best friends got on one's nerves. Rafealla shot Odile a dirty look.

After dinner Eddie Mafair reappeared and hovered at

their table. "We're all going to Annabel's," he said. "Why don't you come with us?"

"Can we?" Rafealla and Odile questioned in unison, turning hopefully to Rupert.

"I don't know." He shook his head vaguely. "I suppose I should drive you girls home."

"Why?" Rafealla asked anxiously. She thought Eddie most attractive, and could imagine nothing better than spending the rest of the evening with him. "My mother and your father are away this weekend. There's nobody waiting up for us."

"True," he said.

"Well?" the two girls demanded.

"All right," he decided. "But you'll both have to chip in on the bill, I'm not made of bloody money."

Annabel's presented a world Rafealla hadn't seen before. It was a sophisticated nightclub, with music courtesy of the Beatles, David Bowie, Aretha Franklin, Jefferson Lionacre, Gary Glitter, Olivia Newton-John, Del Delgardo and the Nightmares—a mixed group—whose records blared forth from loudspeakers stationed above an over-packed dance floor.

"Ohhh! I love discotheques," Odile exclaimed with a delighted smile. "I've been to Le Club in Paris, you know. My mother took me there for my fifteenth birthday."

Rupert raised his eyebrows as if he'd just realized how young they were. "For God's sake," he hissed, "if anyone asks, you're both eighteen."

"Yes, Rupert," Odile said obediently.

"And I'm twenty-one," he added, a trifle sheepishly.

Rafealla nodded, her eyes darting all over the place. "How old is Eddie?" she asked innocently.

"Too old for you," he snapped.

They joined Eddie Mafair and a group of his friends. The girls at the table all resembled the Sloane Rangers Rafealla had spotted strolling in Knightsbridge and the

Kings Road. She was glad she'd chosen to wear a short black skirt and white turtleneck sweater—at least she looked different, and certainly older than fifteen.

"How about some champers?" Eddie offered, already filling her glass with the fizzy liquid.

She decided he liked her too, and felt a shiver of excitement. Rupert was seated farther down the table with Odile next to him, so she was safe. Tentatively she took a sip. It tasted wonderful.

"Drink up. That's my girl," encouraged Eddie, staring straight into her eyes.

She studied his face. He had sharply handsome features, sallow cheeks, and light-brown hair worn appealingly long. He was dressed in a casual blue blazer, a white shirt, dark pants, and a blue-and-red striped tie. She imagined he was only a year or so older than Rupert.

"I say, Eddie," brayed the Sloane Ranger sitting on his other side, "let's trip the light."

"You'll have to excuse me, Fiona. I promised this one to Rafealla."

Fiona pouted, not prettily. "Drat! I simply adore The Who."

Rafealla stifled a giggle. She couldn't imagine Fiona adoring anything other than a walk in the country with a panting Labrador sniffing at her crotch.

"What are you laughing at?" asked Eddie.

"Nothing."

He took her by the hand and stood up. "Shall we?"

"I simply adore The Who," she mimicked wickedly.

"Now, now," he chided, with an amused smile.

They danced the night away. Slow ones, fast ones, sambas, even a waltz! Until at one-thirty in the morning a rather irritable Rupert insisted he drive them home.

"I want to see you again," Eddie Mafair whispered in her ear as they were leaving. "Very very soon. I'll give you a ring."

She nodded, knowing full well her mother would object strongly if an older, sophisticated man like Eddie rang her for a date. She was allowed to go to the cinema with a mixed group, and that was about it. To her chagrin she'd only been kissed once, and it was no big deal. The boy in question was one of the gardener's assistants. Reasonably good-looking, he had a black front tooth and a missing finger, which quite spoiled the effect.

Odile was dying to find out everything but managed to control herself until they got home and Rupert went off to his room.

"Well!" she exclaimed. "Tell me all! And don't leave *anything* out."

Rafealla realized there was not that much to tell. After all, the only thing they'd done was dance. "He wants to phone me," she said lamely.

"Of course he does," Odile enthused. "And he probably wants to make mad, passionate love to you."

"*I* don't know."

"You must know."

"How?"

Odile rolled her eyes. "You had all those slow dances with him. . . ." She hesitated, then rushed on. "Was he . . . you know . . . stiff?"

"What a question!"

"Well, *was* he?"

Rafealla felt a fit of the giggles coming on. She was sure she was blushing, even though Odile was her best friend and they told each other everything.

"Yes," she said at last. "He was stiff as a sergeant on drill parade!"

"Good Lord!" said Odile, collapsing with laughter. "And will you go out with him when he phones?"

"Yes," Rafealla replied defiantly. "Why shouldn't I?"

BOBBY MONDELLA
1975

★ ☆ ★ ☆ ★

"No," Bobby said.

"You're one stubborn son of a bitch." Sharleen replied, dragging nervously on her cigarette. "Why not?"

"We've been over it a hundred times," he said flatly. "You know how I feel. I got loyalty—an' it belongs to Amerika Allen."

"Goddamn!" Viciously Sharleen stubbed her cigarette into an ornate lead-crystal ashtray. "Blue Cadillac and Marcus can do so much more for you. Why won't you listen?"

"Because you're wrong," he replied calmly. "Soul On Soul has been very good to me."

"It hasn't taken you to number one on the crossover charts," she said, reaching out and selecting another cigarette from a fancy silver box on an expensive mahogany coffee table. "What do you have to say about that?"

"You know something?" he said mildly. "You're gonna ruin your voice if you keep on smoking those things."

"Don't wanna talk about it, huh?" she jeered. "Don't wanna admit that Soul On Soul is a little fish in a large pond, an' Blue Cadillac with Marcus Citroen is the goddamn shark."

"Oh, yeah, he's a shark all right," Bobby said quietly.

"You've never even met him," she accused. "Don't assume power equals bad."

He stared at her. In two and a half years she had changed considerably. No longer the wide-eyed, enthusiastic girl he'd first met, she was now a twenty-nine-year-old polished sleek woman. Pretty—yes. Vulnerable—no. Loving—yes. But only when it could get her somewhere or something she wanted.

He was still her friend. He still loved her, but he wasn't sure he liked her any more.

"I spoke to Rocket yesterday," he said, changing the subject.

"*That* bastard!" she snapped.

When had Rocket become "that bastard"? The day she dumped him? Or the day he married Roman Vanders, a black actress ten years his senior?

"I guess you don't want to hear how he is."

"Bobby." She leaned toward him persuasively, close enough so he could study her perfect makeup and observe the unhappiness in her big brown eyes. "All I want is for you to be part of the Blue Cadillac family. It's right for you. I *know* it is. And think how great it will be when you and I can work together. I'd really love to cut an album with you."

"I'll ask Amerika. Maybe she'll have you over to the studio an' we'll do somethin' for Soul On Soul."

Sharleen's expression grew stony. "That's impossible."

"Why?"

"Don't be ridiculous." She got up from the couch and walked over to the French doors of her Park Avenue apartment. Marcus Citroen paid the rent. Marcus Citroen owned every inch of Sharleen.

Throwing the doors open, she strolled outside onto the terrace. A panoramic view of the New York skyline greeted her.

"Come outside, Bobby," she called. "Come and see what you're missing."

The only thing he was missing was a woman in his life, and Sharleen no longer filled the bill.

Following her outside, he had to admit the view was impressive. But what kind of woman sold herself for a view and a couple of hit records?

Oh, yes, Marcus had kept his promise. Sharleen was a rising star, and she loved it. Privately Bobby thought the stuff she was recording was pop crap. While Sharleen had never possessed the greatest voice in the world, she'd always had soul and feeling. Now she sounded as if she was singing by numbers. It didn't appear to be important. The public loved her, and along with Marcus Citroen it had made her what she was today.

He grew restless, standing on her terrace. "I gotta split," he said, pulling up the collar of his jacket.

"Can't you stay for dinner?" she asked, a note of disappointment creeping into her voice.

"I never planned on it. I'm meeting Amerika."

"Of course." She swept back into the apartment. He walked behind her. Suddenly she turned on him. "Are you sleeping with her?"

"That's none of your business, lady," he replied with a sharp edge.

"Obviously she has *some* hold over you. Why else would you turn down the best offer of your life?"

"A little thing called loyalty. L–O–Y–A–L–T–Y. Remember that word—you may need it some day."

Later he met Rocket and his wife, Roman, at a restaurant in the Village famous for its southern fried chicken and black-eye peas.

Rocket looked good. Fame as a New York Method-style actor suited him. He was still short, dark, and moody. But now he had confidence and style, and he was successful enough to pick and choose his roles. He was in demand, and he loved every moment of it.

Roman was a serious-looking black woman who had a fine reputation as a character actress. The two of them had met on location in Georgia. Bobby still suspected Rocket had married her on the rebound from Sharleen.

He remembered the night of the breakup with a sour taste in his mouth. Sharleen had been seeing Marcus Citroen for weeks, arriving home in the early hours stoned and uncommunicative. Bobby didn't know what to do. Finally he'd weakened and called Rocket in L.A., telling him there was a problem.

"I've got two more days dubbing and I'm back," Rocket had said confidently. "No problem."

He was back all right. In time to greet Sharleen as she staggered home at six in the morning.

They screamed at each other for two hours, made love for another two, and later, when Rocket and Bobby strolled down to the corner deli to pick up some cold cuts and potato salad for lunch, Rocket confided that everything was great, Sharleen was sorry, and they were just as much in love as ever.

Somebody forgot to tell Sharleen. When they arrived home with the food, she was packed and gone, courtesy of Marcus Citroen, who had sent his chauffeured car for her. Rocket had sworn he'd never forgive her.

Amerika joined them at the restaurant for coffee. She was full of enthusiasm about Bobby's new single, which was creeping steadily up the black music charts.

"It'd be sensational if it crossed over," he said casually, thinking of what Sharleen had said.

Amerika shook her head. "The most difficult task in the world. You can count the black artists who cross over on one hand."

"Stevie Wonder."

"Dionne Warwick," Roman chimed in.

"Johnny Mathis," said Rocket.

"We are talkin' *mainstream* singers here," Amerika said. "Bobby Mondella is pure soul. He has a hard-core black audience. They love him. Surely that's enough, isn't it?"

For once Bobby thought that maybe it wasn't.

"Lookit, boy—how come we don' never see you? Don' git no word at all. What you think this kinda behavior gonna do to your fine cousin, Fanni? You got a short memory or what? That woman done plenty for you when you was nuttin'. Now you big time an' we don git t'hear no word. What you gotta say 'bout *that,* boy?"

The blustering voice on the other end of the telephone was unmistakably Ernest Crystal.

"Don't call me boy," Bobby said ominously, wondering how Ernest had managed to track him down after almost seven years of silence. "What the hell do you want?"

"What I want? *What I want?*" Ernest's voice reached a falsetto level of outraged insincerity. "You all have family, boy. Relatives who *care* 'bout you."

Sure. When he left Fanni and Ernest's, he'd attempted to keep in touch. But neither of them had shown any interest, and eventually he'd stopped calling.

"How'd you get my number?" he asked resignedly.

"Your record company done tole me—once I tole *them* I was your dear uncle."

"My what?" Bobby spluttered.

"A relative is a relative, boy."

"Didn't you hear me the first time?" Bobby said, his words measured. "Do not call me boy."

"Jest habit, I guess." Ernest cleared his throat, getting ready for the pitch. "Listen t'me. *We* was the ones who done took you in when Mister Leon Rue set you loose on the streets of New York City wit nowhere t'go. *We* was the ones done gave you a bed, an' food, an' a roof over your head. *We* looked after your ass when you was sick, an' never asked for nuttin' in return."

Conveniently, Ernest seemed to have forgotten about the six-thousand-dollar check he'd arrived with, plus a healthy piece of his pay from The Chainsaw every week.

"Cut to the chase," he said abruptly, having no desire to listen to Ernest's whining. If they needed money, he was prepared to give them some. He wasn't rich, but he could certainly afford it, and Fanni *was* his only living relative.

"You talk tough, bo—uh—Bobby. You don' sound like that sweet, fat kiddy we once knew an' loved."

"He died," Bobby said dryly. "How much?"

"Did I say one damn word 'bout money?" Ernest yelled indignantly.

"How much, goddammit?"

"Well . . ." Ernest hesitated. "Since you bein' gentleman 'nuff to ask . . . Fanni bin feelin' bad. She can't work no more. She done gain a pound or two, an' she bin havin' trouble wit her heart."

"Has she seen a doctor? They could put her on a diet, you know."

Ernest rolled his eyes. "She don' have no truck wit them doctors. They jest take your money an' laugh you in the face." He paused, waiting for the right moment to strike. The trouble was, he didn't know how much to ask for. Best to go for high, he decided. "We could sure use . . . say . . . uh . . . twenny thousan'."

Bobby laughed.

"Or fifteen," Ernest added sheepishly. "Wit all the bills we got to pay . . ." He trailed off, waiting for a reaction.

Bobby couldn't believe the nerve of the man. Twenty thousand dollars! Fifteen! He should tell the sonofabitch to take a hike. "I'll send Fanni a check for three thousand.

And you can tell her it would have been nice if she'd taken the time to call me herself."

"Three thousan'!" bitched Ernest. "You all mus' be makin' plenty. An' you're tellin' me all y'kin spare is three thousand—"

"You don't want it, just say so," said Bobby, cutting him off.

"Aw, I guess we'll take it, we'll take it," Ernest whined, an unsatisfied man—but three thousand was better than nothing.

Bobby put down the phone, and for one lousy moment flashed back on life with the Crystals. Their constant fights. The insults he'd endured. His poky back room behind the kitchen, freezing in the winter and hotter than a sauna in the summer. Food. Greasy, plentiful ribs and potatoes and fried chicken. Pies and cakes, cookies and candies. Was it any wonder he'd remained a piece of blubber while living with them?

It was true though—Fanni *had* taken him in, and had defended him many times against the bullying Ernest.

He went to his desk and wrote out a check before he could change his mind. Then he addressed an envelope to Fanni and scrawled a short note telling her to call him and maybe they'd get together.

Needless to say, he never heard a word in return, although the check was cashed quickly enough.

Sharleen, too, was silent for several months. He was used to not hearing from her. She only called when she needed something, and since he'd turned down Marcus Citroen's offer to join Blue Cadillac, he was obviously not on her wanted list. He got on with his life, writing songs, recording, doing quite nicely, dating a variety of girls, and having a good time. Until one summer night, round about midnight, the buzzer sounded on his apartment door and wouldn't quit.

He was alone, watching a late-night movie on television. "Who is it?" he called out loudly before opening up.

The answer was incomprehensible. Instantly he knew it was Sharleen.

Throwing open the door, he was just in time to catch her as she fell into his arms—a beaten, bleeding wreck.

KRIS PHOENIX
1975

★ ☆ ★ ☆ ★

"It's bloody hot here," Kris complained.

"Don't knock it," Buzz replied, a sardonic grin lightening his debauched features. "The booze is cheap. It's friggin' dope paradise. An' the crumpet runs around with nothin' between them an' a cold!"

Kris could see it was going to take quite a speech to get Buzz back to rainy London and work. He had to admit his friend looked great with his gypsy tan, long hair, and single gold hoop earring. In England Buzz was always whiter than white, managing to resemble a walking corpse. Here, at least, his malevolent looks came with a healthy tan, and he didn't appear to be five days away from death, although he was still frighteningly skinny.

"Sounds like your cup of tea, all right," Kris remarked casually.

"I can tell yer, it beats the piss out of spendin' me days an' most of me nights in that stinkin' Volkswagen, with Rasta's smelly feet in me face, and Ollie fartin' the bleedin' night away."

Lounging on faded beach chairs, they both laughed. Flower brought out cans of beer. At twenty-three she was still the perennial hippie—flowing hair and flowing clothes, spacey eyes and an angelic smile. Kris figured she and Buzz had been together a long time—almost eight years. He half expected them to get married and be done with it. "Are you two ever goin' to make it legal?" he couldn't help asking.

"Wot? 'Ave you gone friggin' barmy?" Buzz responded, while Flower just smiled dreamily.

Yes, Kris decided, Buzz certainly had the right idea. Why get married if you didn't have to? Willow had caught him in a trap, and he knew it.

They'd arrived in Ibiza a few hours earlier, after a bumpy flight, Willow complaining all the way.

Buzz met them in an open Jeep wearing nothing but the smallest black briefs and a welcoming leer. Throwing their luggage on the back seat, he said, "Blimey! You're the two unhealthiest-lookin' humans I've ever seen!"

"Thanks," Kris replied. "You always did know how to make a person feel good."

"It's me charm," Buzz said with an evil wink, reaching for Peter John Buddy, who was clutched tightly in Willow's arms. "Let's see the baby then."

"No!" exclaimed Willow sharply, holding on with a sudden show of strength.

Buzz did not back off. He continued to try and pry Bo from her protective grasp.

"Stop it!" she shouted a touch hysterically, turning to Kris for support.

"C'mon, let Buzz hold him," Kris urged. "He's his godfather. He's entitled."

Willow glared at her husband, reluctantly allowing Buzz to take baby Bo for a second or two.

" 'Ello, mate," Buzz said, peering down at the child.

"That's enough," announced Willow crisply, snatching her precious bundle back.

Kris had only met his wife's mother a couple of times, and not under the best of circumstances, but he was beginning to realize with growing dread that Willow was just like the snobbish Mrs. Wigh.

Buzz drove like a maniac, the battered Jeep careening along old, cobbled streets at full speed, his foot jammed down hard on the gas.

Petrified, Willow sat silently in the back, squeezed in next to their luggage, with the baby bouncing around on her knee. "Can't you slow down?" she pleaded a couple of times, but neither of them heard her as the Jeep sped along the increasingly bumpy roads toward its destination.

Their holiday home was a run-down, dusty villa by the sea, and they were not the only occupants. Along with Buzz and Flower lived Inga, a blond, strapping Swedish girl, Klaus, a bearded German who spoke no English, and twenty-year-old American twins, both female, named Chick and Chickie.

"Why didn't you tell me there were other people living here?" Willow whispered angrily.

"How was *I* supposed to know?" Kris replied, dreading what would happen when she found out what was really going on. Buzz had filled him in as soon as they arrived and Willow and Bo were safely deposited in a damp bedroom with a sea view and an old mattress on the floor.

"It's free sex," Buzz had confided with a knowing wink. "You want it—it's yours."

Buzz always had liked the hippie life style, and Flower obviously raised no objections.

Kris knew he was in for trouble—one way or the other.

"You've got a lovely body," Chickie whispered in his ear.

"Smooth skin," murmured Chick.

"When are we gonna get it on?" they asked in unison, a chorus of hope.

Kris knew he was developing a hard-on, no need to

check it out. Christ! Where was Willow when he needed her?

Shifting on the hot sand, he rolled onto his stomach and glanced furtively around. Buzz was lying nearby, wedged between Swedish Inga and delicate Flower. What a picture postcard *that* made, since both girls wore only the bottoms of their bikinis. Inga's huge knockers made an interesting contrast to Flower's small buds.

Willow and the baby were nowhere in sight.

"Well?" teased Chick and Chickie, running their fingers up and down his spine.

This was torture! All he really wanted to do was turn over and ram it into each of them, one after the other. He was so horny it hurt.

Well, who wouldn't be? They'd been on the island for over two weeks, and Willow was consumed with anger about the sleeping arrangements, half-naked house guests, the food, and anything else she could think of.

"I won't tell wifey," Chick whispered, bending over to reach his ear, which she proceeded to nibble, her bare boobs brushing tantalizingly against his back.

Chickie followed suit. "Neither will I."

It was more than any man could reasonably take. "I'm goin' for a swim," he said weakly, getting up and making a wild dash for the sea.

Plunging in, the shock of the cold water abated some of his excitement. Not enough. Especially when Chick and Chickie, full of giggles, bosoms jiggling, ran down the sand to join him.

Jesus! What was he supposed to do? They'd been coming on to him ever since he'd arrived. And, while on one hand he liked the idea of making it with the dynamic duo, on the other he *was* a married man, and his old-fashioned values urged him to stay true—even if Willow continued to deprive him.

Chick swam toward him with Chickie in close pursuit. The two of them wore very determined expressions.

The answer lay with his wife. *Willow, my love,* he thought grimly, *you are just going to have to put out, or else*.

With that he dodged the randy twins, swam ashore, and hotfooted it up the beach toward the villa.

"Where you goin'?" Buzz called out.

He didn't stop. Whatever Willow was doing, she was going to have to drop everything and give him what he wanted. He was her husband. He had his rights.

The villa was peaceful and quiet, which meant baby Bo was asleep. Perfect. Maybe she was taking a siesta too, and he could be all the way to paradise before she even realized what was happening.

Treading quietly, he entered their room. Bo was asleep in his carry-cot, a thin muslin cover protecting him from any marauding bugs or mosquitoes. The kid looked great, suntanned and healthy. *He even looks a little bit like me,* Kris thought proudly. Yeah. Willow might have trapped him, but it was all worth it when he saw his son.

The wife's probably in the kitchen, he decided. She'd spent most of their holiday hunched over the sink, washing anything she could get her hands on. You couldn't even take off a pair of jeans without her grabbing them.

No, she wasn't in the kitchen, nor in the big dusty living room. He wouldn't put it past her to be snooping through Buzz and Flower's room—she had an insatiable desire to know everything about everyone. "Nosy little cow, isn't she?" Avis had said, when she'd caught her going through their bathroom cabinet one Sunday lunch with the family.

She wasn't in Buzz and Flower's room. Chick and Chickie's was also empty. And as Inga slept on the couch, that left only Klaus, and his door was closed.

Kris knocked, and getting no response, he pushed it open.

Spread-eagled on the bed, naked from the waist down, lay Willow. A pillow covered her face, but he would recognize that uptight, suburban pussy anywhere.

Kneeling between her thighs, his bearded face embedded in fairyland, was Klaus, the German.

RAFEALLA
1976

★ ☆ ★ ☆ ★

To Rafealla's consternation and eventual disappointment, Eddie Mafair did not bother to call her. And it wasn't until almost a year later that she bumped into him at the rather elaborate wedding of the daughter of one of her mother's friends. He was the best man, and heading in the direction of being extremely drunk.

"Hello," she said sulkily when he didn't acknowledge her as he attempted to stagger past her table at the reception.

Glancing at her vaguely, he said, "You're going to have to remind me, sweetheart. I'm pissed."

"You certainly are," she replied coldly, aching all over with the desire to be in his arms once more, even if only on the crowded dance floor of Annabel's.

Peering closely at her he said, "Suzanna?"

"No."

"Diana?"

"*No.*"

"A clue?"

"Rafealla."

Her name obviously meant nothing to him either. "Nice to see you," he slurred, and was off.

So much for mutual attraction. She had thought he liked her. In fact she'd been positive, and had made up a million excuses why he hadn't called. Now it was quite obvious he didn't remember her.

Still . . . she wasn't going to let it get her down. After all, she was sixteen now, no more the stupid fifteen-year-old who had fallen for his casual charm. There had been several close encounters over the last year. Stefan, the twenty-two-year-old male nurse whom she'd sat next to at the movies, and had secretly dated for several weeks until he tried to go too far. Jimmy, a young American college student who took her dancing and taught her the fine art of giving what he called a "blow job" because she refused to do anything else of a sexual nature. And Marcel, a young French waiter who worked in a local restaurant. He took her for long walks in the woods and kissed and caressed her breasts for hours on end, bringing her great pleasure. Until in return, after many weeks of pleading, she finally gave him the special blow job Jimmy had taught her, and marveled at his ecstasy and gratefulness.

She wanted to do the same for Eddie. It gave her a grati-fying sense of power and did not interfere with her virgin-ity, which she planned to hang on to until marriage. Odile and she had discussed it many times and decided that everything else was allowed, but going all the way was definitely out. Too risky, for one thing. Unnecessary, for another. Boys were perfectly satisfied with the alternative.

The wedding was a riotous affair, a mixture of young friends of the bride and groom and the older contingent of relatives and close family friends. Rafealla knew quite a few people, and found herself on the dance floor with a variety of enthusiastic would-be suitors. Occasionally she glimpsed Eddie. He seemed to be attached to a sinewy blonde in a minidress who was almost as drunk as he was.

Rafealla stared at him. She was not used to being ig-nored. With her long dark hair, exotic features, and slim figure, she usually received more than her fair share of attention. How *dare* Eddie Mafair not even remember her?

The band began playing Beatles songs—a request from the bride. "Yellow Submarine," "Eleanor Rigby," "She Loves You."

Eddie was crotch to crotch with his blonde on the dance floor.

Feeling the urge to do something to make him notice her, Rafealla brazenly approached the band leader. "Do you know 'Yesterday'?" she asked.

"We certainly do."

"Can I sing it?"

"Can you?" the band leader asked with a quizzical look.

"Of course I can," she replied, full of bravado.

"All right, darling, show us." He handed her the microphone.

Oh, boy! What had she done to herself! She loved singing, but only in the privacy of the shower, with that wonderful echo making every note sound good. Oh, wow! How was she ever going to pull this one off?

"'Yesterday,'" her voice wavered, "'all my troubles seemed so far away.'" Everyone was looking at her. She had to make this good. "'Now it looks as though they're here to stay. Oh, I believe in yesterday.'"

She had it! Sounding good. Getting everyone's attention, including that of her mother, who was staring at her, probably really annoyed that she was making an exhibition of herself.

Her voice was pleasantly low, sounding older than her years. She sought out Eddie Mafair with her eyes, and finally—yes—she had his attention. *Now* he'd remember her.

When it was over, there was applause and a lot of "*I* didn't know you could sing." And finally there was Eddie, who said, "Where have you been hiding all my life?"

Before she could reply, her mother appeared, ruining

everything with news of their imminent departure. At least he now knew she existed. That was something.

Two weeks later she left for France and a summer vacation with Odile. Arriving at Nice airport and rushing outside to find her friend, she felt a surge of excitement, for standing no more than three feet away was Eddie Mafair, arguing in fluent French with an irate cabdriver.

Just along the curb a waving Odile emerged from her stepfather's chauffeur-driven Mercedes.

Rafealla stood transfixed.

Odile yelled, "Kid! Over here."

Eddie stalked away from his cab and marched into the airport without noticing her.

Odile ran over to her. "What's the *matter* with you?" she scolded. "Are you deaf?"

"No," Rafealla replied dreamily, hugging her friend. "Just in love!"

Odile's mother had married into show business. Her husband was Claudio Franconini, an aged Italian crooner with an enormous European following. He had been a star for many years, and reveled in his success. Marrying the widow of the prominent politician Henri Ronet was another plus in his life. Claudio adored the spotlight.

Odile had always considered him to be a bore. And on the occasions Rafealla had met him before, she was forced to agree.

"He still colors his bald spot with boot polish," Odile confided with a wild giggle. "And he still thinks that every woman should fall at his feet with delight. Nothing changes."

"I don't know how your mother stands it," Rafealla commented.

With a Gallic shrug, Odile said, "She doesn't mind. They're good together. Mama is very patient, as you well know."

Claudio greeted Rafealla warmly, kissing her on both cheeks and saying, "Welcome, welcome. What a joy to see you again, my dear. Our humble home is yours."

Their humble home was a magnificent gated château in the hills above Cannes. Guards were on permanent duty. Ten servants looked after the guests. And there was a party every other day. Claudio loved entertaining.

"We'll make our own fun," Odile promised. "We don't have to hang around here with the old fogies."

Rafealla wondered what Eddie Mafair was doing at the airport. Probably on holiday. Too bad he'd left.

The weather in the south of France was glorious. After a rather dreary English summer, Rafealla was delighted to lie in the sun doing absolutely nothing. She found it entertaining to watch Claudio Franconini and his constant stream of guests. Odile and she staked out their corner of the pool and observed the famous come and go. There was a Greek ship owner and his fiery mistress. An American gangster with his very proper English wife. A financier with two girls not much older than Rafealla and Odile. A black female singer and her lover.

"This is what I call entertainment!" Rafealla said. "Is it always like this?"

"Yes," Odile assured her. "Last year we had dozens of movie stars, a President's widow, oh . . . all sorts of strange people. You should've come."

"I wanted to. But as you know, my dear mother always considered I was too young to enjoy the wicked pleasures of the south of France until now."

"I guess sixteen signals wicked pleasures are okay. Right?"

"I bloody well hope so!"

When they got bored sitting beside the pool, the chauffeur dropped them off in nearby Juan-les-Pins, where they wandered around the colorful shops and open sidewalk cafés. Sometimes they water-skied from the beach. Male attention was not lacking, for they made an alluring, if very young, combination. Odile—so blond and innocently pretty. And Rafealla, dark and mysterious. They were the perfect foil for each other as they stalked the beaches in minuscule bikinis, attracting an avid following of admirers.

Odile struck up more than a friendship with a Norwegian law student, and Rafealla found herself practicing the fine art of the blow job with an extremely handsome Swiss medical student. She met him on the beach every evening, and they had a perfectly delightful time. This all had to take place before ten o'clock, when the chauffeured Mercedes would arrive to collect the girls and transport them back to the Franconini home.

"I feel like Cinderella," Rafealla joked. "You know—it's as if we're leading a double life or something."

"We are," Odile said grimly. "My mother will kill us if she ever finds out what we are up to."

"Mine too."

A pause, and then Odile added, "Surely they were young once? They must have done all these things."

"And more," agreed Rafealla, although she could hardly imagine her mother ever doing anything as rude as giving a man a blow job. Come to think of it, she couldn't even imagine her mother making love, and yet it was patently obvious she had—at least once.

Rafealla's medical student decided it was time she went one step further. "Trust me, I'm a doctor—well, almost," he said. "I want to give you pleasure too."

She had never allowed anyone below the belt. Too intimate, too sticky, too embarrassing.

The lure of the white sand, the balmy nights, and the seductive lapping of the sea finally got to her. Besides, he was very good-looking, *and* a medical man. Pushing Eddie Mafair to the back of her mind, she allowed him to embark on a short exploration of uncharted territory.

Removing her jeans and the bottom half of her bikini, he

began gently touching her with his fingers. She had to admit it did feel good, especially when his fingers moved in a strangely soothing circular motion. Automatically she spread her legs, gasping at newfound sensations which suddenly and unexpectedly culminated in a rush of pure pleasure.

"Your first orgasm," he said matter-of-factly.

Her heart was pounding. This was something else. This was *great*.

"Now let me just put it there," he continued, working his way on top of her. "Nothing can happen now."

She felt pressure, and warning signals fired off in her head. "No," she said, quickly shoving him away.

"Yes," he insisted, moving back on top.

"No!" she snapped.

"Do you plan to stay a virgin forever?" he asked nastily.

Absolutely not, she replied silently. *Only until I can have Eddie Mafair. And I will. Oh, yes, I will.*

One morning Rafealla got up very early, before everyone else, and went down to the pool to swim lengths. She was bronzed to perfection, her long limbs oiled and gleaming, her stomach flat and faintly muscled.

"You have a beautiful body, my dear," said a thick male voice with a slight accent.

She turned and encountered Marcus Citroen, a record magnate who had arrived the night before from New York with his ultra-chic wife.

Rafealla grinned—she didn't know what else to do. There was nothing worse than trying to avoid the lecherous leers of dirty old men. "Thanks," she said, and dived into the inviting pool, hoping he would be gone when she surfaced.

To her surprise, when she came up for air, Marcus Citroen was in the pool, close to her.

"Look at this," he said cheerfully, as if he'd spotted some unique form of starfish.

Without thinking she peered below the clear blue water.

Marcus Citroen was taking risks. The man was stark naked, with a full erection.

BOBBY MONDELLA
1976

★ ☆ ★ ☆ ★

It took months of patient handling to nurse Sharleen back to health. Her bruises and cuts healed first, but her pride took a whole lot longer.

"What happened?" Bobby demanded. "Who did this to you? Is it Marcus Citroen, 'cause if it is I'll kill the white sonofabitch."

"No, no," she said, panic-stricken. "It wasn't him. You mustn't get involved."

"I *am* involved. Now you've gotta tell me what went on."

"No way, Bobby. I can't."

There was no use pushing her, but gradually over the next few weeks he heard her story.

At first, she told him, Marcus Citroen was a gentleman. Oh, yes, he persuaded her to join him in cocaine parties, and expected sex. But in return he gave her a lucrative contract with Blue Cadillac, a lavish apartment, and gradually began to build her into a star.

"I'm not naive," she confided tearfully. "I've been around the block an' then back again. But everything that was happening was so good. And I thought I could handle Marcus and his crazy demands."

His demands turned out to be watching her have sex with other girls. And more and more drugs.

"He liked me stoned," she admitted. "That way he could control me."

Stardom arrived, and vainly Sharleen attempted to cut back on Marcus and his perverted ideas. One night she completely rebelled, and refused to go to bed with a man and two other women. Marcus beat her up, and that was when she fled to Bobby.

"I hope I can stay here," she said simply.

She'd been stupid, but she'd learned a harsh lesson. His heart went out to her. "For as long as you like," he said. And concentrated on getting her better.

The trick was to be there for her every minute, supporting her, encouraging her to take a drug cure, watching over her at all times.

After a lot of persuasion she entered a private clinic under an assumed name, emerging weeks later looking like the Sharleen he used to know.

"How're you feelin'?" he asked.

"Great."

"Really great?"

"You gotta know it."

"I'm proud of you, baby. You know that, don't you?"

Smiling wanly, she said, "Thanks. Now tell me, where do I go from here?"

He didn't hesitate. "I've spoken to Amerika. Soul On Soul wants you. I've already written two songs we can record together. How about *that?"*

"Really?" Her smile lit up the room.

"It's done, baby. Sharleen an' Bobby. We're gonna be a team."

It wasn't done at all. Blue Cadillac Records refused to release her from the contract she'd signed, and they also refused to give her songs to record. In other words she was left in limbo, unable to do anything at all.

Bobby was outraged. "I'm going to see this Citroen character," he said angrily. "They can't do this to you. No way."

"Oh, yes," she said softly. "Marcus can do anything he damn well pleases."

Over the months Bobby discovered she was right. Blue Cadillac had her under an exclusive, unbreakable contract, and there wasn't a thing anyone could do, not even the hotshot lawyer Bobby hired at his own considerable expense.

Sharleen, whose star had once shone so brightly, now had to sit back and watch other singers get the attention that was once hers.

After a few months Bobby realized if something didn't happen soon, she was going to revert to her old ways. He'd already caught her drunk a couple of times, and he could see she was restless and getting ready to move on. Their relationship was strictly platonic, even though she was living in his apartment. He wanted to make a move, but somehow, because they had been friends for so long, it wasn't so easy. At this particular time in her life he had no desire to put any more pressure on her. Whatever was going to happen would take place naturally, or not at all.

Amerika Allen said to him one day, "What is it with you an' that girl? You've all but stopped working since she's around. You can't talk about anything except her. To tell you the truth, I reckon you should get on with your *own* life, and let Sharleen do the same."

Amerika was right and he knew it. Too bad. While Sharleen was with him he couldn't change.

Rocket called several times from Europe where he was filming. "How is she?" he always asked.

"Fine," Bobby replied evenly, wanting to say, *What do you care? She's no longer your concern. You're married now. You're out of the picture*.

Without Sharleen's knowing, he tried to call Marcus Citroen on more than one occasion. All he got was "Mr. Citroen's in a meeting." "Mr. Citroen's out of the country." "Mr. Citroen's unavailable."

One morning he awoke to find Sharleen staring into the medicine cabinet sizing up the pill collection. "What are you doing? Planning your death scene?" he joked.

"Yes," she said, deadly serious.

Screw Marcus Citroen. He'd had enough.

Dressing hurriedly, he looked up the address of Blue Cadillac Records and took a cab over there.

He arrived at a minute past 9 A.M., and the receptionist, an attractive black girl with multicolored fingernails, was just settling herself behind the front desk.

"Hello, gorgeous," he said, turning on the charm.

She looked up, her wide red lips breaking into a welcoming smile. "Bobby Mondella!" she exclaimed. "What a nice way to start my day!"

He wasn't used to being recognized, but this couldn't be better.

"I *looove* 'Dream Baby,'" she gushed. "It's a sensational cut."

"Thanks," he said modestly. "Glad you approve."

"I wish you were with *our* company," she said, fluttering extra-long eyelashes."An' then maybe you'd get the attention you deserve."

Shrugging, he said, "Who knows?" Casually leaning across her desk he added, "Is Marcus in yet?"

"Mr. Citroen is always in his office from seven-thirty on," she replied, all of a sudden very businesslike. "Are you his first appointment?"

"Sure am," he said easily.

She glanced down at a large red appointment book, tapping the page with extended fingernails. "His secretaries don't get in until nine-thirty. There's no notation of your name here."

"That's because we made the date late last night."

"*Oooh*." Her eyes gleamed. "I bet you were at the Stevie Wonder party. Am I right?"

"Sure was."

"Lucky *you*."

"Yeah . . . well . . . I'll just go on in. Where's his office?"

"Down the hall, last door on the right. You can't miss it, there's a solid gold record on the door."

"Cute."

"I'll buzz and tell him you're on the way."

"Don't bother. He's probably forgotten. I want to see his face when he realizes *I* remembered."

The receptionist giggled and patted her teased hair. "Keep on makin' those records!"

"Only if you keep on buyin' 'em."

Striding down the hall he tried to decide exactly what he was going to say. What would make a man like Marcus Citroen set Sharleen free?

He remembered their one and only encounter many years ago. The men's room in The Chainsaw. He was the attendant and Marcus Citroen was the customer, snorting cocaine with Del Delgardo. Jeez! That seemed like lifetimes ago.

The door with the gold record attached to the center faced him. The record was larger than the real thing, and boldly printed on the label was MARCUS CITROEN—HIT-MAKER—BLUE CADILLAC RECORDS. Very subtle.

Without knocking, he opened the door and walked right in.

Marcus sat behind his oversize desk, speaking on the phone. He indicated that Bobby should take a seat. There was not a flicker of surprise anywhere on his impassive face.

Bobby didn't want to sit down, but there seemed to be no alternative. What else could he do? Snatch the phone from the man and start berating him?

No way. This had to be a civilized meeting. It had to make sense, and above all, he had to walk out of there with some kind of a solution for Sharleen.

Marcus was obviously talking to someone in London, for he made references to various English events, and he ended the conversation by saying, "I'll be in on the Concorde next week, I expect everything to be worked out by then. Oh . . ." His eyes, behind steely shades settled on Bobby. "And you can tell the motherfuckers that if it's not, someone will be floating in the Thames. And I can assure you, it won't be me."

He hung up.

Bobby cleared his throat, ready to do battle for Sharleen.

Marcus stared at him, put the tips of his fingers together, and continued to stare.

Bobby cleared his throat again. Fuck it. This sonofabitch wasn't going to intimidate him. "You don't know me," he said gruffly. "I've come to see you about Sharleen."

Marcus nodded.

There was something wrong here somewhere: Why wasn't the great Marcus Citroen screaming for his secretary? Why wasn't he telling him to get the hell out?

Bobby pressed on while he had the opportunity. "Uh . . . Sharleen's very unhappy . . . suicidal, in fact. And I think you know why."

Marcus plucked a cigar from a carved box on his desk, reached for a silver table lighter in the shape of a Cadillac, and lit up. Still he didn't say anything.

What kind of game was this man playing? Bobby's voice rose with anger. "The bottom line is, either you let her out of her contract, or I'm gonna see your name in headlines over every tabloid rag in the country, with details of what you made her do."

"Good morning, Mr. Mondella," Marcus said smoothly, the oily thickness in his tone as sweet as syrup. "I've been expecting your visit for quite some time. What took you so long?"

Was this his day for being recognized, or what? And exactly *why* had Marcus Citroen been waiting for him to show up?

"I want you to tear up her contract," Bobby said, feeling a surge of anger overpower him.

"There is an easy answer to all this nonsense," Marcus said calmly. "And if you think about it, you'll find it's the only sensible way."

"What's that?" Bobby asked grimly.

"Why, you, of course. You're the answer."

"I don't get it."

Marcus drew deeply on his cigar, blowing a steady stream of smoke toward the ceiling. "Ah, but you will. Once I explain, you'll understand perfectly." And he proceeded to do just that, while Bobby listened intently.

Marcus Citroen's solution was simple. Blue Cadillac Records wanted Bobby Mondella. Blue Cadillac Records were prepared to offer him an excellent deal, plus they would buy him out of his Soul On Soul contract. Blue Cadillac Records were also prepared to build Bobby Mondella into a big star, and they had the connections and clout to do so.

The deal included Sharleen. Once Bobby signed on the dotted line, her career would automatically be reactivated, and in no time at all they would guide her back to the top—where she rightfully belonged. An album of duets with Bobby was in her future, plus a possible movie for the two of them—depending on how everything went.

"I don't believe this!" Bobby said vehemently. "It's blackmail."

"I would have thought you might jump at an opportunity to get away from a second-rate outfit like Soul On Soul," Marcus said, puffing on his cigar. "They've done nothing for you except squander your talents."

"Hey—listen. They gave me my first chance. They believed in me."

"Ah . . . loyalty. I do admire it. But you must realize *I* believe in you too, Mr. Mondella—or may I call you Bobby?" Marcus rubbed the bridge of his nose, raising his sinister-looking tinted glasses to do so. "I've had my eye on you for quite some time. In my estimation, with your songwriting abilities, your looks, and your talent, you can be the biggest black star in the country. You can be number one. And, with Blue Cadillac to guide you—" he paused, allowing his words to sink in—"there is nothing you cannot achieve."

Bobby was filled with mixed emotions. It wasn't exactly discouraging to hear Marcus Citroen's plans for him—if it wasn't a trap. And yet, he knew he was being manipulated, and that didn't sit well with him at all. Besides, he couldn't imagine anything worse than being in a man like Marcus Citroen's control. And how could he leave Soul On Soul and Amerika after all they had done for him?

Soul On Soul is holding you back, an inner voice warned him. *Amerika Allen says your records can't cross over, and you know damn well they can.*

Yes. He knew it all right. Much as he loathed Marcus Citroen, Blue Cadillac were big enough to do it for him.

Besides, if he wanted to help Sharleen, he had no choice, did he? The decision was out of his hands.

1987
Saturday, July 11th

★ ☆ ★ ☆ ★

The ride down Sunset was long and boring, but Kris didn't mind. The limo was well stocked with every kind of alcoholic beverage, plus a VCR, a stack of tapes, and an excellent sound system including a compact disc player with a selection of the latest discs.

He put on Motown's *Twenty-five Number One Hits from Twenty-five Years,* and would have settled back to enjoy The Temptations, The Four Tops, and Marvin Gaye, if Cybil hadn't decided to be the life and soul of the party and burst forth with a running commentary of her day.

The Hawk seemed interested enough. He leaned forward in the seat facing her, looking immaculate in a white silk dinner jacket, with his perfect tan and ultra-white capped teeth. Tombstone teeth, Kris thought, all the better to gobble you up with.

The Hawk was not a handsome man, but he certainly made the best of what he had. He was married, with a wife who lived permanently in Buenos Aires and only came to Los Angeles once a year. Every six weeks the Hawk got on a plane and visited her for a long weekend—a rather strange arrangement, but one that seemed to work, for they had been together for fifteen years.

176

It did not preclude the Hawk from being a player. He had a stable of luscious girlfriends, none of them a day over twenty-two. Rumor was he merely liked to be seen with them—nothing else.

"So . . ." Cybil continued excitedly, "Jerry doesn't take any shit from anyone—well, maybe from Mick, but that's about it. Anyway, she looked this guy straight in the eye— like a real confrontation stare, y'know what I mean? And then she said in that crazed drawl of hers, 'Honey, the screwin' you'd get ain't *nothin'* compared to the screwin' you'd get!'"

The Hawk laughed. He was amused by Cybil's inside gossip about the world of modeling.

Frankly, Kris didn't want to know. Glancing at his watch he asked irritably, "Are we nearly there?"

"Relax," the Hawk said. "Sit back. Enjoy yourself. It's a beautiful day."

When wasn't it a beautiful day in sunny California?

Fuck it. He wasn't happy about this gig, and nothing was going to improve his mood.

"Name?" barked a fierce-looking guard, as Maxwell Sicily got off the shuttle bus.

"George Smith."

The guard adjusted his opaque sunglasses and checked out a long list. "Okay," he said at last. "Wear this." And he handed Maxwell Sicily a badge with Lilliane's, George Smith, and a number printed on it.

Organized, Maxwell thought, but they would have been better off doing their homework.

"Name?" the guard asked Chloe.

"I'm management. I don't need a badge," she objected, with a haughty toss of her frazzled hair.

"Everyone gotta have one," the guard said grimly. "Otherwise, lady, you ain't goin' nowhere."

"Hah!" she said. "And who's going to stop me?"

"Lady, *I* am. Them's the rules."

Maxwell took the opportunity to move swiftly away, joining a group of waiters busy receiving instructions on where they were and were not allowed to go.

"No cameras. No recording equipment. And no trespassing other than your allocated area," snapped the latest guard.

"What if we wanna take a piss?" asked one of the waiters.

"There's facilities."

"Oooh, and do you come with us, to hold our . . . uh . . . hand?"

The security guard did not crack a smile.

Maxwell followed the group to the back of one of the two main houses on the estate, where a makeshift open-air kitchen had been set up under a large tent. Chefs were busy organizing their equipment, while the waiters were being given a variety of jobs to do.

He got in line and was instructed to help set out silverware. Grabbing a few boxes, he followed a tall woman supervisor shouting out orders as she led the way down a narrow pathway to an enormous sunken area, where there were lots of round tables waiting for decoration and a curved stage that looked like it was balanced right at the edge of the cliff.

By nightfall, with the fairy lights twinkling in the trees, the backdrop of clear sky, and the faint rush of the ocean, the effect was going to be spectacular.

A shame to ruin such a splendid evening, Maxwell reflected grimly. But they deserved it.

All of them.

The attention always made Rafealla faintly uneasy. People jumping at her every command. Didn't they realize she was just like everyone else? Or were stars supposed to be different?

She hadn't been a star long enough to quite get the hang of it. Maybe she should be more demanding, behave like a bitch, have hysterics and scream a lot. But that wasn't her style.

"Do you always do your own hair and makeup?" Trudie, the publicity woman, asked curiously.

"It's easier if I do it myself," Rafealla replied as the limousine turned onto the Pacific Coast Highway. She wished she could tell it to stop. She wanted to get out and run on the beach, or just sit on the sand watching the endlessly fascinating ocean.

For the last few months she hadn't been able to do anything without being recognized. It was an outrageous invasion of privacy, and she didn't enjoy it one bit. And yet she'd wanted it desperately—craved fame with relentless dedication.

"If I had a chance to have professionals get *me* together, I'd jump at it," Trudie admitted, reaching for an M&M set out in a small glass dish.

"I'm sure Rafealla knows what she wants," said one of the record executives, shooting her a warning glare. Rule one: Never criticize anything a celebrity does.

"Uh, you know it's disturbing," Rafealla said, feeling she had to explain herself, "having a stranger paw at your face. I don't like it."

"With a face like yours you don't need it," Trudie observed grudgingly. "Me—they'd have to pile it on with a trowel and then some!"

Rafealla smiled faintly. And wished she was somewhere else.

Speed had no intention of hitting on the Mexican broad in the tight red pants and halter top, but she was coming on to him with such force he'd have to be dead to resist her.

She sashayed past the parked limousine several times, wriggling her big ass and jiggling her tits, before finally saying, "Hiya, handsome. It'sa too hotta day to be sittin' in a car."

It was hot all right. He'd found a nice quiet side street off San Vicente. Residential. Nobody to bother him. First he'd eaten his chicken, then he'd studied both *Playboy* and *Penthouse* cover to cover.

Oh, yes, it was hot. And when Miss Mexico tottered by on stiletto heels, he couldn't help but notice her, and she certainly noticed him. Well, he had this magic with women, didn't he? Sort of a Burt Reynolds magnetism without the looks.

Not that his looks were anything to complain about. Somebody once told him he resembled Roy Scheider on speed.

He didn't do drugs. Well, only sometimes. A few uppers, downers. A snort if he was feeling flush.

He wouldn't mind a snort today, *and* a piece of fine Mexican ass. *Playboy* and *Penthouse* had gotten his engine revving.

Furtively sneaking a look at his watch, he realized there was still time.

Miss Mexico hovered near the window, waiting for a go signal.

Speed knew he was irresistible to women. He also knew this one was a hooker—although what she was doing plying her trade in this respectable area in the middle of the afternoon was beyond him.

"How much?" he asked, trying to make up his mind whether to proceed or not.

"Beeg good time or leetle good time?" The woman leered, suggestively fingering one of her nipples.

"Head."

"What?"

"Suckee."

"Ah." She put a finger to her lips, touching it reverently with her tongue. "Twenny dollar."

"Forget it."

"Fifteen." Her nipple hardened beneath her touch.

Speed let out an anticipatory grunt. He'd always been a sucker for big bosoms. "Get in the back," he said gruffly, springing the locks.

"You no disappointed."

Quickly he got out of the car, glancing up and down the street. It was deserted. Ready to rumba, he joined her on the back seat.

"Money," she said, holding out her hand, palm up.

Struggling in his back pocket he came up with three fives, shoving them in her eager hand.

"Vice," she said, dropping the Mexican accent and miraculously producing a police badge. "You're under arrest, buster."

And so the limousine carrying Bobby Mondella arrived at checkpoint number one on the vast oceanside estate. A guard spoke to the driver and then peered inside.

"What's happening?" Bobby asked. This is what he hated more than anything, having to ask about every little thing.

Sara laid a reassuring hand on his arm. "Just a security check."

"What for?"

"I don't know. I guess they have to be careful at an event like this."

"Sure," Bobby said acidly. "Someone might try to blow Marcus Citroen's ass sky-high—an' not a moment too soon."

"Bobby! Don't talk like that."

What did Sara know? Exactly nothing. She had no idea how evil a man like Marcus Citroen could be.

The car moved smoothly off, up a steep incline and along a narrow private road which would eventually lead the way to Novaroen.

Bobby took a deep, strangled breath and remembered Nova Citroen. The bitch of all time.

"I'm not a fucking maid," Vicki Foxe wanted to say to the bossy housekeeper who seriously thought she was Joan Crawford reincarnated. However, she could not say that because, right now, she *was* a maid, or at least playing the role. So instead she said, "Yes, Mrs. Ivors, as soon as I've finished cleaning the silver champagne goblets for the guest house."

"Mrs. Citroen needs attention *now,*" the Ivors woman snapped, scarlet lips and heavy eyebrows a fond tribute to Mommy Dearest. "Those goblets should have been polished days ago. I don't know what you girls do with your time."

Vicki didn't say a word. Thank God this was the last day she would have to put up with this unbelievable crap.

"Go to Mrs. Citroen. Now," instructed Mrs. Ivors. "And when she's finished with you, come right back here. I don't want to find you cozying with the guards. You're much too familiar with them. We'll have to have a talk about attitude if you're to continue in this job."

How Vicki longed to say, *Get stuffed, you silly old cow. You can shove this crappy job right up your drawers—and watch out for moths.* Smiling serenely, she said, "Yes, Mrs. Ivors. I'll be right back, as soon as Madame lets me."

Madame! What a great touch! Even Mrs. Ivors shut up.

Vicki made her way upstairs to the master suite, humming softly to herself. Within hours it would be all over. And not a moment too soon.

"Good afternoon, Mr. Citroen."

"Nice day, Mr. Citroen."

"Delighted to see you again, Mr. Citroen."

Minions. All of them. Worker ants. The guards. The gardeners, the staff, the security. The place was a swarm of activity. If he'd had his way they would never have thrown open their home for such an event.

"It's not our home," Nova had reminded him scornfully when he'd voiced his objections. "Merely a weekend shack. And if *I* want to have the party here, this is where it will be."

Sometimes she challenged his authority. Not too often. Nova knew exactly how far she could go. Only as far as he'd allow her to. If she stepped beyond the bounds he punished her.

Nobody took punishment the way Nova did. Nobody. . . .

As far as Marcus was concerned it made their relationship perfect.

For a moment he thought about Rafealla. So young . . . so spirited.

It had been a very long time since he'd been forced to wait for a woman. But Rafealla was going to be worth it. Of that he was sure.

Nova Citroen glanced up as the maid entered after knocking discreetly. "What took you so long?" she asked irritably.

"Mrs. Ivors only just told me you needed someone—"

"Yes, I do," Nova interrupted rudely. "Get down and find my ring. I think it rolled under the bed."

Find it yourself, you spoiled bitch, Vicki thought to herself as she dutifully assumed the position and scanned the dusty underneath of Mr. and Mrs. Citroen's custom-made bed. She spotted the ring immediately—a huge solitaire diamond. What would happen if she slipped it casually down her cleavage and claimed she couldn't find it? It was a thought—but too risky today of all days.

"Here we are, Mrs. Citroen," she said brightly, scooping it up.

Nova took the ring, slipping it back on her finger.

The maid was staring at her. Nova hated scrutiny. She was perfect from a distance, but up close sometimes the cool perfection cracked. "You can go now," she snapped. Stupid bovine creature. Take your eyes *off* me. God! She was getting too thin; that was why her ring had fallen off. As one grew older, svelte turned into scrawny, and when rings started slipping off one's fingers it was time to do something about it.

"Thank you, Mrs. Citroen." Vicki bobbed a curtsy, another perfect touch. She was almost beginning to enjoy this!

As soon as the girl left, Nova resumed her agitated pacing. She twisted the magnificent diamond on her finger and thought about its history. Marcus had bought it for her. A blood present between the two of them, and only she knew why.

KRIS PHOENIX
1977

★ ☆ ★ ☆ ★

The noise was a deafening roar. A cacophony of excited sound.

"KRIS! KRIS! KRIS!"

"BUZZ! BUZZ! BUZZ!"

One of the roadies had told him there wasn't a dry seat in the house when they were finished, just like it was when the Beatles were performing.

They moved together, the four of them, The Wild Ones, surrounded by their people: a makeup girl, a hair stylist, Mr. Terence, a couple of bodyguards, and the ever-present Flower.

Buzz swigged from a bottle of Scotch, shoving it toward Kris, who drank his share, before passing it on to Ollie and Rasta.

"WE WANT THE WILD ONES," chanted the crowd. "WE WANT THE WILD ONES!"

"Yeah," muttered Kris. "An' you're gonna get 'em."

As they neared the side of the stage, Flower passed Buzz a joint. Taking a couple of deep hits, he automatically handed it on to Kris, who did the same.

Mr. Terence pretended not to notice.

Kris held up the roach, waving it at Ollie and Rasta. "Anyone?"

"Naw," said Rasta. "I'm high enough, man."

"Let's go get 'em then!" shouted Kris, adjusting his guitar. "Let's go rock the shit outta 'em!"

"We're goin' in for the kill!" yelled Buzz.

And the four of them ran frantically on stage as the screaming reached fever pitch.

"KRIS. WE LOVE YOU!"

"BUZZ! BUZZ! BUZZ!"

"KRIIIIIIIIIS!"

It had been that way from the beginning of the incredible relaunching of their stalled careers. Within a fast eighteen months they had become media superstars, roaring a path to fame and glory with nothing and no one to stop them.

The Wild Ones. White-hot and ready to play. Sexy. Talented. Four likely contenders in the rock & roll sweepstakes.

While Ollie and Rasta were considered cute, and definitely necessary to the overall picture, it was Kris and Buzz who culled all the major attention.

Kris Phoenix. How the little teenyboppers loved him. They went crazy for his irreverent looks, his spiky dirty-blond hair, his ice-blue eyes, and his wiry body. They especially liked his wiry body.

Buzz attracted the slightly older fans. Suntan long gone, he was back to his usual whiter-than-white pallor. And with his long raggedy black hair, oblique unsmiling expression, and skinny snake-hips, he had a certain satanic quality parents feared and loathed. Therefore rebellious teenagers worshipped him.

Kris Phoenix and Buzz Darke. Two new English heroes for the seventies—a triumph over punk music, which was all the rage, with groups like the Sex Pistols, the Jam, and the Damned getting most of the attention.

The Wild Ones were no way punk-influenced. All four

of them hated the tuneless, mindless music of the "fuck you" generation of punk musicians. The Wild Ones took their influence from a combination of early rhythm & blues, Buddy Holly, Chuck Berry, Sam Cooke, and Otis Redding. They threw in a little of the Rolling Stones drive, the melodies of the Beatles, the guts of Joe Cocker's vocals, and the pure guitar genius of Eric Clapton.

What emerged was a distinctive sound, especially as they only performed their own compositions.

In eighteen months they'd made it—quickly enough for some of the music press to label them an overnight success.

"Overnight bleedin' success, my arse!" sneered Buzz. "What about the friggin' sloggin' years nobody would friggin' look at us? What about explorin' England in a friggin' Volkswagen?"

True words. But now they were stars. In England. They hadn't cracked America yet. They hadn't tried.

Flash! Photographers captured that initial crazy moment as they launched into their first hit record—"Dirty Miss Mary." Kris had written the lyrics to go with Buzz's melody. It was a quirky tune, reminiscent in a way of the Beatles' "Eleanor Rigby."

Kris and Buzz sang it together, sharing the center microphone for effect, working off each other, singing the hell out of the sardonic lyrics.

Kris felt the adrenaline pumping through his system, charging him up, making him razor-sharp and ready for anything. Christ! There was no feeling in the world like performing for an appreciative, yelling, stamping, screaming audience of fans. Hell, no.

And yet it had almost never happened. Buzz hadn't wanted to leave Ibiza, where he sat around stoned all day with naked girls to satisfy his every need. It had taken a great deal of not-so-gentle persuasion. In fact, they'd almost come to blows, with Kris calling him every name he could think of. Well, he had to have *someone* to vent his frustration on. Once he'd packed Willow and the baby back to England, he took it all out on Buzz. They fought for five long weeks, arguing back and forth, until finally Buzz gave in. "Fuck it!" he'd said bitterly. "I can see I'm never goin' t'get any peace again if I don't do it."

"Bloody right," Kris agreed.

Since Willow had left he'd been to bed with Inga, the strapping Swede, both Chickie and Chick, and a variety of other females. Oh, yes, and he'd taken part in his first orgy, which didn't thrill him one little bit. "Too messy," he informed Flower, when she invited him to attend another one.

"Don't be so silly!" she chided lightly. "It's fun!"

His idea of fun was not squirming around on the floor with a bunch of sweaty, maybe disease-ridden, strangers. Buzz and Flower got off on it at least twice a week. Kris couldn't understand why.

Catching goody-goody Willow with Klaus, the German, was a real downer. He couldn't remember having felt such rage over anything. After discovering the two of them, he'd dragged her out of the room, slapped her stupid face, and told her to get packed. Then he booked a flight for her and the baby, drove them to the airport, and put them on the next plane to London.

Willow cried. "Please come too," she begged.

"I'll be back when I feel like it," he said without emotion.

"I'm sorry," she whimpered.

Was she sorry she'd been caught? Or sorry she'd done it? He didn't know and he didn't care. He felt betrayed. But he wasn't going to let it ruin his life.

Working on Buzz to come back kept him sane. And sleeping around restored his ego. By the time they arrived in London he'd decided to forgive Willow for the sake of their baby. After all, they were even now.

He was too late. She'd gone. Fled home to Mummy and Daddy in Esher, taking baby Bo with her. Divorce papers awaited him.

He didn't waste time worrying about it. But he did get hold of a lawyer to make sure he could visit his son regularly.

From then on it was all work. Once they'd rehearsed the new material, they went out on the road to try it out. The old, familiar Volkswagen van transported them up north.

"Bloody hell!" Buzz grumbled. "Is this what I bleedin' dragged meself back for?"

Audience reaction was great. Mr. Terence came down for the concert when they reached Scotland. He liked what he saw so much, he arranged for a well-known booking agent to fly in and see them the next day.

Within a week they had signed on to open for Del Delgardo and the Nightmares, the big American group who were due to do a two-week tour of England.

Night after night they stole the show from Mr. Delgardo and his Nightmares, causing major friction and a rapid payoff after only one week. Kris couldn't care less. Del Delgardo was a prick. Besides, a scout from Force Records had seen them and signed them to make an album of original material. The power of positive thinking obviously worked. Kris had instinctively known that this time it was all going to come together.

Force Records put a strong P.R. push behind them when they released the first single from the album. There were interviews, photo sessions, promotional appearances, and radio shows. When "Dirty Miss Mary" began to climb the English charts, they got on *Top of the Pops*, the record plugger's dream television show. Within weeks "Dirty Miss Mary" went to number one. The Wild Ones were a hit!

Kris often thought about his mother's face when he told her. She'd gone quite pale and clutched the sleeve of his shirt. "Does number one mean it's selling more than any-fing else?"

"Yes."

"More than Johnnie Ray?"

"Ma—Johnnie Ray was a long time ago."

She'd beamed. "I'm proud of yer, lad. We all are."

And they all were, except Brian, who still treated him like his snotty-nosed kid brother. "You'd better save your money," Brian had said airily. "It won't last."

It had lasted long enough to give them two more hit singles and a successful album. Now they were on the last leg of a sold-out European tour. Next stop—London. After that Kris planned to sit down and discuss how they were going to conquer America.

America was the world.

And he wanted it.

RAFEALLA
1977

★ ☆ ★ ☆ ★

Mother decided finishing school was in order. Preferably Switzerland. And she finally settled on L'Evier, an exclusive, expensive all-girls school nestled deep in the lush green countryside.

"Why finishing school?" Rafealla complained. "I'm nearly seventeen. I'm too old for school."

"One year, and then we'll send you to a suitable American college. You're looking forward to that, aren't you?"

"If I survive a year in Switzerland," Rafealla groaned.

Touching her lightly on the cheek, her mother smiled. "You'll survive, my darling, you're just like your father."

It pleased Rafealla when Anna spoke of her father. She cherished every mention of him—after all, she had been so young when Lucien died, and her memories were vivid and very precious.

She often wondered how different her life would have been were he still alive. No England. No castle in the country. No stepfather. No Rupert.

Ah . . . Rupert. He truly was like the brother she'd never had, and she loved him very much. Right now he was traveling across America with a backpack and the daughter of an earl. Everyone hoped they would marry.

Everyone except Rafealla—in her mind, she was saving him for Odile.

L'Evier turned out to be a strict prison, with lights out at ten, and a formidable headmistress. Rafealla took classes in English literature, languages—Italian and Spanish—cooking, singing, social graces, and history of the arts.

She hated every minute. What kind of life was she preparing for? She had no desire to marry some rich titled man and live in luxury, giving great charity.

Phoning Odile in Paris, she complained bitterly. "This is a real crock."

"Leave," Odile said simply. "My design college is the greatest. Ask your mother if you can come here with me. You don't learn much, but the male talent is *vroooom!*"

"She'd never let me. Not after I made the mistake of telling her about that New York flasher in the south of France."

"Stupid old Marcus Citroen. He does it to everyone, including the maids. You shouldn't have told your mother."

"I know. Now she thinks you're all a bunch of perverts!"

"How crazy. Maybe I'll have Mamma telephone her and beg for your freedom."

"Would you?"

"Why not?"

Isabella Ronet and Lady Anna Egerton had a long chat. The result was Rafealla stayed in Switzerland. Both mothers decided that the two girls, although lifelong best friends, were not always the greatest influence on each other.

So Rafealla slogged it out at L'Evier, loathing it more and more as each day passed, enjoying only her singing classes and choir practice. She had a strong, deep voice, a talent obviously inherited from her father.

Some of the girls at school were unbearable little snobs who ostracized her because her skin was darker than theirs.

"Touch of the tar brush, dear?" Fenella Stephenson, one

of the ringleaders, asked one day as they stepped out of the communal showers.

"Sorry?" said Rafealla, reaching for a towel and tying it across her chest.

"I thought they had a policy here," Fenella sneered. "No *blacks* allowed."

Rafealla felt a rush of color sting her cheeks. Fenella was unpleasantly plump. "Funny," she said, keeping her voice nice and even. "And I thought it was *fatties* they didn't allow in."

The ensuing fight would have thrilled any voyeur of young girls. They went at each other with no thought of modesty as their towels fell off and they rolled on the cold stone floor.

"Black bitch!" Fenella yelled.

"Fat white tub of lard!" Rafealla retorted, as they kicked and thrashed, pulling at each other's hair.

A crowd of enthusiastic girls gathered, cheering them on with pithy comments. Nothing like a good fight to break up the monotony.

"What *is* this fiasco?" raged the piercing voice of the principal as she pushed her way through to reach the scene of the crime.

Quickly Rafealla grabbed her towel. "Sorry, ma'am," she said. She had a split lip and the beginning of a black eye. "I slipped on the tiles, and Fenella was helping me up."

"Is this true, Fenella?" thundered the principal, not believing a word of it.

"Yes, ma'am," said Fenella, struggling to cover herself, obviously relieved at Rafealla's discretion.

"Golly!" said Rafealla, innocently widening her eyes. "You should do something about these slippery tiles. Wouldn't it be awful if someone *sued* the school one of these days?"

The principal glared at her, pursing thin lips. She hadn't

liked Rafealla from the moment she'd arrived. She reminded her of another girl quite a few years earlier, a girl called Lucky Saint—or Santangelo, as it turned out. A gangster's daughter of all things, and a troublemaker from the beginning. Because of Lucky they'd had to have extra locks fitted on all the windows to curb any nocturnal wanderings.

Yes. Rafealla had that same dangerous quality. She'd probably end up getting expelled just like Lucky, in spite of being Lord Egerton's stepdaughter.

As it turned out, Rafealla lasted the term, gaining top grades in languages and English literature, and great praise from her singing teacher. She also became good friends with Fenella, and organized a diet for her that really worked. After their unfortunate introduction, they found they had mutual acquaintances and lived quite near each other in the English countryside. With prejudice out of the way, they got along extremely well, although no one could ever replace Odile as Rafealla's best friend.

When vacation time rolled around, Fenella invited her to spend a weekend in Oxfordshire at her family's estate. Her father was a property tycoon, and her mother a society butterball. Rafealla had to control her laughter when she met Lady Stephenson. The woman was outrageous—dressed in more frills and flounces than a drag queen!

On Saturday night Lady Stephenson had a fancy-dress ball for five hundred of her most intimate friends.

"Mummy does this twice a year," Fenella revealed. "She says she sees everyone in a different light when they're wearing costumes."

Rafealla dressed up as a Chicago gangster in one of Fenella's brother's suits, which was several sizes too large for her, a black shirt, bold white tie, and beige fedora—under which she stuffed her long, dark hair. With no makeup she looked like a beautiful, fierce young man.

When Eddie Mafair appeared in a pirate costume, she sighed deeply—she knew he was never going to recognize her.

On the contrary. One look and he was by her side.

"What a bore these things are," he muttered. "How about you and me taking off early?"

She could hardly believe her luck. "Yes," she said quickly.

Glancing around, he said, "Meet me here in an hour. I suppose I must be sociable. Bloody boring way to spend an evening."

A cryptic exchange, to say the least. No *Nice to see you again*, or *How have you been?*

With difficulty she managed to get through the next hour, checking her watch every ten minutes. It seemed like an eternity. At the alloted time she was ready and waiting.

Eddie Mafair appeared twenty minutes late, unapologetic and flushed. Taking her arm, he guided her outside to an open sports car parked along the edge of the driveway. Hopping around to the driver's side, he failed to open the passenger door for her.

Opening it herself, she climbed inside, wondering if she should have told Fenella of her adventure. Wouldn't they worry when they couldn't find her at the end of the party?

What the heck! She was past caring. She had thought about Eddie Mafair for almost three years, and now the great moment was here. Nothing was going to spoil it.

Casually turning the ignition with one hand, and reaching for a cigarette with the other, he said, "Eton or Harrow?"

"Sorry?"

"Which *school* do you go to?"

"Oh. L'Evier in Switzerland."

Pulling the car to a sudden halt, he said in a surprised voice, "Isn't that a *girls'* school?"

"Of course it is." With a gesture she pulled off the fedora, and her long hair tumbled loose.

"Jesus Christ!" he said.

"What?"

Choking on his cigarette, he managed, "Nothing, nothing."

"You *do* know who I am, don't you?" she asked suspiciously.

Quite indignantly, his choking fit having abated, he said, "I most certainly do."

"Rafealla," she reminded.

"I know," he said testily.

Eddie Mafair was a strange one. The sooner she gave him a blow job and got him under her spell, the better.

Two hours later they lay naked under tangled sheets in Eddie Mafair's mews house in Chelsea.

An hour to get there, driving at breakneck speed. A glass of neat vodka and Billy Joel on the stereo repeatedly singing, "Just the Way You Are." And then sex. No kisses. No lingering buildup. No caresses. Just straight to it.

Inexperienced as she was, Rafealla soon realized something was wrong as he jabbed away with a soft penis. Eddie Mafair had what Odile crudely described as "two inches of cock and dynamic fingers." Only he didn't have dynamic fingers.

Far from being dismayed, Rafealla knew she had to help him over this unfortunate hurdle. Instinctively she said what he wanted to hear. "I'm a virgin. I've never been to bed with a man before."

Well, the virgin part was accurate. And she'd never actually been in bed with a man. The beach—yes. The woods —yes. And many other places. But never bed.

"You're so . . . manly," she breathed. "I love being with you."

And that did the trick. Eddie Mafair performed as he hadn't performed in a long time. And Rafealla let all thoughts of saving herself for a husband drift by the wayside. All she could think about was Eddie. She loved him. It was as simple as that.

BOBBY MONDELLA
1977

★ ☆ ★ ☆ ★

"Black," Nova Citroen said. "Silk."

The tailor nodded.

"And white. All white. Very clinging."

"I understand."

"A dozen shirts. A dozen pairs of pants. No colors."

"Yes, Mrs. Citroen."

"Oh, and he dresses to the left."

The tailor didn't miss a beat. "Yes, Mrs. Citroen."

A flick of her elegant wrist dismissed him.

When he was gone she paced around the living room of the Century City penthouse, with views stretching all the way to Catalina. Picking up a cigarette, she didn't light it, merely held it thoughtfully between her manicured fingers.

Today was the day.

She had waited long enough.

Bobby, sweat dripping from his body, begged for mercy. "Enough," he pleaded.

"More curls," his personal exercise instructor insisted. "Those arms need it."

"*Nothing* else needs it," Bobby gasped, dropping the weights and flopping on his back.

"Tomorrow," his instructor said, a short man with formidable muscles and a torturous smile.

"Can't wait!"

So . . . Bobby thought. *This is what it's like to be number one.* Hell—he'd had more fun when he was fat and a men's room attendant.

Life, at the moment, was nothing but work—backbreaking, gut-busting, getting-ready preparation.

His daily grind included dancing, voice practice, movement, and weight training for the ultimate body.

Then there were publicity photos to do, hair stylists to see, nutritionists to consult, and daily jogging for hours on end.

And then, of course, there was Nova.

Nova Citroen.

What an incredible woman!

Closing his eyes, he thought about the past year.

He'd shaken hands with the devil, and his whole world changed overnight.

Amerika wasn't pleased when she heard about Bobby's defection. She was angry and hurt—most of all incredulous. "How can you do this to yourself?" she asked, her lower lip quivering with emotion. "Don't you have any black pride? Marcus Citroen is a *killer*. He'll own you, exploit you, then drop you."

"No way," Bobby argued.

"What makes you think you're so different?" she spat, her voice shaking. "And how can you walk out on me?"

"Blue Cadillac is willing to pay you a lot of compensation."

Her eyes flashed. "They'd better."

He didn't know what else to say. Light conversation was out of the question, and he couldn't explain about Sharleen.

"I suppose it has something to do with that tramp," Amerika said icily, reading his mind.

Springing to her defense, he said, "C'mon. Don't call Sharleen names just 'cause you're mad at *me*."

"Hey—Bobby," Amerika jeered. "Why don't you admit she's got your balls in her pocket, and be done with it?"

He'd given her the courtesy of telling her himself. Now he walked out with a clear conscience.

Sharleen bubbled with joy when he gave her the news. *"Oooh,* Bobby, Bobby, Bobby! You're wonderful! The best!" She hugged him tight. "An' it'll be good for you too, honey. Just wait. If Marcus says he'll make you number one—well, baby, he's gonna do it."

"I just want to be certain you'll be all right," he said, full of concern.

Kissing his cheek, she murmured, "I've learned my lesson. I won't make a mistake again." A pause. "Do I get my apartment back?"

"Who cares? It's better you stay here where I can watch out for you."

"You're right," she agreed demurely.

A week later came the bombshell. Blue Cadillac wanted him in L.A. where he would undergo intensive training for major stardom.

He burst into Marcus's office. "What is this shit? I don't wanna go to L.A."

"Insurance," Marcus said mildly.

"For what?"

"For both of us. Like a world-class fighter, you have to train to be at peak performance level. In September of next year we present you to your public at the Hollywood Bowl. Bobby Mondella. In Concert. A three-night sold-out engagement. Rave reviews. A television special. All *you* have to do is deliver."

Marcus Citroen seemed to have it all planned. He

wanted Bobby to drop out of sight and reappear like the brightest meteor in the sky.

"Your album will reach the stores that same week. A single from it will already be a smash," Marcus assured him.

"What album?" Bobby asked, perplexed.

"The one you're going to write and record in L.A. You have a year to do it. And a magnificent penthouse apartment in Century City ready for your arrival."

"How about Sharleen?"

"She stays here."

"Why?"

"Because she wants to."

"And if she doesn't?"

Marcus did not waver. "Nobody's stopping her from doing anything she cares to do."

"You mean if I persuade her to come with me, you won't object?"

"Absolutely not."

The choice was Sharleen's, and she wouldn't budge. She had a new single to record, a video to make, and a hundred and one interviews. Her career was back on track and she was happy.

"Be careful," Bobby warned. "Stay away from Marcus Citroen."

Indignantly she said, "You really think I'd ever get involved with him in a personal way again? Are you nuts? After what I went through?" Dancing around the apartment, she added, quite sternly, "Now, Bobby. I want you to take off an' stop worrying about me. Think about yourself for a change. Promise?"

There was no point in fighting it. Deep down he knew the best thing was to get away. Sharleen was becoming an obsession, and now that he'd helped her straighten her life out, there *should* be space between them. Only then could he put their relationship in proper perspective.

*   *   *

Los Angeles was a revelation. The wide, clean streets. Sunshine and palm trees. Friendly people and a kind of laid-back ambience he wasn't used to after the frenetic activity of New York.

Walking into the apartment Blue Cadillac had rented for him, he couldn't believe it was his. After all, he hadn't done anything to deserve it. But he would. Their confidence in him was going to pay off.

The months spent recording an album with a top producer and great musicians in a first-class studio were the most exciting of his life. Unlike New York, there was no watching the clock because studio time was so expensive —here there was just an easy, relaxed atmosphere, with plenty of good-natured banter, and a certain amount of pharmaceuticals passed around. Usually Bobby didn't approve of drugs, but recording late into the night it made sense to get a little high—keep the energy level really up.

The album material he had written worked. The songs, arrangements, everything came together perfectly.

In New York, Marcus decided to combine the talents of Bobby and Sharleen on a duet. Bobby wrote a song called "Baby— I Care About You." And Sharleen arrived in L.A. to record it with him.

She looked spectacular, glowing with success. Accompanying her was a female bodyguard who never left her side.

"Don't I get to see you alone?" he joked.

"Why, honey," she replied, affecting a heavy Southern drawl. "You're so *biiig* an' *baaad* an' *haaan'some*. I don't think I'd trust myself alone with you at all!"

She stayed three days, gave an impeccable performance —her vocals weren't great, but what she lacked in voice she made up for with sensational style—and flew back to New York.

And then Bobby met Nova Citroen. The kind of woman he had never encountered before.

Nova Citroen traveled in a chauffeured Rolls-Royce, wore only the most expensive designer clothes, real jewelry, and smelled of big bucks. Bobby was dazzled.

She arrived at his apartment one afternoon, unannounced, with an executive from Blue Cadillac Records who jumped nervously at her every command.

"I'm Mrs. Citroen," she said, a slight accent coloring her speech. "I hope you're comfortable in this apartment. I chose it from several. I meant to visit you before, but I have only recently returned from Europe."

"*You* found me this apartment?" he asked in surprise.

She smiled faintly. "The apartment, the body expert, the nutritionist—all of them. I hope they're doing a good job. Hmmm . . ." She narrowed her quite amazing violet eyes, allowing them to sweep over him from head to toe. "Yes. I can see they're doing an *extremely* good job, Mr. Mondella—or may I call you Bobby?"

In spite of his nine-year crush on Sharleen, he was not exactly inexperienced when it came to women. They hit on him all the time, and he knew how to handle any situation.

This one was different. This one was a lady. She was also Marcus Citroen's wife, and therefore untouchable.

In spite of that, he found her powerfully attractive.

"Yeah, please do," he said, meeting her direct gaze with one of his own.

"Thank you." Amusement glinted in those mesmerizing eyes.

The executive from Blue Cadillac Records said, "Mrs. Citroen was anxious to meet you, Bobby. Word has it everyone loves the album material in New York. Are you nearly finished?"

"Two more tracks to go."

"Perhaps I can come to the studio," Nova said. "I always enjoy watching the creative process."

He enjoyed watching her, with her drawn-back white-blond hair and slim figure. Nova Citroen presented class with a great big capital C.

"It gets kinda rough in the studio," he said.

"Really?" Holding him tightly captive with her eyes, she paused before saying, "Well, Bobby, if things get *too* rough I'll just have to leave, won't I?"

She turned up on two successive nights, each time with a different male escort. She stayed fifteen minutes in the recording booth watching him intently through the glass and left before he took a break.

It was annoying. He wanted to talk to her, find out more about the mysterious Mrs. Citroen. For she *was* mysterious—nobody seemed to know much about her except that she moved in high society and had been married to Marcus for a long time.

She vanished after that, and did not reappear until six weeks before his Hollywood Bowl debut.

By this time his duet with Sharleen was number one on the soul charts, and steadily climbing the mainstream list. Things were going as planned.

He couldn't help being in a nervous sweat, even though he'd never looked and sounded better in his life. The Hollywood Bowl concert was make-or-break time. He knew he could perform on records, but a stage performance was a whole other deal.

No one could say he wasn't prepared. He was at fighting weight and raring to go.

Nova arrived at his apartment one morning—again unannounced, and this time alone. She wore a white silk suit, a green blouse, and crocodile accessories. "What are you planning to wear?" she asked coolly, as if they had just paused in the middle of a conversation.

"Huh?"

"At the Bowl."

"Uh . . . the stylist has a selection of leather suits for me."

"Leather?" She raised an elegant eyebrow.

"It's sexy." He laughed, sending himself up. "Or so they tell me."

"It's sweaty."

He challenged her. "It's what I'm wearing."

A faint smile. "I don't think so."

Bobby stretched and slowly sat up. The workouts were hard, but the rewards were worth it. In fact, the entire year had been quite something. And now Nova Citroen was in his living room instructing her own personal tailor to measure him for size.

He would wear whatever she wanted. Instinctively he knew her choice would be the right one.

The tailor entered the mirrored workout room armed with a tape measure and a determined expression. "Mrs. Citroen knows exactly what you want," he said, busily unrolling the measure.

"Yeah, an' I know exactly what *she* wants," Bobby muttered under his breath.

KRIS PHOENIX
1977

★ ☆ ★ ☆ ★

The cavernous dressing room was filled with people all milling around a long wooden trestle table piled high with cans of beer, paper cups, dishes of crisps, and several plates of stale sandwiches. Hardly luxury, but The Wild Ones were finishing their first tour, and had not yet learned to make demands.

Buzz had his own bottle of Scotch, given to him by an admirer. He sat in a corner swigging blissfully.

"He'll get drunk," Mr. Terence fussed.

"No way," argued Kris. "It'll improve his voice."

Mr. Terence raised a disbelieving eyebrow. "Go and talk to that girl over there. She's from the *Evening News*. Say something witty." He mopped his forehead with a polka-dot handkerchief.

"Shit!" muttered Kris. He hated this socializing bit before a concert. Why did he have to make nice to reporters and other assorted hangers-on, when all he wanted to do was concentrate on the performance ahead of him? He'd tried to explain to Mr. Terence on numerous occasions, but Mr. Terence insisted that the press was too important to shut out. How come everyone expected *him* to do it, and not the rest of the band?

"Kris!" The reporter from the *Evening News* had lank hair, buck teeth, and an upper-class accent. "*Do* tell me how it feels to be number one?"

"Bloody marvelous," he replied.

"Super!" She jotted something down in a loose-leaf notebook. "And *do* tell me, when the critics knock your music, does it upset you *terribly?*"

"I didn't realize we were bein' knocked," he said, helping himself to a soggy potato chip.

"There's a review of your Manchester concert in the current issue of *N.M.E.* Let me see. . . ." Cocking her head on one side, she sucked on her pencil. "I think it said something like Kris Phoenix sounds like a cross between a sore throat and a foghorn in a bad storm."

"Charming!"

Pencil poised, buck teeth facing him like a firing squad, she said, "Any other comment?"

"Fuck 'em. It's not the bleedin' critics who are buying our records."

Scribbling furiously, she agreed with an enthusiastic "Quite. I like your attitude."

He wandered off, looking for Mum and the rest of his family. They were all supposed to be here tonight, the lot of them—including dear old brother Brian. He'd given Avis backstage passes and told her exactly where to go, but he couldn't spot any of them.

Rasta rushed over. "You see those two little darlin's over there?" he said, pointing out two girls hovering on the edge of the crowd. "How about one for you an' one for me, I'll book 'em in now, while I can. If Buzz spots 'em, it's all over."

Kris glanced across the room, checking out two very attractive but extremely young females. "Juveniles," he said dismissively.

"Leave it out," Rasta complained. "I bet they're at least sixteen. That's old enough."

"I like 'em over twenty, and smart," Kris said firmly. No more Willows in *his* life. For the last year he'd bedded a variety of girls, scrupulously steering clear of teenagers or any girl who didn't look like she knew what she was doing. His opening line was always, "Are you takin' precautions or shall I?"

It got the ball rolling nicely, in more ways than one.

Willow was behaving like a right cow. When he was nothing, she'd been only too happy to agree to a quickie divorce. But as soon as he started to make it, she was there with a sharp lawyer and a suitcaseful of demands. Bitch! What had *she* done to deserve any of his hard-earned money? He didn't mind supporting Bo, but Willow's demands were ridiculous. It wasn't as if he were making a fortune. Everything he earned, except the publishing, had to be split four ways, and that was after Mr. Terence had taken his fat 35 percent. And then there were all the expenses—including travel, roadies, a sound man, lighting, publicity, clothes, a secretary, bodyguards, etcetera, and finally, the dreaded tax.

As a matter of fact he was almost as broke as he'd ever been.

Every day he realized more and more if they wanted to score big, America was the place.

Tonight Mr. Terence had promised several hotshots from American recording companies would be in the audience. *Okay, we're gonna show 'em what we can do*, Kris decided. *We're gonna really rock 'n roll!*

"Christopher!" shrieked a fat butterball of a woman in a flounced lavender dress. "Your music sends me!"

"Kris," he corrected, backing away from her overzealous approach.

"Ah . . . but short for Christopher, dear boy. Am I right?"

Who the fuck was this weird old bird? "No," he said, looking around for someone to rescue him.

"We're having a little thingie at Annabel's later. Simply marvelous fun. Can you join us?"

Annabel's. He'd heard of it. The poshest nightclub in London, where all the chinless wonders and their birds hung out. Royalty, too.

Annabel's. Yeah! But not with this apparition, who was old enough to be his mother.

"Can't make it, luv," he said, trying to sound regretful. "Sorry. Gotta take me mum out."

"Shame!" brayed the fat lady. "Fenella is *dying* to meet you."

"Well, she'll just havta wait, won't she?" Edging away, he bumped into a red-faced Mr. Terence.

"What did she say?" Mr. Terence asked anxiously.

"Who?"

"Lady Stephenson."

"Is *that* who she is when she's at home?"

"Well?"

"Wanted me to join her at Annabel's, didn't she."

"Just you?"

"I dunno."

Mr. Terence did a nervous jig. The Wild Ones making it so quickly and with such strength had left him out of his depth. He wasn't quite sure how to deal with it. Too much was happening too fast. Half the offers he received on their behalf he didn't even tell them about. America was begging for attention, and yet he'd done nothing, because knowing Kris and his raging ambition, he figured they'd run off to the States and never return. A contract was no real protection once those beady-eyed Yank lawyers got their hands on it.

Mr. Terence was in a turmoil. Snatching a quick peek at Buzz lounging happily in a quiet corner swigging from his bottle of Scotch calmed him down. Buzz would hate America and the gaudy razzmatazz that went with it. In fact, he was doing Buzz a favor by keeping all the lucrative offers to himself.

"C'mon." Ollie grabbed Kris by the arm. "Let's get out of here. This circus is no good before a show. We should be tuning up."

Ollie, the perfectionist. So straight and serious. He'd found himself a redheaded girlfriend who played the cello and hated what she termed as "the pop business."

"Right," agreed Kris. "Let's grab the others an' find a quiet corner backstage."

"I'll round up Rasta, Buzz is all yours," Ollie said.

"You got it."

Lady Stephenson grabbed his arm as he walked by. "Kris, dear," she said, as if they were old and intimate friends, "do say hello to my daughter Fenella and her friend, Raffi."

He was face to face with the two baby girls Rasta had fancied earlier. "Hello," he said, hardly noticing them.

"Now Kris, dear," Lady Stephenson continued, double chins wobbling above lavender and lace frills, "if you *can* get away later, do join us. You might find it to be rather an interesting group. Quite a few American music people who I'm *sure* you *must* know. The Dorfmans, Marcus Citroen. Oh, and Sharleen, the famous"—she lowered her voice— "black singer."

"Maybe," Kris said. Now he was *really* interested in going, but he had promised his mum and the family a night on the town, and he couldn't dump them.

"Cheers!" gushed Lady Stephenson. "Don't forget. Annabel's. I'll leave word at the door."

The concert was a blast. Finally, London—and the fans loved them.

What a raw sense of power! What a roller-coaster high!

Kris knew there were a lot of important people there watching them live for the first time, and he really let rip, straining his gravelly voice to the limit, performing virtuoso guitar solos, taking turns with Buzz, who was full of piss and sardonic strut.

The crowd yelled, cheering and stamping its approval. The usual chants rose above the yelling and clapping.

"KRISSS . . . WE . . . LOVE . . . YOU!"

"BUZZZZ . . . WE . . . LOVE . . . YOU!"

Kris leaped across the stage, his energy level at an all-time peak. He wore high-top sneakers, skintight faded jeans, and a T-shirt with THE WILD ONES '77 emblazoned across the front.

Buzz weaved back and forth, picking at his guitar with talented fingers, face impassive, body clad in black footless tights, his mangy long black shirt hanging loose.

"'Ere," Rasta had said, observing them before the show. "Wot you two doin' then? 'Aving a whose-got-the-biggest-cock contest?" He'd broken up at his own rather accurate observation.

Mr. Terence had wanted them to wear matching blue gabardine jumpsuits. "You know where you can shove that idea," Kris told him. Kris ran the group now as far as what they played, how they played it, and certainly what they wore.

"Why the frig we payin' Mr. T. bleedin' thirty-five percent?" Buzz bitched. "Whyn't we dump 'im?"

The thought *had* occurred to Kris. But he knew there was bound to be a big legal hassle, and their timing wasn't right. Also, they owed Mr. Terence *something*. After all, he was the one who'd bankrolled them when they had nothing, even though he was deducting every penny of his initial investment from their earnings, on top of his hefty percentages. No wonder they were still broke.

The money was rolling in, but not in their direction.

There was a rumor backstage that Princess Anne was somewhere in the audience. The blinding lights prevented them from searching the rows of eager faces—although

Kris had noticed, at all their gigs, the rows in front never contained the swooners and the screamers.

"That's because they're comps," Ollie had explained.

"Wot's that?" asked Buzz.

"Complimentary. Free seats for the managers, theater owners, promoters, record execs, and all their friends."

Kris decided that when he had enough clout, comps would be moved to the middle of the venue, and only the real fans would be allowed up front.

Triumphantly they launched into their last song. A fast-driving rocker written by Kris and Ollie called "Skinny Little Slider."

It brought the house down. The audience was on its feet, yelling and clamoring for more.

They did two more choruses of "Skinny Little Slider," and then they were off, running from the stage, sweat-soaked and ecstatic.

"Fuck me!" screamed Rasta. "This is better 'n sex any day!"

"Bloody right!" agreed Kris.

Who needed one woman when there were sixty thousand lusting after your body?

"You looked like a bunch of tatty layabouts," brother Brian said, shoveling spaghetti into his mouth. "Can't you afford decent outfits?"

Jennifer, his wife, agreed. "Oh, yes. Matching outfits would be ever so nice, wouldn't they? The Beatles always appeared so smart. . . ." She trailed off, silenced by the look Kris gave her.

He sat with his mum, Horace, his two sisters and their boyfriends, and Brian and Jennifer in Trattoria Terrazza, an Italian restaurant in Soho.

What a group! What a letdown! Why he had arranged a family outing on a night like this was beyond him. Christ! This was the downer of all times, and he'd asked for it. Set it up. While everybody else went off to parties and celebrations.

He'd done it for his mum, really. Avis, so proud. The matriarch of the family, with her loud voice and work-worn hands.

She was beaming with pride, ignoring Brian for once. "I never thought I'd see the day," she said, craftily snagging a half-eaten roll, wrapping it in a tissue and sliding it in her bag.

"Mum!" Kris objected. "I can buy you all the bread you want."

"Not like this, lad. Nice an' fresh. It'll go down a treat in the mornin' with a bit of marge, a dab of jam, an' a nice cuppa tea." She smiled contentedly.

"Take one for me," Horace said irritably. "'Struth! I've got an 'orrible 'eadache after all that noise."

"Me too," agreed Brian. "Give me Barry Manilow any day." He threw his younger brother a smug look. "No offense, Kris. But even *you* have to admit that it's a bloody awful racket you make up there."

The evening went from bad to worse as Brian got into his stride, complaining about everything. Horace joined in, and his two sisters stared at him like they'd never really noticed him before. Meanwhile Avis went on a food-stealing binge the likes of which he'd never seen. After the rolls, she laid claim to a slice of veal Jennifer left over, almost an entire salad, and a large piece of chocolate rum cake.

"Ma," Kris pleaded. "Let 'em pack the stuff up for you. I'm payin' for it, y'know."

"That's all right, dear," she said cheerfully, having a wonderful time. "It's better this way. Don't want to embarrass you, do I?"

Oh, sure. She had a bag full of food wrapped in a few soggy tissues, and she didn't want to embarrass him. Great! At least she was happy.

A girl at another table recognized him and scurried over, asking for an autograph.

"She probably thinks you're Rod Stewart," sneered Brian.

"Thanks," Kris snapped, and called for the bill.

By the time he reached Annabel's he was well gone. Once the family were dispatched into the night, he'd stopped by Rasta's party, held at a rowdy pub in Brixton. Several beers and a few vodkas later he arrived at the exclusive Berkeley Square establishment, his only claim to respectability being the chauffeured Daimler he'd hired for the night.

"I'm sorry, sir," the doorman said, with frosty politeness. "This is a membership only club."

"Yeah." Kris swayed slightly, cleverly concealing a burp. "The thing is, I'm joinin' Lady Stephenson. How's that for gettin' me in?"

"You'd better speak to them downstairs," the doorman said regally, indicating that Kris should descend the open stairway.

"Bloody basement," Kris muttered, holding onto the banister for support.

Downstairs, inside the entrance to the club, a manager in evening dress greeted him. "Sir?"

"Uh . . . Kris Phoenix, that's me. I'm s'pose to be joinin' uh . . . Lady Stephenson."

"Ah, yes, sir. Mr. Phoenix from The Wild Ones. Lady Stephenson is expecting you."

"Yeah?"

"Yes, sir." Lowering his voice, the manager added discreetly, "We do have a dress code, Mr. Phoenix. If you follow me I'm sure we can put that right."

"A what code?"

"Dress, sir. Jacket and ties for the gentlemen. Suitable attire for the ladies."

"You're kiddin'?"

"This way, sir."

The manager ushered him into a side room where he offered him a white shirt, a blue jacket, and a red tie.

"I feel like a bleedin' Union Jack!" Kris joked, putting the outfit on.

"We'll turn a blind eye to your bottom half, sir," said the manager with a benevolent smile. "Perhaps you can sign my daughter's autograph book. She's quite a fan."

Ego was slowly being restored. Kris took the autograph book with a flourish. "Certainly, mate. An' what's the little darlin's name?"

RAFEALLA
1977

★ ☆ ★ ☆ ★

Lady Stephenson, Fenella's mother, was the most amazing woman. She knew everyone and was invited to everything. Film premieres, the best parties, restaurant openings, art galleries. If there was a gala occasion, it was a safe bet that Lady Stephenson, in her frills and flounces, would be there.

Fenella did not often accompany her, but when she heard that The Wild Ones were doing a one-night concert in London, and that her mother, as usual, was invited, she telephoned Rafealla and said enthusiastically, "I'm going to ask Mummy if we can go too. Are you on?"

"You bet!" Rafealla replied. Both she and Fenella were crazy about The Wild Ones. At finishing school they'd played "Dirty Miss Mary" whenever they could. Fenella quite fancied the black drummer, and Rafealla thought Buzz Darke the most interesting, with his sinister looks and I-don't-give-a-damn attitude.

They set off for the concert full of great expectations. Rafealla was relieved to get out of the house. It was three weeks since she'd slept with Eddie Mafair, and she had not heard one word from him since. She couldn't believe it. What a bastard!

"Why don't you phone *him?*" Fenella suggested helpfully.

Phone him! Ha! She'd sooner die. He had her number, she'd scrawled it in his phone book herself.

He was a jerk anyway. After sex he'd fallen asleep, surfaced three hours later, and summoned a cab to spirit her back to the country. The cheapskate didn't even offer to pay for the taxi, so she'd had to borrow the money from the Stephensons' butler. Men! What a bunch of insensitive creeps.

And yet . . . she loved him, in spite of the fact that going all the way with Eddie Mafair had not been as physically fulfilling as the playful necking sessions she'd indulged in with her other boyfriends. It didn't matter. She still loved him.

So what? He obviously couldn't give a damn about her.

In her head she went through the excuses he might come up with.

Too busy at work.

What did he actually do? She had no idea.

Sick.

Did that mean his dialing finger automatically stopped functioning?

On vacation.

Well, he would have mentioned *something* about going away, wouldn't he?

It was not a happy time for her. But he would phone. If she just sat it out and waited patiently, she knew he would.

The venue for The Wild Ones concert was crazy time. Lady Stephenson had special stickers attached to her car, and parking attendants waved her chauffeur-driven Rolls through the unruly crowd to a VIP roped-off parking area.

"Come along, everyone," she trilled. "Let's go backstage and have a drink."

"Divine, darling," said Pierce, her faithful walker, who did double duty as her interior designer. Lord Stephenson only made rare forays into his rambunctious wife's social activities. He infinitely preferred the quiet life.

The backstage party was an experience. Lady Stephenson and Pierce vanished into the melee, while Rafealla and Fenella stood at the entrance taking it all in. Rock & roll was a whole new world.

"Wow!" Fenella breathed. "Don't stare, but that's him. That's the drummer. And I think he's looking over here!"

"Hmm . . . whatever happened to 'black bastard'?" Rafealla asked coolly, checking out the cheeky-looking drummer.

"Oh, God! Don't bring that up," Fenella groaned. "You can't imagine how embarrassed I am. How could I ever have said that?"

"What's his name?"

"Who?"

"The guy on the drums, idiot."

"Rasta. Sounds interesting, huh?"

"Yeah, your mother would find it *veree* interesting if she knew you fancied him."

"Girls!" The piercing voice of Lady Stephenson filled the air, rising above the clamor, followed by a frilled and flounced wave of the hand. "Over here!"

They edged their way toward the makeshift bar, where Pierce supplied them with two paper cups filled with flat Coca-Cola.

Another exciting evening, Rafealla thought. *Why hasn't Eddie Mafair phoned me? Why?*

"Isn't this fun?" Lady Stephenson shrilled.

> *She's a bank clerk's daughter*
> *An' y'know what I mean*
> *Y'see when I met her she was barely eighteen*
> *So I took her to my bed*
> *An' I gave her some . . .*
> *LOVIN'*

218

YEAH!
LOVIN'
YEAH!
Y' know what I mean
Oh yeah, y' know what I mean . . .

Screams rang through the air as Kris and Buzz gave it their all, sharing the microphone with a certain vagabond intimacy. Two talented likely lads on the make.

She's a bank clerk's daughter
So pretty an' sweet
Innocent as an angel with exceptionally small feet
Long yellow hair an' big blue eyes
An' I gave her some . . .
LOVIN'
YEAH!
LOVIN'
YEAH!
Y' know what I mean
Oh yeah, y' know what I mean

Every girl in the audience knew what they meant. The excitement factor ran high.

Rafealla found herself swept away by the sheer energy of their performance. Buzz Darke and Kris Phoenix made a formidable combination. Whether they were singing, or playing brilliant guitar riffs together, or merely running and jumping around, they both projected pure animal magnetism. The whole group was great. It was an exciting concert.

Afterward, at Annabel's, where they were joined by several Americans in the music business, plus Sharleen, the famous recording star, there was much discussion about exactly how good The Wild Ones were.

"*I* think they're the new Rolling Stones," announced

Lady Stephenson knowledgeably—she liked to keep up with what she termed "the youth culture."

"No!" Pierce disagreed. "They're much sexier. And Kris Phoenix doesn't scream and make faces like that awful Mick Jagger."

"Mick Jagger's adorable," defended Lady Stephenson, fluttering fake lashes as she ordered champagne from an attentive waiter. "I will not listen to a word against him."

To her surprise, Rafealla discovered one of the Americans in their party was Marcus Citroen—her very own flasher from the south of France. He did not appear to remember their brief encounter and merely nodded when introduced, turning his full attention on the startlingly pretty singer, Sharleen, who appeared to be his date.

Stifling a giggle, she whispered the story to Fenella, who heaved with silent laughter.

Being in Annabel's reminded her of Eddie Mafair, and the night they first met.

I'm nearly eighteen, she thought despairingly. *My life is ahead of me. I have to forget about Eddie, he's just a creep.*

Lady Stephenson was a wow on the dance floor, twirling and twisting until her chubby cheeks were red with exertion. Pierce made a suitable escort in his Doug Heyward suit.

"Haven't we met before, young lady?" Marcus Citroen asked Rafealla, as soon as Sharleen went to the ladies' room.

"I don't think so," she replied shortly, wishing he would go away, for she would never be able to erase the mental picture of Marcus Citroen, naked, with an erection, in the Franconinis' swimming pool. When it happened, she had merely swum away, climbed out of the water, and vanished into the house, hoping their paths never crossed again.

"What do you do?" he asked.

"I'm a student," she mumbled.

"A student," he repeated her words, staring straight at her. "A very unusual and beautiful student, if I may say so. I'm sure I've seen you somewhere before."

She returned his stare, saying nothing, refusing to look away, challenging his intent scrutiny.

"If I can ever help you in any way, please call me," he said, handing her his engraved card. "I mean it."

Accepting it reluctantly, she stuffed it in her purse, and hurriedly turned to speak to Fenella, who was sitting down after a hectic session on the dance floor.

"Guess who's here?" Fenella whispered excitedly.

"The Queen Mum."

"Very funny."

"Who?"

"I don't think I'll tell you now."

"Who?"

"You're not going to like it."

"Will you stop playing games, and *tell* me."

Before Fenella uttered his name, she knew.

"Eddie Mafair," said Fenella.

Oh, no! Her stomach knotted up. "Alone?" she asked wanly.

"He's with Fiona Ripley-Hedges. She looks like the back end of a bus, but her father owns most of London, and we all *know* how attractive *that* must be. Especially since there's a rumor going around that he's broke."

By the time Kris Phoenix made his entrance, Rafealla was ready for him. She was ready for anyone, actually, having surreptitiously drained every glass of alcoholic beverage in sight.

As soon as he sat down she was on to him, wasting no time in forcing the rock star to pay attention and notice her. "I loved your concert," she said. "You were fantastic."

"Thanks, luv."

"I honestly mean it."

"Great."

"Before I saw you I used to think Buzz was the star of the group, but now . . ."

"That's nice."

He wasn't interested, dammit. He had eyes for the record moguls and Sharleen. Especially Sharleen.

Without a doubt he regarded her as just another boring fan. Well, she would show *him:* Mister Star—Mister Who-Did-He-Think-He-Was.

Marcus Citroen had his attention now, but it kept wandering toward Sharleen. Helplessly Rafealla watched the eye play between Kris and the pretty singer. Sharleen was coming on to him. Licking full red lips, touching fluffy hair, eating him up with those big brown eyes.

Rafealla stood up. She had youth on her side—that had to count for something. "Can we dance?" she asked aggressively.

"Uh"—Kris glanced around, hoping she was talking to someone else. The kid was a looker, but just a kid, and he'd had that scene.

No escape was in view, so, getting to his feet, he staggered a bit and followed her onto the packed dance floor, where she pulled him into a close clinch, grinding her body into his. He immediately got a hard-on. Some men couldn't get it up when they were drunk. He was just the opposite—all that booze went straight to the old bone.

Rafealla experienced a moment of power. Young as she was, she already realized the sexual hold she had over men.

Screw you, Eddie Mafair. I can have anyone I want.

And then she saw him dancing nearby, with horse-faced Fiona held tightly in his arms. He was laughing at something and didn't even notice her.

Determinedly she moved closer to Kris Phoenix as, inexplicably, her eyes filled with tears.

BOBBY MONDELLA
1977

★ ☆ ★ ☆ ★

"Drink?"

"Pernod."

"I don't think I have any of that, Mrs. Citroen."

"Yes, you do. Look in the cupboard under the bar, you'll find it's fully stocked."

He was the occupant of the apartment, and *she* was telling him where to find things. Goddamn it, this woman was too sure of herself by far.

"Maybe you can fix it yourself. I'm gonna shower an' put clothes on," he said, feeling at a disadvantage because she was fully dressed and he was still clad in his workout clothes—shorts and a cut-off T-shirt.

She raised an elegant eyebrow, unused to being told to do things for herself. "Fine," she said coolly. "And can I make something for you while I'm playing barman? Or should that be maid?" she added sarcastically.

"Orange juice."

"My oh my. We *are* on a health kick."

"Your idea."

A slight smile. "In that case, one drink a night *is* allowed."

"Scotch."

"How about champagne?"

"I don't have—"

"Ah, but you do," she interrupted. "So why don't you go shower, and simply leave everything to me?" A glimmer of a smile. "I'm *very* capable when I have to be."

Walking into the bedroom, he was aware of a distinct feeling of anticipation. The tailor had left, and they were all alone in the apartment. Mrs. Citroen was not staying around for her health. The lady was hot for action, and if that's what she wanted . . .

No! an inner voice warned him. *This is dangerous territory. The lady is the boss's wife.*

Yeah? he answered himself. *So what?* He was just about ready for a touch of danger.

Stripping off his sweaty clothes, he entered the bathroom, turned on the shower, and stepped under the invigorating needles of spray.

Mrs. Citroen. With her ice-queen looks and cool demeanor. The same Mrs. Citroen whose husband had played games with Sharleen, nearly finishing her off. What did the lady want from him?

C'mon, Bobby—you know what she wants.

He almost laughed aloud. Yeah, he knew what she wanted, and if she was very patient . . . yeah, really patient . . . then maybe, only maybe, mind you . . .

Naked except for a black lace G-string and spike-heeled shoes, Nova got into the shower behind him, carrying an open bottle of Cristal. She nuzzled the cold bottle against his back. "I never really welcomed you to Blue Cadillac properly, did I?" she murmured in her husky voice.

He'd known she was going to come on to him, but not this strong. And not this soon. She was not a patient woman.

"Don't turn around," she commanded, placing the bottle on the tile floor. "Just relax."

Sure. He could certainly relax with a naked married

woman cozying up behind him, running talented and expensive fingers along his spine.

He thought about what to say, but it was too late for words. With great confidence, she was reaching for his balls, cupping them delicately, applying just the right amount of tingling pressure before falling to her knees.

"Now!" she said urgently. "Turn around *now!*"

He did as she asked, plunging deep inside that elegant mouth ready and waiting to taste and tease him with feathery jabs of her tongue and a low, animal, groaning sound.

Eat your heart out, Marcus, he thought. *I'm getting my own back for Sharleen.*

He surrendered to sensation. There was really nothing else he could do except lean back and enjoy it.

LOS ANGELES 1987
Saturday, July 11th

★ ☆ ★ ☆ ★

The security checks aggravated Kris. "What is this shit?" he demanded. "Don't they know who I am?"

"Of course they do," the Hawk said soothingly. "They're merely following orders. You can't be too careful with the number of terrorists around today."

"Yeah," Kris replied sarcastically. "We really look like a terrorist group, don't we? Y'know, in the limo an' all. Just ridin' on up to rip the bleedin' place to pieces."

"Have you been to Novaroen before?" the Hawk asked, quickly changing the subject.

"Once," Kris replied vaguely.

"You didn't tell *me* that," squealed Cybil. "One of the girls did a shoot here for that perfume Nova Citroen was pushing, and she says the place is amazing."

"It is," the Hawk assured her. "They have two houses, both decorated in different styles. The main house is Colonial, while the guest house is—"

"Christ! Not again!" bitched Kris, as the limousine stopped for a third security check.

"Lighten up," Cybil said, laughing gaily. "This is an adventure. *I'm* really enjoying it!"

He stared at his California girlfriend, all bright eyes,

226

glossy hair, and whiter-than-white teeth. It didn't take much to make her happy, did it?

Sometimes she got on his nerves.

It was amazing how inefficient security became once the guards were sure everyone was doing something.

Maxwell Sicily surveyed the scene. The workers were all in place, name-tagged and running here, there, and everywhere like an army of robots. Access between the makeshift tented kitchen and the open-air dining area, was no problem. Now that there were over a hundred catering personnel busying themselves on the premises, a party atmosphere prevailed. Waiters and busboys were whistling and cracking jokes. The chefs were slicing and pounding as they prepared gourmet delights. The dessert cooks were hard at work creating creamy concoctions. And an army of barmen was unpacking crates of the finest champagnes and wines, plus a dizzying assortment of other beverages.

Maxwell picked his moment before slipping quietly away. He knew exactly where he was going. Thanks to Vicki Foxe, he was aware of every inch of Novaroen.

Alighting from her limousine, Rafealla took a deep breath. The sea air was invigorating. If only the circumstances were different she might be enjoying herself.

"Here comes the greeting committee," warned Trudie, as a dapper man with owl-like glasses and a pleasant smile stepped forward.

"Welcome to Novaroen," he said, in a clipped English accent. "I'm Norton St. John, personal assistant to Mrs. Citroen. Please allow me to escort you to your suite."

"He makes the joint sound like a hotel," Trudie said in a low aside.

"Rafealla would like to do a sound check immediately," announced one of the record executives. "Are the musicians ready?"

"I believe they're planning a run-through with Mr. Bobby Mondella," Norton St. John replied. "However, since each artist is only performing two songs, it shouldn't take long."

"Rafealla wants to do her sound check *now,*" said the executive testily. "You *do* know that Mr. Citroen has given strict instructions for Rafealla to have everything—"

"Forget it," she interrupted quickly. "I can wait. In fact, if Bobby doesn't mind, maybe I'll watch him."

"Certainly, Miss Rafealla." Norton shot the bad-tempered executive a triumphant look. "I will show you to your suite first, and then I will ask Mr. Mondella's representative. If everything seems to be all right, I shall return for you immediately."

"Shit!" Speed exclaimed for the tenth time. "I'm tellin' ya, the broad set me up. She wiggled her fat ass in my face an' demanded money. So I gave her a few bucks, just t'get rid of her. Big deal. Ya only gotta look at the witch t'know I wouldn't touch her with somebody *else's* hot rod! Shit!"

A bored detective burped in his face.

"I gotta warn ya—I know people," Speed said, rapidly changing tactics. "I got solid connections. My lawyer'll make fartheads outta all of ya with this dirtbag bust."

"Don't threaten," said the detective mildly. "Or I'll knock your yella molars outta the backa your dumb head."

"Huh?" demanded Speed, snapping to attention. He had lovely teeth. His incisors were a bit too pointed—but yellow? No way.

"I don't believe this crapola!" he said indignantly. "I'm just an honest citizen who's bin set up, an' I wanna call my lawyer. You got no right t'hold me."

The detective burped a second time, leaving no doubt in anyone's mind that he loved garlic. "Fuck!" he said mournfully. "I hate these Mickey Mouse arrests."

* * *

Bobby could smell the sea as Sara led him down a winding pathway. He could hear noise and bustle, the sounds of clinking cutlery and glasses being placed on tables.

God! Since the loss of his sight, he depended so much on smell, and feel, and sound and taste. He knew everything that was going on around him—he just couldn't see it.

"What does it look like?" he asked, yearning for information.

"Beautiful!" Sara replied. "We're balanced on top of the world."

Very descriptive. What the hell did she think he was going to get out of that? Maybe he should employ a person who was only there to be his eyes. A soothing voice to give him an account of every little detail without him having to ask.

"Sara," he said simply. "What color is the sky? Can you see the sea? Are there clouds? Is the grass green? *Tell* me, goddammit, I need to know."

Nobody could imagine what it was like. A world of darkness, with no way out.

Sara stopped walking. He felt her tension. And then a soft, insistent hand touched his arm, and the familiar scent of danger wafted through the air.

"Hello, Bobby," said the unmistakable voice of Nova Citroen. "How very nice to see you again."

"Everything going okay?" Vicki Foxe asked, creeping up behind Tom and treating him to a little back rub with her massive bosom.

"You're not supposed to come in here," Tom said sternly. "This is security headquarters."

"Don't be silly," Vicki scolded. "You sound like a spy movie! Who do you think *cleans* in here? Anyway, I've brought you a nice cold beer and a roast beef sandwich. You must be starving."

"I am," he admitted, his eyes automatically fixing on her

outsize attributes and swiveling away from the bank of television monitors covering every key location on the estate.

"I knew you had to be a hungry boy," she purred, taking the sandwich from the plate and feeding him a bite.

"You're some damn hot woman," he said, consecutively chewing and feasting his eyes.

"And you're some *big* man." Innuendo was thick in the air.

"How would you know?" he asked, a red flush suffusing his bull neck.

"A girl can—well," she giggled, "sorta tell."

His attention was all hers as Maxwell Sicily appeared on monitor three. Tom didn't see a thing as furtively he darted a nifty hand up her skirt.

Parting her legs she allowed him a quick feel of warm thigh before squeaking with feigned indignation and slapping his hand away. *"Bad* big boy."

"Ya love it."

"Maybe. Maybe not," she responded tartly.

"When am I gonna find out?" He was almost panting with anticipation.

Licking her lips, she promised, "Tonight, if you're real lucky."

Out of the corner of her eye she watched Maxwell Sicily disappear from the monitor.

Timing perfect.

Mission accomplished.

"See you later, Tommy, baby, when you're not quite so busy. We'll have a very good time." Blowing him a juicy kiss, she undulated out of the room.

Nova Citroen stared at Bobby Mondella. Three years, and he still looked exactly the same.

The body. Tall, powerful, sexy.

The face. Strong, handsome, carved-ebony perfection.

His eyes were covered by dark glasses. She had no idea what was hidden beneath them.

"How are you?" she asked.

He felt the rage seethe up inside him as this woman—this bitch—casually inquired after his health.

Where had Nova Citroen been when he needed her? Where the hell was she then?

"Fine," he said, remembering every inch of her pampered body. The smell of her special scent. The raw hunger of their lovemaking.

"I'm glad you could come," she said.

Hey—lady. I didn't have a choice. I had to face you.

"C'mon, Sara, let's move it," he said impatiently.

"Yes." Nova withdrew her hand from his arm and looked directly at Sara. "The musicians are waiting for Mr. Mondella. Be sure to let my people know if he needs anything."

"Hey, Mrs. C. If I need anything you'll be the first to get the message," he said roughly. " 'Cause I sure know I can depend on *you* anytime . . . anywhere. . . ."

His sarcasm was not lost on either woman.

Feeling uncomfortable, Sara began to move off, guiding Bobby away from trouble.

Nova watched them as they walked away. She wondered if he was sleeping with the pretty black girl. If he was—what a waste. Bobby Mondella deserved a woman—in bed and out. He might be blind, but he was still all man.

Nova felt the thrill of stalking the forbidden and shuddered with anticipation.

As Marcus Citroen sat in his spacious study overlooking the ocean, a cigar in one hand, a Chivas Regal on the rocks in the other, he was savoring the moment. The peace before the storm.

The wheels were in motion, and there was no going back.

For anyone.

KRIS PHOENIX
1979

★ ☆ ★ ☆ ★

For nearly two years Kris had been having an on-off affair with Sharleen. Not easy when an ocean separated them, and she was a big star in America and the The Wild Ones hadn't cracked it yet. Not easy when her main man was Marcus Citroen, the record tycoon—and if Marcus found out, Sharleen assured him, Kris would have both legs broken and a face full of smashed teeth. Charming! Nothing like living a dangerous life.

"Whyn't you get the fucker t'sign us to a record deal?" he suggested one day as they lazed on the big bed in her Dorchester hotel suite.

Sharleen rolled over on her stomach and smiled lazily. "Are you shittin' me, man? One mention of your name an' he'll suspect for sure. Marcus has an antenna for these things."

Sliding his hand beneath her stomach and down toward her furry warmth, he asked wryly, "How many of *these things* have there bin?"

Giggling huskily, she said, "Let's put it this way, honey —what Mr. C. don't know ain't gonna burn his balls!"

"Mebbe it'll burn mine," he retorted.

She laughed. "Oh, sure! I just know, when I ain't around, you got it wrapped in cotton an' outta action."

"Shit! Somebody told you!"

They both started to laugh, secure in the knowledge that what they had together was great sex. And neither of them made any other demands.

Sharleen turned him on with a vengeance. She was devastatingly pretty, a big star, and old enough to know what she was doing without bitching about a commitment. Every time he climbed into bed with her he couldn't believe his luck.

How had they met? He vaguely remembered meeting her in Annabel's the night of their first big London gig. Sharleen, all eyes and teeth and come-on looks. But somehow he'd ended up with yet another enthusiastic groupie, making it in the back of his car, as the chauffeur drove slowly around Berkeley Square, sneaking surreptitious looks in the rearview mirror.

He'd seen Sharleen again a few nights later at a Queen concert. This time she was without Marcus Citroen, who had flown back to New York. She was wearing a startling red dress and a wide smile.

He was with Buzz and Flower and a group of hangers-on, and she'd invited them all back to her hotel, where she'd plied them with food, booze, and the finest Colombian Gold grass, until eventually she'd taken Kris to one side and said, "Get rid of the entourage an' let's *really* party."

He didn't need asking twice.

Now they got together every time she came to London, and she flew in whenever she could. She was a favorite of Prince Charles, and always obliged when he asked her to appear at one of his special charity events. Her records in England automatically went to number one, and the public adored her. This time she was visiting for a television appearance on the popular *Top of the Pops*.

Kris had decided to use his connection. Mr. Terence was getting nowhere with the Americans. Frankly, Kris suspected that when it came to the States, old man Terence didn't know his ass from a hole in the ground. It was time for some long-overdue action. Maybe dumping Mr. Terence was the first move. He'd been thinking about it on and off. Timing was everything.

There was no doubt that Marcus Citroen and Blue Cadillac Records would be a great label for The Wild Ones. They were among the best, along with Atlantic, Capitol and Warners. Kris wanted only the best. He'd turned down several offers from half-assed companies who wouldn't guarantee shit on advertising and promotion. Without the right launch behind them they were nowhere.

Sharleen didn't seem inclined to help, and he could understand why. He'd been toying with the idea of flying to New York himself.

"Forget it," Buzz had said dismissively, when he'd mentioned it to him. "Doin' things ourselves is strictly amateur night. *You* know that better than anyone."

Buzz was perfectly happy with their present situation. They were big stars in England. Europe too. Buzz's attitude was, "Who needs the bleedin' Yanks? We're makin' it here. What's the panic?"

Kris wanted America. He wanted it so bad it made his teeth ache whenever he thought about it.

Every Sunday he visited his son at his in-laws' house in Esher. Bo was a strapping three and a half years old. A nice-looking kid, but Willow and her uptight parents were making the boy into a wimp. He could see all the signs.

"I want to take him out on my own," he informed his ex-wife.

"No," she said stubbornly. "I can't allow that."

"A court'll bleedin' allow it," he argued hotly.

"Take me to court then," she replied, red-cheeked and self-righteous. "We'll *see* what a judge will allow."

He couldn't be bothered. It wasn't worth the public hassle. Maybe when the kid was older.

Groupies were knee-deep. He couldn't move without

falling over them. They gathered outside the tiny house he'd bought in a quiet side street near Hampstead Heath. They phoned at all hours of the day and night, forcing him to change his number every two weeks. They followed him along the street whenever he ventured out, and sent him passionate handwritten notes chock-full of all the lustful things they would like to do to him.

Buzz and Rasta reveled in the attention.

Kris and Ollie hated it.

Ollie was on the verge of getting married to his cellist girlfriend.

"Do it!" Kris urged, because deep down he knew the rock & roll life wasn't really Ollie's thing, and his girlfriend seemed perfect for him.

"Are you friggin' mad?" exploded Buzz.

"Not *another* wife to hide," groaned Mr. Terence.

Ollie did it on a summer's day in the English countryside, with only close family and friends present. The news hit the press two days later, causing a cyclone. The Wild Ones belonged to the female population of England. This was a hostile act, and the screaming teenyboppers were furious —Ollie, in his own quiet way, was very popular.

Hate mail rained down on Ollie's new wife and her unassuming middle-class family.

Within a week, Ollie made a momentous decision. He resigned from the group.

They were all shocked except Kris, who calmly accepted the fact that Ollie considered a life more important than rock stardom.

Ten days after Ollie's defection they were auditioning for a new keyboard-and-bass player. Inadvertently, that was how Doktor Head entered their lives, and America became more than just a possibility.

RAFEALLA
1979

★ ☆ ★ ☆ ★

"C'mere, bitch."

"Eddie—you're drunk. Leave me alone."

"I said, Come here. You *do* it. *Now!*"

He was shouting, his eyes angry slits, his mouth slack and mean, as he sprawled on the chintz-covered couch in his mother's sitting room, a full glass of vodka balanced precariously in one hand.

Warily Rafealla approached the couch. She hated Eddie when he was drunk. He turned into an appallingly rough animal, and she had no idea how to handle him.

As soon as she was within reach he grabbed her wrist, spitefully digging his nails into her soft flesh.

"Hello, whore," he mumbled with a sick grin. "Wadderya goin' t'do for me today?"

"Eddie." She could hear the pleading tone in her voice and loathed herself for it. "Why don't we go to bed? It's late, and your mother will be home soon. You don't want her to see you like this, do you?"

He laughed. An empty laugh, full of venom. "Fuck both of you cunts. I don't give a damn what either of you whores think of me."

"Please, Eddie," she whispered. "Don't talk like that—"

236

Abruptly he yanked her down on top of him, roughly pushing her skirt up and tearing at her panties.

"Open your legs," he commanded coldly.

"No, Eddie. Not like this. No."

Her objections only served to excite him, and pinning her down, he managed to free himself from the confines of his trousers and thrust toward her.

She struggled for a moment, finally going limp, allowing him to jab away until he lost his erection and pushed her to the floor in disgust. Then he started to cry. As usual, she felt sorry for him, and with difficulty managed to help him from the couch, guide him along the corridor to their room, and dump him on the bed, where he promptly fell asleep.

Throwing a blanket over him, she hurried back to the living room and tidied up—just in time, for Lady Mafair made a noisy entrance with her beau of the moment, an ex-member of Parliament, with several chins and a penchant for discipline.

"Oh!" exclaimed Lady Mafair, hardly concealing her annoyance. "You're still up."

"I'm just off to bed," Rafealla said quickly.

"No hurry, dear," said the ex-politician, helping himself to a large glass of brandy.

"She's tired," Lady Mafair insisted. "Let her go."

"Yes, I'm very tired," Rafealla replied. "Please excuse me."

Walking rapidly from the room, she knew that everything was her own fault. With a sigh she thought about the events of the past two years, and realized with a feeling of deep despair that she had nobody to blame but herself.

The day Eddie Mafair announced his engagement to Fiona Ripley-Hedges in *The Times* was the day Rafealla found out for sure she was pregnant.

After her initial shock and horror, it occurred to her she

was carrying Eddie Mafair's baby, and therefore they were irrevocably joined, and nothing and nobody could ever change that.

For several days she nursed her secret, not even confiding in Odile or Fenella—until eventually she went to her mother and confessed everything.

Anna was horrified. "You're barely eighteen," she said. "A mere child. Who *is* this Eddie Mafair? What kind of despicable man takes advantage of a *child?*"

"I'm not a child," Rafaella stated firmly. "And he *didn't* take advantage of me. I love Eddie, and I want to marry him."

Anna was even more horrified. "Marriage! At your age. I *cannot* say yes."

"Mamma. Eighteen is old enough. In some countries girls get married at thirteen."

"Uncivilized countries."

"Ah, but you don't seem to understand. I will *not* have an abortion. So . . . you see . . . marriage is the only answer."

There was never any doubt in her mind what she wanted. Marriage. Eddie would marry her—*should* marry her. And they'd live happily ever after.

Anna and Rafealla's stepfather, Lord Egerton, met with Eddie's widowed mother, Lady Elizabetta Mafair. She was a formidable-looking woman in her late fifties. Once a great beauty, with a scandalous divorce behind her, she was still fiercely attractive, with dyed raven hair, scarlet lips, and piercing dagger eyes. "I can't tell Eddie what to do," she said unpleasantly. "He's over twenty-one, and already engaged to some other girl."

"But you *can* influence him, can't you?" said Cyrus, a man used to getting his own way and determined to do so now.

Lady Elizabetta reached for a cigarette, leaning forward

so Cyrus could light it for her. The swell of her breasts fell into view.

Anna looked away. It offended her the way this woman was flirting with her husband.

"Perhaps," Lady Elizabetta said casually, drawing smoke deeply into her lungs.

"I've done a touch of investigating," Cyrus said, getting up and pacing around the room. "It seems that your son has gambled his inheritance away and does not stand to gain another penny until you—please excuse me for saying this —pass away. Fortunately," he added, with a dry laugh, "you appear to be extremely healthy to me."

"I am," Lady Elizabetta said. "*Un*fortunately for poor Eddie. Although I understand this girl he's engaged to comes from a wealthy family."

"I gather that *is* the main attraction."

"Hmm, you seem to know all the answers, Lord Egerton. I wonder why our paths never crossed before."

"Well, you see," Cyrus said wryly, "when you were coming out as debutante of the year—"

"Please don't say *what* year," she interrupted, with a tightly controlled smile.

"I wouldn't dream of doing so," he replied, being charming because Anna wanted him to settle this matter, and whatever Anna wanted, he would do. "As I was saying," he continued, "when you were being honored, I was just a copy boy, running errands on Fleet Street."

"How you've risen," Lady Elizabetta mocked, blowing a stream of smoke in his face.

"It took me many years of hard work."

"I'm sure it did."

Anna rose from the couch. "Let's get to the point," she said forcefully.

Cyrus glanced at her in surprise. It was unlike his darling Anna to assert herself. And then he realized she was jealous, and it pleased him, puffed him up.

"The point is money," he said, taking an authoritative tone. "If Eddie is willing to marry our daughter, I will immediately settle a million-pound trust fund on their unborn baby. Plus I will give Eddie a worthwhile job and a bonus payment of two hundred and fifty thousand pounds a year for the next five years."

"How generous," remarked Lady Elizabetta. "Your daughter must really love him."

"She does," said Anna. "That's the only reason he was able to take advantage of such a very young and innocent girl."

Lady Elizabetta raised a sardonic eyebrow. "We're living in the seventies, Lady Egerton. I doubt if Eddie took advantage of anyone. From what I read about girls today, quite the reverse is probably true."

A faint blush of anger suffused Anna's pale cheeks. "Nonsense!" she said vehemently.

"Ladies," Cyrus interrupted, "shall we get to the reason for this meeting? A marriage between our daughter and your son. Let us not waste any more time. Is it arrangeable or not?"

The wedding of Rafealla Le Serre Egerton and Eddie Mafair was a glittering social affair. Rafealla wore a stunning white satin Norman Hartnell wedding gown, and Eddie looked very handsome in his dark morning suit.

The bride's mother was clad in pale blue, and the groom's mother favored attention-getting scarlet.

As bridesmaids, Odile and Fenella were pretty in pink. And Rupert was best man.

The ceremony took place in church, and the reception was held in the ballroom of the Grosvenor House hotel on Park Lane, where Eddie had booked a suite for their honeymoon night before their flight to Acapulco the next day.

Rafealla was intensely nervous. She'd hardly spent any time with Eddie alone while the wedding was being hurriedly planned: two dinners with her mother and stepfather present; tea with Lady Elizabetta; and one lunch with Eddie in San Lorenzo, where he'd drunk too much wine and failed to tell her he loved her.

Hardly the perfect beginning, but they had their whole lives ahead of them, and things could only get better.

The wedding passed in a blur of faces. So many people, and only a few she knew. By the end of the day her cheeks were aching from smiling so much.

Eddie behaved impeccably. He didn't drink and was polite to everyone. How handsome he looked in his morning suit! With a shiver of pleasure Rafealla knew she had made the right choice.

Eddie mumbled in his sleep but didn't wake. Fortunately. For Rafealla was too exhausted to deal with any more of his vile behavior tonight. She brushed her long hair and thought about their baby—Jonathan, or Jon Jon as everyone called him.

Their baby . . . the only reason she and Eddie were together. The only reason she could never leave him.

Soon Jonathan would be two years old. And he looked exactly like Kris Phoenix.

BOBBY MONDELLA
1979

★ ☆ ★ ☆ ★

"*They want you for a cover on* People. *Do you realize what that means?*"

"*The week in England is a sellout. The tickets have only been on sale three hours.*"

"*Can you make the July fourth weekend in Washington? The President's wife requested you personally.*"

Stardom.

How sweet it is.

Bobby Mondella lived in Los Angeles in a Hancock Park mansion with eleven bedrooms, eleven matching bathrooms, several huge entertaining rooms, and a lush landscaped garden.

He lived alone, except for six servants and two fierce German shepherds.

Outside the house there was a dark-green Rolls-Royce, a white Porsche, and a 1959 vintage pink Thunderbird.

Whenever Rocket Fabrizzi was in town he stayed with Bobby. Rocket was also a star, a movie star. But since his divorce from the serious Roman Vanders, he shunned possessions, preferring to live out of a couple of suitcases and bed down in friends' spare rooms when necessary.

"Wadderya need all this garbage for?" he often asked

Bobby. "You're not married. You have no kids. I don't get it."

"Why not?" Bobby replied. "I can afford it. I like havin' stuff. It's a kick."

Rocket shook his head. "I guess we've come a long way from Greenwich Village," he said, with a bitter twist of longing.

"The further the better," Bobby responded sharply.

Bobby Mondella, just as Marcus Citroen had predicted, was a superstar. He was Stevie Wonder with more sex appeal. Michael Jackson with balls. Teddy Pendergrass with a mainstream connection. He was that rare happening—a black star who had crossed right on over to white America and was immediately accepted. In the two years since his debut concert at the Hollywood Bowl he'd had two smash albums, and seven hit singles culled from these—an unheard-of accomplishment; most artists were lucky if they got one or two hits off an album.

He'd received six Grammy Awards—another unheard-of achievement in such a short period of time.

"You're the greatest!" everyone told him. It was a soothing mantra.

Rocket never told him any such thing, and when Bobby jokingly complained, his friend laughed. "I'll cut a deal with ya," Rocket said easily. "You don't buzz me 'bout bein' the new Marlon, an' I'll never give ya any of that 'you're wonderful' crap. 'Cause, Bobby, ya gotta remember where we're both comin' from, an' never—like I mean *never*—get caught up in the bullshit. It don't mean nothin', man, an' it ain't gonna last."

Once every six weeks, Nova Citroen flew into town. She and Marcus owned a Bel Air estate and had recently purchased a huge piece of property at the beach. Nova came in to meet with architects and designers. Marcus usually stayed in New York—he was not overly fond of Los Angeles.

Nova had rented a small house in the Malibu colony under an assumed name. Having embarked on an affair with Bobby, she was quite strict about absolute secrecy. During her brief visits they usually got together for several hours of unadulterated lust. She was a very sensual woman, with extremely sophisticated sexual tastes. Bobby tried to discourage her overt kinkiness.

"Wouldn't you like to have me and another woman together?" she often teased. "I can arrange it very easily, you know. Most men would kill for the opportunity."

"No way," he replied. "You're enough for me."

Usually she smiled and called him her "suburban lover."

"Don't you wish!" he boasted jokingly. "I'm a star, baby. I can have any woman I want."

"Never forget," she said quietly, "Marcus makes stars, and he can break them. For instance," she paused meaningfully, "if he ever found out about us . . ."

She never had to say any more than that.

Sometimes he thought he was crazy for continuing the affair. But there was something about her that had him hooked. He needed Nova—this classy rich woman with the hungry body and cool personality. And it was no longer a grudge fuck against Marcus. It was much more. She was so different from all the other women he'd had—the females who gathered around a star, anxious for any crumb of affection.

When Nova wasn't in town he forced himself to date other women. Currently he was seeing a bubbleheaded actress who couldn't pronounce her "th"s properly and was considered adorably cute, and a forty-year-old black feminist.

Rocket was dating no one. "Sometimes I like t'save it, man," he explained, when Bobby tried to fix him up. "Y'know—put it all into a performance."

Privately, Bobby thought Rocket still had a case on Sharleen. Well, he was too late. Sharleen had just announced her engagement to a well-known clothes designer in New York. Bobby wondered how Marcus Citroen felt about that. The rumor was that she and Marcus continued to be an unspoken item. Bobby had lost touch with her a long time ago. He'd realized life was too short to live it for someone else.

Rocket wandered into the bedroom as Bobby finished dressing. They'd been invited to a party for the opening of Nichols Kline's new discotheque in Beverly Hills, and neither could resist the temptation of seeing their former boss from The Chainsaw.

Nichols had done very well for himself. He was the biggest concert promoter on the West Coast, and he'd started Nichols Hit City, his own extremely successful record company. Now he was opening "Nichols" as an ego trip.

Bobby wore an immaculate white suit, while Rocket looked suitably scruffy in creased chinos and a work shirt.

"The odd couple," Nichols said, greeting them both at the entrance of his new club with overly familiar hugs.

Settling them at his own table, where there was champagne, caviar and there were plenty of pretty women on tap, he gripped Bobby by the arm. "I gotta talk to you, it's important," he said, nose twitching with the smell of money. "Hear me out, Bobby baby, 'cause this'll make us *both* billionaires. You can count on it, my man. Have I got a deal for you! Infuckin'*credible!*"

KRIS PHOENIX
1979

★ ☆ ★ ☆ ★

Doktor Head was a flamboyant character. In his mid-thirties, he was six feet four inches tall, and portly. He had wild shoulder-length flaming-red hair, an out-of-control beard, permanently bloodshot eyes, and a crazed facial tic, which gave one the impression that every few minutes he was winking obscenely.

An American citizen, he had lived and worked in England for ten years, originally going there with Nellie and the Knockers, an all-girl group he had managed for three rambunctious years. When Nellie decided to become a nun and the group disbanded, he'd taken over the career of Michael Hollywood, a young solo artist. Under Doktor Head's management, Michael Hollywood became very big very quickly—and for several years the unlikely combination of the laid-back young singer and his outrageous manager flourished.

Michael Hollywood was killed in a plane crash in 1974, at the peak of his career. Doktor Head never forgave himself for not being on the plane. He went on a four-year rampage of drugs and booze, and when he walked into the hall where The Wild Ones were auditioning for a musician to replace Ollie, with his new discovery—a female keyboard player whom he'd named Fingers—he'd been straight for exactly five weeks.

Kris, grabbing a can of Coca-Cola from a machine in the back of the hall, noticed the odd duo first. Thinking that Doktor Head was the one preparing to audition, he figured he'd do him a favor and tell him to forget it.

"Hello, mate," he said casually.

Doktor Head fixed him with alarmingly bloodshot eyes. "Where can I take a piss?" he demanded.

Kris was tired. It had been a long day, and not one of the people who'd auditioned was up to par. "I dunno," he said irritably.

"In that case," Doktor Head replied grandly, with an unpreventable wink, "I'll give this plant the gift of life." And with that, he unzipped and proceeded to deliver a steady stream of urine to a wilting fern in a large clay pot.

Fingers, a tomboyish American girl in faded blue jeans and a sweatshirt, yawned. She had obviously witnessed Doktor Head's eccentricities before.

"Go ahead," Kris said sarcastically. "Take a slash wherever y'want. Don't mind me."

"Thank you," Doktor Head replied, zipping up with a satisfied expression.

"Listen—I may as well tell you now," Kris continued. "Don't bother to stick around for the audition. You're too old, an' even if you're the greatest keyboard player in the world, y'ain't got the look we need."

"I'm so glad you told me that," Doktor Head said gravely.

"Yeah, well at least y'got a piss outta it!" Kris joked, and wandered back to the others, busily watching an acne'd youth do a major kill on "Dirty Miss Mary."

Half an hour later Fingers jumped up on the stage ready to show them what she could do. She sat down at the piano and immediately began to rock and roll.

"Hold it!" Buzz yelled. "What the frig—it's a bleedin' girl, ennit?"

Mr. Terence came to life. When Buzz spoke, he jumped. "We're not auditioning females, dear," he said tartly.

Fingers made a rude gesture and began to play the hell out of "Skinny Little Slider."

Her talent was formidable—a fact Mr. Terence ignored. "Enough!" he shouted, going red in the face. "We don't have time to waste. Get out of here."

"Wait a minute, hold on," Kris began. "She's good."

"Leave it out," sneered Buzz. "That's all we need—a fuckin' *girl*."

Kris hadn't really thought about it, but why not, if she was sensational?

Doktor Head strolled into the picture, waving his arms in the air. "If you want her you'll have to act fast," he said with studied authority. "She doesn't come cheap, but she'll be worth it to you."

"Who the hell are *you?*" demanded Mr. Terence, bristling because he sensed competition.

"Her manager," Doktor Head replied, gesturing for Fingers to cease her frantic pounding. Fixing Kris with bloodshot eyes he handed him his business card. "Call me," he said. "Soon."

They auditioned for another three days, and not one applicant sparked any excitement. Kris kept on thinking of Fingers with her tomboyish looks and fast talent. He got the lowdown on Doktor Head and was impressed with his background. Michael Hollywood and Nellie and the Knockers had both been big at one time.

Without telling the others, he called Doktor Head, who calmly informed him he'd changed his mind. The Wild Ones were not the right group for Fingers.

Kris was perplexed. "Are you crazy?" he asked in amazement.

"So I've been told," replied Doktor Head. "But then crazy is merely a state of mind, isn't it?"

They met for a drink in a Hampstead pub. Kris got plastered, while Doktor Head drank only warm milk, which stuck disconcertingly to his beard. He gave a long discourse on the pursuit of real stardom in the rock world and the perils of booze and drugs in general. "I survived the sixties," he noted with satisfaction. "A lot of people in rock 'n roll didn't." He then proceeded to relate the story of how he had acquired the name Doktor Head. It seemed at one time he was famous for giving young ladies haircuts, specializing in a certain part of their lower anatomy. "Wonderful days," he sighed reverently. "Ah . . . the sixties . . ."

"So what's Fingers gonna do?" Kris asked, avoiding eye contact with the barmaid, who wanted more than an autograph.

"There's a new group—The Mission. I'm thinking of managing them. If I do, Fingers will join them. She's only eighteen, you know. She has a big future."

Laughing disbelievingly, Kris said, "So like there's this unknown new group, an' you reckon she'll have a better future with them? Come on, man—where are *you* at? We're friggin' huge."

"In England."

"An' Germany."

"Holland too, no doubt."

"Yeah, an' bleedin' Finland, *an'* Denmark."

"Congratulations," Doktor Head said dryly. "And if you stay with Terry Terence, that's about as far as you'll go. You should have conquered America years ago."

Kris swigged his beer. "Tell me about it," he said glumly. "America ain't that easy."

"Especially when you've got a manager who sells you short."

"What?"

"Terry Terence fucked you over."

"No way. He's always done his best for us."

"Really?"

"Yeah."

"Remember 'Lonesome Morning'?"

"How could I ever forget it? Our first recording."

"And a big hit for Del Delgardo."

Kris grimaced. "Distribution. He had it. We didn't."

"Not at all. Your great manager sold out on you. The American record company didn't want your version on the market. A deal was made. You got shafted."

Kris felt the anger begin to build. "How do you know?"

"Everyone in the industry knew. Ask around. Ask your producer at the time—what was his name? Sam something?"

"Yeah. Sam Rozelle."

"That's right. Call him. He'll tell you the truth. He wasn't happy about it, I can assure you."

They closed the pub, went back to Kris's house, and talked until four in the morning.

The next day Kris went to see Sam Rozelle and learned the truth for himself. Terry Terence *had* sold them out on what could have been their first big hit. "He just didn't have enough faith in you," Sam said, too embarrassed to look Kris in the eye. "When Marcus Citroen said jump, he did so. I'm sure he regrets it now."

"He'll regret it all right," Kris said grimly.

Without hesitation he called a meeting, summoning Buzz and Rasta to his house. There he told them the truth —and that it was time to get rid of Mr. Terence.

"The old geezer's done okay for us," Buzz argued. "It don't seem fair." He quite liked the fact that Mr. Terence hero-worshipped him and treated him like a god.

"He's screwin' up our chances of makin' it in America," Kris pointed out. "We need someone who knows what it's all about over there."

"Who?" asked Rasta, casually lighting up a joint.

"Yeah, who?" Buzz joined in.

"Doktor Head," Kris announced with confidence.

"Fuck me!" exclaimed Buzz. "An' who's 'e when 'e's at 'ome?"

"We gotta trust him," Kris said urgently. "He's where we want to go. Believe me. I know when something smells good."

After a long-drawn-out battle, Doktor Head took over the management of The Wild Ones, Fingers joined the group, and Mr. Terence, unhappy with the financial settlement suggested, instigated a heavy lawsuit.

Kris didn't care. He was positive they were making the right move, and within weeks Doktor Head had an American record deal for them with Nichols Hit City, a hot new company. The deal met all their requirements.

The night before leaving for New York to meet with producers and writers, Kris went to his mother's flat.

Horace was slumped in front of the television watching *Charlie's Angels*. His sisters were out, and Avis sat in the kitchen drinking endless cups of strong, sugary tea. Smiling wanly at her youngest son, she imparted a few words of useless advice. She looked tired and older than her fifty-one years.

Kris handed her a thousand pounds in crisp new ten-pound notes. He had planned the gesture for weeks.

She pushed it away, saying, "I don't want your money, luv. Keep it, you'll need it."

Her words aggravated him. Why would he need it when he was on his way to making a fortune? Didn't she have any faith in him?

"Go on, take it," he insisted. "There's goin' t'be plenty more where that came from."

"Well . . . ," she hesitated, thinking it over. "Maybe Brian could use a little help. . . ."

Fuck Brian! "It's for *you*, Ma," he said pointedly.

"I'll put it away for a rainy day," she decided at last, shuffling the money into a neat pile.

At least she'd accepted something from him. For a year now he'd been begging her to give up work. Avis didn't want to listen. "I can't let my people down," she'd explained. He'd wanted to say, "Ma, you clean their bloody bogs, you don't perform frigging brain surgery." But he'd refrained from doing so. She had her reasons. He respected that.

"So . . . I guess I'll see you in a few months," he said, kissing her on the cheek, anxious to get out of there before his sisters came home. He hated goodbyes.

"America," Avis said with a sigh. "I stepped out with a Yank once. He was ever so nice. 'E 'ad lovely shiny fingernails."

"Sounds like a real winner."

"I fink 'e liked me too. Asked me to go an' live in Nebraska." She gulped her tea. "Where's that?"

He had no desire to listen to Avis's true confessions.

"I'll have t'let you know, Ma. Hang about—I'll be in touch."

And so he said goodbye to England with no regrets. Christ! He was twenty-nine. No time to waste. His future was America. And he was more than ready to ride the wave.

RAFEALLA
1979

★ ☆ ★ ☆ ★

"I'd like to get a job," Rafealla said one day. "It'll help us out, and I'd enjoy meeting new people."

"What the hell do you think *you* can do?" Eddie sneered derisively. "And who will look after the baby? If you're thinking of my mother—forget it. She's not the maternal type. Take it from me, I really know."

"Eddie," Rafealla said, very quietly, "I'm going crazy, stuck in this flat every day with only your mother to talk to. There's an art gallery in Duke Street. The owner has a notice in the window for someone to work there. I know about paintings. I can easily do it."

"No."

"What do you mean, no?"

"You happen to be my wife—your choice, I might remind you. And no wife of mine is going to take a job."

"I want to," she said stubbornly.

"Too bad," he replied.

She stared at her husband. His eyes were too small, his cheeks sallow. Why had she once thought him so handsome?

Oh, God! What a trap she was caught in. Married to a man she didn't love. Stuck in an apartment with his loathsome mother because he'd lost all the money her stepfather had given him at the gaming tables, and they'd been forced to leave his mews house in a hurry. Eddie loved to gamble. It seemed to be his one and only true passion.

She was too ashamed to tell her mother. She even colored her stories to Odile and Fenella, telling them married life was great, and they were only living with Lady Elizabetta while they looked for a house of their own.

Lies. All lies. Married life was abominable, and had been ever since the first night they spent together in their suite at the Grosvenor House hotel after their lavish wedding party.

"I feel so wonderful. This is like a marvelous dream, isn't it, Eddie?" Rafealla floated around their honeymoon suite in a white lace peignoir, her long hair loose, a smile on her lips.

Eddie had already summoned room service, and when it arrived, he managed to consume three neat vodkas before getting undressed.

Rafealla climbed into bed and waited for her husband. Legal sex. She could hardly contain herself!

Eddie stripped down to his shorts. He had a strangely hairless body, with a thin white scar running from below his breastbone to his navel.

"How did you get that?" she asked curiously.

"One of these days, when you're a big girl, I'll tell you."

She reached up her arms for him. Ignoring the gesture, he grabbed a nearby newspaper.

"Eddie," she murmured softly, "it's our wedding night."

Carefully putting the newspaper down, he stared at her with a cold expression. "Does that mean you want another fucking? Didn't the first one get me in enough trouble?"

For a moment his words did not sink in. And then she

could only imagine he must be joking. "Don't be so nasty," she said.

"Nasty, my sweet?" His tone was pure acid. "Is *that* what you consider being nasty?"

"Eddie, I—"

Without warning he pounced on top of her, pinning her hands above her head, tearing her nightdress, exposing her breasts.

With studied cruelty he bent down and bit one of her nipples.

She screamed with pain.

"Now *that's* nasty," he said with a bitter laugh. "Isn't it, darling?"

For a moment she lay there, too stunned to respond. And then with a supreme effort she brought her knee up, catching him firmly between the legs.

Swearing angrily, he rolled across the bed clutching his balls. "You little cow."

"I thought we were playing nasty," she said innocently.

"One of these days I'll *really* show you how to play. You'd better watch out, bitch."

Not the ideal start for any relationship.

Their honeymoon in Acapulco was a disaster. The surroundings were beautiful, but that was about it. Eddie drank all day and gambled all night, while Rafealla consoled herself with the thought that once the baby was born he would change.

Back in London things worsened, and by the time they moved into Lady Elizabetta's flat, she had grown to hate her husband, and yet she had no idea how she could escape.

"Jon Jon doesn't look like Eddie, does he?" Odile said, bouncing her godson on her knee. "And he doesn't resemble you either. Who *does* he look like? Your mother? No.

Your father? Hardly . . ." She giggled. "Probably some sailor you forgot to mention, right?"

"The entire merchant navy, actually," Rafealla replied casually, her heart beating fast.

Fortunately nobody knew of her one-night stand in the back of a chauffeured car with Kris Phoenix. Not even Fenella. She'd been so ashamed of her rash behavior she'd confided in no one. And quite honestly, when she discovered she was pregnant, it had never occurred to her that Kris Phoenix might be responsible.

Looking at Jon Jon now, there was no doubt in her mind. He looked exactly like the famous rock star. Same eyes, same nose, same stubborn little mouth. He even had the same spiky hair.

God! What a bizarre twist of fate.

Odile glanced around the stuffy living room. "When are you moving out of here and getting your own place?" she asked. "Isn't it terribly awkward living with his mother?"

Rafealla shrugged. "Not too bad. It won't be long now. We look at houses every week."

"I hope you find something soon."

"So do I."

"You're too thin," Odile said, her eyes suddenly very concerned and knowing. "Are you *sure* everything's all right?"

Rafealla stood up and smoothed down her blue cashmere dress. If only Odile could see the bruises covering most of her body, she would know that everything was certainly not all right. "Of course it is. I couldn't be happier."

"Good," said Odile, also rising. "Whoops! I think dear little Jon Jon just peed on me. Do you want to change him or something?"

Rafealla took the baby in her arms and hugged him tightly. She was glad he wasn't Eddie's. And one of these days she would tell the world.

BOBBY MONDELLA
1979

★ ☆ ★ ☆ ★

The throb of Aretha Franklin filled the discotheque. Aretha singing "Respect." Nobody did it better.

The dance floor was packed with couples in various stages of getting it on. Smoke filled the air, and champagne flowed freely.

"Some place, huh?" sighed Nichols, glancing proudly around his glitter palace of art deco and twirling mirrored lights. "Some classy joint, huh?"

"Yeah," Bobby agreed.

"Beats the fuckin' Chainsaw, any day," Nichols boasted.

Bobby drained his champagne glass and nodded. He was still thinking about Nichols Kline's ridiculous offer. Well . . . jeez . . . it had to be ridiculous. If he said yes to it, Nichols was offering him the earth and the sky, plus the moon and the stars. It was, as Nichols had said, infuckin'*credible*.

Of course, he'd said no. Had to say no. After all, he had a contract with Blue Cadillac.

"No problem." Nichols had seemed unperturbed when he'd turned him down. "My backers in the record company and the club, they're good guys—businessmen. They'll buy you out of Blue Cadillac. All you gotta do is give me the word."

"I'll think it over."

He'd left it at that.

Now Nichols was playing Mr. Genial Host, catering to their every need, including trying to push a succession of available bimbos onto them.

"The guy was a creep way back, an' he's still a creep," Rocket muttered irritably. "Exit time is comin' up. Wadderya say, Bobby?"

"Sure. Whenever you're ready."

But they were too late—a TV camera crew was upon them, with Nichols saying, "C'mon, guys, do me this little favor for old times. Say the place is the hottest club you've ever been in. Okay?"

Nichols was sweating profusely in brown leather pants and a pink ruffled shirt, worn with a selection of solid-gold chains clinking around his neck. His once rust-colored curls were dyed a spiffy bright auburn, and had been straightened. His once Captain Hook nose had been straightened too. He was forty-seven years old and still a stud, although he had swapped a different girl a night for a faded English bottle-blonde with a thick Cockney accent and floppy tits.

"This is Pammy," was his proud introduction. "We're engaged to be engaged."

Pammy Booser was a would-be photographer, former nude model (T and A only, dear, no bush shots), and all-around loser. She came on to every male in sight the minute Nichols's back was turned, just as long as she thought they could do her some good.

Nichols liked her because he imagined he had found himself a classy English broad with brains. She called herself a writer, but all she had ever written was a pornographic piece on male prostitutes (she'd sampled three) for a cheapo girlie magazine. In her time she'd been into girls, guys, all together please, bondage, water sports, S&M, and now she'd decided to write a book about it. The only problem was, she couldn't write, so she'd latched onto Nichols to pay the bills.

Tonight she was having difficulty making up her mind whether to hit on Rocket or Bobby. She vacillated, finally centering her attention on Rocket, because in the long run a movie star was better pickings than a rock star.

While Bobby was being interviewed, she whispered in Rocket's ear, "I'm not Nichols's private property, y'know."

As if he cared. Her grating, whiny voice was enough to put anyone off. And she was no chicken—this one had been around the track and then some.

"Back off," he warned in a low voice. "I'm not into used goods."

"Charmin'!" she snapped.

He squashed her with a look, exchanging eye signals with Bobby that it was certainly time to beat it.

The television interviewer zeroed in on him the moment Bobby was through. "Please!" she begged. "Just one comment— you don't know what a coup it'll be for me to get you on the program."

She was black and pretty, just his style. He acquiesced.

Grinning, Bobby headed for the men's room, where he was surprised to discover Seymour. Good old Seymour. King of the VIP men's room when The Chainsaw was at its peak. "Hey—how're y'doin', man?" he greeted, with genuine pleasure.

Seymour, well into his sixties now, bobbed his head respectfully. "Evenin', Mr. Mondella. Anythin' I kin do for you—just say—just say, sir. I'm here for you."

The old man didn't remember him. And indeed, why should he? They'd hardly ever spoken. Seymour had been the King upstairs, and Bobby had just been the fat boy catering to the masses down below. He liked the fact that

Nichols had hired Seymour all these years later. It indicated a certain loyalty.

After relieving himself, he slipped the old man a hundred-dollar bill, remembering how Jefferson Lionacre had once done the same thing, handing him the money when he was at a particularly low point in his life. He'd never forgotten that night, and Jefferson Lionacre's encouraging words—"Today the crapper—tomorrow the world." How right the famous singer had been.

"Thank you kindly, Mr. Mondella," said Seymour, bowing and scraping a touch too much.

Outside the men's room lurked Pammy Booser, trying to appear casual. "Bobby," she greeted cheerfully, as if they were old and dear friends, "why don't you an' I take off somewhere for a private nightcap, just the two of us?"

What a cheap and obvious bimbo she was. "How about Nichols?" he asked, curious to hear what she'd say.

"Him," she spat scornfully. "He can get along without me for one night." Throwing Bobby a coy come-hither look, she added, "Or longer . . . depending."

Women! This was a real douche bag.

"I was just thinkin' about loyalty," he said. "Nichols has it, why don't *you* learn it?"

When he got back to the table, Rocket, true to style, had vanished with the television interviewer.

"He says he'll call you tomorrow," Nichols guffawed. "What an operator!"

"He always was," Bobby agreed.

"Yeah, remember him and Sharleen? Look what happened to *her*," Nichols said, plunging into an ice-cream sundae with double chocolate sauce. "Y'know somethin'? The Chainsaw was like a breedin' ground for raw talent. You—Rocket—Sharleen—me. What a team!"

Bobby nodded, although he could hardly remember them as one big happy team.

"I guess I inspired everyone to get their act together," Nichols bragged, with a sigh of satisfaction.

"You fired *me*," Bobby reminded him.

"Naw."

"Sure you did. Short memory, Nichols?"

"Naw. Whatever I did was for the best. Look at you today."

"Thanks a lot."

"Sharleen's the one I remember," Nichols said, lasciviously licking his lips. "Now she was one *juicy* piece of ass. Man, I'll never forget givin' her the jism for three solid hours."

Bobby went cold. "What?"

"I screwed that sexy piece for longer than I ever did any broad before. Holy shit! My pecker needed a fire hydrant to cool it down!"

"When?" Bobby asked, quite sure the creep had to be lying.

"When? How do I know? Back when she first came to work for me." Shoveling more ice cream into his mouth, he added, "She was always an ambitious little lady, that one. I knew she'd make it." Ice cream dribbled from his lower lip. "Now I can't even get her on the phone. I wanted her to fly out for tonight, make it a proper reunion."

The thought of Sharleen with Nichols Kline turned his stomach. He had no wish to hear any more. "Listen," he said, getting up. "Tonight was uh . . . interesting. But right now I gotta date with my pillow. I'm recording tomorrow."

Nichols looked dismayed. "You're leavin'? So early? The place hasn't even started to jump yet."

"It'll have to jump without me."

Abandoning his sundae, Nichols rose also, grabbing Bobby's right hand in both of his. "Baby, you're a real friend. I appreciate you comin' by tonight. An' don't be a stranger. Wendy!" He signaled a tall waitress in a skintight silver-lamé cat suit. "Go to the front desk an' bring me Mr. Mondella's membership card. Number one. Make sure it's number one."

"I gotta go," Bobby said.

"Yeah. One minute. Where's my Pammy? She'll want to say goodnight." Stopping another waitress, he said, "Where's Miss Booser?"

False eyelashes fluttered. "I don't know, Mr. Kline."

"Find out an' get her for me."

"Yes, Mr. Kline."

"Bobby—" Nichols leaned toward him, confidentially lowering his voice to a hoarse whisper. "Think about my offer. It's the greatest. *We're* the greatest. What a combination we'd be!"

"Sure," Bobby said dully. He'd had it with the noise and the smoke and most of all Nichols's stinking revelations.

Pammy appeared, fake smile in place, lipstick smudged. Nichols would never know she'd been giving the disc jockey head in the storeroom during his ten-minute break. "'Bye," she said with an affected wave.

Nichols pinched her cheek. "What a girl!"

Out of there, in the limo, home and bed. Smokey Robinson on the stereo, and a glass of Scotch by his side.

Bobby tossed and turned, unable to sleep. It had been a disturbing evening. Too many memories. Too many old times.

Eventually he had to get up and take a comforting, warm shower. Only then did he feel better.

Finally he fell asleep.

LOS ANGELES 1987
Saturday, July 11th

★ ☆ ★ ☆ ★

"I'm not doin' press," Kris said stubbornly. "No way, José. You can take the reporters an' shove 'em up your ass."

"Thank you *so* much, Mr. Phoenix," Norton St. John replied politely. "And if *only* I had the room, I'd be more than happy to oblige."

Kris couldn't help cracking a grin—after all he was dealing with a fellow Englishman, and he'd always had a soft spot for the gay brigade. Not that he'd ever been tempted to join them, but most of them were witty and well-informed, and knew a hell of a lot more about what was going on in the world than the civilian population. Also, they loved his records. He even had a gay fan club based in Denmark.

"Look," he said, trying to explain. "Talkin' to reporters wasn't part of the deal. Tell 'im, Hawk."

The Hawk nodded. "Whatever you want, Kris," he said smoothly, pausing for a moment before adding, "Although with the release of the new album, *and* the film talks taking place right now, it wouldn't be a *bad* move. This is such a prestigious event. And I'm sure that Rafealla and Bobby Mondella will be speaking to the press."

263

"They certainly will," Norton St. John said confidently, in spite of the fact he had not received a yes from either of them. His demeanor was cool and collected—although what exactly was he supposed to say to a select group of press and television interviewers when he couldn't come up with one star willing to answer their questions?

"*I'll* meet them," Cybil suggested brightly. "They love me. I don't mean to sound immodest, but ever since the *Sports Illustrated* cover, they're all over me."

"No!" Kris said, picking at a bunch of grapes.

"Why?" pouted Cybil.

"'Cos *I've* decided t'do it. I'll give 'em five minutes." He turned to the Hawk. "An' set some ground rules. I'm not gonna answer any questions about The Wild Ones, Buzz, Doktor Head, or her." He jerked his head in Cybil's direction.

"Why not me?" she demanded hotly.

"My fans don't like it."

"How ridiculous!"

"An' all those assholes jerkin' off over your picture probably don't like it either. Single is sexy. I learned that one a long time ago." Swooping a whole bunch of grapes from the dish, he crushed them into his mouth. "Saw this in a French movie once," he explained between chews. "It's the only way to eat 'em."

The Hawk tried not to look offended at his star's lack of etiquette. Rock stars. They were all the same. Street kids with money to burn and the manners of pigs.

Norton St. John heaved a hidden sigh of relief. "May I suggest we get it over and done with? The press are all assembled."

"Okay. You come too, Hawk. Cybil, plant your ass here. I mean it."

She wanted to argue, it was written all over her pretty

face—California golden girls were always supposed to get their own way. This just wasn't fair.

Maxwell Sicily, ever watchful, fell back into position without anyone noticing he had been missing for over twenty minutes.

Chloe found him shortly after. "Quick," she said, tugging anxiously at his sleeve. "Bobby Mondella's rehearsing, come and watch."

"I'm working," he said, shaking her hand off.

"That's all right. *I* say you can take a ten-minute break."

The woman was a pest. She'd better stop bothering him, for there was no way he was going to allow her to screw up his plans.

"I'd better tell you something," he said shortly. "I'm married."

Without hesitation she jumped in with, "An' I bet your wife don't understand you."

"Yes, she does," he answered quickly.

Disappointment crossed her puffy face, but it didn't stop her. "I can't spot a wedding ring," she said accusingly.

Anger flickered behind his blank eyes. "Neither of us believe in useless symbols."

"I bet you don't believe in weddin' certificates either. On your fact sheet—the one you filled out when you came to work at Lilliane's—you said you was single. What is it? One of them hippie marriages?"

She was asking to be broken in pieces. "I guess you could call it that."

Chloe grimaced, all crooked teeth and a crafty expression. "Well, George, let *me* tell *you* somethin'. As long as it's not legal, you're fair game." Once more she grabbed hold of his arm. "Come on, we're gonna see Bobby Mondella rehearse. An' *that's* an order from management."

* * *

"He's something, isn't he?" Trudie sighed, watching Bobby Mondella as his powerfully haunting voice filled the air.

"Yes," murmured Rafealla, "he really is."

"I guess this is his first appearance in public since the accident."

Rafealla nodded.

"Do you know him?" Trudie ventured.

"Uh . . . I used to."

What kind of a reply was that? Either you knew someone or you didn't. "Well . . ." Trudie said. "I never saw one of his concerts before, but I've heard he had the horniest act going. I expect he'll have to change that now."

Rafealla didn't bother to reply. She was too caught up with the joy of seeing him again. He looked wonderful. Thank God—above all else, Bobby Mondella was a survivor.

Speed couldn't believe it. His luck he had to pick a street where the Mexican houseman of some rich couple who were away jiving in Europe had set the place up as a brothel, with three underage illegal aliens doing duty as flavors of the month. What a break! The street was crawling with vice, busting asses. They wanted it all. The houseman. The girls. Even the clients. He made it in the third category.

Finally, after hours of dumb questions, they allowed him to call a lawyer. He knew this one guy, a shyster—charged a month of steak dinners, but he was fast.

"Get me the fuck outta here," he pleaded on the phone. "Like yesterday."

"I'm in the middle of a family reunion," the lawyer said testily, wondering how a weasel-shit client like Speed had managed to obtain his home phone number.

"I don't give a piss if you're jerkin' off the President!

Get me outta here!" screamed Speed. "I'll pay double—treble. Just *do* it!"

> *An' there's heat*
> *An' there's woman*
> *An' then . . . baby . . . there's you . . .*

Bobby sang the song with as little effort as possible, saving himself for the real thing later on—just going through the motions to make sure the excellent musicians hired for the evening had his arrangement down pat and everything sounded right. Sara had told him Rafealla wanted to watch him rehearse. "That's okay," he'd said. He had to face people sometime, and tonight was as good a time as any.

He felt strong and fit. Ready for anything.

Successfully he'd passed test number one. A confrontation with Nova. Short. Not so sweet.

Sara hadn't commented. She just led him quickly away when he told her to. He wished she *had* said something. A bitchy remark would be better than her long-suffering silence.

These thoughts went through his mind as he automatically sang the lyrics.

Was Nova standing out there watching him?

Stop thinking about her, man.

Was Marcus around? Was the sonofabitch watching too?

He blew the lyric, touched his dark glasses, and tried to concentrate on the music alone. It wasn't as easy as he made it seem.

Vicki mingled, enjoying the frantic activity and general hubbub. Working as a maid at Novaroen was dull stuff up until today. If she breathed very deeply she could smell freedom. Wow! The first thing she was going to do was pile on the makeup, get dressed up in her fanciest outfit, and go out and get laid.

Bobby Mondella was rehearsing. What a voice! What a guy! Now she wouldn't mind a piece of *that*.

Grinning to herself, she spotted Maxwell Sicily with some blowsy redheaded broad clinging to his arm.

That stopped her in her tracks. Maxwell hadn't mentioned anyone else being involved. Dammit! Why was she feeling sharp stabs of jealousy?

"I'm going to change," Nova Citroen said to her husband. "Our guests will be arriving soon. May I suggest you do the same?"

Marcus stared penetratingly at his wife. She was still an extremely attractive woman, no doubt about it. Even in her forties she had lost none of her seductive allure—the same allure that had first attracted him to her all those years ago in Hamburg.

If only the world knew what the elegant Mrs. Citroen was when he initially set eyes on her. A whore. A *putain*. Highly paid and highly skilled, a mistress of her art.

The first time he went to bed with her was almost a religious experience. She allowed him the freedom of mind and body women had always denied him. She encouraged him to live out his fantasies with an abandon he had not thought himself capable of. She coaxed him further than he had ever been before. And he loved every moment of her relentless discipline.

When she returned to visit him the next day, she maneuvered a delicate switch of roles. Somehow she psyched into exactly what he needed, and this time he became the pain master, and she took what he handed out with exactly the right degree of controlled anguish.

A week in her company, and he'd thought that would be it. But upon returning to America, he found he couldn't get her out of his mind. Nobody had ever satisfied him the way Nova did.

Of course, she was not called Nova then. Her hair was dark. Her nose was hardly the fine patrician shape it was today. And she was much heavier.

He'd brought her to Paris, where he set her up in a secluded apartment, and exposed her to beauty experts in every field, one by one.

At the same time he hired a language teacher and an elderly English woman who was most discreet and specialized in etiquette. He also engaged several other experts on everything from paintings to wine.

The one thing he could not teach her about was sex. When it came to pleasing him, her instinct was always right.

He married her exactly eighteen months after their first encounter. By that time she was a lady.

Just what he had always desired. A lady in the drawing room and a whore in the bedroom. He had the best of both worlds.

Now he wanted Rafealla. And whatever Marcus Citroen wanted, he got. Always.

KRIS PHOENIX
1981

★ ☆ ★ ☆ ★

" '**E**re," slurred Buzz. "There's more 'igh-class pussy lyin' around in the other room than *I've* ever seen. An' askin' for it. Bleedin' beggin'. Wot we gonna do, mate?" he asked gloomily. "I only got one cock."

"Yeah," replied Kris, staring at Buzz's reflection in the mirror of the luxury-hotel bathroom in Chicago. "And I'm surprised y'can still get it up, the amount of blow you're doin'."

Buzz laughed, a crazed, satanic laugh, touching his forehead with a gesture of deference. "I forgot, didn't I? I'm in the presence of Mister Friggin' Clean. Smokes a *joint* an' freaks out."

"I don't get off on drugs," Kris said wearily. "How many times d'you want me to say I'm sorry for not rollin' around like some piss-assed zombie? Screw it, man. Sometimes you get on my fuckin' nerves. All you wan' to do is get stoned an' laid."

Buzz made a face. "'Ave you come up with any better ideas?"

"Yeah. Take some time out to rehearse. The other night in Boston, you played like some sloppy kid auditioning for his first gig."

"Crap!"

"Think about it."

"Bullshit. We just got the best friggin' review of our lives in friggin' *Newsweek*. The Yanks love our limey asses. We're friggin' superstars here. Just wot you wanted, huh?" As if to bait Kris, he took a small packet of cocaine from the pocket of his leather jacket and laid out several lines of the loose white powder. Then he rolled a hundred-dollar bill and snorted each thin powdered strip with greedy satisfaction.

Kris turned away. He knew what was happening to Buzz. He didn't have to watch.

Worldwide fame.

American fame.

Success.

Adulation.

Yeah, they had it all now. Everything he'd always dreamed of. And it was a kick. If you wanted to spend your life joined at the hip to three other people—plus Doktor Head and an ever-growing entourage.

The Wild Ones.

Supergroup.

With an appeal somewhere between the Beatles—long broken up—and the Rolling Stones—still rocking when they felt like it.

The Wild Ones.

They covered every base.

Kris Phoenix. Raunchy rocker, with a charismatic stage presence, a wild, throaty voice, and a magic touch on his guitar.

Buzz Darke. He inspired a cult following. The Americans loved his devilish looks and brilliant guitar work.

Rasta Stanley. Black. Funny. Sexy.

And Fingers. A tough little female with a genuine rock & roll talent.

We couldn't have put it together any better, Kris thought. *We're the mix everyone was waiting for.*

Buzz flipped up the collar of his leather jacket, pushing his way to the bathroom door. "I'm joinin' the party," he said. "Whyn't you do the same? It's wot it's all about, ennit?"

Yeah. Maybe, Kris thought.

When they'd first hit it in America, he'd gone crazy, just like the rest of them. He'd laid his way from New York to Los Angeles with absolutely no problem at all. Amazing groupies. The supercunts, as Doktor Head endearingly christened them. Luscious lovelies with nothing on their minds except climbing into bed with a rock star. In the sack they name-dropped as much as they could.

Well . . . when I was in San Francisco with Mick . . .

Keith was the greatest. I'm telling you, that man could party till he dropped . . .

David is the most brilliant human being I ever met . . .

Buzz and Rasta completely freaked. They couldn't get enough. But after the initial thrill of having more or less any girl he wanted, Kris grew bored, preferring to hang out with the roadies, drinking beer and watching sports on TV. American television blew his mind. So many stations to choose from, and twenty-four-hour action. Horace would have a heart attack. In England the three channels shut down before midnight with a stern newscaster daring you to argue.

Goodnight.

Sleep tight.

Fuck that for a lark!

He'd seen Sharleen a couple of times when they'd first arrived in America, but she wasn't the same on home ground, and she told him she didn't think they should get together any more. Fine with him.

Lighting a cigarette, he leaned on the marble sink. It was time to rejoin the party—only he had no desire to do so.

A walk would be nice.

Impossible. Riffraff groupies staked every hotel they stayed at, waiting to pounce with their blank, starey eyes, quivering lips, and voracious appetites. They would do anything to get near one of the stars of a successful group, and invariably did. The bouncers, equipment drivers, and roadies had many a bawdy tale to tell of teenage girls willing to perform whatever was required—and all for a mere backstage pass.

Buzz and Rasta had worked out a crafty system for picking the girls they fancied out of the audience. During the course of their performance they were able to give a series of hand signals to a roadie standing at the side of the stage, pinpointing the females of their choice. He, in turn, contacted a second roadie sitting in the audience. By the time the show was over, the chosen girls were assembled in a room waiting for the stars to take their pick. The leftovers were divided among the crew. And the girls seemed perfectly satisfied. They were thrilled to have been noticed at all.

Kris had no desire to go along with that kind of soulless action. Random sex had lost its thrill. How about a relationship for a change? Someone who cared about Kris Phoenix the person—not the rock & roll image. The supergod in black leather with a red-hot guitar between his legs. Jesus—that's what he needed, someone who really cared.

America.

It was theirs.

And he wasn't fulfilled or satisfied or any of the things he knew he should be.

Rasta banged on the door. "Are you bleedin' comin' out or wot? Mikki's goin' spare. She says you promised 'er tonight's the night."

Michelle Hanley-Bogart of New York City. A former deb of the year, an heiress with a penchant for rock stars.

She was twenty-three, exceptionally pretty, and self-titled queen of the groupies. According to Mikki, she had been collecting notches on her Gucci belt since the tender age of thirteen. "Honey," she was fond of saying in her uptown, gravelly voice, "you ain't a star until Mikki *says* you are."

Whispers informed him Michelle Hanley-Bogart made no false claims to fame. She'd been to bed with all the greats, and had never been proved wrong. Once in Mikki's bed, and there was no limit.

Buzz wanted a crack, but since she'd joined the entourage in Philadelphia, she had eyes only for Kris.

Pretty as she was, infamous as she was, he found himself holding back. On this, their second tour of America, he did not have jet lag, he had groupie lag.

Mikki waited patiently, endearing herself to the rest of the group and the roadies by picking out the best girls, the best restaurants, and the best places to have fun in as they trekked through city after city. Mikki would have made a sensational tour manager—she knew it all.

Buzz was insulted that she hadn't chosen him. She'd share a joint, but nothing else. "I'm waiting for Kris," she'd say simply, when pressed. It had become the tour joke. When was Kris going to get a leg over?

He'd promised her it would happen in Chicago. Now he felt like a reluctant bridegroom.

"Wot the fuck you *doin'* in there?" Rasta demanded.

"A tribal marriage dance," Kris replied dourly, and reentered the real world.

The party was going strong. The Temptations blasted forth from the stereo. Wine, beer, and champagne flowed. There were plenty of couples in advanced stages of necking, and joints were being passed back and forth like dimestore candy. Buzz seemed to be buried beneath two busty blondes. Flower was safely stashed in London, but even if she were present, she wouldn't object, as group sex was her hobby.

Mikki stood serenely next to the stereo, wearing a tur-quoise minidress with patterned stockings and black pat-ent-leather pumps. Her straight blond hair was parted in the middle and held back with a neat barrette. The word "vir-gin" came to mind. Mikki looked like she'd never done it in her life.

Kris grinned. He couldn't help liking her. She had a terrific personality, always up, always fun. If she hadn't slept with a virtual Who's Who of the rock world, he could quite fancy a steady relationship.

"Hello—star," she said, her knowing voice arguing with her pretty image.

Why didn't he just close his eyes and think of England? Not such a great hardship.

RAFEALLA
1981

★ ☆ ★ ☆ ★

Escape had been on Rafealla's mind for many months. The only reason she'd stayed around so long was because of Jon Jon, now a robust four years old. Life was a series of dangerous skirmishes. She had to be on her guard at all times, ready to deflect Eddie's vicious temper tantrums and bouts of cruelty. She kept an old Turkish dagger in its tooled-leather case under the bed—one of the few souvenirs of her father that she had. Once she had taken it out and threatened him. The beatings had to stop. It seemed a suitable way to warn him.

"You wouldn't dare use that thing," he jeered.

"Just try me," she said grimly, her eyes explosive pinpoints of trouble.

The beatings stopped. The verbal abuse and the gambling did not.

Lady Elizabetta obviously knew what was going on, but said nothing. They had moved from her apartment into a Chelsea service flat, and she visited every few weeks to see her grandchild and criticize. Anna, Rafealla's own mother, suspected all was not well, but Rafealla refused to break down and tell the truth. She had too much pride. After all, the marriage had been *her* idea, and to admit defeat, even to her own family, was humiliating.

Odile guessed. "Eddie's not perfect," Rafealla admitted reluctantly. "We're working things out."

The truth was that Eddie Mafair was a sadistic, gambling drunk, and Rafealla had finally faced up to the fact that things were never going to change. She had given him more than four years of her life. It was enough.

Leaving him was going to be no simple task. He depended on Lord Egerton's money to support his gambling habit. And even though he had never availed himself of the job Lord Egerton had offered him, it suited him to know the opportunity was always available.

No, Eddie would not take kindly to her departure. He professed to love his son, although she had never seen any proof of it. He ignored baby Jon Jon, bitterly complaining when the child made too much noise or messed up the apartment.

Rafealla didn't mind. *He's not your son,* she thought triumphantly. What a thankful twist of fate *that* was.

Their sex life was almost nonexistent. It had been that way from the beginning. When they did sleep together, it was merely a physical release and, as far as Rafealla was concerned, not a very satisfactory one. At first she had tried to talk to him, make some sense out of their relationship.

"It's what *you* wanted," was all he would say. "You forced it on both of us, so don't whine—because it's too late."

True. But she was older and wiser now. Her life was ahead of her, and four years was enough of a chance to give anyone.

Odile and Rafealla's stepbrother, Rupert, shocked everyone with the news of their quickie marriage in Rio de Janeiro. Odile phoned with the good tidings.

"It's wonderful!" Rafealla exclaimed, genuinely thrilled.

"How come you didn't tell anyone? Mamma will go crazy, and so will your mother. You know how they both love big weddings."

"Exactly what we wished to avoid," Odile giggled. "I'm so happy! We want you to come and visit us, and bring Jon Jon."

"I'd love to," Rafealla said quietly, thinking this might be exactly the opportunity she'd been waiting for. Rupert had been living in South America for two years, working on a mammoth engineering project.

Brazil. On the phone he spoke about it glowingly.

Brazil. It could be the perfect escape.

"How long will you be away?" Eddie asked churlishly.

Forever. "Three weeks."

"That's far too much time," he said, swigging on a third after-dinner brandy.

"It's a great distance," Rafealla replied carefully. "I can't just go there, then turn around and come right back."

"And who's supposed to look after me while you're away?"

"You'll manage."

"I know I'll manage," he said petulantly. "But why should I? That's what I married *you* for."

"Thanks," she said, and did not regret her decision to leave one little bit.

She packed carefully, taking only her very favorite things. It wouldn't do to make him suspicious.

As she was filling the last suitcase, he came into the bedroom and stared at her. "You're taking a hell of a lot of stuff for three weeks," he said accusingly.

The fumes of his breath hit her in the face. She almost gagged. In an even voice, she said, "I'm leaving you, Eddie. I'm never coming back."

For one split second he took her seriously, and then

began to laugh. He was quite convinced she couldn't live without him; he'd told her so on many occasions.

"I couldn't get rid of you if I tried," he said, with immodest confidence. "When you tricked me into marrying you it was a life sentence, wasn't it, sweetheart?"

You wish. "Yes," she said dully.

"C'mere."

Automatically she backed away.

His tone was threatening. "I . . . *said . . . come . . . here.*"

"Eddie, I'm tired—"

"Oh, it's Eddie I'm tired now, is it? I can remember when you never stopped complaining because we *didn't* make love as much as you wanted."

"It's just that—"

"It's just that what, sweetheart?" He grabbed her around the waist and pressed his lips down hard on hers.

She wanted to scream. All the times she'd yearned for his attention, all the lonely nights and frustrating encounters that started off hopefully and ended in drunken bouts of cruelty.

Now he seemed in control. He was not quite drunk enough to cramp his style; she could feel his erection pressing insistently against her thigh, and his hands creeping under her sweater.

Oh, Eddie, once you were my dream lover. What happened?

In spite of herself she began to respond to his practiced touch. Her physical needs swept away their cloudy past, and she opened up to pure, unbridled passion as he made love to her.

With perfect precision he brought them to mutual orgasm, kissing her on the mouth as it happened, murmuring words, unspoken before, of great love and tenderness.

"Eddie . . ." She gasped his name, filled with confusion

and guilt. Could it be that after all this time she had finally touched him? And now they could live happily ever after?

No. Absolutely not. Pure fairytale time. But she fell asleep full of doubts, wondering if leaving was the right thing to do.

In the morning he woke her with gentle kisses and clean breath. He made love to her again, bringing her to new heights of dizzying sensation.

"What's going on?" she asked wonderingly.

"I simply realized how much I'm going to miss you," he said, kissing her face. "Hurry home, sweetheart."

Jon Jon was staying at her mother's. She had arranged to meet them both at the airport. Her mother knew nothing of her plan to stay in South America. Nobody did. It wasn't too late to change her mind. . . .

Eddie insisted on driving her to the airport. He took care of the luggage and porters, then escorted her to the VIP lounge, where he proceeded to play with Jon Jon, making the child scream with delight.

Anna smiled. She was relieved to witness such a happy family group. Sometimes she wasn't so sure all was well with her headstrong daughter's marriage, but today her doubts were firmly put to rest.

When their flight was called, Eddie drew Rafealla over to a quiet corner. "I never learned to express my positive feelings," he said, staring intently into her eyes. "However, somehow, with you going away, everything's fallen into position, and I know I'm going to make it better for you. Trust me, sweetheart. Come home soon. I miss you and little Jon already."

By the time she was on the plane, belted in and ready for takeoff, she was a nervous wreck. What was she doing? Running off halfway around the world to escape from what? It seemed too good to be true, but in a miraculously short period of time, Eddie honestly appeared to have changed.

So, the voice of reason told her, *go for three weeks and come back.*

But I want to be with him now, another voice cried.

Forget it, see what happens, cautioned the sensible voice.

The large jet taxied down the runway.

Too late now, kid.

Three hours later they were still on the plane, which had not left the runway due to some kind of technical difficulty. The passengers were hot and impatient; every half hour they had been promised an imminent takeoff. Jon Jon was restless, tired, and flushed with excitement.

Rafealla summoned a flight attendant. "Can you tell me exactly what *is* happening?" she asked.

The flight attendant shrugged. "I wish I could. We know as much as you."

Eventually an official announcement was made. The airplane was not going anywhere, and the passengers were offered alternatives. Everyone disembarked.

Rafealla found a helpful ground clerk and inquired if she could take the same flight the following day.

"Certainly," he said, wishing she would take a flight into his life. This was some great-looking female.

"Keep my luggage and book us on it," she said, hurrying for a cab, with Jon Jon running happily beside her, his short little legs doing double time to keep up.

After dropping Jon Jon back at her mother's house, a mere twenty minutes from the airport, she borrowed her stepfather's Aston Martin and drove in high spirits to the Chelsea flat she shared with Eddie. By the time she arrived it was early evening and already dark. She'd had all day to think things over and felt good about getting another chance to be with her husband before her vacation. Because that's what she'd decided it was going to be. A vacation. A break. And in three weeks they would both be ready to start their marriage afresh.

Placing her key in the lock, she heard the muted sounds of Manhattan Transfer—one of her favorite groups. As she entered the apartment the record changed to Lou Reed's "Take a Walk on the Wild Side."

Funny, Eddie never played records. He never lit candles either, and the living room was alive with small black votive candles in stylish art deco holders.

She immediately knew he had someone there, and her stomach turned.

Resolutely she marched toward the bedroom, determined to confront the woman face to face.

Just get out. What are you pushing it for?

Why should I?

Because he isn't worth it.

She burst into the bedroom and felt sick.

The woman wasn't a woman. The woman was a man with silky pale hair, a boyish face, and a hairless, naked body.

"Excuse me," the creature said tartly. "Might we have a touch of privacy?"

Eddie did not say one word.

BOBBY MONDELLA
1981

★ ☆ ★ ☆ ★

Bobby Mondella arrived at the wedding of Nichols Kline to Pammy Booser in a metallic-gold Mercedes limousine with tinted bullet-proof windows, and three personal body-guards in close attendance.

Hey—he'd figured it out. When you're a star—go for it. Live the life. His public expected it. Indeed they loved it. And so did he.

He wore a black sharkskin suit with a Russian-style silk shirt and a long, masculine-cut sable coat thrown casually over his shoulders. Accompanying him was Zella Raven, a six-foot black performance artist with a *Playboy* centerfold body and a marine crewcut. Zella wore thin strips of rubber and thigh-high boots.

The photographers and television crews went crazy as their feet hit the ground outside the private Pacific Palisades home where the wedding was to take place. They paused, in perfect sync, to allow exactly eight seconds of frantic picture taking. Then they were on the move, flanked by bodyguards, the crowd of star-watchers cheering hoarsely.

That's why Bobby liked taking Zella to public events. She had the routine down pat, never put a foot wrong. She had the right image, and it really steamed Nova when he was seen out with her. The claws emerged with a vengeance.

Nova Citroen. The woman had him under her spell. But he was gradually breaking away, and he'd finally decided that if she didn't want to go for some kind of commitment, it was over. He was a *star,* for crissakes. A superstar. Not the fledgling, uncertain twenty-seven-year-old she had first come on to. It was about time she realized that.

Bobby Mondella. Sex symbol. Thirty-one. Rich. Handsome. Powerful.

Yeah—powerful. Because with great fame came the power to do whatever you damned well pleased. He said "Jump" and people jumped. He told a joke and everyone broke up. He demanded pizza at 4 A.M. and there it was. He pointed out a woman—any woman—and she was usually obtainable.

Hey, hey, hey—he could have anything and anyone he wanted. Except Nova. She might share his bed on occasion, but she belonged to Marcus Citroen, and up until now she had exhibited no signs of moving on.

Bobby knew it was because as far as she was concerned they both belonged to Marcus. She was married to the man, and he was under contract to him.

A breakable contract. He had been meeting with Nichols Kline's lawyers for months, trying to work out a way to go. After all, Nichols Hit City was offering him a better deal than he'd ever had with Blue Cadillac. With Blue Cadillac he was the singer they'd discovered and made into something. With Nichols Hit City he had no history; he was a world-famous superstar, and the contract they were tempting him with reflected that.

"There's no contract can't be broken," said Arnie Torterelli, one of Nichols's business associates. "You want out of Blue Cadillac—you got it. Leave everything to our lawyers. They'll spring you. No fuckin' problem."

Now the day was drawing near, and Bobby was ready to fly.

All he had to do was hope Nova would fly with him.

The turnout for Nichols Kline's marriage to Pammy Booser was eclectic—a mixed group of guests ranging from bank presidents and captains of industry to rock stars, well-endowed starlets, and representatives of life in the Hollywood fast lane. Neither marital candidate appeared to have any family. Nichols's best man was a long-time friend of his from Miami, Carmine Sicily, a stooped, gaunt man, in his late fifties, with sinister slitted eyes and gray hair. Bobby remembered seeing him in The Chainsaw with Nichols all those years ago. He had the sort of face it wasn't easy to forget.

"Keep your eyes on that dude," Zella whispered to Bobby, as they watched Nichols and Carmine make the walk to take up their positions in front of the Justice of the Peace who was to perform the nonreligious marriage ceremony in the garden of Arnie Torterelli's house. "He's a major Miami drug king. And I mean Mister Big."

Bobby nodded, although he didn't believe her. Zella liked to think she knew everything about everybody. Sometimes she was wrong.

Looks-wise, Zella Raven was sensational. Conversation-wise she did not grab his attention. In his entire life there had only been two women he'd seriously wanted. Sharleen. And now Nova. Unfortunately he'd never been more than friends with Sharleen, and although Nova and he were lovers, up until now she had remained elusive, running the relationship on her terms.

No more. The choice would soon be hers.

Pammy Booser appeared on the arm of Arnie Torterelli. She tottered on stiletto heels, her white lace dress a Frederick's of Hollywood dream come true. Behind her trailed a gaggle of over-age girls about town, all with their eyes open for the main chance.

"No style," muttered Zella. Sometimes she was right on.

Pammy Booser and Nichols Kline were pronounced man and wife, and the wedding party progressed.

Married for the first time at nearly fifty, Nichols proceeded to get well and truly drunk. The many guests had now taken over the tented reception area of Arnie Torterelli's large house. Seated at round tables, they dined on lobster cocktail and veal in a rich cream sauce. Bobby found himself at the head table, with Arnie's large wife on one side and Zella on the other. Beside Zella sat Arnie himself, and then Pammy with a proud and flushed Nichols next to her. Her maid of honor, a fading beauty with stoned eyes and slack lips, kept Nichols's other side warm, while the sinister-looking Carmine Sicily patted her on the knee with less than fatherly intent. Rounding out the table of twelve was a sexy female singer with enormous breasts and a voice to match, her manager husband, and Kris Phoenix, star of Nichols Hit City's premier recording group, The Wild Ones. He was with a girl called Mikki.

Zella was more than pleased to be seated beside Kris Phoenix, but she couldn't wait to inform Bobby that Mikki was a world-famous supergroupie. "I'm real surprised she hasn't given *you* a whirl," Zella drawled.

"Maybe tonight I'll get lucky," Bobby commented dryly, motioning for the waiter to refill his glass of bourbon.

"Over my dead tits an' ass, baby!" Zella joked threateningly.

After dinner there was dancing. And in between there were speeches. Arnie made a lengthy speech, followed by his wife, and then Carmine Sicily, whose ponderous voice nearly sent everyone to sleep. Pammy stood up next, cloying insincerity at its very best. And finally Nichols, a drunk, sentimental, and genuinely happy man. "To my lovely bride," he said, raising his glass in a final toast.

Both Bobby and Kris Phoenix observed Pammy surreptitiously groping Carmine Sicily under the table. They caught each other watching and laughed.

Kris leaned across and shook Bobby's hand. "S'good t'meet you, mate. I'm a fan."

Bobby smiled. "Hey—that's real fine t'know, because it's mutual. I really like your songs, in fact I wish I'd written some of them."

Pleased and flattered, Kris said, "Yeah? Which ones?"

"'Skinny Little Slider' is a big favorite. Oh, yeah, and 'Lonesome Mornin'.' I like those words, man. Shades of early Otis Redding."

"I wish," Kris said ruefully.

"No—really, I mean it."

Kris couldn't hide his delight. This was the kind of recognition he really appreciated. "Yeah?"

"You got it, man, you got the talent."

"That's somethin', comin' from you."

As soon as Zella and Mikki went off to find the ladies' room, Kris moved over next to Bobby. Soon they were talking in earnest about writing and songs, early influences, and the magic of the late great Sam Cooke and other legends. By the time the girls returned they were too interested in each other to stop.

"Wonderful!" sighed Zella, turning her attention to Arnie, who, if he could shake his plump wife, would be hers forever.

Mikki spotted Del Delgardo across the room, and sidled over.

Pammy hit the dance area with Carmine. His bony hands dug into not-so-firm flesh beneath tight white lace.

Nichols danced with every one of Pammy's sad-sack girlfriends, including her maid of honor, who whispered in his ear that if he was ever lonely, unhappy, or merely horny, he should call her, as she had the perfect cure for such maladies.

Looking around, Bobby decided if he ever got married it would be a strictly private affair. Then again, who needed marriage anyway?

"You ever bin married?" he asked Kris.

Kris grinned. "Once, mate. Once was enough. Y'can take it an' shove it. *That's* what I think of the whole bleedin' institution."

Bobby laughed. "Right on!"

They cemented their newfound friendship with a conspiratorial wink in each other's direction.

KRIS PHOENIX
1981

★ ☆ ★ ☆ ★

To everyone's great surprise, Michelle Hanley-Bogart became a fixture in Kris's life. It happened after Chicago. And by the time the tour reached New York City, where The Wild Ones were due to play two sold-out performances in Madison Square Garden, they were inseparable.

"Jesus Christ!" Buzz complained jealously. "She's a friggin' slag. She's gotta bead on everyone's friggin' dick except the Pope. An' if 'e sang, she'd 'ave 'im too!"

"Very funny," Kris replied. "You're just pissed because she doesn't want to know about you."

"Yeah. Fuckin' her must be like doin' it with the rock 'n roll hall of friggin' fame. You're welcome, mate. She could suck the chrome right off the bumper of a 1958 Cadillac!"

In New York Mikki introduced Kris to her disparate circle of friends. They included a tall gay clothes designer of international repute, a wild-eyed cabaret singer with spider eyelashes who snorted cocaine for breakfast, a decadent European princess who lent her name to a line of expensive cosmetics—and China Wallineska, her best friend, a short girl with a wiry mass of frizzy hair and generous curves.

China was an artist, and lived untidily in a Greenwich Village loft.

"She gives great parties," Mikki informed Kris. "And if she likes you—she'll paint you."

"What makes you think I'd fancy being painted?" he asked warily.

"Because it's an honor," Mikki replied, adding casually, "China's quite famous, you know. Kind of a female Andy Warhol."

Madison Square Garden was the thrill of a lifetime. Their latest single, "Dirty Bits," was number one, and the album of the same name was just entering the stores in huge amounts. Nichols Hit City was doing the job. Kris couldn't help being pleased with its distribution and sales, but deep down he wished The Wild Ones were with one of the giants. Blue Cadillac, for instance.

When he mentioned his thoughts to Doktor Head, the man laughed. "You can't get any higher than number one," he said. "What's the difference?"

"I think it's the difference between driving a Ferrari or a Ford," Mikki joined in. "They both get you there, but only one gets you there in style."

"Yeah, that's it," Kris agreed. "Exactly what I was tryin' to say."

Doktor Head glared at Mikki. He'd had enough trouble with her when, at the tender age of sixteen, she'd attached herself to Michael Hollywood. They'd had five months together, breaking up a few weeks before his death.

At sixteen she'd been a pain. At twenty-four she was impossible. There was nothing worse than a rich groupie with connections.

"I know Marcus Citroen, the president of Blue Cadillac, very well," she said, as if reading his thoughts. "Why don't I set up a meeting?"

"No," Doktor Head replied vehemently. "Any setting up I can do myself."

"Hey, listen, if she knows Marcus Citroen—" Kris began. "As a matter of fact, I met him myself once."

"Forget it," Doktor Head snapped, grimacing wildly. "You think I just came over on the banana boat? I can get to Marcus any time I want. Right now we're with Hit City. Our record's number one, and we are staying right where we are." He glared at Mikki, who glared back. "And another thing, don't forget you promised to show your ugly face at Nichols's wedding tomorrow. I've booked you on a Pan Am flight first thing in the morning."

"Mikki too?"

"Considering you're joined at the hip," he said sarcastically, "would I do anything else?"

"How about Buzz?"

"He won't go."

"Why not?"

"Ask him."

"Are you coming?"

"You'll be back here within twenty-four hours. Do you really need me to hold your hand, or can I stay here and take care of business?"

"You can go fly a fuckin' kite for all I care."

On the plane Mikki started. She had been leading up to it for some time.

"How come you let your manager tell you what to do?"

Kris shrugged. "It's what a manager's for, ennit?"

"A manager is supposed to do what *you* want him to do."

"It's not just me. There's the rest of the group."

"Oh, yes, I forgot," she said sneeringly. "Everything you make has to be split four ways. Very smart."

"It's only fair."

"To whom? You're the main talent."

"We're a group."

"Listen to what I'm saying, Kris. *You're* the star. *You*

write the best songs. *You* sing them. Really it should be Kris Phoenix and The Wild Ones."

He grinned, liking the thought, but knowing they'd all freak. "Sure, Buzz would really love that. It'd go down a treat."

Mikki wasn't about to quit. "Remember Diana Ross? Originally she was just a Supreme. Teddy Pendergrass was one of Harold Melvin's Blue Notes. Rod Stewart was a Small Face, and David Ruffin a Temptation. You want me to go on? Or are you getting the message?"

Yes, he was getting the message—loud and clear. And quite frankly, by the time they reached L.A. he realized she did have a point. Kris Phoenix and The Wild Ones. It sounded good, and maybe he deserved it. After all, he was the one doing most of the work, *and* receiving the bulk of the fan mail. Buzz was out of it most of the time, too stoned to take anything seriously. Rasta played his drums with no great outstanding talent. Fingers was good, excellent in fact. But they weren't screaming and yelling for Fingers. The truth of the matter was, Mikki happened to be right. And when they got back to New York he was going to insist that his name precede The Wild Ones.

"If they don't like it you can always leave and become a solo artist," Mikki suggested slyly.

He'd never thought of that before.

At Nichols Kline's wedding, Bobby Mondella fired Kris with enthusiasm. The guy was the greatest—they had so much in common, and although their styles were completely different, it would be a real blast to try something together one of these days.

"Where's your base?" Kris asked.

"Here in L.A.," Bobby replied. "I've got me a little shack over in Hancock Park. Maybe you and your lady would like to drop by later."

"We'd love it," Kris replied, looking around for Mikki, who appeared to be on the missing list.

"She's talkin' to Del Delgardo," Zella offered. "Shall I get her for you?"

Del Delgardo. The enemy. Del Delgardo, who'd dumped the Nighmares quite sometime ago, and was now a big solo artist. Fucking poxy-faced wanker. Kris felt the burn. After Willow, he'd promised himself he would never get jealous over any woman again.

Too late. Mikki had him. She was addictive.

He wondered if Del Delgardo was part of her past, or maybe she had him in mind for her future. Goddamn!

Zella unwound her rangy body from the chair. "I'll tell her we're splitting."

"Don't bother," he said quickly. He had no intention of chasing. "If she wants to come, she will."

"Yeah, but how's she gonna know we're leaving?" Zella asked logically.

"She'll know," he said, rising, just as Pammy Booser Kline grabbed him from behind.

"Kris Phoenix," she slurred, rubbing herself against him. "One dance for the bride, huh, baby?"

"I don't do this sort of dancin', luv."

"One dance," she insisted, giving him no further chance to get out of it as she dragged him toward the dance floor, where she ground her crotch against his and whispered suggestively in his ear.

He tried to distance himself, but she was having none of it. "I've always fancied you, didja know that?"

"Leave it out, darlin'," he said firmly. "You only just got married, or did you forget?"

What a slag! A few whirls and he made his escape, said goodbye to Nichols, and found Mikki back at their table where she belonged. "Having a good time?" he asked casually, waiting to see if she volunteered any information.

"Not bad," she replied, hugging his arm. "Zella tells me we're going over to Bobby's."

Why did he have to get involved with a girl who had once whiled away the years as groupie numero uno to the entire rock world?

Just lucky, I guess, he thought grimly.

Bobby Mondella's house was a revelation. Kris was impressed.

"You mean people really live like this?" he asked, after a tour of the mansion.

"Remind me never to take you home to Mommy and Daddy," Mikki murmured with a secret smile.

"Yeah, man," Bobby replied. "It's the rock star dream come true. You gotta get yourself the house an' the pool an' the cars. The whole bit. You can't miss out."

"I still live in England," Kris reflected glumly. "By the time I've paid taxes, livin' expenses, and slipped a few bob to my family, I'm broke."

"You've gotta be kidding."

"Don't forget, what I make gets shared with the guys and Fingers. An' what with road costs, lawyers, my ex-wife, my kid, accountants, our manager . . . ," he trailed off. "Life's a bitch."

"And then you die!" chorused Mikki, Zella, and Bobby, breaking up.

They spent the rest of the night listening to soul and blues records while sharing a joint or two. Sam Cooke and Otis Redding, Chuck Berry and Jackie Wilson. All the old-time greats. Kris couldn't remember when he'd had a better time.

"I'm pleased to see you can relax," Mikki said, on the limo drive back to the hotel.

"Who, me?" He laughed. "I'm always bleedin' relaxed."

"No, you're not," she chided gently. "You spend your whole time worrying about something. It's either Buzz or your son, where your record is on the charts, concert dates, backup musicians—"

"Whoa! You makin' me sound like a neurotic nut."

"Well, you are."

"No, I'm not."

"Yes, you are."

"Mikki, luv?"

"Yes, Kris?"

"Whyn't you just shut up, an' get down on your knees where you belong."

She began to giggle. "I like a man with nothing on his mind but sex!"

"On your knees."

"What about the driver?"

"Fuck the driver. He can find his own blow job later!"

In the morning they had to leave the hotel at 9 A.M. to fly back to New York in time for a limo ride to Philadelphia and a late concert. At exactly ten to nine Mikki dropped her bombshell. "I'm not coming," she said, wrinkling her pretty nose.

"What are you talkin' about?" he demanded angrily.

She wouldn't look him in the eye. "I've got business to do," she said vaguely.

"*What* fucking business?"

"Like family stuff. Trusts, investments. I really should take care of it while I'm out here."

He threw her a disgusted look. "I don't believe this crap."

Smoothing down her skirt, she said, "I'll meet you in Washington."

He knew she was staying for Del Delgardo. This made him determined not to mention his name. Why give her the satisfaction? "Suit yourself," he said, switching to don't-care tactics.

Women. Fuck 'em. He could live without their shit.

He returned to New York alone; performed in Philadelphia; partied with buxom twins; caught Buzz shooting heroin; told Doktor Head from now on it was going to be Kris Phoenix and The Wild Ones; ended the American tour in Washington, where Mikki never showed. And flew back to England.

Another change was in the works. He could feel it coming on.

RAFEALLA
1981

★ ☆ ★ ☆ ★

Within six months Rafealla was settled in Rio de Janeiro as if she had lived there forever. "I love this place," she told Odile. "Love it, love it, *love* it! I never want to leave."

Odile smiled wisely. She was pregnant with her first baby and quite content and happy herself. "Never is a strong statement. I'll tell you something, if it wasn't for the dreadful poverty all around us, *I* wouldn't want to leave here either."

Rafealla nodded. It was true. Such an affluent society, living in such an exquisite city, ringed with the most appalling slums she had ever seen. These were called *favelas*. Muddy hillsides packed with ramshackle tin huts. Slum dwellings that housed generations of families living side by side in rat-infested hovels.

"I know," she agreed. "It's shocking."

"But not our problem," sighed Odile. "So we mustn't let it bother us."

"I guess," Rafealla said uncertainly, although deep down she felt there must be *something* they could do.

When they had first arrived in Rio, she and Jon Jon lived with Odile and Rupert in their comfortable house, but after six weeks she felt they were imposing and began to look for an apartment of her own. By this time she had phoned her mother in England to tell her she was staying, and was instructing her lawyers to begin divorce proceedings against Eddie.

Anna was more than relieved. "I sensed all was not well, my darling," she'd said sympathetically. "But why run so far? Couldn't you have just moved back to the country with us?"

Rafealla decided it was too complicated to start explaining that she needed the distance, the breathing space. For once in her life she wished to be completely independent.

Money was no problem. At age twenty-five she was to inherit a large trust fund from her father, and even though she was only twenty-one, it was not difficult for her lawyers in England to arrange for an adequate advance.

She found a modern sunny apartment with a magnificent sea view near Copacabana Beach, and she and Jon Jon, plus a stern English nanny Anna sent over, moved in.

Free at last! She hadn't heard a word from Eddie, and was not surprised. What could he say? Getting caught in the act was hardly conducive to a long, meaningful discussion about their future together.

"What actually happened?" Odile kept on begging for information.

Rafealla merely shrugged. "I don't know and I don't care. I never want to set eyes on Eddie again."

"Hmmm . . ." Odile said. "You'll have to let him visit Jon Jon."

Rafealla knew she would have to do no such thing. "We'll see," she said mysteriously.

She did not reveal the discovery of her husband's homosexuality to anyone. It was her secret, and as long as he caused her no trouble, it would remain that way. For six months his silence had been constant. Their divorce was proceeding without any problems.

In Rio she met a lot of new friends. At first she hung out

with Odile and Rupert's affluent group of young marrieds, fending off the advances of all the eligible bachelors Odile regularly produced. But she soon grew bored, and got herself a job in an art gallery—the same sort of job she had wanted in London. This led to her meeting a different mix of people—artists, designers, and art collectors. She found most of them interesting, in fact, she went out on a few dates. However, once a man wanted more than conversation, it was over.

The owner of the gallery, a soigné divorcée in her forties, suggested she try older men. "You'll enjoy yourself *so* much more, my dear. A mature man *knows* how to treat a woman."

Reluctantly she allowed herself to be fixed up with Jorge Maraco, a man old enough to be her father, and found him comfortable to be with. He didn't jump on her at the end of the evening—which made a refreshing change. His conversation was interesting. And in his own rather staid way he was reasonably attractive.

On their second date she discovered he was a billionaire industrialist whose wife of eighteen years had tragically committed suicide four years earlier.

"I'm sorry," she said quietly. "It must have been a terrible ordeal."

Six weeks later he announced that he wanted to marry her. "The time has come for me to start my life afresh," he said gravely. "And you—Rafealla, my darling—are the woman for me."

Her refusal startled him—he was a man used to getting his own way. He began to pursue her in earnest, showering her with expensive gifts—all of which she returned—and dozens of red roses daily, which gave the apartment a delightfully festive appearance.

"What *is* going on?" Odile asked, anxious for a full report. "He's a very important man, you know."

"And a very nice one," Rafealla replied truthfully. "Only not for me."

"Too old, I guess. I hear he has a daughter our age."

"Age doesn't matter."

"Sure it does."

A week later, Odile gave birth to her first baby, a ten-pound girl with blue eyes and no hair. Rafealla rushed to the hospital. Rupert needed her support; he was a nervous wreck, especially when they took the baby home and discovered the young local girl they had hired to look after her didn't have any experience.

"What are we going to do?" wailed Odile.

"No problem," Rafealla said calmly. "Jon Jon's nanny will come and work for you, and I'll take your girl. After all, Jon is at nursery school most of the day—so he doesn't really need a proper nanny anymore."

A very sensible solution. Everyone was happy except Jorge, who kept asking Rafealla to find out who this strange girl was she'd brought into her home to look after Jon Jon, this girl with no experience and no references.

"She's okay," Rafealla insisted. "Her aunt works for Rupert's partner."

"That's not good enough," he said sternly.

The girl's name was Juana. Small, slight, and quiet, she worked hard, cleaning the apartment as well as taking care of Jon Jon, who took to her immediately. All week she lived in, and weekends she went home, returning early Monday morning. As far as Rafealla was concerned, it was the perfect arrangement. She loved being alone with her son on weekends. It was fun to take him to the beach, swim, and play games.

Jorge Maraco hovered on the sidelines of her life, waiting patiently to be more than just a charming escort. She met his daughter, Cristina, and many of his friends. She spent time at his magnificent heavily guarded mansion— Jorge had a macabre fear of kidnappers. Being with him was safe and unthreatening. He could protect her from the world, and maybe she *would* marry him when her divorce was final. Why not?

So far she had not slept with him, and he didn't push. If nothing else, he was a patient man, prepared to wait.

Both Odile and Rupert were fiercely against it. "He's much too old for you," they both said. "Are you mad? You don't need his money. What's the big attraction?"

Ha! Big attraction. She'd had that with Eddie, and look where it got her.

One Monday morning Juana didn't show up. By Wednesday Rafealla was worried, for she had no idea how to contact the girl—she only knew that her family lived in the notorious *favela*.

"You're lucky she's gone," Jorge said in an "I told you so" voice. "What did she steal?"

"Nothing," Rafealla replied hotly. "Don't be so quick to judge."

"You, my dear, do not understand," he said pompously. "Stealing is a way of existence for the slum people. It means nothing to them."

"How would *you* know?"

"Because I have lived next to these peasants all my life."

"Then it's a shame you haven't done anything to help them with all your money and all your power. I think the contrast between the very rich and the very poor in this country is disgusting."

"Oh, do you, young lady? And I suppose you *think* you know exactly what you are talking about."

"I know what I see."

"Perhaps you only see what you want to."

Soon they were embroiled in a fierce argument, with Jorge finally stalking from her apartment.

She made Jon Jon dinner, bathed him, and tucked him safely into bed—her little spiky-haired boy with the bright blue eyes. He was her life, her future. And whatever she did had to be the very best for him.

For a moment her mind drifted back to that cold London night four years ago. Kris Phoenix, brash and cocky—a typical rock star without a care in the world except for himself. A ride around Berkeley Square in a chauffeured car. Hot, sticky, fast sex, and everything changed. . . .

Perhaps marrying Jorge Maraco wasn't such a brilliant idea. Maybe she should try having a life first.

The doorbell rang, and thinking it was probably Jorge returning to apologize, she did not bother to check the peephole.

Upon opening the door, she came face to face with the best-looking male she had ever seen. He was Brazilian, about her age, with long black curly hair, green eyes, and a mouth she wanted to touch. He wore blue jeans, a work shirt, and sneakers. With a jolt she realized their outfits were matching.

For a moment there was silence as they both checked each other out. He was obviously as struck by her looks as she was with his. Instinctively she touched her hair, tied back in a ponytail.

"Uh . . . are *you* Mrs. Le Serre?" he asked at last.

Recovering her composure, she nodded. Mrs. Mafair was a name she'd dropped as fast as she could.

He smiled. White, even teeth. A devastating smile.

Once she had thought Eddie handsome. He was nothing compared to this man.

"Can I help you?" she asked, trying not to stare.

"I'm Juana's brother."

"Who?"

"Juana. Your girl. She work for you."

"Oh, Juana," she said vaguely.

"Maybe you are wondering why she hasn't come in this week."

"Is she sick?"

"Food poisoning."

"How awful."

"Shrimp. She eat the shrimp and swell up like a basket-ball."

They were having this perfectly simple conversation about Juana and her problem, but really they were having a completely different conversation as their eyes met and spoke a secret language.

Rafealla felt uncomfortably warm. Her eyes darted down to his jeans and quickly observed he felt as hot as she did.

"Would you like a cold drink?" she asked quickly.

"Maybe a beer," he replied, "before I go to work."

"What do you do?"

"I'm a musician."

"How interesting. What instrument do you play?"

"Many things. Guitar, drums, flute, and I sing."

She grinned. "Multi-talented, huh?"

He grinned back. "If you say so."

"I'll get your beer," she said, wondering why her heart was pounding so fast. "Please come in."

He followed her into the apartment, looked around and gave a low whistle. "Nice."

"I like it," she said, going to the fridge. "Is American beer okay?"

Nodding, he walked over to the counter that separated the kitchen from the living room.

Clumsily she pulled the ring on the can, and before she could prevent it, the beer frothed over the top. They both reached for a nearby box of Kleenex and felt the burn as their hands touched. Hastily she pulled away, pouring the golden liquid into a glass, which she passed to him.

"I tell you something, you're not like I expected," he said, sipping his drink.

"What did you expect?"

"Juana. She always talk about the grand English lady she

303

work for. I imagine you older. Another thing—you don't look English to me."

"A quarter. My mother is half English and half French, and my father was half American and half Ethiopian. He died when I was seven. We lived in Paris, and then London."

Why was she telling a complete stranger her life history?

Gazing at her with disconcertingly direct green eyes, he said, "Juana will be back next Monday. Fine for you?"

She nodded, remarking, "Your English is very good."

"Not bad. I taught myself."

"Was it difficult?"

Shrugging, he said, "Sometimes. But nothing good come easy. Right?" Finishing his beer, he walked toward the door. "So I say goodbye, Mrs. Le Serre."

"Goodbye," she said, breathlessly flustered.

When he'd left the apartment she realized she didn't even know his name.

"God!" exclaimed Odile. "What a fuss! *Why* do we have to go to this funny little nightclub? It's not one of the in places, you know."

"Don't be such a snob," Rafealla replied. "I've heard it's great."

"From whom?" Rupert inquired. "Not Jorge, I bet."

"She's put Jorge on hold, thank goodness," said Odile. "Her apartment looks like a florist's shop. The poor man is obviously distraught."

"Oh, it's 'the poor man' now, is it?" Rafealla said tartly. "Make up your mind. Last week you thought he was the worst thing that ever happened to me."

"He *is* one of the richest men in South America," Rupert remarked.

"So what?" Rafealla replied defiantly. "I'm fed up with you two. One minute he's right for me, the next he's wrong. And you've both said I don't need his stupid money."

"True," said Odile.

"Very true," agreed Rupert.

"Can we go now?" Rafealla asked impatiently.

She had found out Juana's brother's name—it was Luiz Oliveira—and where he worked—a club called "Pussy Satin." Further inquiries revealed it was a tourist joint, featuring nude dancers and gambling in the back room. Hardly a place she could take Jorge to—which is why she had conned Odile and Rupert into going with her.

The Pussy Satin lived up to its name. Gaudy and noisy, it was a beehive of frantic activity. Colorfully dressed hostesses were scattered around the place in scanty, body-hugging clothes. There was a long, crowded bar, and up on a small stage a combo of musicians played lively samba music. On the dance floor, sweating, happy bodies swayed to the beat.

"Good God!" exclaimed Rupert. "Some dive!"

"Hiya, honey," greeted a comely woman in red ruffles and a turban, her tanned, plump midriff temptingly exposed. "Wanna table?"

"I suppose so," Rupert replied gruffly.

"For three," added Odile, trying to avoid the eye of a fat man who leaned against the bar winking suggestively at her.

The woman in red ruffles passed them over to a young, undersized waiter. He led them to a table at the front, demanded an exorbitant cover charge, and asked Rupert if he required a hostess.

"Certainly not!" Rupert snapped, affronted.

The waiter shrugged. What did he care as long as they tipped well? "Champagne?" he asked automatically.

"No," said Rupert.

"Yes," said Odile. She turned to her husband with a winning smile. "Let's enjoy it now we're here. At least it's different. I'm so fed up with all those boring business dinners we have to go to."

"All right," Rupert relented. "Bring us a bottle of Dom Perignon."

"House champagne only," the waiter said stoically.

"Bring it anyway," Odile said.

Casually Rafealla glanced beyond the milling bodies on the dance floor to check out the musicians. There were five of them, and none of them were Luiz. Concealing a sharp stab of disappointment, she turned to Odile. "I told you it was different," she said, trying to sound cheerful.

"You don't have to convince me," Odile replied enthusiastically. "I adore the place. It's got such atmosphere, and the music is wonderful."

"Wanna dance, hansome?" A frizzy-haired hostess in a blue fishnet dress approached their table, her flashing eyes settling on Rupert.

He pursed his lips. "No, thank you."

"Go *on*. Live dangerously," laughed Odile.

"Yes. Do it!" encouraged Rafealla. "I can remember when you used to be fun. Now you're becoming a boring old fart!"

"Thanks a lot, little sister."

"Go for it," urged Odile.

"I dare you!" added Rafealla.

"Right!" Rupert said, jumping up. "You asked for it, you two nags."

The woman in blue fishnet beamed, revealing a single gold front tooth in a sea of crooked white ones. "C'mon, honey-pie," she tempted, wiggling her fat bottom. "Let us go *shake* it *out!*"

Without further hesitation, Rupert hit the dance floor, his English manners loosening up considerably as the samba beat enveloped him.

"Come on," giggled Odile, leaping to her feet. "We'd better join them before he gets into trouble!"

Unable to resist the sensuous rhythm, Rafealla rose also and began to dance. It didn't matter that she had no partner, the music was companion enough, the melodious Brazilian beat soon sweeping over her.

Several glasses of champagne later, the three of them were feeling no pain. Rupert was methodically dancing with each and every hostess at five bucks a throw, while Odile and Rafealla warded off the amorous attentions of several stray men who hovered near their table. When Madame Red Ruffles announced it was cabaret time, they were reluctant to settle down.

"This is the best bloody night I've had in years," Rupert raved. "We've got to bring *everyone* here."

Rafealla collapsed in her chair, fanning herself with the drinks menu. When she looked up, Luiz was sitting on a stool at the side of the stage, tuning his guitar.

"An' now—ladies an' gennelmen," said Madame Red Ruffles, "we are delighted to welcome 'Miss Top of Pussy Satin'—the wunnerful 'Eve.'"

A tall, over-made-up woman in a spangly outfit descended from a suspended birdcage. She was clad in silver from head to toe, including a cloche hat and very high-heeled shoes.

While Luiz picked out a soulful rendition of "The Girl from Ipanema" on his guitar, Eve very slowly began to take it all off. She started with her hat, from which she shook a mane of dyed silver hair, ending up in nothing but high heels and a minute G-string, along with sparkling pasties covering each large breast.

"What an amazing piece of crumpet!" breathed Rupert admiringly.

"Do shut up," scolded Odile. "They're probably silicone."

Eve paused, striking a wide-legged pose, suggestively fingering the two pasties concealing her nipples from an expectant audience. And then, with a sudden flourish, she removed the stuck-on devices, exposing darkly swollen nipples.

Rupert gulped, nearly choking on his drink.

"Typical!" Odile snorted.

Eve smirked knowingly, flicking a hidden catch, allowing her G-string to fall away.

Total nudity for several seconds, then the stage went black.

When the lights came on again, Eve was gone, but Luiz remained, singing of lost love and balmy nights in an appealingly husky voice.

Rafealla's heart went out to him. He looked so handsome, and his voice was so terrific—but who cared? Everyone was recovering from Eve—the big horse. He deserved better than this.

Over the next few weeks she went back to the Pussy Satin quite a few times, dragging into service anyone who would go with her. Although she never got a chance to speak to Luiz, he was well aware of her presence. Their eyes conducted a private, intimate conversation, of which they were both excruciatingly aware. Seeing him made her happy and sad, crazy and calm. She was almost in love with a man she'd hardly spoken to. Oh, God! It could never work out. They came from two different worlds. And yet . . .

Jorge continued to pursue her hotly. He was determined they would be together, and she found it difficult to deflect his insistent attentions—but right now she wasn't ready to make any lasting decisions.

Odile and Rupert were going on a trip to England with their new baby to show him off to the grandparents. Rafealla and Jon Jon were supposed to accompany them, but at the last minute she declined, finally allowing them to take Jon Jon without her.

That night she hired a car and a chauffeur and went to the Pussy Satin alone. Her heart was bouncing around like a Ping-Pong ball, but instinctively she knew Luiz would never make the first move—and someone had to do it.

By this time she was known in the club and she was given a front table. Nervously she ordered champagne and waited.

As soon as he was finished onstage, Luiz slid into the empty chair beside her. "It seems you like it here," he said. "I am sorry you do."

"Why?" she challenged.

"Because it is no place for you. You don't belong with these people."

"God! You're not a snob too, are you? Rupert is bad enough."

"Who is Rupert?"

"My brother."

"A smart man."

"Bullshit!"

Fixing her with an intense look, he said, "What do you want from me?"

"Take me home and we'll talk."

"Seriously."

"Yes, we can talk seriously if you like."

"Don't play with me, English lady."

"I'm *not* English," she said furiously. "Do I look English?"

Softening, he said, "You look beautiful." With a deep sigh of regret he added, "Too beautiful, too rich. And whatever we may both feel, we should not be together. I know these things."

Persuasively she gave it her all. "Take me home, Luiz. Please—take me home now."

Antonio Carlos Jobim on the stereo, more champagne, the apartment lit only by the glow of the streetlamps.

Just kissing was a trip she'd never experienced before. His lips so cool, his tongue so hot. They stood up against each other in the dark apartment exploring, tasting, indulging in long, lingering soul kisses.

He was in no hurry and neither was she. They'd waited since the first moment they'd met, and now the time was here and there was no rush.

Running his hands through her long hair, he softly murmured her name. "Rafealla, ah . . . Rafealla."

"Luiz," she whispered back, feeling the soft, fine curls at the base of his neck. "Ah . . . Luiz."

Slowly his hands moved down to her shoulders, and tantalizingly played with the thin straps of her dress, pushing them up and down.

She wanted him to pull the damn dress off. She wanted to feel his hands on her skin. She just wanted him. . . .

Slowly, at last he peeled the top of her dress down, caressing her breasts, gently at first, his fingertips barely brushing her nipples, until finally his touch grew stronger, and soon he replaced his fingers with his mouth.

Sighing with pleasure, she reached toward his hardness, releasing him, murmuring his name.

Together they sank to the floor. Cosmic twins, alike in every way. Somehow she knew exactly what would please him, while he anticipated her every need.

They were together. As far as she was concerned, it was all that mattered.

In the morning he was gone. She waited for him to come to her apartment or call. He didn't. She went to the Pussy Satin, only to be told he no longer worked there. Meanwhile Juana had packed up and left with no explanation or goodbye.

One night, and it was over.

Luiz was gone, and she had no way of ever finding him again.

BOBBY MONDELLA
1981

★ ☆ ★ ☆ ★

"You're making the biggest mistake of your life," Marcus Citroen said. His voice on the phone was tempered steel, but it didn't frighten Bobby—nothing could frighten a superstar. Goddamnit! He was too big to be touched by anyone or anything. Right now he was merely angry that Marcus had him trapped. He didn't need this. The dumb lawyers were supposed to have handled everything without him getting involved.

"Hey," he said calmly. "It's my mistake, an' if I wanna make it, I guess I can."

"You're screwing me, Bobby. I want you to be fully aware of that."

I'm screwing your wife, just like you screwed Sharleen for all those years.

"Yeah, well, life goes on. I'm sorry you're not happy, Marcus, but business is business."

"You have a lesson to learn, Bobby." Marcus sounded ominous. "And believe me, you'll learn it with Hit City— the hard way. You have no idea what you're getting into with those people." He hung up, leaving a sharp dial tone in Bobby's ear.

Who the fuck did the dude think he was? Some asshole

311

businessman, that's all. While he, Bobby Mondella, was a star, and let no one forget it.

Whistling quietly to himself, he checked out his image in the mirror. Nova was on her way over. Confrontation time was here, and he wanted to be sure he looked his very best. She'd never been to his house before, and the fact that she'd agreed to meet him on his own territory was a coup.

Mrs. Citroen was coming to tea, and everything had to be just right.

Taking another sip of bourbon, he decided to change from the all-white outfit he had on to an all-black one. She preferred him in black, said it gave him a sleeker look.

Sleek, hell. Nobody could beat Bobby Mondella when it came to looking sleek. He was the biggest superstar soul singer in the world, and soon he would be moving on. Nichols Kline had so many great plans—number one being a movie in which he would star.

Hey—Bobby Mondella, movie star. Yeah! He could go for that.

The new deal and getting away from Blue Cadillac had taken some working out. Fortunately Arnie Torterelli's lawyers were that rare combination—street smart and college educated. They'd handled everything, and Bobby was delighted. Moving to Nichols Hit City was about the best decision he'd ever made.

More bourbon soothed his throat. Lately he'd taken to waking up with it and keeping a glass nearby at all times. Booze did not affect him, just kept him nicely mellowed out, because the pressures of superstardom were unbelievable!

Hey—he didn't do drugs—just cocaine once in a while before a show. So what was wrong with drinking, as long as he never took it too far?

The all-black outfit suited him admirably. He glanced at

his solid-gold Rolex. Nova should be arriving any minute. She knew the score. All he needed was an answer.

"You look tired, Bobby."

"I do?"

"Yes, you do."

Is that all she had to say? *You look tired, Bobby.* How about *Your house is sensational* or *I'm thrilled with the news* or even *Yes I've made my decision—I'm leaving Marcus*.

"I guess it's all the hard work I've bin doin'," he replied.

"Maybe even all the alcohol you're consuming."

She should talk. She drank champagne by the bucket.

It had been six weeks since he'd seen her. She was elegant, as usual, in a beige suit, with her usual crocodile accessories and striking gold jewelry. Her white-blond hair was pulled back into a neat chignon.

Mrs. Citroen did not have matching collar and cuffs— between her classy legs there was a patch of thick black hair, overgrown and dense, and sexy as hell. The contrast was a real turn-on.

"How was your trip?" he asked, changing the subject.

"The Orient is always fascinating," she replied, reaching for a cigarette.

"So I've heard."

Gazing directly into his eyes, she said, "You're a fool, you know."

He leaned toward her, lighting her cigarette. "Why's that?"

"Because you left Blue Cadillac without asking me. You did something extremely stupid."

She talked to him as if he were a child. It burned the hell out of him. "Tell me what you think's so stupid?"

"Leaving Marcus."

"Fuck Marcus," he exploded. "I don't give a shit about him, and neither should you. He's screwed around on you

313

since the day you married him. You've told me about the games he plays with you, and his sick carryings-on. Maybe *you* can forgive and forget, but, lady, *I* certainly can't."

Drawing deeply on her cigarette, she said, "I've managed to live with it."

"Yeah, well maybe *you* can. Let me repeat myself—*I* can't. So I've done something about it. I've gotten out. An' now I want you to come with me. Don't you understand, woman? I'm giving you a chance to escape."

Shaking her head ruefully, she said, "Bobby, when we started this affair, that's all it was—an affair. Somehow it grew into something more. But *never* did I say I would leave Marcus."

"You don't have to say it. Just do it. I've got everything you'll ever need, baby. We can have a great life together."

"Don't you understand? Marcus won't allow me to go."

"What kinda crap is that? I'll get a tough lawyer on the case—I know just the right guy. You won't have to deal with a thing."

Stubbing out her barely smoked cigarette, she sighed deeply. "You don't know Marcus at all, do you?"

"What's to know?"

Her tone was very measured. "If I ever left him he'd kill me. And whoever was responsible for my leaving would be dead meat too. Just remember what I'm saying, Bobby. Marcus Citroen would have us both killed."

LOS ANGELES 1987
Saturday, July 11th

★ ☆ ★ ☆ ★

The four subjects the press wished to discuss were The Wild Ones, Buzz, Doktor Head, and Cybil. Kris blanked them nicely. He hadn't been in the business for so many years without learning a thing or two. With a cheeky grin, he could joke them out of anything. "Cybil, who's she?" he asked, jollying them along when they inquired if he had any marriage plans. Skillfully he turned the question-and-answer session around, directing it toward his soon-to-be-released new album, *Long-Legged Blondes*.

"Is the title track about Cybil Wilde?" demanded an English woman reporter with scraggly hair and bad teeth.

Kris knew her—Cyndi Lou Planter. She was always digging for the dirt—her weekly page in a national British newspaper brought frustrated bitchery to new heights.

"C'mon, Cyndi luv," he said good-naturedly, hoping to endear himself to her by remembering the old bag's name. "You know me—I never favor anyone. The song's dedicated to every long-legged blonde I ever fancied."

"*That* certainly covers a lot of ground," Cyndi Lou Planter said with a knowing smirk. "Aren't you at an age when you should start thinking about settling down? What about marriage?"

Screw the stupid cow. What did age have to do with anything?

"I reckon I got a few years left in me yet," he joked.

"You're nearly forty," Cyndi Lou persisted. "How long can you continue to jump around on stage? There's nothing worse than an aging rocker, is there? You said so yourself in an interview we did three days before your thirtieth birthday."

"I'm *just* thirty-eight," he snapped back. "That's hardly senile. An' I'm in the best shape I've ever bin in."

"What about Buzz? Do you miss him?"

"Excuse me," he said, smothering a strong desire to bash her face in. Spotting Jeanne Wolfe from *Entertainment Tonight,* he thanked the press and walked over to do the TV spot. Television was a lot fairer than the written word. At least on television you could defend yourself. He could just imagine Cyndi Lou Planter's opening paragraph when she wrote her piece: "Aging rocker Kris Phoenix, who reluctantly admits to being nearly forty, has no intention of marrying his long-legged blonde, Cybil Wilde. The aging Romeo prefers to play the field, even though he's over the hill."

"Tell me, Kris?" Jeannie asked. "Is *Long-Legged Blondes* a summary of your love life?"

Bloody Albert! What was it with him and his love life? That's all they wanted to know about lately.

"The music comes first, Jeannie," he said sincerely. "It always has an' it always will."

Yeah, now he was *really* telling it like it was. He'd fooled around plenty, but there'd never been a woman who was more important than his music.

A sad fact of life. Sometimes he wished there had been.

As soon as Maxwell Sicily could shake the clinging Chloe he did so, leaving her with the excuse he had to take a leak. The woman was a pest.

Time was passing, and there was a lot to think about. With the help of Vicki Foxe, he knew the layout of Nova-roen backward. Ten days ago Vicki had got him on the estate on the pretext that he was a plant specialist. She had the head of security hot for her, and the guy didn't even question it when she'd told him Mrs. Citroen had specially requested that her plant doctor from Beverly Hills was to have full access to the grounds.

He'd spent over an hour finding his way around. Fortunately there were no problems. In this business you could never be too sure of anything.

When she was finished watching Bobby rehearse, Rafealla went for a walk, accompanied by Trudie and the two Blue Cadillac executives, who didn't seem prepared to let her out of their sight. They were probably working under Marcus's strict instructions.

She had wanted to stay and talk to Bobby, but his personal assistant, a pretty black woman, had said a polite but firm no, Bobby did not wish to speak to anyone.

At least he was alive, looking great, and sounding sensational. Seeing him was enough for now.

They tried to lure her into the press-room to meet the media. Now it was her turn to say no.

"Mr. Citroen will expect you to," one of the executives said, rather edgily.

"Then let him ask me himself," she replied defiantly.

After her walk, she did her sound-check, then went back to her room and relaxed.

One entire house had been turned over to the three stars and their entourages. The guest house was balanced on the side of a cliff, with breathtaking views of the ocean spread out below. It was away from the main mansion and the frantic activity taking place all around. There were brightly colored golf carts to transport them to and from the center of activities should they wish to be part of the action.

"I've never seen anything to match this setup," Trudie exclaimed. "I can't believe people really live like this."

Rafealla quite liked the publicity girl, but right now she wanted to be alone. "I'm going to rest," she said. "If you can let me know an hour before I'm on, that'll be perfect."

"Sure," Trudie said. "When you need me, I can be buzzed in the fun room. I always fancied playing Pac-Man!" Opening the door, she was just about to leave when she spotted Marcus Citroen coming up the stairs. Darting back, she said, "The Big Boss is on his way. Do you want me to go or stay?"

"Marcus Citroen?"

"Yup."

Rafealla's face clouded over. "Can you stay? Please?"

"You got it."

Patience had never been one of Speed's virtues. Pacing the holding cell, waiting for his lawyer, he almost began climbing walls.

If he blew this one . . . Jeez! It didn't bear thinking about. His name would be mud-slime in the business. Who would hire a douche-bag driver who never even showed up for his own job?

Nobody, that's who. Reliability was the key to success, and if he didn't break out of this shit palace soon, his reliability was about as hot as an Eskimo's ass.

Sugarbush would love this. Sugarbush, his ex-wife—the balls-breaking Las Vegas tootsie roll, with knockers to send a man to heaven and back. She got off on watching him fail. This one would really be a crowd pleaser.

"Listen, I gotta make another call," he yelled, rattling the rusty bars of the holding cell.

Everyone ignored him.

So what else was new?

* * *

"You *should* meet with the press," Sara insisted. "They're here, and they're on your side."

"What makes you think that?" Bobby asked moodily.

"I don't think—I know. You're a survivor. You're right back at the top where you belong. Everybody loves a winner. Now go for it."

"Hey babe, I'm just not sure . . ."

"Trust me, Bobby."

"It's not you I'm worried about."

"Please."

"I don't want anyone feelin' sorry for me," he warned.

"Sorry for you!" she shrieked. "Are you a crazy man? You're tall, you're handsome, you're singing better than you ever did before. Honey—*you* are right up there."

"Well . . ."

She picked up the phone. "Mr. St. John. Bobby Mondella is ready to meet the press. Can we do it right now before he changes his mind?"

"Who's the fat dingbat?"

"Get away from me," Maxwell snarled.

"Who is she?" Vicki fumed.

"Get the fuck away from me. Anybody could be watching."

"Not until I know who she is, and if she's in on it."

"She's not in on anything," he said, his eyes darting furtively around. "She works at Lilliane's."

"So what?"

"So she likes me."

"Can't you dump her?"

"That's what I'm trying to do."

Vicki chewed on her lower lip, automatically thrusting her breasts forward as far as her confining maid's uniform would allow. "Shall I deal with her?"

His voice was a deadly whisper. "Just get back to doing

what you're supposed to be doing, and don't bother me again."

"There's nothin' wrong with a maid talkin' to a waiter."

"Get lost before you blow it."

Reluctantly she moved away. There was zilch going on between Maxwell and her, but she certainly wasn't going to stand by while some other bitch invaded what could be her future territory. After all, she was putting a lot on the line for Maxwell Sicily.

Walking away, she came face to face with Tom, her own special security guard.

"What are you doing down here?" he asked.

Suggestively licking her lips, she lightly touched his arm. "Lookin' for you, sugar."

He was pleased. A woman hadn't paid this much attention to him in years. "Well," he said happily, "you've found me."

"Later, I'm *really* gonna find you," she said, with a promising nudge.

Taking a risk, he patted her on the ass. "Who were you talking to?"

"When?"

"Just now."

"Was I talkin' to someone?" she asked innocently.

"A man."

"Oh, him. Some wop waiter needing directions."

"Where to?"

"The men's room." She laughed aloud. "Do I look like an information booth?"

"You look good enough to eat," he said, his eyes bulging.

"Keep the thought." She winked. "I'll catch ya later, lover."

"Welcome to Novaroen, my dear," Marcus Citroen said, taking Rafealla's hand in a courtly old-world gesture and kissing it. With a dismissive wave in Trudie's direction, he coldly added, "You can go."

"Marcus, this is Trudie," Rafealla said quickly. "She works for you."

"Publicity." Trudie held out a hand to introduce herself —yet again—for she had met the great boss on countless occasions, although he never remembered her. "I handled Del Delgardo's last tour."

"Did you?" His interest was at zero level.

"I heard you were very pleased."

"I'm sure I was. You're still working for me, aren't you," he stated flatly.

"Trudie wants me to go to the press-room," Rafealla announced, jumping up. "We were just on our way."

"Uh . . . yes," Trudie agreed, catching on quickly. "I know her sales are going great, but publicity never hurt anyone. Right, Mr. Citroen?"

With an effort he concealed his irritation. "I wish to talk to Rafealla now. She can meet the press later."

"No can do," Trudie contradicted gamely, quite enjoying a chance to put Marcus Citroen in the backseat for once. "Governor Highland is giving a press conference at five o'clock." She consulted her watch. "Which allows us twenty-five minutes of fun and games before he takes over —just enough time to answer every question you've answered eight hundred thousand times before, huh, Rafealla? But these things have to be done. That's the great old world of show biz."

Happily Rafealla played along, gathering her purse, glancing in the mirror to check her hair and makeup.

Marcus was furious, hiding his anger because there was no way he was going to give the loudmouthed publicity girl tales to tell.

"I'll see you later," he said tightly. "Do you have everything you need?"

"Thank you, Marcus. Yes," Rafealla replied. And without further hesitation she left with Trudie.

Marcus Citroen waited a few moments, his eyes scanning the room. He must be crazy, wasting his time pursuing this girl. What was the matter with him? He was Marcus Citroen. He could have any woman he wanted.

And yet . . . there was something about her. Something about the tilt of her head and the sway of her body that he simply had to possess.

Did the girl really think she was going to avoid him forever? Did she imagine he was a complete fool?

Ah . . . extreme youth. Rafealla had so much to learn. And he would teach her.

Yes. Eventually he would teach her.

KRIS PHOENIX
1983

★ ☆ ★ ☆ ★

For two years it had been Kris Phoenix and The Wild Ones.

For two years it had been war between Kris and Buzz.

For two years the group had continued to grow and soar, with Kris at the helm.

Tensions simmered. Egos raged. Vicious fights and arguments were a daily occurrence.

Doktor Head had just about managed to keep it all together—with difficulty. Everybody wanted to take off on his own, but, as he'd patiently pointed out, they were The Wild Ones. One of the biggest rock groups in the world. And to break up would be sheer lunacy.

To add madness to madness, Buzz had recently taken up with the infamous Mikki—Michelle Hanley-Bogart—who had only just ricochetted out of a stormy on/off two-year liaison with Del Delgardo.

Kris still carried a slight grudge about the way she'd treated *him*. Having her hanging around with Buzz wasn't the ideal situation.

Flower had finally been put out to pasture. An aging child of the sixties, she wasn't happy about being given the boot after fifteen years of togetherness with Buzz. Within weeks, she proclaimed herself an expert on The Wild Ones and their early days and proceeded to write a book about them. When it was finished, excerpts were headlined in a four-page story in an English tabloid. They were all dragged through the mud, especially Buzz and Kris, whom she labeled drunken, drugged sex fiends, with nothing on their minds except groupies, orgies, and dope.

Kris read it with mounting anger. It was true about Buzz —but how had *he* managed to get in on the act? First of all, he hardly ever doped. Groupies were out. And he'd only attended one orgy—and that was at Flower's invitation—hated it, and left immediately.

No. He was not at all like the crazed egomaniac Flower portrayed. Music was his main passion. He was a serious musician, and more and more people who knew what they were talking about acknowledged that fact. His guitar work was acclaimed almost as widely as Eric Clapton's, and along with the young and very accomplished Eddie Van Halen, he was becoming a guitar legend—much to Buzz's fury. Buzz was brilliant but sloppy. His work had a blurred edge, although sometimes—not often—he could take off into genius, playing a solo so wild and so perfect, nobody could match him.

Unfortunately his talent was not consistent. Heroin ruled his life. He seemed to like it that way, in spite of everyone's efforts to wean him off the killer drug.

Mikki was no help. Her stint with Del Delgardo had turned her into a doper herself. At twenty-five she looked years older, a brash, over-made-up woman of the world. Before taking up with Buzz she'd tried another shot at Kris. He'd brushed her off so fast it made the Concorde seem slow. Somehow he knew she was only with Buzz in a pathetic attempt to annoy him. It was working, but not for the reasons she had in mind. Addicted to her as he'd once been, it was a short-term addiction, and when she ran off with Del Delgardo, he'd soon forgotten her.

Mostly he went out with an assortment of girls—usually models or actresses, because they looked good, loved the publicity involved, and, like him, had no need of any heavy involvements, for they had their "careers" to think of. Occasionally one came along who wanted more. Then it was "Wham Bam Thank You Ma'am" time. In and out and on to the next.

He was getting slightly paranoid about herpes, the latest sexual disease doing the rounds. Unlike the rest of the group, he was lucky enough to have never caught anything, and he certainly didn't plan to start now. Ladies of his choice were asked to submit to a quick visit to his doctor. Most of them agreed. And the ones who didn't lost out.

"You're a fuckin' chauvinist pig," Fingers informed him one day as they all sat around in the studio.

"Isn't everyone?" he asked, feigning surprise.

"Well y'can count *me* in," Rasta said, laughing.

"You—you're just a slag," Fingers said in her direct way. "If it can't run fast enough, you'll fuck it."

Buzz surfaced. "I thought that's what chicks was for."

Fingers threw a glass of beer in his face.

Another normal day in the studio. Constant bickering was a way of life.

In spite of massive American success, The Wild Ones still lived in Europe, and all owned homes in England, registered under company names, as they were tax exiles and only allowed to spend a certain amount of time a year there. Kris had purchased a large apartment in Grosvenor Square. When his mother saw it she almost fainted. Upon recovering, the first thing she said was, "It's luverly, son. When can the others come over?"

The others meant Horace, his two sisters and their respective husbands, plus brother Brian and his lot. Family never went away, it just got bigger.

"I'll arrange it," he'd said, with no intention of doing so.

As long as Avis was happy, he had no particular interest in the rest of them. He sent lavish presents—color televisions, a washing machine, a dishwasher, even a car. He'd offered to buy his mum a house in the country, but she declined, saying, "I like me little flat, with all me friends nearby. It suits me nicely, lad."

At least he'd persuaded her to give up work and accept a monthly sum of money from him. He suspected most of it went in Brian's direction.

So what? He could afford it. Brian was still the world's worst jerk—a fussy, bitter man, with never a good word to say about anyone or anything. Instead of being proud of his younger brother, he was pathologically jealous, belittling Kris and his career at every opportunity. Finally it got so bad that Kris was forced to tell Avis to keep Brian away from him. She wasn't pleased, but she'd done as he asked, and he hadn't had the pleasure of his brother's company in over eighteen months. What a joy!

Apart from the Grosvenor Square flat, he had a small farmhouse in the south of France, just outside St. Tropez. It was a good place to get away from everything, an enjoyable retreat where he could write songs with no interruptions, although the more famous he became, the more difficult it was to cut himself off.

Once a week, he took out his son, who now lived with Willow and her new husband—a chinless-wonder stockbroker—in a large house just outside London. Because of his limited time in England, it was not an ideal arrangement. His weekly outings with Bo were inconsistent, to say the least, and Willow was being a real bitch, labeling him an uncaring father, when she knew there wasn't a damn thing he could do about it because of his tax situation. She would have made a perfect wife for Brian—two miserable human beings together.

Bo suffered. He was turning out to be a real sissy. At eight, he was frightened of everything, whined a lot, and ate too much. The kid was a right little pain in the neck. When Kris tried to talk to Willow, she laughed in his face. "Hah! The caring father. Where were you when he was growing up? Sleeping with slags and making money." He'd written a song called "Making Money" for the new album, and another titled "Does Your Mother Know You're Pregnant?" They were both secretly dedicated to Willow. She wouldn't even allow him to take the kid away with him to France for a few weeks. His lawyer had been working on it, but now, with Flower's choice revelations in the newspapers, it didn't seem likely.

The Wild Ones were making a video in Paris. They had taken over one entire floor of a hotel, and Doktor Head was going crazy trying to keep everyone on speaking terms.

Buzz had his own press conference, with Mikki by his side. The two of them, in dusty black outfits, paraded in front of the press announcing their future plans. "I won't be stayin' with the group much longer," Buzz said, attempting to control a continual sniff with the back of his hand.

This caused much excitement, especially when the news reached the others. Kris and Buzz had their usual confrontation, with Mikki standing defiantly by, and Doktor Head acting as mediator.

"If you wanted to leave, why didn't you have the balls to tell me before shoutin' it out to the world and its bleedin' mother?" Kris demanded.

"So he's tellin' you now," Mikki said, glaring at him fiercely.

"Yeah, man," Buzz agreed, all stoned, bloodshot eyes and snakehips, his dirty black hair pulled back into a scruffy ponytail. "I'm tellin' yer now."

"Thanks a lot," Kris said sarcastically. "The Wild Ones

are breakin' up after fourteen years together, and you're lettin' me know as an afterthought. *Very* nice."

"The Wild Ones don't have to break up if Buzz decides to do other projects as well," Doktor Head said, still trying to keep the peace.

"Aw, shit, leave it out," Kris said disgustedly. "It's over, man. Me and Buzz started the group, an' if he wants to go, it's all right with me." Shaking his head, he added, "I'm tired of pickin' up after him anyway. Mikki, baby, he's all yours."

"Wait a minute," Doktor Head said quickly. "The new album comes out in a few weeks. We have four live shows to do in Australia next month, and there's the video we have to finish. Oh, yes, and another album commitment to Nichols Hit City. He can't walk."

"He can do what he wants," Mikki said grandly. "Del Delgardo did when he left the Nightmares."

"I don't give a fuck about Del Delgardo," Doktor Head said, getting forceful. "Buzz has commitments, and if he doesn't care to keep them, he'll get the ass sued off him. Is that what he wants?"

"I'll finish the friggin' video," Buzz mumbled, "an' the Australian dates, but that's it. After Australia I'm gone. Use someone else on the album. I don't give a frig."

"You can work everything out with me," Mikki said, very businesslike, shooting Kris a spiteful look. "*I'm* his new manager."

After that, Kris and Buzz went out of their way to ignore each other. For years Kris had been trying to save his friend from himself. It was no good. Buzz was on a path to destruction, and now he had the perfect partner.

Early one evening Doktor Head arrived at the hotel with a pretty Danish girl. He introduced her to Kris as Astrid. "She makes the best leather pants in the world," he said. "You'll love her work, especially the way *you* jump around on stage. I'm going next door, I'll be back in a minute."

Kris was used to male designers, and Astrid looked too young to know what she was doing anyway. Lounging on the sofa, he said, "I don't need anything, luv. But hang about, we'll have dinner."

"No, thank you," she replied, with only the trace of an accent. "I have another engagement."

He was surprised. "No, thank you" was a phrase he rarely heard. "Break it," he said, testing her.

She smiled. "I can't. It's with my fiancé, and I don't think he'd understand."

A turndown! A genuine turndown! This was interesting.

"Maybe I will have some pants made," he said lazily. "What d'you suggest?"

She was pretty in the way that only Scandinavian girls can be. Clear-skinned, with a smattering of light freckles, wide gray eyes, a snub nose, and long straight flaxen hair.

He noticed, beneath the pale blue track suit she had on, promising breasts, a small waist, and exceptionally long legs. Not bad. Not bad at all.

Approaching the back of the sofa, she asked, "Do you like leather?"

He gave her a shot of the intense, blue-eyed Phoenix gaze and said, "Only if it's *very* soft, luv. Know what I mean?"

She knew what he meant all right, but she chose to ignore his double-entendre. Opening her sizable purse, she produced swatches of various colors. "The pale beige is nice. This particular leather is very comfortable to wear."

Fingering the material, he wondered if she'd agree to a quick medical check.

"Maybe the orange," she pressed. "Or is it too hot for you?"

Was she, in her own not so subtle way, coming on to him?

"Nothin's too hot for me, darlin'," he said, grabbing her and tumbling her over the top of the sofa. Scandinavian lips were hot lips, everyone knew that. Grabbing a tit, he tried to kiss her.

"What are you doing?" she yelled indignantly, pushing him off and standing up. "How dare you! I'm not one of your groupies." Snatching up her swatches, cheeks red with genuine anger, she stalked to the door, opened it, and slammed out.

Kris felt like a fool. When Doktor Head reappeared, he said, "What was *she* all about?"

"Who?" Doktor Head asked vaguely.

"The Danish bit."

"Oh, Astrid. She's the greatest. You'll be very pleased."

"With *what?*"

"The pants she designs for you. When Michael Hollywood was alive she made all his stuff. He swore by her."

"You mean she really makes things?"

"Yes." Doktor Head began to laugh. "You didn't come on to her, did you?"

"Why would I do that?" Kris asked sarcastically. "You parade her in here—a blonde with a body—an' then you piss off. What was I supposed to do, play chess?"

"Berk! You were *supposed* to order some pants."

He did. He ordered pants in every color of the soft leather she'd shown him. And he sent her twelve dozen yellow roses along with a pair of trousers he wanted copied.

An assistant delivered the finished goods in three days with a hefty bill. Twelve pairs of perfect leather pants.

Before he could decide what to do about Astrid, he was summoned to London. His son had been in a car accident and was in the hospital. They didn't think he would live.

RAFEALLA
1983

★ ☆ ★ ☆ ★

After her divorce from Eddie Mafair was final, Rafealla still refused to marry Jorge, but she did eventually move in with him. The pressures of being a young and beautiful woman in a big city with a small child to look after finally got to her. She didn't need his money, but she did need his protection. Besides, it suited her. After Luiz, she had decided there was no future with anyone else. The most painful thing of all was that she'd never heard from him again. Two years of silence. What was it with her and men? Did she turn them off to such an extent that after they slept with her, they never wanted to see her again?

Jorge didn't feel that way. Jorge couldn't get enough.

Odile was disapproving. "If you're sleeping with him anyway, why don't you get married?"

"Because I don't ever want to be tied to a man again," she explained. "I need to be free."

"Why?"

With a shrug she said, "Who knows? Just to ride the rainbow without anyone stopping me."

"You're crazy." Odile shook her head.

"I know," Rafealla replied, perfectly happy.

She had taken up singing again, and that pleased her.

Twice a week her voice coach, a stout Viennese woman, arrived at Jorge's mansion to put her through a vigorous practice routine. She loved the discipline and the pleasure. Singing was her joy. Having given up her job in the art gallery, she now spent the rest of her days shopping, going to the beach, lunching with Odile, and playing with Jon Jon, a sturdy six-year-old with a tough, stubborn streak. In the evening there were numerous parties and social events to attend with Jorge. He enjoyed entertaining and was a gracious host.

"You're only twenty-three," Odile said to her after one of Jorge's dinner parties. "Why are you mixing with all these old people? You'd better watch out or you'll turn into one of them."

"I happen to enjoy their company. There's nothing wrong with being older, you know. I'm learning a lot."

"Like what?"

She sighed. "Odile—get on with your own life and leave me alone."

"My life is going back to England soon," Odile replied, determined to get her point across. "I'm worried about *you*. You're just drifting along. You and Jon Jon should come with us. This place is fabulous for a few years, but surely you miss Europe?"

Yes. She did miss London and Paris and the south of France and her mother and stepfather and their big house in the country, and the horses she used to love to ride. But how could she leave Rio? If she left, there was no way she would ever see Luiz again. While she stayed there was always a chance. . . .

Carnival time took place in February, and the entire city went crazy, getting ready for the few days of frantic pleasure with overwhelming zeal. Carnival time in Rio was the culmination of months of preparation. There were amazing flower-bedecked floats for the incredible parade, out-of-this-world costumes, and a glut of wild parties. For once the poor felt rich and the rich felt richer, and out on the streets there was a wild tangle of half-naked Cariocas, handsome young men, fat mammas, sparkling transvestites, hustlers, pimps, con men, hookers, tourists, and a general assortment of outrageous characters. The streets were alive with the samba beat, the sweet smell of flowers, and a swaying, singing, celebrating mass of people.

Parties were an everyday affair, starting early and going on all day and all night. Odile and Rupert threw a fancy-dress farewell celebration the night before the big parade. In two weeks they were moving back to England. The thought depressed Rafealla, for they were her family, and she knew she was going to miss them terribly. It couldn't be helped—she would just have to learn to manage without them.

For the party she dressed as Nefertiti, the Egyptian queen, and Jorge, after much persuasion, dressed up as a Roman general. They took little Jon Jon, clad as a Yankee baseball hero. He had the greatest time and didn't want to go home. When they finally persuaded him into the chauffeur-driven Mercedes, he fell asleep across their knees.

This was her family, she suddenly realized. Why wait any longer? She would marry Jorge and give Jon Jon a real father.

"Congratulations, darling!"

"Wonderful news!"

"How wise of you to wait. Now you're *really* sure."

"When is the wedding?"

Jorge had wasted no time in presenting her with the most magnificent solitaire diamond ring. The moment she'd said yes, he'd produced it from the safe, proudly telling her he'd bought it the day she moved in. Now she wore it to the big parade, where she was safely cloistered in a special box overlooking the route with a dozen or so of Jorge's friends and business acquaintances, who had flown in especially for the evening of festivities. Special boxes had been erected for watching the parade, enabling the rich to see and be seen without ever really becoming involved.

Looking around, she was quite surprised to spot Marcus Citroen, the American record magnate, with his wife, Nova, an elegant, cold woman. She hadn't seen him since that fateful night in London at Annabel's, which he obviously didn't remember, for when they were introduced by one of Jorge's friends, he showed not a flicker of recognition.

That's twice he hasn't remembered me, she thought, her mind quickly darting back to their first encounter at Odile's stepfather's house in the south of France where he'd flashed her in the swimming pool. He was a dirty old man then, and nothing had changed.

As they were introduced, his hooded eyes lasciviously stripped off the gypsy outfit she wore, checking out every inch of her body.

When Odile arrived she didn't wait for an introduction. "Mr. Citroen," she exclaimed, winking at Rafealla with a certain amount of wickedness. "I bet you don't remember me."

Turning, he acknowledged Odile's blond prettiness with a perfunctory nod. "You'll have to assist my memory, my dear."

"Isabella and Claudio Franconini's daughter, Odile. You came to stay at our château in France one summer. Don't worry if you've forgotten, it was a long time ago."

"Indeed I do remember. What a pleasure to see you again. Tell me, are your parents well?"

"Very well." Unable to resist, gamely stifling a giggle, she added, "And surely you remember my best friend, Rafealla? She was staying with us at the time."

Rafealla could have kicked her grinning sister-in-law.

Fortunately Jorge appeared at that moment, putting a

possessive arm around her shoulders as he said, "So, Marcus, you've met my soon-to-be bride, the most beautiful woman in Rio."

"Child bride," murmured Marcus, gazing at her reflectively, with a *Haven't I seen you somewhere before* look in his eyes.

Rafealla shifted uncomfortably. There was something about Marcus Citroen that filled her with dread.

The gaiety and wildness of the night excited everyone. It was impossible not to get caught up in the delirious goings on. Carnival fever was catching, what with the noise and the smells and the insistent music. Pulsating bodies and decadent faces were everywhere. A heavy sexual feeling pervaded the air as Rio forgot about the rest of the world and surrendered to Carnival.

Odile was in an adventurous mood. Several glasses of champagne always made her a little crazy, and combined with the heady atmosphere of the evening, an earlier fight with Rupert, and the fact she would soon be leaving Rio, she was ready to do the forbidden.

The forbidden was leaving the rarefied atmosphere of the boxes where the rich people experienced Carnival without getting too close.

"Why don't we skip out of here?" she whispered. "I can't stand being confined like this."

"No," Rafealla whispered back. "Jorge said it's dangerous."

"Please! Now you're beginning to *sound* like him. What happened to the girl who wanted to be free? This is a holiday—a festival. Let's go have fun for ten minutes. Nobody'll miss us, they'll think we're in the loo."

To dance in the streets was a tempting prospect. Being a spectator wasn't the same as participating. Why the hell shouldn't they?

Sneaking from the box, they hit the street like two

naughty schoolgirls, falling in with a swaying group of half-naked bodies snaking along the side of the parade, giggling with the sheer energy and exhilaration of it all.

"We'll just go a couple of blocks and then back," Odile promised.

"Sure." Rafealla laughed as a masked stranger grabbed her arm, propelling her along.

The crowds were dense and unruly. It took only moments for the two friends to get separated and lose sight of each other, but neither really cared—they were having too enjoyable a time. The music was loud and sensual. Inhibitions were left behind as they joined the swaying, laughing throng.

It wasn't until Rafealla began to lose her breath that she realized they should go back. When she looked around for Odile, she couldn't find her.

"Damn!" she muttered, knowing there was no way she could return without her. Rupert would be furious.

Now she tried to ignore the samba beat and the oscillating mass of bodies as her eyes began to search for Odile. An impossible task. Should she turn around? Continue forward?

Oh, God! What to do?

A creature in an orange satin bikini, trailing ruffled skirt, and exaggerated makeup, pounced upon her. "Dahling!" the creature shrieked in a distinctly male voice, even though it had jutting breasts. "Dahling! Dahling! Dahling!"

Breaking away, she tripped and almost fell. The creature pursued her.

"Go away!" she yelled.

"Be . . . ooo . . . tiful! *Sooo* be . . . oo . . . tiful."

She didn't feel beautiful; she felt nervous. Suddenly all of Jorge's warnings came back to her.

The Carnival is dangerous . . .

Murders . . .

Assaults . . .

Pickpockets everywhere . . .

The thieves wait all year for these few days . . .

And most chilling of all: *Lepers walk the streets during Carnival. . . .*

With a sudden shiver she twisted the huge diamond on her finger so it didn't show, clenching her hand shut.

The creature waved gaily and danced off. Was she being paranoid? How could anything happen to her with all these people around? Resolutely she pressed on, furious with Odile for getting lost and just as furious with herself for allowing it to happen.

An hour later she had no idea where she was. All she could do was wander the crowded streets like a zombie. Hot, tired, despairing. If only she could get a cab, she would throw herself in it and go home. Odile had probably found her way back to the box ages ago, and Jorge, no doubt, had bodyguards combing the city for her. She felt like a fool, as all around her the big street party went on, getting louder and wilder and more out of control.

Men were hitting on her from all sides. She was hearing everything from obscenely suggestive whispers to bold outright come-ons.

Hands reached out to touch as she hurried by.

Stay calm, she told herself. *Don't panic.*

Two men slammed into her, pushing her up against a wall as their rough hands roamed her body.

"Leave me alone," she shouted, bringing her knee up and kicking out as hard as she could.

Right on target. One of the men howled with pain, as the other snatched the gold beads from around her neck, and dragged off her gold hoop earrings.

The man she had kicked suddenly went crazy, his ugly face contorted with rage. "Amerikain feelth!" he roared, just before smashing her in the face with his beringed fist.

She slid to the ground, unconscious.

BOBBY MONDELLA
1983
★ ☆ ★ ☆ ★

"Hiya, Bobby."

"Hey, Sharleen baby, you are lookin' great!"

His words were strictly automatic. She looked terrible, overweight, with bloated features.

Touching her hair, she laughed self-consciously. "Never bullshit a bullshitter. I know what I look like—an' Diana Ross it ain't. I gotta lose a pound or two."

"Hey—she's nothin' but a skinny little thing," he joked, trying to warm her up. "I like a woman with some flesh on her bones."

"I heard you just like women—period."

"That's my life style, baby."

"I also heard you like one special woman a whole lot. An' honey, I am here to tell you it ain't exactly peachy for your health."

They faced each other in his suite at the Helmsley Palace in New York. Sharleen had called and asked if she could come over. He hadn't seen her for two years, and since she was an old friend, he'd said yes. Usually it wasn't that easy to get an audience with Bobby Mondella.

"How about some champagne?" he asked, cradling a glass of bourbon—his constant, soothing companion.

"Why not?" she said, throwing off her fur coat.

With a gesture he summoned one of his bodyguards lurking at the back of the large living room.

"Champagne for Sharleen."

An impassive nod.

"And I'll have another bourbon."

"Bobby, Bobby, Bobby," she singsonged. "You really made it, didn't you?"

"That's kind of an old story," he remarked. There was nothing he hated more than being reminded of his humble beginnings. Nichols was always trying to pull that garbage, until one day he'd told him if he ever mentioned The Chainsaw and how he was a men's room attendant one more time, he would seriously think about switching record companies again.

"You don't wanna discuss old times?" she asked, smoothing her dress down over too-generous curves.

"I don't get off on that. Do you?"

"When I'm feelin' blue I can get a real kick goin' back over it. Y'know, thinkin' 'bout how I'd change things, maybe do it differently."

The bodyguard handed her a glass of champagne and she began to sip the cold bubbly liquid. Bobby noticed her hand was shaking—ever so slightly, but it was still a shake. He'd heard her marriage had broken up and she was still involved with drugs.

Funny. Once Sharleen had been the most important person in the world to him; he would have done anything for her. Now she was just another face from his past—and who needed to be reminded?

"So . . ." he said, hoping she wouldn't stay too long. "And what can I do for you, pretty lady?"

Glancing at the two bodyguards stationed at the back of the room, she said, "Can we talk . . . privately?"

He gestured to the guards. "Come back in ten minutes."

The two burly men left.

"Wow!" she exclaimed sarcastically. "Ten whole minutes. I'm honored."

Ignoring her sarcasm, he said, "Gotta get a lot done before I fly back to L.A."

Glancing around the luxurious suite, she said, "They're sure travelin' you in style."

"Better than Blue Cadillac ever did."

"Blue Cadillac made you the star you are today."

"I could have done it without them," he replied evenly.

"You really think that, huh? I guess you're forgetting that after strugglin' with Soul On Soul for all those years, you were still just another black singer. Marcus Citroen put you where you are today. He *made* you. Surely you gotta admit that?"

"What is this?" he asked restlessly. "A pitch to get me back with Blue Cadillac?"

"No, honey. It's a pitch to get you to stop leanin' on Marcus's wife. He doesn't like it, an' Bobby, I'm warnin' you, you'd better quit, otherwise you're in real trouble."

Was she serious? How dare she come to him with this? "Still keepin' the old man warm at night, huh?" he asked with a mirthless laugh. "You haven't had a hit in two years, I would've thought he'd have dumped you by now. But I guess he figures he can still use you to run his dirty errands, huh?"

Carefully she placed her glass of champagne on the table and reached for her fur coat. "I knew you'd be too stubborn to listen."

"You can tell your fine friend Mr. C.," Bobby said angrily, "to take his warnings an' choke on 'em. You can tell your motherfuckin' *friend* to dance at his own funeral. Because I *don't care*. One of these days Nova's goin' to leave him. An' when she does, I'll be waitin'. An' all the threats in the world ain't gonna change that. So, woman, shift out of here with your man's messages. I don't like bein' threatened. Especially by you."

Brown eyes flashing angrily, she said, "Thank you, Bobby. What a prince! Only thing is—Marcus never sent me, I came on my own, because once—a very long time ago—we were friends, an' I felt I owed you. But, honey, you are one changed person, an' I don't like what I see."

"Shove some more coke up your nose an' tell me what you don't like," he said harshly.

"Hey, man, last night I shoved it all over your girl-friend's pussy while Marcus eyeballed me licking it off. How does *that* grab you?"

"You're a lying bitch!"

"No, I'm not. I may be a doper, but baby, I don't make things up. Nova plays games with people. It's her kick. You'd better remember that's all you are to her—another kick. A big black stud she can control. So don't go gettin' no ideas 'bout how she loves you—'cause, baby—you are on the *wrong* track. She'll *never* leave Marcus, you can bet on it. Only I'm here to tell you—you're pissin' him off, man. So I've warned you, an' that's all I can do."

She slammed her way from the suite.

Goddamn her! Why was she coming to him with her filthy lies?

Maybe Marcus forced her to do it. Yeah. That was it. Marcus wanted to make Nova look bad, and what better way than to have Sharleen say she was rolling around on the bed making out with Nova.

Angrily he picked up the phone and called Nova on her private line.

"Hello." She sounded guarded.

"It's me," he said.

Her voice was brisk and to the point. "I can't talk now. My dressmaker is here."

"One question."

A testy "Yes?"

"What did you do last night?"

341

"I told you yesterday. We had a business dinner at Le Cirque."

"Who with?"

"Several people."

"Was Sharleen one of them?"

A pause. "I think so."

"You *think* so. Either she was there or she wasn't."

"Yes, she was there. Why?" Nova asked curiously.

Was she licking your pussy while Marcus watched? He didn't believe it. Not for a moment.

"Hey—it's not important. I'll see you at our usual place."

"Five o'clock?"

"You got it."

Hanging up the phone, he wondered how he could have ever doubted her. Sure Sharleen was there. Why not? She was still a Blue Cadillac star, even if a slightly tarnished one.

As soon as the moment was right, Nova had promised she was going to leave Marcus. "Don't force me into a corner," she'd said. "You have to let me do it my way."

True, he was still waiting after giving her an ultimatum two years ago, but what choice did he have, other than giving her up? And he couldn't do that.

They still saw each other as often as possible. In Los Angeles they met at the secret beach house, and in New York at a small apartment he'd rented under an assumed name in a discreet building off Madison Avenue.

Arriving at the apartment ten minutes before five, he was there before her. Time to fix himself a drink and put on some music. Today he chose Teddy Pendergrass.

Nova appeared promptly at five o'clock wearing a belted mink coat, dark glasses and a headscarf.

"I wish you wouldn't call me at home," was her opening line. "Staff gossip, you know. I can't trust anyone."

He hadn't seen her in six weeks. Her greeting could have been warmer.

Walking into the bedroom, she started unbelting her coat, throwing it onto the bed. And then she began unzipping her dress.

They did have a very sexual relationship. But was that all it was—sex?

"Hey—hold it a minute," he said.

"I have exactly one hour," she replied crisply.

Sharleen's words taunted him: *That's all you are to her —another kick. A big black stud she can control.* "How's the move going?" he asked.

Stepping out of her dress, she said, "What move?"

"Your move out of Marcus's life an' into mine," he said tightly.

"I'm working on it."

"You're always workin' on it, babe. The thing is, I can't understand why it's takin' you so long. It's not like you have kids to think about."

"Ah, but we do have property, and I want to make sure I walk away with my fair share."

"*I* can give you everything you'll ever need. How many times do I have to tell you that?"

Reaching toward him, she fiddled with his belt, softening her tone. "Let's go to bed, Bobby, I've missed you."

He moved away from her. "Nova, I'm not in the mood."

She laughed disbelievingly. "You're always in the mood."

How come she sounded so sure of herself? Was he that easy? "I am?" he asked coldly.

Confidently she tugged at his belt. "You certainly are."

Drawing even farther away from her, he said, "Today I want to talk."

About to argue, she changed her mind and sat down on the side of the bed, primly crossing her legs clad in sheer black stockings fastened by a lace garter belt. "Go ahead," she said in a resigned voice.

"I think"— his words were measured—"that you're givin' me a runaround."

She tapped her long, scarlet nails on the side of the bed. "Really?"

"Yes, really. Because I can't see why it's takin' you all this time to leave Marcus."

"Hmmm . . ."

"What's that supposed to mean?"

"It means," she said with a slight pause, "I'll do it when I can."

Switching the subject, all the better to catch her off guard, he said, "Were you in bed with Sharleen last night? Was Marcus watchin' the two of you?"

The look of guilty surprise that swept across her face told him everything he needed to know.

"Aw, shit," he said wearily. "You never had any intention of leavin' him, did you?"

Recovering her composure, she said, "There are things I do with Marcus that mean nothing. Last night was one of them." She paused. "With you, it's different."

Bitterly he said, "Sure."

"I told you once, and you refused to listen to me. If I ever left Marcus he'd have us both killed. He can do it, you know. He can arrange anything."

This was all getting to be too much. "Nova, put your clothes on an' go home. I've just about had it with you."

For once in her life she looked vulnerable, the veneer of sophistication stripped away. "I was only protecting us, Bobby."

"Yeah, I bet."

"One day perhaps you'll understand."

"Goodbye, baby, goodbye."

KRIS PHOENIX
1983

★ ☆ ★ ☆ ★

For three weeks Kris kept vigil in the hospital while his son lay in a deep coma. Willow and he put their differences aside and sat by the child's bedside day and night, until one afternoon—miraculously—Bo's eyes fluttered open and he said, "Hello, Dad."

Willow burst into tears. Kris put his arms around her, cradling her sadness and joy with a great deal of tenderness. It had taken an almost-tragedy for both to realize how unimportant it was to bicker and fight over minor things, when all that really mattered was their son's well-being.

"You can take him away with you to France," Willow offered. "Twice a year if you like. I'm sure he'd love to spend his holidays with you."

"And I'll try to visit him more," Kris promised.

"He adores seeing you," she admitted. "He's very proud of his famous dad."

They were now okay together; however, their families remained a pain, fussing around, full of unwanted advice. Avis insisted the accident was the fault of Willow's mother, with whom the boy had been staying at the time.

"How *dare* that dreadful woman accuse me," Mrs. Wigh screamed, when she heard what Avis was saying.

"Who's that old bat calling a dreadful woman?" yelled Avis.

It became the battle of the grandmothers.

Kris couldn't hang around to watch. Bo was out of the hospital in time for him to take off to do the Australian concerts—The Wild Ones' last stand. Buzz hadn't changed his mind about leaving, and in a way it was a relief. Working with him was like working next to a pressure cooker—any moment he could blow.

Doktor Head had negotiated some kind of record-breaking deal for them to appear down under. It was a fitting finale to fourteen years of madness.

Their opening concert in Melbourne almost caused riots. The fans were out in force, blocking the streets, charging the Festival Hall, where they were due to appear, holding aloft banners proclaiming

WE LOVE YOU KRIS!

THE WILD ONES FOREVER

BUZZ BUZZ BUZZ!

Locked in their suites at the Rockman Regency Hotel, they gave interviews and partied with the local so-called "in" group.

Buzz and Mikki declined any invitations. Instead they contacted their friendly neighborhood drug dealer and spent all their time in a vague stupor.

Onstage Kris found himself covering up for Buzz more and more. He was glad it would soon be over.

After two days in Melbourne they flew to Sydney, where it was more of the same.

Kris complained hotly. "I've come halfway round the bleedin' world, an' all I've seen of Australia is the inside of a hotel room."

Doktor Head suggested he try to disguise himself, and then maybe he could go on a short sightseeing trip.

With the help of the daughter of their Australian tour promoter, they dressed him up as a girl, replete with long blond wig, granny glasses, and a dirndl skirt.

"You're the ugliest bird I've ever seen," choked Doktor Head, spluttering with laughter. "I wouldn't want to cut *your* hair!"

"Get fucked. You're just jealous," Kris said, smearing on a liberal amount of bright-red lipstick.

"Yeah, especially of your hairy legs. Nice touch, that."

The disguise worked, and he got to see Sydney—a beautiful city. In the morning they took a water-taxi around the harbor, admiring the modern architecture of the all-white Opera House. Then the taxi dropped them off in Watsons Bay, where they lunched at Doyle's, an open-air restaurant situated next to the water, with delicious seafood and a friendly ambience.

"This is more like it," Kris said, sitting back and enjoying the freedom for a change.

"Give us a kiss, darlin'," joked Doktor Head. "You're looking better every minute!"

That night, their concert at the Horden Pavilion was another riotous success. Afterward, Kris was tracked backstage by a beautiful, if somewhat older, French ex-movie star, who was traveling the world compiling a book of photographs. She wore a gold-sequinned dress and clutched a Nikon camera close to her voluptuous cleavage. "I weel photograph you, no?" she asked, after her manager had inveigled a yes out of him.

"Sure," he agreed. "Only not here, luv. You'd better come back to the hotel. There's a party."

There was always a party. It was the rock & roll life. Booze, girls, drugs, food, music. Everything on tap. If you want something—just ask. For a star nothing is too much trouble.

The French ex-movie star took a few photographs. She had once been a great beauty—a world-class sex symbol.

Kris could remember seeing her in movies when he was a kid. At thirteen he'd really lusted after those huge tits. They still looked in pretty good nick to him, although she had to be close to his mother's age.

After a while she asked, "Can we be more—how you say?—preevit?"

"Private," he corrected.

"No?"

"Yeah, okay."

They went to his suite, where she took a roll of film of him lounging on the couch. Then she asked if he would mind removing his shirt.

She was beginning to get him going. He kept on thinking of this one film he'd seen her in where she'd played a slave girl, and she'd had this little pearl in her navel, and, oh, shit . . . here came the old trouser puppet, alert and ready to play "You show me yours and I'll show you mine."

She was no slouch in the noticing-what-was-going-on department. Putting down her camera, she undulated toward him, placed her arms around his neck, and planted the biggest, wettest kiss he had ever experienced on his hardly unwilling lips.

They indulged in erotic tongue play for a few moments, until he decided enough was enough, and slid his hands between flesh and gold sequins, peeling the top of her dress down, and flipping as much of her breasts as he could over the top of a tight corselette.

She had the biggest nipples he'd ever seen atop her magnificent bosom. Large, ripe, peaked cherries. He couldn't decide what to do first—unzip himself and get some well-needed freedom; try to figure out how to ooze her out of the corselette contraption; or place those delectable cherries right into his mouth where they belonged.

Before he could make up his mind, it was all over. There was a wild, familiar throb in his pants, and to his eternal humiliation Kris Phoenix, rock star supreme, came in his pants. "Je . . . sus!" he exclaimed. "I don't believe it!"

The French ex-movie star smiled comfortingly, as if this mishap was an everyday occurrence—and around her, it probably was. "Now we do eet properly," she said, reaching behind her back to deal with hooks and eyes and God knows what else was keeping the gold dress up. "We go in zee bedroom, no?"

"Yes," he mumbled, feeling about fourteen. What a berk! He'd better make up for it or his reputation was shot to hell.

"I'll be right back, darlin'. Don't go away," he said, diving into the bathroom, stripping off his clothes, and throwing himself under a quick shower.

Once, when he was a teenager, he'd sent away for some kind of erection cream he'd seen advertised in a nudie magazine. It was called "Stiff Stuff," and the instructions were to rub it on your cock just before making love. It promised hours of uninterrupted pleasure. He'd been over at this girl's house ready for action. Her parents were out, and they'd started to neck. When the time was right, he'd run into the bathroom, pulled out his tube of Stiff Stuff and rubbed it on. Two seconds later he came all over the bathroom floor. Wonderful!

In a funny way, this reminded him of that night.

When he returned she was lying across the rumpled bed, the top sheet carefully arranged as if she were preparing for a pinup session. Her breasts were covered, but one leg emerged from the sheet in a delicate pose.

He was naked, everything on show, and why not?—he certainly had nothing to hide.

"Beeg!" she exclaimed admiringly, which of course made him even bigger.

Without further ado he jumped on top of her, pulling the sheet away, exposing prime French ex-movie-star skin.

Stripped of gold sequins, she was pleasantly rounded,

completely unlike his usual bed companions, whom he liked long and lean—although large breasts were generally an essential part of the package.

Making love to her was all flesh and pulsating sensuality. After Daphne Darke, Buzz's mum, she was his second older woman, and he wasn't complaining. It was a bit like pigging out on a lusciously rich ice-cream sundae. You wouldn't want to do it all the time, but oh, boy, was it good while it lasted!

Arriving back in New York to do a week of promotion on the new album, the shit really hit. Buzz was arrested at the airport for possession of heroin. Fingers publicly declared herself a lesbian. And Rasta was slapped with two paternity suits—both by white girls.

It was the end of The Wild Ones. The end of an era.

Kris didn't regret it one bit.

RAFEALLA
1983

★ ☆ ★ ☆ ★

Drifting in and out of consciousness, Rafealla was vaguely aware of the sound of voices—murmurs from another world. Her eyelids fluttered, and she made a half-hearted attempt to open her eyes. She couldn't do it. Why should she?

"Why should I?" she mumbled. And then she groaned, for there was a sharp, stabbing pain on her left cheek. Instinctively her hand reached up and felt a soggy bandage. With a supreme effort she opened her eyes.

A woman dressed in white peered down at her.

She couldn't remember a thing. Where was she? What happened? Why wasn't she at home in bed?

"Have I been in a car accident?" she asked, very slowly. Her lips were dry and her voice sounded more like a frog's croak.

"You were robbed and beaten," a male voice said. A disturbingly familiar male voice.

Luiz! Was it Luiz? Quickly she tried to sit up, but the room took off, an alarming kaleidoscope of flashing colors. Sinking back down, she asked, "Where am I?"

"In a bar. The back room. Some people carried you in here for safety."

She was drifting. "Luiz? Is that you?" she whispered. "Luiz . . ."

The next time she woke up she was in a hospital room, all pristine white, with the smell of antiseptic in the air. Once again she was completely disoriented. She lay with her eyes wide open trying to figure out what had happened.

"Thank God you're all right, my darling," Jorge said, looming over her. "It was a nightmare." He clutched her hand. "We were so desperately worried."

Gradually it all began to come back. Carnival. Carnival. Carnival. Ah . . . and she and Odile out on the street, laughing, dancing.

"Odile," she mumbled anxiously. "What happened to her?"

"She's fine," Jorge assured her. "Repentant, naturally, but much better once you were found."

"Found? Where was I?"

"On the street where those animals left you."

"On the street . . ." she repeated vaguely, becoming aware of a pounding, relentless headache and a painful throb down one side of her face. Automatically her hand reached up and touched the bandages covering her cheek. "I thought I was in a bar."

"A bar? What are you talking about?"

"They carried me into the bar . . . for safety."

He bent to kiss her. "Darling, you're still groggy—understandably so. You were found on the street by some American tourists. They brought you straight here."

Closing her eyes, she thought, *Luiz. What about Luiz?* Was it a dream? Had she just imagined his voice?

"You're badly bruised," Jorge continued, matter-of-factly. "And your face is cut—nothing that a touch of plastic surgery can't take care of when the time comes. My own personal physician will visit you later; meanwhile, the doctors here feel you should stay in the hospital for a few days of observation, just in case."

She tried to nod, couldn't quite make it, and drifted back into a deep sleep.

"Good morning, Miss Le Serre." So spoke a crisp nurse in a virgin-white uniform. "You slept through the night. I am sure you are feeling better this morning."

She might be sure, but Rafealla felt like she had the world's worst hangover. However, as soon as she opened her eyes she was functioning, which was an improvement.

"I want to go home," she said groggily.

"We'll see," replied the nurse, with an officious toss of her head.

An hour later Rafealla had her wish. Jorge and Odile came to fetch her, and soon she was settled in her own bed, with Jon Jon playing happily nearby.

Odile sat with her, while Jorge, having plied her with dozens of pink roses, went off to his office.

"Sorry," Odile said, in a small voice.

"Don't be silly. It was just as much *my* fault. I *wanted* to hit the streets, you didn't force me."

"How's your face?"

"I'll live—it's just a scratch. The creep who bashed me apparently had a pinky ring which cut my cheek open. Jorge is talking plastic surgery, but I rather like the idea of a small scar. It's mysterious, don't you think?"

"Certainly not. Who wants to be reminded? You could have been killed."

"For what? A pair of earrings and a necklace? You know, they really were a couple of inept jerks—they didn't even look at my fingers." She held up her hand, staring at the huge ring Jorge had presented her with. "My diamond is intact."

"That's good."

"It doesn't really matter, does it? Jorge could buy me dozens of these and not even feel the pinch."

"Lucky you. A far better situation than Eddie Mafair, sponging off your family and gambling it all away."

"I guess."

Odile, curled up at the edge of the bed, hugged her knees and said, "Well, we'll soon be off, and I've made Rupert promise me faithfully that we'll come back for your wedding. Have you decided on a date yet?"

Rafealla shook her head. "Jorge and I will discuss it. Naturally, as soon as we decide, you'll be the first to know. Isn't it always that way?"

Odile smiled. "I hope so. I'd hate to be left out."

Two weeks later the drama of the Carnival was forgotten. Only the scar on her cheek reminded Rafealla that during one moment of violence her life might have been over. It made her think very carefully about her future, and what she really wanted. Her one great achievement had been giving birth to Jon Jon. No big deal, millions of women had babies every day. Was she just going to marry a rich man and settle into a life of safe, secure luxury? For Jorge continued to press about a date for their wedding, even though she had told him she thought they should wait.

No. She had to try to achieve something on her own before committing to marriage again.

Every day she woke up with a renewed sense of determination and vigor, until one day it came to her: What was she really good at? What did she honestly love to do?

"Jorge," she said very quietly, "I've decided I'm going to try a career as a singer."

He was barely awake. "I beg your pardon?"

"A singer," she repeated slowly. "As in 'entertainer.'"

He struggled to sit up. "Are you feeling all right?"

"Perfectly fine."

Deciding to humor her, he said, "If it amuses you, my darling, you can do whatever you wish."

She frowned. "I wasn't asking your permission."

"I realize that. I was merely giving you my blessing."

Sometimes Jorge turned into that rare commodity, an understanding man. It hadn't always been that way—he had mellowed as the years passed.

The months that followed were exciting. Now that she'd made up her mind to do something, there was no way she could be swayed. A singing career was the perfect choice. In a way it brought her closer to her father. He'd been one of the most famous operatic tenors in the world, and maybe she'd inherited some of his talent, although opera wasn't her style—she was drawn more toward the soft, lilting sounds of samba, with an infusion of mellow jazz.

Her father had been an avid collector of blues and jazz records. His particular favorites had been Billie Holiday, Dinah Washington, and Sarah Vaughn. Rafealla had inherited his collection, and had always been attracted to the rich, melancholy sounds of their voices. She didn't care for the heavy metal, rock, or punk influences of today, finding them too hard-edged. The Brazilian flavor combined with soothing jazz and blues suited her nicely. And it also fitted her low, smoky voice to perfection.

Jorge wanted to help her, but she'd told him up front she did not require his assistance. If she was going to achieve anything it had to be on her own or not at all; so, reluctantly, he stood back, allowing her to do things her way.

At twenty-three, Rafealla embarked on a career. She was determined to succeed.

BOBBY MONDELLA
1983

★ ☆ ★ ☆ ★

They were sitting around in Nichols Kline's Century City penthouse office when Bobby reached over and poured himself another bourbon.

"You're drinkin' too much," Nichols said bluntly. He was the only one who dared talk to him that way. Everyone else kissed ass.

"Gee. Sue me," Bobby said sarcastically.

"Take a look in the mirror," Nichols pressed. "You got sleepin' bags under your bloodshot eyes a Boy Scout group could camp out in."

"Very funny, man."

"And you're gettin' a gut."

"Tough shit. Nobody said I had t'be perfect."

Nichols leaned back in his custom-made leather chair. "For the Leibovitz photo session you've got to be. The cover of *Rolling Stone* still means plenty."

"Big fuckin' deal. I don't need it," Bobby replied confidently.

Bobby Mondella, Nichols decided, was beginning to believe his own publicity. "A cover on *Rolling Stone* you always need, and don't you forget it."

"Yeah, where's it written?" Bobby challenged.

"In small print. On your ass."

"You're turnin' into a comedian, Nichols."

"An' you're turnin' into an asshole."

It occurred to Bobby that he didn't have to take this kind of disrespectful shit—not from anyone. It was bad enough Nova was still giving him a runaround. Why should he let Nichols get away with talking down to him?

"Hey—" he said threateningly. "You want me to split from Hit City—keep on needlin' me an' you got it, man. I can walk into Warners, Motown, any place I want. They'd get down on their fuckin' knees to have me."

"Really?" Nichols asked snidely.

"You'd better believe it."

"You can't walk, Bobby," Nichols said, his tone hardening. "You belong to Hit City. You can't walk anywhere." He paused, allowing his words to sink in. "Which reminds me—Carmine's comin' to town for his goddaughter's twenty-first birthday party. He's requested that you sing."

Bobby frowned. "What are you talkin' about?"

"Sing. Entertain. Make nice to his friends."

"Are you shittin' me? I gave up weddin's and bar mitzvahs a long time ago."

"This is a favor. A very personal favor for Carmine. He owns most of the company, you know. So I suggest you take it seriously."

Bobby walked to the window, staring out at the view. He could see the apartment building he used to live in—the same apartment where Nova first came on to him. "Why's that?" he asked, not really interested in Nichols's reply, because he had no intention of singing at anyone's twenty-first birthday.

Nichols pressed his fingers together, forming a dome. "Have you ever studied your contract? Like I mean looked into the small print? I'm sure you're aware that when Hit City bought you out of Blue Cadillac you signed yourself into a new deal—right?"

357

Bobby nodded.

"A dynamite deal with everything you ever wanted, huh?"

"What is this—rerun time?"

"No. Just a reminder. Hit City is owned by Arnie Torterelli, Carmine Sicily, and a syndicate of investors. I have a piece of the action—naturally."

"So what the fuck are you gettin' at, Nichols? Don't be shy. Spit it out."

"Check your contract. If Carmine or Arnie don't want you to work for ten years, there's not a damn thing you can do about it. Because *this* contract is unbreakable. There's *no* gettin' out unless we say so." A meaningful pause. "If I was you, I wouldn't make Carmine mad. Keep things nice an' smooth, know what I mean, Bobby?"

He didn't answer. Instead he studied Nichols Kline, sitting behind his desk so full of his own importance, and he tried to decide whether the jerkoff was actually *threatening* him.

No. He was too big to be threatened by anyone.

"The party is next Saturday," Nichols said mildly. "How about it?"

It started with one simple twenty-first-birthday party. A favor. For Carmine Sicily. He did it, why not? It was better than getting into a hassle.

And then there was Arnie Torterelli's parents' wedding anniversary in Florida. They made it very easy for him. A private jet, the whole bit.

A week in Las Vegas at the Mirage Hotel he fought against. "I'm not a Vegas performer," he insisted. "Get Lionel Ritchie or Jefferson Lionacre."

"They want *you*," Nichols insisted. "They'll pay whatever we ask." And then the ominous words, "It's a favor for Carmine. He's promised you'll do it, you can't let him down."

Bobby felt like he was living two lives. On the one hand he was this enormous superstar. And on the other—every time the word "favor" was whispered, he was expected to jump.

Nichols Kline had turned out to be right. His contract *was* unbreakable. Professionally he was completely in Kline's hands. When he consulted a sharp, independent lawyer, the man said, "There's only one way you can break *this* contract. Kill yourself."

Very funny.

He raged at himself for having been so stupid. Money and artistic control had led him into the biggest trap of his life. The favor trap. He was their pet superstar, wheeled out for weddings, birthdays, and anniversaries.

He hadn't seen Nova in months and he missed her. Not that she cared. If she did she would have contacted him. When he'd told her goodbye at their last meeting she'd obviously taken him at his word. For compensation he moved Zella Raven into his house. Zella, the amazon. It was better than sleeping with a different girl every night. It was better than being alone.

Hey—he was a star—what did anything matter? As long as he had lots of money to throw around, an entourage of yes people, plenty of booze, and the more than occasional snort of cocaine—what did *anything* matter?

Bobby Mondella was a superstar. That was the bottom line. And the bottom line was all that counted.

1987
Saturday, July 11th

★ ☆ ★ ☆ ★

"I don't know why I couldn't go to the press conference with you," Cybil complained. "You know, Kris, sometimes you act like you're ashamed of me."

"Don't be daft."

"It's true. You never include me in anything that's important to you."

"Sure I do."

"Like what?" she demanded belligerently.

"The Song for Food gig. I took you with me."

"Big deal. The world was at that."

"It was a very special session."

"I know. So special that I got completely left out. I was hanging around like some kind of—" she gulped, hardly able to say the word— "groupie!"

"C'mon, luv." He touched her hair. "Nobody would mistake *you* for a groupie."

She had been saving the next bit of information, knowing it would aggravate him. "Well, Del Delgardo did."

"Did what?"

"Thought I was a groupie. I was so humiliated."

She'd aroused his interest. "When?"

"At the Song for Food recording session."

"What did the bastard do?"

"He came on . . . you know."

She was just trying to get him going. Why was he falling for it? "You're probably imagining it," he said, dismissing her accusation.

"Kris," she replied in a hurt voice, "I do know a come-on when I see one. He asked me back to his house for a party, like I was just some cheap little bimbo standing around waiting for him to notice me. When I told him I was with you, he laughed."

"Laughed, did he?"

"Don't you care?"

"I've got more important things on my mind right now."

"Like what?"

"Like gettin' this bleedin' gig over an' done with, an' gettin' the hell out of here."

As the start of the evening's gala drew closer, things were heating up. The chefs were busily preparing hundreds of tantalizing appetizers for the early part of the event, and screaming at any waiter they could catch. The tables were set with pale-pink cloths, fine silverware, and an assortment of crystal stemware. Waiters and busboys were diligently placing the centerpiece flower arrangements and slender pale-lilac candles.

Soon the guests would be arriving and gathering on the tented tennis court, where they would sip cocktails and nibble on elaborate hors d'oeuvres before sitting down to dinner.

"You!" One of the chefs caught Maxwell's attention with an authoritative snap of his fingers. "Take this tray over to the guest house for Bobby Mondella. Make it quick."

"Where's the guest house?" Maxwell asked blankly, although he knew perfectly well.

"Ask someone else," yelled the chef. "Can't you see I'm busy?"

Maxwell took the tray. On it was a covered dish, under which was a plain omelet with an accompanying order of crisp french fries. Balancing it on one hand, he headed in the wrong direction. A uniformed guard stopped him. "Where are you going?"

"Delivering an order for Bobby Mondella."

The guard said, "Wait a minute," and consulted a special map. "The big guest house. Take one of those golf carts over there. Follow the main path all the way past the swimming pool and you can't miss it."

"Thanks," said Maxwell, thinking that a golf cart in his possession was exactly what he needed. Placing the tray on the passenger seat, he got behind the wheel. This was probably going to be the last errand he would ever have to run.

Trudie was dying to ask Rafealla what the deal was, but she didn't quite dare. It wasn't like they were girlfriends or anything. Rafealla was the star, and Trudie merely publicity. They had common ground—but it didn't include the true scam on Marcus Citroen.

Trudie would give anything to know the real story. She'd worked at Blue Cadillac for five years and heard *the* most outrageous stories about her boss. Maybe Rafealla could enlighten her.

"Uh . . . how long have you known Marcus Citroen?" she asked, on the way back from the pressroom. It was worth a shot.

Rafealla blanked her with a look, ignoring the question, and saying instead, "Are you pleased with how everything went in there?"

"Considering you weren't prepared, I thought you were brilliant," Trudie replied. "Especially the way you handled that English bitch, Cyndi Lou whatshername."

"Thank you. I've come up against her before. There's no

point in answering her questions, she's already decided what she's going to write."

"One of the guys was telling me she gave Kris Phoenix a hard time. Do you know him?"

An innocent enough question. Did she know him? No, she didn't know him at all. But she did have his son. God! What a secret to live with. *Her* secret, for she had never told another soul.

She wondered if they would come face to face tonight, and shivered. "I'm hungry," she said. "Do you think we can get something to eat?"

Rafealla had a disconcerting habit of not answering direct questions. Trudie was becoming quite used to it. "In this place? Are you kidding me? I think we can get anything we damn well please."

"What the fuck took ya so long?" Speed demanded, a nervous tic dominating the left side of his face.

The lawyer stared at him coldly. Clients like this he could do without. He would most certainly charge an exorbitant fee.

"I got here as soon as I could."

"Don't jerk me around, ya took ya freakin' time."

"I'm here. You're out. That's good enough, isn't it?"

"Fuckin' lawyers," Speed mumbled under his breath, as they both left the police station.

He'd rehearsed. He'd run the gamut of the press, and now he just wanted to take it easy before performing.

"Sara, babe," he said, "I'd like to be by myself awhile. Do you mind?"

"Not at all," she said brightly, although of course she did. It hurt her when he shut himself away. She was happy to be in his company twenty-four hours a day. Why couldn't he feel the same?

"Shall I come back in an hour?" she asked.

"Yeah, that'll be fine."

"Maybe I should wait until your omelet arrives."

"I can handle it."

"There's a small table next to the door with a bowl of flowers on it. If you walk over, be careful—"

"I *said* I can handle it," he interrupted, aggravated by her fussing.

"I know, I know."

"Then get the hell out." His tone was joking, but she knew him well enough to exit fast.

He felt her absence by the silence. People didn't have to speak when they were in a room with him. He always knew they were there by the sound of their breathing.

Getting up, he made a tour of the room, leading with his hands. Once Sara had suggested he use a white stick. "Never!" he'd told her vehemently; he also rejected the idea of a Seeing Eye dog—not that he disliked animals, it was just that he had to be responsible for his own safety, he wanted no props.

A knock on the door heralded the arrival of the food he'd ordered.

"Come in," he said, groping his way to the couch.

Her perfume reached him first, the rich, sensual, unmistakable Nova Citroen musk.

He'd known instinctively that once he'd got rid of Sara, she would come.

"Hello, Nova," he said quietly.

"What's your name, honey?"

The sudden influx of able-bodied men to Novaroen had Vicki in hot demand. For weeks all she'd seen were Mexican gardeners, a few gay housemen, plus Tom and his merry band of security heavies. Now the place was crawling with out-of-work actors, male models, and the like, all doing double duty as waiters. And a good-looking bunch they were too. The barmen weren't bad either.

Vicki decided if a girl wasn't working she could have a real peachy time.

"Don't you worry 'bout my name, sailor," she said sassily, fixing the waiter who was coming on to her with a flirtatious look. He had a yellow cowlick and a body that would have fitted nicely into Chippendale's. "Just get on with what *you're* supposed to be doing."

"Talkin' of gettin' it on—" He winked suggestively.

"Forget it," she replied shortly.

"You can't blame a guy for tryin'."

Maybe she didn't look as bad as she thought. Tom certainly had the idea she was Marilyn Monroe back in business.

Moving right along, she walked back toward the main house, where Mrs. Ivors, the Joan Crawford housekeeper, waited impatiently.

"Go over to the guest house," Mrs. Ivors ordered. "And stay there until further notice. If any of the celebrity guests need anything at all, see they get it. I may as well warn you, Mrs. Citroen will fire anyone who is caught not doing their job tonight. That is official. Do you understand?"

Vicki bobbed her head. "Yes, ma'am. I'll make sure I do my job *real* good!"

Marcus Citroen could be the most charming man in the world when he wanted to. Smooth, knowledgeable, a man of taste and money. Most women found him attractive, even though he was not good-looking in the traditional sense. With his bald, egg-shaped head, dark-hued skin, and hooded eyes, he had the look of a Middle Eastern potentate. Power was his main attraction. It radiated from him, drawing people toward him like a magnet—especially women. And Marcus was used to women being available at his command. Like Sharleen, who'd needed him to guide her career. From the very beginning she'd understood the game. And he'd made her a star. It wasn't as if he'd used her and not done as he'd promised.

Rafealla was something else. She was an obsessive challenge, and he looked forward to breaking her in.

Nova had always understood the game—far better than anyone else. In her own peculiar way, Nova was the female equivalent of him—which was why they were irrevocably tied together, sexually and otherwise.

As far as Marcus was concerned, most women were dispensable. When they played their role correctly he kept them around. When they didn't, he discarded them without a second thought.

Over the years Nova had come close, very close. But she'd always known when to draw the line.

Tonight was a testing time. He wanted to see if she had learned her lesson.

He had to make absolutely sure.

KRIS PHOENIX
1984

★ ☆ ★ ☆ ★

They were shooting the third video from his first solo album, *Erotic,* on the grounds of Novaroen.

"Bloody hell!" Kris exclaimed. "This is some place!"

Doktor Head nodded his agreement.

"I wouldn't mind movin' in," Kris joked.

"Put in an offer."

"Ha ha!"

A trio of girls in extremely brief bikinis paraded past. They were extras, hired for background. Once Kris would have had them, one by one, but not now that he was older and wiser and living in a world where AIDS was the killer everyone feared.

He sat back in his canvas chair with his name stenciled on it, and merely watched.

"Hi, Kris," one of them said boldly, with a cute little wave.

"Hello, darlin'," he replied, though he had no idea who she was.

"Watch out," Doktor Head muttered. "Here comes the lady of the house. Make nice, she runs the show."

Kris stood up. He had heard plenty about the alluring Mrs. Citroen and was interested in meeting her.

She walked briskly toward them, cool in linen slacks and a silk shirt, her white-blond hair a startling contrast to her lightly tanned skin.

"Mr. Phoenix," she said graciously. "What a pleasure to meet you. And belated congratulations on joining Blue Cadillac. I've just returned from Europe. Now that I'm back, I'd love to give a dinner for you."

"Sounds great."

"Tuesday?" she questioned.

"That's good for me."

Doktor Head rose also, a fierce sight with his wild mass of flaming red hair and messy beard. "Madame," he said politely. "I'm Doktor Head. The manager."

She raised a cynical eyebrow. "Doktor . . . *Head?*"

"A strange name, I know. Bestowed on me many moons ago. But fitting, I can assure you."

Kris had never seen Doktor Head grovel before. He tried not to laugh.

Nova didn't seem to find him particularly amusing. Dismissing him with a perfunctory nod, she turned back to Kris. "Where are you staying?"

"The Westwood Marquis."

"I'll send a car for you. Seven-thirty on Tuesday. Casual. Will you have a young lady with you, or shall I arrange a selection?"

It sounded as if she were talking about a box of chocolates! "I'll be alone," he said.

She smiled. "In that case I'll put together an interesting group. Seven-thirty. Don't forget. Oh, and please enjoy yourself today—if there is anything you need—anything at all, don't hesitate to ask."

She strolled over to talk to the director, a young hotshot who knocked off videos in between making hugely successful feature films.

"And what exactly am I? Chopped liver?" demanded

Doktor Head, twitching and winking overtime. "Why didn't you tell her to invite *me?*"

"Because I hardly reckoned it was your kind of deal."

"Oh, and I suppose it's yours?"

"I can go to a dinner party without you comin' along to hold my hand, can't I? It was bad enough when I had the whole mob to think about."

The second assistant hurried over. "Mr. Phoenix, we're ready for you now."

In just over a year he'd made it on his own. Thank God he'd listened when Mikki told him all that time ago to tag his name onto the front of The Wild Ones. When they split, everyone knew who he was—there was no great identity crisis. The other three had not been so lucky. Buzz was deported from America and stormed back to England with Mikki in tow, where he'd eventually formed a new group called Mania. They'd disbanded after six months, and Buzz occasionally did gigs on his own.

Rasta was keeping a low profile while he fought his two paternity suits.

And Fingers had become a sort of underground cult figure.

The main problems had been sorting out the legal hassles involved with breaking up a successful group. Kris had taken Doktor Head's advice and hired the best lawyers to look after his interests. Meanwhile, he'd gone to his house in France, with Bo and an au pair girl.

It was a soothing transition period. After all, he'd been twelve years on the road on and off, with hardly a break. During that time The Wild Ones had become public property, and their lives reflected that. Not to have any commitments was sheer bliss.

While Bo was staying with him they spent all their time together, swimming, going out on the powerful Riva he'd bought, snorkeling, and water-skiing—which they both learned to do together. At the end of three weeks he felt a lot closer to his son, and more at peace with himself because of it. Then, like a fool, he shattered everything by inviting his mum to come for a visit.

"Can I bring Brian and 'is family?" she pleaded. The brothers were talking again since Bo's accident.

"Why?"

"It's all right fer you, lad. You've got everyfing. Brian 'asn't. Brian packed in 'is job, 'e *needs* a holiday."

Some holiday. Brian arrived, more pompous than ever, complete with Jennifer—who had turned into the stereotype of a nagging wife—and their two whining kids. He wasted no time in launching straight into his pitch. "I've left the bank, as you already know," he said imperiously. "And I've been thinking, now that you're on your own, you need new management."

"I'm stickin' with Doktor Head."

"No, no. You should have new representation. I've decided to help you out."

"What are you *talkin'* about?"

"I'll be your manager," Brian announced magnanimously.

Kris doubled over laughing. "You?" he exploded with mirth. "Fuck me!"

"Naturally," Brian said, ignoring his brother's outburst, "it's a sacrifice on my part. But I decided blood is blood. Who can run your affairs better than me?"

"Jesus Christ! You've really flipped, haven't you?"

"Obviously I'll need to learn a thing or two about the music business. But working in a bank for the last nine years, I certainly know how to deal with people."

"Leave it out, mate. I'll bust a gut laughin' if you keep this up."

Brian was affronted because Kris didn't jump at his offer. He complained to Avis, who in turn complained to her youngest son. "If yer can't give yer own brovver a job, I don't know what," she said huffily.

They accepted his hospitality for two weeks, and then returned to England, not a moment too soon as far as he was concerned. He later heard from one of his sisters that Brian was claiming Kris had *asked* him to leave his job to come and work for him and had then changed his mind. Now he was the family villain. Charming!

Finally, when everyone, including Bo, was gone and he was alone, he started to write, composing the words and music for several new songs.

Things were going so well that he wanted to share them with someone. One day he thought of Astrid, tracked her down, and called her in Paris. "You still engaged?" he asked.

"Yes," she replied.

"I need some pants."

"I'll mail them to you. What color?"

"No good. I've put on a pound or two. I'll have to get a fitting."

"Really?"

"No kidding. I'm in the south of France. Can you fly down?"

A long thoughtful pause. "Okay."

"I'll send you a ticket. Bring a bikini."

"I can't stay."

"Bring a bikini anyway. You've got time for a swim, haven't you?"

She arrived for a day and spent the summer. They'd been together ever since. Right now she was in London keeping the Grosvenor Square flat warm and overseeing the renovations to the country house he'd bought.

Astrid was a calming influence. It was nice to have someone to confide in and share things with. She was also a right little raver in bed, once he finally got her there.

The breakup of The Wild Ones made worldwide headlines and caused a lot of heartbreak for their legions of fans. Kris refused to give interviews or talk about it, and when intrepid reporters turned up on his doorstep in France, they were turned away.

One weekend Doktor Head arrived with news of a solo deal he was negotiating with Blue Cadillac.

"I don't want to get caught into anything long term," Kris warned. "Just make it for one album an' I'll see if I'm happy."

He was happy. *Erotic* was his first album with Blue Cadillac, and it was a smash—not only a huge commercial success but critically acclaimed also.

Yes, Kris Phoenix was extremely happy indeed.

Nova Citroen's dinner party took place at her Bel Air house, an enormous mansion with startling views and an army of servants to attend to the sixteen guests' every need. Marcus was not in residence.

"He's in London," Nova explained, when Kris arrived. "Business, as usual."

She introduced him around to a group that included two movie stars, a writer, a couple of important producers, *the* personal manager Hawkins Lamont, and several gorgeous, apparently unattached blondes. When Nova Citroen said she'd arrange a selection, she knew what she was talking about.

One of the blondes, clad in a short leather dress, slinked over to him. "Hi," she said with a welcoming smile. "Didn't we meet at Allan Carr's last week?"

"I was in London last week," he replied, wondering if the pushed-up tits were silicone or real.

"Shame! Think of the fun we could've had!"

The leather dress, appealing as it was, put him off. It reminded him of Astrid, waiting patiently in London. They'd promised each other there would be no screwing around. It just wasn't fair any more with all the diseases lurking about. Not that any of Nova's guests looked disease-ridden. But that was the whole point—with AIDS you couldn't notice a thing. Having sex with strangers nowadays was like playing Russian Roulette.

Two handsome waiters served drinks, while Nova flitted among her guests. Kris found himself making conversation with a man he had grown up watching on the movie screen. The man, once a matinee idol, now had yellowing teeth, gray hair, and a large paunch, but he was pleasant enough—especially when he started to carry on about how much he liked Kris's music.

Funny, Kris had never considered he appealed to old people too.

Hang about, a little voice warned him. *What's old? You're bleedin' thirty-six.*

Christ! Thirty-six. He was getting up there. A nerve-wracking thought. In his mind he'd always imagined when he reached forty he would quit. But forty was creeping closer every day, and he had no intention of going anywhere. Look at Mick Jagger—over forty and still prancing about like a teenager. And Rod Stewart—he had to be around the dreaded Four O mark, not to mention Paul McCartney, Pete Townshend, and a whole slew of aging rockers.

"I think I need another drink," he said, grabbing a glass of champagne from a moving waiter.

Nova took him discreetly to one side before they went into the dining room for dinner. "I've put Hawkins Lamont on your right—he's the most fascinating man, and certainly the right manager for you. Unfortunately he's not taking on any new clients right now. But I felt you should meet him. Tell me, who would you like on your other side?"

"You," he said, without thinking.

The shadow of a smile. "I was hoping you'd say that."

RAFEALLA
1984

★ ☆ ★ ☆ ★

I fall in love too easily
I fall in love too fast
I fall in love too terribly hard
For love to ever last . . .

As Rafealla sang the poignant Sammy Cahn and Jule Styne song, there was rapt silence in Julio's, the small, discreet supper club she had begun to call her second home. Originally booked to appear once a week, she was now performing nightly, singing her particular blend of popular American classics set to a throbbing jazz/samba beat.

Clad in a simple white dress, her long hair loose around her exotically beautiful face, she sang of undefined yearnings and intoxicating passion. Her voice, low and smoky, was filled with bittersweet sensuality.

After only a year of performing professionally, Rafealla was a hit. She had an appeal that struck home immediately, and whether she was singing in Portuguese, which she'd learned in Brazil, or English, the Brazilians loved her.

Recently she'd been offered a recording contract and a permanent singing spot on a popular television show. She could hardly believe it, everything seemed to have happened so fast.

Although Jorge gamely tried to pretend, he was not happy. He'd lost his would-be bride to a career, and it did not sit well with him. A month ago she'd moved out of his mansion, taking Jon Jon with her. "I can wait," he'd said bravely. "You'll come back."

Rafealla had shaken her head as she kissed him sadly. "It was never meant to be. You'll find someone who loves you more than I ever can."

She left behind her huge diamond ring, plus all the other gifts he'd lavished upon her. And once again it was just her and Jon Jon, who accepted the move without complaint. Now nearly seven, he combined the best physical qualities of both parents. Tall for his age, he had Rafealla's deep-olive skin and high cheekbones, along with Kris Phoenix's intense blue eyes and spiky blond hair.

"You're such a good-looking kid," she told him every day, accompanying this with a big hug. "How did I ever get so lucky?"

" 'Cause you got *me me me!*" he yelled happily.

Yes. She had Jon Jon. And a career. And an agent/manager—Tinto Reuben—who looked after her well. Life was pretty good.

Once a week her mother phoned from England. "When are you coming to visit, dear?"

"Soon," Rafealla replied dutifully.

They had the same conversation every time. Rafealla didn't want to go home. Going back would only remind her of Eddie Mafair, and God forbid he would try to see Jon Jon, although up until now he'd made no attempt. Odile had bumped into him at Annabel's one night, and apparently he hadn't asked after either of them. Great! She couldn't be happier. Hopefully, she would never have to set eyes on him again.

Her manager was waiting when she finished her set. Tinto

Reuben was a short, jolly man of fifty with chubby cheeks and a chipmunk grin. He had been recommended by her singing coach, and they'd hit it off at once. Tinto was married, with seven children. He'd once been a singer himself, and he understood the business thoroughly. No big-time agent, he was well respected and liked, with a middle-of-the-road client list. Rafealla, he knew, was on the verge of making it in a big way. When she had first come to him, the beautiful young girl had everything except experience. Now, a year later, she was ready for anything.

"What's up, Tinto?" she asked, lighting a cigarette as she sat down.

"You smoke too much," he scolded.

"I've got to have one bad habit." She laughed. "It's a hangover from my school days when smoking was the most decadent pursuit around."

Tinto smiled. He had good news. "Next week there's a very special song festival in São Paulo. You are invited to appear."

Her face lit up. "I am?"

"It's an honor."

"Why me?"

"You're becoming popular, my dear."

"I love it!"

"Wait. This is only the beginning."

São Paulo was a lovely city. Flying in at noon, Rafealla gazed out the window of the airplane, absorbing the panoramic view spread out below.

"You've never been here before?" Tinto asked.

"I've always wanted to."

"My wife was born here. She wanted to come with us. Not so easy with seven children to look after, eh?"

"Plus one of mine."

"She loves having Jon Jon to stay. Maria is mother earth." He beamed, a contented man.

After checking into the hotel, they were due to go to the rehearsal hall and meet Rafealla's backup musicians. She preferred the minimum of help—just guitar and keyboard, sometimes a touch of percussion. Originally she'd asked if she could bring the musicians she usually worked with, but Tinto thought the cost too prohibitive to fly them in for one night's performance.

The weather was hot and sultry. Arranging her long hair in a thick braid, she put on loose cotton pants and a sizes-too-big T-shirt. Tinto was clad in his usual pale-pink suit—he had several of them—and a brown shirt that strained across his protruding stomach.

"Tell you what," Rafealla said, as they entered the rehearsal hall. "You give up eating and I'll stop smoking."

"You have a deal!"

"When?"

"When what?"

"When are you going to start dieting?"

"After Christmas."

"That's eight months away!"

Innocently he said, "Really?"

Shaking her head, she couldn't help smiling.

Tinto introduced her to several of the organizers of the festival. She made polite chat about nothing much until a svelte woman dressed in red said, "Ah, here come your backup musicians—Carlos Pinafida on the piano and Luiz Oliveira, guitar. Luiz is a very talented young man. He has a wonderful style. Later in the concert he will be performing his own composition—'English Girl.' He's very popular locally."

And so Rafealla came face to face with Luiz once more—three years after their last encounter.

Holding her breath, she stared straight at him.

He stared back.

The air was charged with electricity.

BOBBY MONDELLA
1984

★ ☆ ★ ☆ ★

The success trip. He'd climbed to the top of the mountain, taken a deep breath, and found the air stank. Why wasn't it cool and clear and pleasant? How come everything was such a fuck-up?

Bobby Mondella stared at his photographic image on the cover of *Rolling Stone* and wondered why it didn't thrill him. You're a handsome sonofabitch, he told himself dispassionately, reaching for a drink.

Zella Raven floated into the room—a black superwoman in leopard-print leather. Zella enjoyed the high life. Zella snorted coke for breakfast and finished the day with a touch of free-basing.

In the back of his mind he knew he had to get rid of her; she was dragging him down. Once, long ago, he'd been anti-drugs. He, more than anyone, had seen how they destroyed people.

Now he let it go on all around him, and he wasn't averse to joining in occasionally, because drugs gave him even more power and strength, and, fuck it—when he was high he owned the whole world, and nothing and no one could bring him down. Including Nova.

Ah . . . Nova. His obsession. How come he had everything, and everything wasn't enough, because he would give up everything just to possess the one woman he couldn't have? It didn't make sense.

When he was drunk or stoned it didn't even matter.

He knew one thing: *Rolling Stone* was correct when they said he couldn't write any more. The songs stopped coming one day—just like that.

No inspiration. No drive. *No shit?*

Hey—*Rolling Stone* had written that Bobby Mondella was not the talent he once was. What did he care? He'd reached the top, and it was a long fall down.

Zella liked to party. Every night they hit a new club or restaurant. They *owned* Las Vegas, where he regularly appeared—a favor for Carmine, his best friend, Carmine—or was it Arnie?—good old Arnie.

"How come y'all's lookin' like you're dead in the water?" Zella asked, fluffing out a wild Afro wig that perched atop her head like a frothy cake. "An' you're not even dressed."

"Why should I be dressed? We're not goin' anywhere."

"Sure we are, sugar. You all forgotten? It's Arnie's big party at the beach."

Another party. Another lousy time. And everyone would probably have read the put-down piece in *Rolling Stone,* which he chose to ignore because who gave a shit? Fuck it! What did he care? They'd only remember seeing his picture on the cover. Another cover. More fame. And he was a handsome sonofabitch. . . .

Yeah. Mister Soul Superstar was a handsome sonofabitch. . . .

And so fuckin' what?

Women always came on to him. It was a fact. They smiled and tried to act normal, but Zella had captured it like it was when she'd said, "Honey, they are creamin' their scanty lace panties, *whatever* damn stuff they're talkin'."

Sex symbol.

Black sex symbol.

A double hit.

"The storms were quite devastating," said a beautiful woman with a diamond the size of an acorn on her finger. "But we'd never sell."

"You wouldn't, huh?" commented Bobby, swaying on his feet.

"Never," she replied, gazing at him steadfastly. "Malibu is the best."

Was she hot for him? Was she steaming?

Oh, yeah, he could tell.

"Bobby, darling!" Greetings from Poppy Soloman, the ebullient wife of a studio head. "How nice to see you again. Thank you, thank you for appearing at my charity. Everyone was thrilled."

Did she want him? Was she ready?

A simple yes would do it.

He watched Zella, taking off across the room. Ever since landing the villainess role in a Rambo-type film she was Miss Movie Star, playing the role on screen and off, and loving every minute.

At least someone was happy.

"Hey, man—long time, how're ya doin'?"

He turned to face his old friend Rocket. The same old scruffy Rocket, with his long, greasy hair and beat-up clothes. The same Rocket who last year had been nominated for an Oscar, honoring his fine performance in a stark movie about corruption in politics.

Bobby was pleased to see him. They'd lost touch and hadn't run into each other for a long while. With genuine camaraderie they exchanged hugs.

The beautiful woman with the diamond and the wife of the studio head waited anxiously to be introduced to the moody actor, who was not known for his social graces. Since Bobby couldn't remember either of their names, he didn't bother

380

with introductions. Instead, he grabbed a fresh drink and walked outside with Rocket to the pool area.

"Will ya look at this?" Rocket said, exasperated, throwing his arms wide. "Whadda they need a pool for when they have a whole ocean?"

"Hey, man." Bobby shrugged. "That's show biz—if ya got it—put out."

Rocket wrinkled his face in disgust. "One hell of a philosophy. Whyn't they jam some of their big bucks back where they belong—with the people?" Taking a crumpled joint from his pocket, he lit up.

"What are you doin' in L.A. anyway?" Bobby asked. "I thought you hated it."

"Another movie. It's a true story about a Hollywood cocaine freak who snorts his life away. This guy has the world by the balls an' screws everything up. Real powerful stuff."

"You get off on those kind of roles, huh?"

"A lot of people out here are goin' to identify with this one." He dragged on the roach, then passed it to Bobby, who declined. "I forgot, this ain't your thing, is it?"

"I'll take some blow if you got it."

Rocket raised a cynical eyebrow. "I wouldn't touch that poison for a million big ones."

Why did Rocket always make him feel like a loser? He was more famous than his actor friend would ever be. Or was he?

"Didja see me on the cover of *Rollin' Stone?*" he found himself asking.

"Why d'you do that stuff?" Rocket said, his voice full of contempt. "You're bendin' over an' beggin' for the screwin' they're gonna give yuh. It don't make no sense to set yourself up for it. Y'should do what I do. Nothin'. No press. No shit. *Nada.*"

Before he had a chance to defend himself, Zella was upon them. She was all over Rocket like a sinuous, gleaming snake.

Bobby left them to it. He'd had it with Rocket and his superior attitude. Who the fuck did the prick think he was anyway?

Finding a group snorting cocaine in a bathroom, he joined them.

It didn't matter. Nothing really mattered. Being a star meant never having to explain anything to anyone.

KRIS PHOENIX
1985

★ ☆ ★ ☆ ★

Bedding Mrs. Citroen might not have been the greatest idea in the world, but he'd done it—once—and there was no going back.

When Kris reflected on it—which wasn't often—he realized it had not been his fault. After all, what was a guy supposed to do when faced with the wife of his new boss wearing nothing but stiletto heels and an icy smile? "Sorry, no, thank you" wouldn't have seemed polite, especially when she'd just given a dinner in his honor and sat him next to one of the most sought-after personal managers in the music business.

Once was enough, thank you. Kris knew a ballsbreaker when he saw one.

Mrs. Citroen. She didn't give up easily. She called him. Sent him presents via chauffeured Rolls-Royce. Tried to pressure him.

He didn't weaken. No way. In fact, what he did do, just to prevent any future complications, was tell Astrid as soon as he got back to England. She was cool—broke some furniture and chipped one of his teeth, but basically she took it well.

This had all taken place a year ago, and a lot had happened in that year. The big news was he'd been forced to get rid of Doktor Head. It was a move he hadn't been happy making, but it was inevitable once Doktor Head started drinking again—for when he drank he became an uncontrollable maniac, and Kris wanted none of it. As far as his career was concerned he had a killer instinct, refusing to allow anyone to fuck it up. He gave Doktor Head several chances and then fired him. Fortunately they had no contract. Theirs was a handshake arrangement—unwise, but that was the way they'd both wanted it.

Two days after the firing, Kris called Hawkins Lamont. "I need someone to take me higher," he'd said.

"Come into my office and we'll talk."

They met. They talked. They both had the same desire. To make Kris Phoenix into the biggest rock star in the world.

A deal was set.

"You'll move to America," the Hawk had said. "If we intend to make you into an international star you have to be based in the States."

"Astrid'll hate that."

"Don't bring her. Leave her in England. It's better for your image if you're unattached and available."

An excellent solution. Astrid loved the English countryside, she'd be quite happy pottering about there. And he'd spend plenty of time visiting because of Bo.

"Sold!" he'd said.

Six weeks later he said "Sold" again when he purchased a vast house in Bel Air.

True to his word, the Hawk set about making Kris Phoenix into the biggest rock superstar of all. He renegotiated Doktor Head's deal with Blue Cadillac. He put Kris in the hands of one of the hottest and most prestigious P.R. companies on the West Coast. He suggested a theme for the new album. And planned a special tour across fifteen key cities to set America alight.

"We have to forget The Wild Ones ever existed and start afresh," he announced, with all the enthusiasm of a general going into battle. "From now on it's Kris Phoenix all the way. Go home, sit down, and write the best songs you've ever written. The theme is family. Don't forget—family and roots and relationships."

Kris flew back to England, holed up at his country estate, shut off the phones, and went to work, emerging seven weeks later with twelve gritty, truthful songs full of everything the Hawk had asked for.

The new album was called *Gettin' Down*. The tour was called simply KRIS PHOENIX '85. Both broke every existing record.

The Hawk had done as he promised. Within one year Kris Phoenix was the hottest name to hit the rock world since Bruce Springsteen.

RAFEALLA
1985

★ ★ ★ ★ ★

There were moments when Rafealla couldn't keep her hands off Luiz, and fortunately he seemed to feel the same way. Bumping into him by chance made her determined never to be apart from him again. A year had passed, and she had her wish.

At first they were both uncomfortable with each other and after the initial shock, stiffly polite.

"I didn't know you sang," he'd said.

"And I didn't know you lived in São Paulo," she'd retorted accusingly, longing to say, "Why did you disappear? How come I never heard from you? How dare you treat me like that!"

They'd rehearsed with all the warm interaction of a suspicious Siamese cat and a fierce Doberman.

"What's the matter, Rafealla?" Tinto had asked. "Do you two know each other?"

"Yes," she'd snapped, at the same time that Luiz replied with a sharp "No."

"Ah . . ." Tinto had sighed wisely. He knew exactly what was going on.

Finally, music brought them together. The caressing, insinuating strum of his guitar melded perfectly with her low, sensual voice. By the time they did the concert, they still weren't friendly, but they were in tune.

The next morning, shortly before she and Tinto were due to leave their hotel for the airport, Luiz turned up.

"I think we must talk," he said.

"A little late for that," she replied.

Tinto rolled his eyes and handed over her ticket. Rafealla was all work and no play; it wasn't natural. "Yes, talk," he'd encouraged, nodding understandingly. "Catch the later plane."

By later, he hadn't meant two weeks later. But that's the way it was. And when she returned to Rio she was glowing, as only a woman in love can. Luiz, she had discovered, was a very intense, complex young man. His original disappearance had not been because he didn't like her, but because he liked her too much. "I had nothing to offer you," he explained simply. "We would not have been happy."

"Yes, we would," she argued.

"No," he insisted. "I had to leave the city. For if I hadn't, the temptation would have trapped me."

So he'd had his reasons: pride and such. In São Paulo his career progressed, and when they met again he felt ready to accept the challenge of a relationship.

Within weeks of her return to Rio, he followed her, as Tinto had promised he could get them work as a duo. It was an easy promise to keep. They had a magic between them that the public loved. Luiz settled into her apartment and her life as if it were destined, and they were inseparable. Soon, due to the success they enjoyed, he was able to afford his own place. Once again Rafealla gave up her independence, and along with Jon Jon moved in with him.

They made a beautiful trio—Rafealla and Luiz, both so dark with their matching green eyes and jet-black hair, and Jon Jon, blond and tanned with his shining, innocent blue eyes.

Now, for the first time in her life, Rafealla truly knew what happiness was. She had a career she loved, a man she adored. And Jon Jon.

Odile phoned often. "You have to come home for a visit soon," she insisted. "Or your mother will have a positive cow!"

"Yes, soon," Rafealla promised, not meaning it at all. For one thing, she had no intention of ever letting Luiz out of her sight again, and for another, the thought of his meeting her family was hardly one she relished. Not that they were snobs—the very opposite. But Luiz had come from the favela; it would be difficult for him to understand her background; he would feel intimidated and out of place on her stepfather's enormous country estate. Meanwhile she sent home her records and press clippings, leaving out the ones that mentioned she and Luiz were living together. Even though she was now twenty-five, she knew her mother would be shocked, especially because of Jon Jon.

They lived an idyllic existence. Working together, playing on the white sandy beaches, enjoying their leisure time and work equally. Luiz was terrific with Jon Jon—just like the father he'd never had.

Their singing success was particularly rewarding. Not only were they both doing something they loved, they were also getting paid for it—and handsomely. In Latin America they were fast becoming famous and had enjoyed several hit records.

Tinto sat back like a proud father as he watched and helped their careers grow. When he'd first taken Rafealla on, he hadn't planned on handling her as a double act. But she and Luiz were perfect together. Their love shone through everything they did.

"I think we might get married," Rafealla confided to Tinto one day. "Only don't tell Luiz, he doesn't know."

"My lips reveal nothing."

"Good. Keep it that way."

To celebrate the fact that Luiz's latest composition had hit number one—a song he and Rafealla had recorded together, and their third consecutive hit—Tinto threw a big party. Rafealla sat back, allowing Luiz to bask in the limelight and enjoy most of the attention. He was so handsome and exhilarated. He deserved this success.

Proudly she watched him circulate, charming press and guests alike. He had never mentioned marriage, but lately it had been on her mind a lot. Oh, sure, she was happy just being with him; marriage, however, was a more permanent commitment, and since she never wanted to be apart from him again, it seemed like a good idea. Determined not to be the one to bring the subject up, she longed for him to ask her. He remained silent, obviously quite content with things the way they were.

Other women threw themselves at him. During the course of the party Rafealla noticed several females coming on strong. Luiz had a way of deflecting their advances without hurting their feelings. He was studiously polite and well-mannered, which of course made him all the more interesting. Nothing turned women on more than a man they couldn't get through to. Especially when that man was talented, young, and extraordinarily handsome.

Rafealla couldn't hold back. In the car on their way home she hugged him warmly. "I've got a fantastic idea," she said.

"What?"

"A sensational idea."

He smiled—white, even teeth and emerald-green eyes she couldn't resist. "Tell me, my Carioca," he encouraged, his hand lingering on her knee.

"Let's get married."

A silence. Too long a silence. A *dangerous* silence.

Before he even spoke she knew something was wrong.

He hesitated, and then falteringly said, "I was going to tell you."

She could hardly breathe. "Yes?"

"Uh . . . how I say this?" He paused again, and then, very slowly, "Rafealla, you know that I love you . . . but this is the thing—I am already married."

BOBBY MONDELLA
1985

★ ★ ★ ★ ★

The crowd at Rio airport greeting Bobby Mondella was gratifyingly large. It took several bodyguards and security police to get him through safely. In the Rolls-Royce sent to meet him he sat back with a satisfied sigh. "Y'see, they still love me," he said.

Nichols Kline, momentarily unnerved by the massive crowds and roaring fans, said, "Sure. This is a foreign country. They're a year behind."

"You're a real downer sonofabitch," Bobby responded angrily. "One record doesn't make number one, an' in your book I'm finished."

"Your last *three* singles," Pammy corrected with a toss of her dyed-blond hair.

Bobby couldn't stand the phony bitch. How come Nichols put up with her? She'd laid every one of his friends and treated him like dirt. But Nichols hung in there, thinking he'd found himself some kind of English princess instead of dumb cunt of the year.

Bobby ignored her. He'd grown expert at pretending she didn't exist. God! he needed a drink. "How far is the hotel?" he asked brusquely.

"Do I look like a fuckin' tour guide?" Nichols snapped. "Ask the driver."

They were all tired after the long journey from Los Angeles. Hey—Bobby didn't give a damn—he hadn't asked Nichols to come, especially with Miss Congeniality in tow. Nichols had insisted on making the trip. Carlos Baptista, the Brazilian concert promoter, had been begging him to visit for years, and with Bobby due to do three concerts at the Maracana stadium, he'd grabbed the opportunity—with a little persuasion from Pammy.

Bobby half-wished Zella was with him—at least he'd have an ally. And then again, he was relieved she wasn't. Zella was crazy—certifiably so. She'd freaked out on the set of her latest movie and beaten up two petrified makeup men before being subdued and ultimately carted off to the Betty Ford Center for a spell of drying out.

Zella was bad news; she would drag him down with her if he wasn't careful. It wasn't her fault, the woman just couldn't resist causing trouble.

He'd visited her at the clinic before leaving. With a weary smile she'd said, "Hey—superstar—maybe you should be here with me, huh?"

Why the hell should he be? Yeah—he drank. Sure—he did cocaine. But he could control it. He knew exactly what he was doing. And any time he wanted to stop, no problem.

Deep down, he was well aware of what he really wanted—to dump Nichols Hit City and get back to his roots. Nine months ago he'd run into Amerika Allen at the Grammy Awards. She'd done pretty well over the years. Soul On Soul was second only to Motown, with the cream of black recording artists.

He was pitted against one of her people for Best R&B Vocal Performance, an award he'd won several times. Her star got it—a fresh-faced kid with long, corn-rowed hair and a toothy grin, full of enthusiasm and sass.

Bobby applauded along with the rest of the audience. It was the first year since 1977 he'd won nothing, and it hurt.

On the way home he had his driver go into Tower Records on Sunset and buy the kid's record. Back at his house he played it. Some monster hit, with synthesizers and a mesmerizing African beat. It sounded new and hot.

Then he put on *his* last record. The same old thing. Throbbing, sensual soul. Maybe it wasn't enough anymore.

He'd been using a producer Arnie Torterelli had thrust upon him instead of doing it himself. Another favor. It was time to make some changes.

Insisting on a new producer, he'd said, "I'm tryin' out somethin' different."

Something different hadn't worked. As Pammy so kindly pointed out, his last three singles had failed to hit the number one spot, although the album from which they were pulled had achieved fairly respectable sales.

"Respectable" didn't cut it. Where were the regular number ones? Where were the album mega-sales he was used to? He was a superstar, for crissake, there was no coming down from that.

Bobby Mondella was on a slide, and he didn't like it one little bit. He especially didn't like it when he had to hear about it from Nichols's moron wife.

He knew what the problem was—he'd been pushing himself too hard, appearing here, there, and everywhere, making too many records without concentrating on the content. Bobby Mondella was overexposed. He needed to lay back and return to the people who really cared. Nichols Hit City was money-oriented, that's all they took notice of—making the buck, and pushing, pushing, pushing. They were worse than Blue Cadillac in that respect.

Soul On Soul was interested in quality and style and nurturing the performer. Amerika was an inspiration to work with, and yet he'd dumped on her, walked when she could have used the support. It was to her credit she'd behaved so cordially when they ran into each other.

He'd made up his mind that on this Rio trip he was going to tell Nichols he wanted out. If he offered Hit City some kind of override deal where they would still continue to get a piece of his future, he was sure they'd let him go. Enough weddings and Vegas stints and doing goddamn favors. He needed time to straighten out and get back into the flow of writing and performing music he had a genuine feeling for. With Zella out of the way, he could do it.

The Copacabana Palace was a swank, glitzy hotel, overlooking the ocean and the famous white sand Copacabana Beach. Bobby was installed in a magnificent suite on the top floor. There was champagne on ice, a huge basket of fresh fruit, and several elaborate flower arrangements in both the bedroom and living room, with cards attached.

First he reached for a drink, then glanced at the cards. CARLOS AND CHARA BAPTISTA WELCOME YOU TO RIO . . . WITH THE COMPLIMENTS OF CARLOS BAPTISTA AND HIS STAFF . . . And so on.

That night there was a dinner planned for him to meet the concert promoter. To Nichols's and Pammy's fury he canceled out, climbed into bed with a bottle of bourbon and a plate of room-service chicken, and watched television. New rule—he was sick of doing what everyone else wanted. No more favors. In the future he was going to do exactly what *he* wanted, and if they didn't like it, fuck 'em.

Maybe he'd even try to lay off the booze and drugs for a while. Not that he couldn't stop any time . . . any time at all.

Carlos Baptista phoned. The man was polite and concerned, not pissed off like Nichols had been. "We are so sorry you cannot attend our dinner for you. Is there anything you need?"

"I guess I'm just tired," Bobby explained. "The flight an' everything."

"Carlos understands perfectly. Maybe a young woman to massage away the tensions . . ."

"I'm not into arranged sex."

"I didn't mean to insult you."

"Hey, man. No insult. Everything's cool."

Idly he flicked the channels on the television, stopping to watch a young couple sing together. They were fresh and innovative, the girl exotically beautiful and the man darkly handsome. Their Brazilian blend of samba and jazz was soothing and yet upbeat and very sensuous.

With a burst of interest he sat up. Could this be the inspiration he was looking for? Soul with a mix of samba and jazz? *His* kind of soul done *their* way?

Suddenly he was high. This was it. He knew this was the sound he'd been looking for.

As the credits rolled at the end of the show he searched for their names.

Rafealla and Luiz. Reaching for a pad he scrawled them down.

Rafealla and Luiz, he thought, *you may just have hit pay dirt. Oh, yeah, baby. Oh, yeah!*

Rio was his salvation. Rio, with its laid-back ambience and wonderfully friendly people. His three concerts at the Maracana stadium were a smash, and he reveled in the adulation. The South Americans certainly still loved Bobby Mondella.

After much thought, and to Nichols's great consternation, he told him he'd decided to stay in Rio for a while.

"You can't do that," Nichols objected harshly. "We got commitments to fulfill."

"Cancel 'em."

"Are you insane?"

"I like it here. This place is good for me. I'm not drinking. I'm relaxing. And oh, yeah—I'm stayin'."

Nichols was furious; the muscle in his cheek twitched as he attempted to remain in control. "For how long?"

"For however long I feel like."

"I'm tellin' you—no can do, Bobby. You have a contract."

"Fuck the contract, an' fuck you. I've had it with bein' maneuvered into position every time I breathe. You know something? I've worked for people since I was twelve years old, and now I've decided to do nothin' for however long it takes to get my head straight. We had a contract, so I'll give you a piece of whatever I decide to do in the future, but right now I want out. You got it?"

"You'll regret this," Pammy shrieked, suddenly joining in.

"Shut up, you dumb broad," yelled Nichols, taking his frustration out on her.

The result was that a very flustered Nichols and a sulking wife were forced to return to L.A. without Bobby.

Six months passed, and in spite of numerous threats and angry phone calls from Nichols, Bobby was happy. He'd arranged for his business manager to sell his Hancock Park mansion and all his possessions. He'd told Zella it was over; she wasn't surprised. And he'd started afresh.

For a while stardom had caught him in its trap and sent him spinning out of control. Now he was back on the ground and he liked it. He had a nice apartment in the Chopin Building, next to the Copacabana Palace, a variety of girlfriends—nobody special. And most important of all, he was drug-free, and hardly drinking at all.

Leisure, he discovered, was very pleasant. And because he didn't *have* to write, the songs began to flow, and his creative juices went into overdrive.

Shortly after seeing Rafealla and Luiz on television, he'd arranged a meeting. Over the following months they became his good friends as well as musical collaborators, and although they were unable to record together because of his battle with Nichols Hit City, occasionally they sneaked in a performance somewhere, just for pure enjoyment.

The moment he thought his life was settled, Nova reappeared. Two years of silence, and one day she phoned him on his private line as if they'd been together all along. "I'm at the airport. I must see you," she said urgently.

"Come right over," he replied calmly.

His heart didn't give him a choice.

Just like old times, she walked back into his life. Cool, classy Nova Citroen. The Ice Queen to those who didn't know her. The love of his life.

Like a replay, he opened his door to a woman he hardly recognized, and she almost fell at his feet. Sharleen, all those years ago, a beaten wreck—and now Nova in the same condition, her face puffed and swollen. She was wrapped in a mink coat, dark glasses covered her eyes, and she was shaking.

"Jesus Christ!" he exclaimed. "What happened to you?"

As if he didn't know. Marcus Citroen.

"Bobby—" her voice was shaking. "Oh, Bobby! I got on a plane and came straight to you. I didn't know where else to go."

They'd had a long relationship, and not once during the times they were together had she ever shown any vulnerability. Nova had always been on top of things.

He opened up his arms and she walked right into his embrace. "C'mon, baby," he comforted her. "It's okay, I'm here for you. Everything's gonna be fine." It was if they'd never been apart.

She began to sob, long drawn-out cries of pure anguish. "I never thought I'd find you. It wasn't easy. God, Bobby . . . I hate him, I've always hated him. . . ."

He led her into his apartment, removed her coat, settled her on the couch, and poured her a large glass of brandy.

"Calm down, baby," he said soothingly. "Just take it easy, an' tell me everything."

Slowly she recovered her composure. She removed her dark glasses. Her eyes were swollen slits, the skin beneath them black and blue.

"That sonofabitch sadistic bastard!" he said angrily.

"I've left him." Her voice was hardly more than a whisper. "And now he'll try to destroy me."

"Destroy you? Are you *crazy? He's* the one in big trouble. Look at yourself for crissake. Look at what he's done to you."

"You don't understand," she said despairingly. "He *can* destroy me. And I know Marcus. He will."

"How's that?" he asked, humoring her.

"He's going to tell the world the truth about me."

"And what's the truth?"

Lowering her eyes, she said, "That when he found me I was a whore."

He looked at her disbelievingly. "Come on—"

"It's true." Her voice was bitter. "The Mrs. Citroen everyone knows—the *elegant* Mrs. Marcus Citroen—was once a highly paid, highly skilled whore in Germany. Marcus . . . discovered me. He . . . changed me. He molded me into the woman he wanted, and then, when I was exactly the way he desired, he married me."

Bobby's throat was dry; for the first time in months he needed a drink. "Nova," he said, "there's no way I believe this."

"Why not?" She gazed at him dispassionately. "It's true. Does it disgust you? Are you sorry we had an affair?"

He shook his head—he didn't know what he felt. For years he'd begged Nova to leave Marcus, and now this.

"There's more," she said. "I need to to tell you everything, Bobby, because I have to know how you feel." She paused, and gave a brittle laugh. "All I want from you is the truth."

Taking a deep breath, he said, "Whatever it is, babe, you're building it way out of proportion."

"Like hell I am," she shot back, staring at him defiantly. "Bobby, I'm half black."

"What?"

She touched her white-blond hair. "Oh, you'd never guess it, would you? No one could ever tell. When Marcus sent me to Paris to be worked over, he had my skin bleached along with my hair. Not that I was ever noticeably dark. My mother was white. My father was a black G.I. she had a drunken one-night stand with. Unfortunately she waited too long for an abortion, and the result was me."

"Je—sus!"

"So you see," she continued in a flat voice. "I am not the woman you imagined me to be. I'm a half-black whore from Germany. Not the ritzy lady who appears on the front pages of *Women's Wear Daily* and gives the best parties in town. I'm a fraud, Bobby, and Marcus is going to expose me because I've dared to leave him."

He canceled all his arrangements and summoned a doctor to check Nova over. The man glared at Bobby with accusation written all over his face.

"I didn't do it," Bobby explained quickly. "She's runnin' from her husband."

"What's her name?" the doctor asked, filling out a prescription for sleeping pills.

"Margaret," Bobby lied. "Margaret Smith."

"She needs rest. There's no internal damage. Cold compresses on the eyes, and plenty of liquids." A pause. "I really should report it. This woman has been badly beaten."

"Come on, Doc. She's had enough trouble."

Another accusatory look. "Very well."

Gradually Bobby pieced together the story. One of Marcus's friendly visits to a whorehouse in Paris. He liked to watch his wife with hookers. She obliged. It was part of their agreement. Later he invited two of the girls back to their apartment. For once Nova objected. But Marcus insisted. The girls were street tarts, they stole clothes and jewelry. Nova said she'd had enough. Marcus said she'd take whatever he handed her. They fought, and he beat her with a golf club, then walked out. As soon as he was gone she'd grabbed a few things, taken a taxi to the airport and boarded the next plane to Rio. Marcus had no idea where she'd run to.

"How come you finally did it?" he asked.

"It was time," she replied simply.

Now she was in his apartment and he didn't know how he felt any more. He needed a while to work out his true feelings. Hell! She couldn't expect to walk back into his life and find nothing changed, could she?

On top of everything else, he got a surprise phone call from Carmine Sicily. "We want you to go back to work, Bobby," Carmine said pleasantly. "We want you on a plane to L.A. this week. I mean *this week,* otherwise you might never go on a trip anywhere ever again. Do we understand each other?"

"I'm not comin' back, Carmine. Don't try to push me. Talk to my lawyers."

"You're playing fuck-you games with the wrong people," Carmine said mildly. "It's my sister's birthday next Tuesday. She likes you, Bobby. She thinks you're handsome. Be there. Be smart."

Bobby didn't mention the phone call to Nova. Screw Carmine Sicily and his threats. They couldn't touch him, they were all talk.

For days, Nova lay in the center of his bed watching television. Her bruises began to fade. He cooked her scrambled eggs and soup, and brought her magazines. The one thing he couldn't do was make love to her. He needed time.

She waited patiently. She said nothing. It was her way of testing him, and he knew it.

Nova, baby—he wanted to say—I don't give a damn about your past, it doesn't matter to me. What I do care about is the hold Marcus has had on you all this time. How come you didn't break out when I gave you the chance two years ago? What made you keep on doing the things he forced you to do?

Why, baby?

Why?

The *why* stood between them like a brick wall.

After a few days he felt he had to get out of the apartment for a while, go for a walk, grab a beer, anything.

"Hey—will you be okay?" he asked solicitously. "I'll be back in an hour."

She nodded.

He left and went straight to Luiz and Rafealla's. They were delighted to see him.

"We've missed you," Rafealla said. "Where have you been?"

He shrugged. "Nowhere. I've got a friend stayin' with me from the States."

"A lady friend?" Rafealla asked playfully.

"Yeah."

"Anything serious?"

Making light of it, he said, "Let's put it this way—I'm not gettin' married."

He didn't stay long; he was too restless. He couldn't help thinking of Nova lying in his bed, waiting for him to make a move, show her his support.

So she was a whore once upon a time. Did it really matter?

No. But what she did with Marcus mattered.

They had to talk. Decisively he headed home.

The apartment was dark when he let himself in; the flicker of the television from the bedroom was the only light. The sound on the TV was loud, too loud.

He knew something was wrong a moment too late, for as soon as he sensed danger, he was grabbed from behind, his arms twisted in an immovable lock, and the struggle began. Bobby was strong, six feet two inches of powerful muscle. But there was more than one man behind him, two, maybe three. He could hear them grunting, smell their lousy breath.

Thoughts flashed through his head. Nova. Was she all right? Shit! If they'd hurt her he'd fucking kill them.

They were trying to propel him forward—kicking, thrashing. A heavy object crashed down on his head, his skull exploded, lights flashed. So it was true—you did see stars.

Jesus, blood was trickling down his face, and so was something else. He could smell liquor. What the fuck did they want? They were half-dragging him now, across the thick-pile carpet, toward the balcony.

Terror swept over him.

They were going to throw him over the fucking balcony.

They were going to kill him.

Jesus!

JESUS!

He screamed, but it was too late. He was falling . . . falling in space . . . falling. . . .

It was all over.

LOS ANGELES 1987
Saturday, July 11th

★ ☆ ★ ☆ ★

The parade of chauffeur-driven Rolls-Royces, Mercedeses, and other expensive automobiles arriving at the Citroen beach estate was impressive. Each car was stopped at the point of entry and the occupants identified and checked off a master list. Then a numbered sticker was attached to the windshield, and the driver was allowed to take the guests up to the main house, where they were dropped off. After that, the chauffeur drove the car back to an allocated parking lot five minutes away. When guests were ready to leave, their car would be summoned by number.

Several parking valets were in charge of this operation, making sure everything ran smoothly and there were no traffic jams.

The guests then went through a second security procedure as they entered the reception hall of the main house. Their names were double-checked on another list, and then they were escorted outside to the tented tennis-court area, where the party really began.

Wearing an immaculate dinner suit with a white silk jacket especially tailored for him in Hong Kong, Hawkins Lamont circulated among the guests. Cybil Wilde was by his side, not really dressed for the occasion, but it didn't matter. Cybil was so stunningly pretty that nobody noticed what she was wearing. Hawkins had no objections to squiring her during the cocktail hour; she made a delightful accessory.

"Take her out there for crissakes," Kris had grumbled. "She's gettin' on my nerves."

Hawkins obliged. That was what a personal manager was for, wasn't it? To take care of all the things the star couldn't be bothered to deal with himself, including girlfriends.

Smiling wryly, Hawkins wondered if perhaps Kris might like him to make love to her too. He would not oblige on that score. Hawkins liked to be seen with pretty girls. He even liked to watch them play together. But he didn't care to take them to bed. He'd lost interest in sex when he'd discovered business. Money, it turned out, was the greatest satisfaction of all.

"This is fantastic!" Cybil enthused. "Have you seen who's here? I think I've spotted my *favorite* Italian movie star."

"Yes, it's quite a group," agreed Hawkins. "Leave it to Nova, and they're here in force."

"Did these people really pay one hundred thousand dollars a couple?" Cybil gasped.

"It's only money," Hawkins replied sensibly. "They can afford it. And if the Governor ever makes it to the White House, he'll owe them all a seat at his dinner table."

"Wow! I'd love to meet him. Then he can owe *me* a seat too!"

"I'm sure Governor Highland wouldn't mind meeting you," Hawkins replied, knowing full well the Governor would adore being introduced to a luscious California blonde—just his type. "Come." He offered his arm. "Let us go and find the gentleman."

* * *

Alone at last, Kris brooded about Cyndi Lou Planter, the moon-faced English journalist and her dumb questions. Why did he let reporters bother him? Why did he waste his time burdening himself with negative thoughts?

Kris Phoenix was at the top. Naturally everyone wanted to drag him down. It was only human nature. . . .

Maxwell Sicily passed among the illustrious guests, his tray held aloft, bearing small squares of pizza covered with smoked salmon and golden caviar—the chic L.A. snack. Bejeweled fingers grabbed. Hairy wrists wrapped in ten-thousand-dollar watches propelled bony hands in the right direction.

He hadn't even gotten halfway around before his tray was empty. With a purposeful step he returned to the supply bar and picked up a fresh load of hors d'oeuvres. This time he was given tiny crab cakes with a dipping sauce.

"How delicious!" exclaimed a fat woman in a pink satin ball gown, grabbing two. She stuffed one in her mouth, dipping the second one in the zesty red sauce. Maxwell observed a splodge of the stuff fall upon her ample bosom as the crab cake vanished into her mouth. Too bad.

He moved away, listening to fragments of conversation, checking out the lavish jewelry. Why did party guests treat waiters as if they didn't exist? Hands grabbed, eyes rarely met, and a thank you was out of the question. Fucking rich parasites.

Fortunately he didn't have to do this for a living. Thank God he was smarter than everyone at this party put together.

Maxwell Sicily was one of life's winners. By the end of the night he was going to be richer than all of them.

Marcus Citroen's voice on the phone was commanding. "Rafealla?"

"Yes, Marcus."

"I wish to see you after the concert."

"Surely you'll be busy with your guests?"

"Kris Phoenix will appear after you. And then there'll be speeches and the auction. We'll have plenty of time. When you finish, you will return to your room. Get rid of the publicity girl and anyone else hanging around. I will see you then. Alone. Do you understand?"

A feeling of dread swept over her. But there was a price, and she had promised to pay it. "Yes, Marcus."

Racing down San Vicente toward the beach, Speed glanced at the clock on the dashboard. He was running late. Jeez! His freakin' luck.

He put his foot down hard, and the sleek limousine surged forward, overtaking a yellow Porsche with a blonde driving. He slowed down just long enough to check her out in his rearview mirror.

Hot! A blonde in a Porsche. His kind of babe!

As he hit the accelerator again, the big limo sped down the highway.

If only I could make it with a fox the way I make it with a car, Speed daydreamed, any broad would be in freakin' sex heaven! Take Sugarbush, his ex-wife. That barracuda didn't break balls, she crushed them in a blender and drank 'em for freakin' breakfast!

Sugarbush. What a flashy cooze-machine *she* was, with her zoomer tits and bright-red hair—pussy hair too, because she dyed it down there. Every guy who eyeballed her—and they all did—tried to give her a roll.

The trouble was, she let 'em. Which is why he'd dumped her one steamy Vegas night with ten thousand winnings in his pocket and a stacked blonde on each arm.

Unfortunately the bucks didn't last, nor did the blondes.

Thinking of his ex always jerked his blood pressure way up. Sugarbush was something else—she gave *hookers* a bad name.

Jamming his foot down, he shot through an amber light.

A police vehicle swept out of a side street, settled in behind him, and began to flash its lights.

Holy shit! What was this? Rent-a-cop city? They were freakin' everywhere.

Reluctantly he pulled over to the side.

Bobby Mondella paced around the room. He had a headache, a throbbing, skull-shattering ache that was driving him crazy. Damn Nova Citroen. Damn her! She thought she could walk back into his life as if everything was still the same. As if Rio had never happened.

Well, she was wrong. He was no longer her own personal sex-machine. As far as he was concerned, he couldn't care less if he never spoke to her again.

Vicki made sure the three celebrities were settled in their rooms. Big deal. Famous people were no different from anyone else. They went to the bathroom, didn't they? Just like the masses.

Vicki was not awestruck by any means. She'd had a few famous ones in her time. Well, not exactly *worldwide* famous—more like an L.A. disc jockey with pimples on his ass and a rubber fetish. Also a very rich Hollywood realtor who claimed to know absolutely everybody. Oh, yeah, and she'd once had a senator from the East who was staying at a local Holiday Inn. At least he'd *said* he was a senator. He'd made her get down on her knees and pledge allegiance to the flag, and then he'd made her pledge allegiance to something he obviously considered far more important.

Men! What a bunch! And yet, she had to admit, she loved 'em—they were so goddamn *easy!* Tom was the perfect example. She'd had *his* balls in an uproar with just one glance.

She looked around, making sure nobody was observing her as she slid into the unoccupied guest suite. Opening the closet, she checked that everything was in position—the empty Vuitton bag she had placed there yesterday and Maxwell's small hold-all, pushed out of sight. Everything was in place.

With a quick glance in the mirror, she made a few adjustments to her personal appearance. Oh, was she going to be happy to shed the godawful maid's uniform she'd been forced to wear for six long weeks!

Quickly she undid a few buttons, hiked the skirt shorter, fluffed out her hair, and applied a liberal amount of jammy red lipstick.

"That's better, sweetie-bird," she murmured to herself.

It was almost showtime, the props were all in place, and she couldn't wait.

Marcus Citroen caught the eye of his wife as she moved graciously among her guests. An impressive woman, Nova Citroen. Elegant, assured, the perfect partner. He'd made the right choice when he'd picked her, although it had meant taking a very calculated risk, and it could have backfired—badly.

In all their years of marriage there had only been one dangerous period, a time he preferred to forget. But he had dealt with it just as he'd dealt with everything else in his life. Quickly. Expertly.

Marcus Citroen knew exactly when to be ruthless. Nobody crossed him. Nobody dared. Not even Nova.

KRIS PHOENIX
1986

★ ★ ★ ☆ ★

The girl on the television commercial had big blue eyes, a wide smile complete with all-American teeth, a pert nose, cascades of pale honey-gold hair, and a sensational body.

"I want to meet her," Kris Phoenix said. "Find out who she is."

That didn't take much doing. She was Cybil Wilde—a hot new model, with a Christie Brinkley/Cheryl Tiegs future.

She was in New York. Kris was in L.A.

"Fly her in," Kris said.

She said, Thank you, but no, thank you.

"I want her for the cover of my new album," Kris told his people. They replied that she was very expensive, three times the price of an ordinary model.

"Fuck it. Pay her," Kris said.

A photo shoot was arranged, and Cybil Wilde flew into L.A. Kris made sure there was a limousine filled with white roses to meet her at the airport, and a note from him asking her to join him for dinner. He also made sure the record company paid.

She had her mother phone him to make an excuse for not joining him for dinner. Her *mother!* It turned out she was a

California girl who'd migrated to New York, and her family lived quite comfortably in Encino.

Kris decided he wanted her before they even met. Astrid was settled in England, she hated America and what she referred to as the rock & roll circus. He was perfectly happy with Astrid, but he needed a woman in America, and from the moment he spotted Cybil in her TV commercial—which, incidentally, was for yogurt—he knew she was the right girl.

One of his minions was put in charge of compiling a dossier on her. The night before the photo shoot he sat in bed and studied it.

> *The Cybil Wilde Fact Sheet*
> AGE: 18
> HEIGHT: 5'9"
> MEASUREMENTS: 36, 22, 36
> HAIR COLOR: Honey blond
> WEIGHT: 120 pounds
> EYE COLOR: Cornflower blue

She'd attended a local high school, gone steady with the boy next door, kept two dogs and a pony, and had been an A-plus student. When she was sixteen her boyfriend entered a photograph he'd taken of her in a "model of the year" magazine contest. She won a trip to New York and an introduction to one of the best model agencies in town. A year of training. A year of learning on the job. And then she hit it. Along the way she'd broken up with her boyfriend and had dated a variety of men. Nothing serious.

Kris decided he would be her first something serious.

Antonio was a famous photographer. Italian by birth, American by choice, he practiced his craft with impeccable style. He'd recently had a book of his work published—a weighty tome of portraits entitled *Antonio—The Face*. On the cover was a glorious shot of glamorous television star Silver Anderson in a dramatic pose. The book lay casually in the dressing room, awaiting inspection.

Cybil arrived at the studio first. Scrubbed and shining, she could easily be mistaken for a teenage cheerleader.

"Hmmm . . ." Antonio inspected her, hands on hips, a critical look in his beady eyes. "Antonio think *mebbe* the raw material okay."

Cybil twinkled; she'd been warned what a pain in the ass the temperamental little photographer could be. "Only maybe?" she asked nicely.

"Fernando!" Antonio snapped his fingers for the hairdresser. "José!" Another snap to summon the makeup artist. "Paulette!" The stylist came running. "What we do weeth thees plain leetle creature?" The three of them waited for Antonio to answer himself. Which he did. "We make her *bellissima,* no?"

"Yes," they dutifully chorused.

"Bene, bene," Antonio said, with a satisfied clap of his hands. "Go to work. Make the child deevine. *Pronto!*"

Kris arrived a couple of hours later, by which time Cybil was certainly divine, although closeted out of sight with Fernando, José and Paulette.

"How're you doin', mate?" Kris asked, casually putting an arm around the diminutive photographer's shoulder.

"Kreees," purred Antonio, becoming quite skittish. "How sexy you are. I *looove* your leetle tight ass!"

Antonio had photographed Kris for his last two album covers, and the two of them had a playfully wary relationship.

The famous Phoenix grin. "Yeah, well, *you're* not gettin' any."

Antonio pursed his lips. "You have no idea what you miss, dear boy."

"Let's just keep it that way, mate."

"As you weesh," Antonio said, lascivious eyes roaming over his favorite rock star, who stood before him in jeans and a sleeveless black T-shirt with GOLD'S GYM emblazoned on the front. "You seem to be so . . . hmm . . . how I say it?" A meaningful pause. "Strong."

"Yeah, well, I've bin workin' out, haven't I? It's my new thing. Good for the old muscles, huh?" He flexed an arm, just to get the randy little photographer going.

"*Bene!*" exclaimed Antonio admiringly. "*Sooo* athletic."

"All the better to beat you up with if you ever lay a finger in my direction," Kris joked. "Not that you ever would, of course." Plucking an apple from a nearby bowl, he crunched into it. "Is the girl here yet?"

Antonio sighed. "We try to make her eento sometheeng."

Spud, Kris's English hairdresser, brought over for every important photo session, whistled as Cybil emerged from the dressing room flanked by Fernando, José and Paulette.

Looking sensational in a cutaway yellow swimsuit, her hair styled into a wild mane, and a startling makeup on her face, she smiled.

The all-American teeth attracted Kris like a flash of lightning. *All the better to eat you up with!*

"Hello, darlin'," he said. "How do you feel about moving to L.A.?"

Cybil was no pushover. He had to work on her. He had to turn on the charm. He even had to follow her back to New York.

"I don't like rock stars," she announced.

"What kind of stupid remark is that? You might just as well say you don't like policemen or kids or any sort of group. What's a rock star, anyway?"

"A guy who thinks he can get anything he wants just by winking."

"I winked. I didn't get *you*, did I?"

Gradually he won her over, and within several weeks convinced her that life in his Bel Air mansion was exactly what she wanted.

She came to stay. Gorgeous Cybil, with the hair and the teeth and the body. It was fun having her around, she was a real upper, full of enthusiasm and high spirits.

What with Astrid, no slouch in the looks stakes herself, stashed safely in England, and Cybil, the lady of his Bel Air mansion, he felt pretty settled. Not bad for a working boy who started out with zilch.

Kris Phoenix. Rock superstar.

He'd been on his own for three and a half years. Long enough to have had three smash solo albums, each one breaking records and outselling the last. First there was his debut album, *Erotic* in 1984, followed by 1985's *Gettin' Down*, and later in the year *Busted!*, a real breakthrough, putting him up there with the best-selling albums of all time. And now *Poor Little Bitch Girl*, on which he was just putting the finishing touches. One of the finishing touches was having the luscious Cybil Wilde on the album sleeve. She was an asset, no doubt about *that*.

He didn't love her.

He didn't love Astrid either.

He was thirty-seven, soon to be thirty-eight, and he had no idea what being in love was all about. Oh, he'd been in lust many times, but love—no—he'd never had that insane, urgent longing to spend the rest of his life with one woman.

And yet he knew it existed. He could write about it, think about it. Probably it was something that was never going to happen to him. He had his music, his guitar, his creativity. It was enough. Or was it? Sometimes at night he'd lie awake and think of all the things he'd achieved, and it was at those times he wished he had someone to *really* share it with. Often he thought he might have quite fancied having more kids. Bo had a stepsister, courtesy of Willow and her stockbroker husband. What might have been if he hadn't discovered Willow cheating on him?

No—that wouldn't have worked either.

Deep down, he had to admit he really missed Buzz. They'd grown up together, shared each other's lives, including the back of that horrible Volkswagen for months on end. Buzz had been closer to him than a brother could ever be. They'd had some good old times together. One of his favorite memories was their early sessions in the old dusty garage, with only Buddy Holly and Otis Redding for company. And with a great deal of nostalgia he remembered traveling through Europe screwing everything that moved —and even a few that didn't!

Finally success, and all that came with it. After that, things began to change.

Not only did he miss Buzz as his closest friend, he missed performing on stage with him. God! They'd had some great times, writing their songs, hanging out, just being together.

Now it was all over. Their past was gone. Recently Buzz, who'd formed another new group—his fourth since The Wild Ones had split—had been interviewed for *Rolling Stone*. "Kris Phoenix is a wanker," he'd said. "All he ever wanted was the money and fame. Look at him now, with his big mansions and Hollywood life style. He's success crazy. As far as I'm concerned his music is bubblegum pop shit. The wanker sold out."

When Kris first read it he'd been angry and then hurt. The Hawk had advised him to take no notice. "Everyone knows Buzz Darke is a burned-out junkie and just about finished," he'd said. "Ignore it. Don't dignify his jealousy of your success with any comment at all."

So he hadn't. But it still hurt.

Occasionally he saw Rasta—the same good-natured joker. Rasta had weathered his bad publicity, married a pretty German actress, and bought a song-publishing company that kept him busy. "Don't you miss being up on stage?" Kris often asked.

Rasta always came out with the same stock reply: "When you've had the best, why go for seconds?"

Rasta was right. Kris realized how lucky he was to have made it twice. No wonder Buzz was bitter. Every group he'd put together had turned out to be a dismal failure, mainly because most of the time he was so stoned he had no idea what he was doing. Plus he couldn't get back into America due to his drug bust. Strangely enough, he was still with Mikki, his partner in crime. Whenever Kris read about their public antics he felt sorry for both of them. A couple of losers.

Shortly after Cybil moved in, he persuaded Willow to let Bo make his first trip to America. She said no at first, having returned to her usual mean-spirited self six months after their son's accident was history, but Kris was insistent. The boy was twelve, hardly a little kid anymore.

Bo arrived, very much the proper English schoolboy, with a posh accent to go with his neat appearance. Willow was doing a great job of squeezing out any individuality the kid might possess. Kris remembered himself at the same age—a right little tearaway, guitar-crazy, with the rock star dream.

"Well, son, how's it going?" he asked, strangely uncomfortable.

"Fine, thank you, sir," Bo replied stiffly.

Sir! What was this sir shit? Three years ago they'd shared a wonderful time together at his house in the south of France. They'd swum and snorkeled and done all the good father-and-son things. Then Willow had insisted on enrolling Bo in a strict naval academy—and look at the little wanker now.

"Don't call me sir," he said tightly. "Don't call *anyone* sir."

"Yes, si . . . er . . . Dad."

The visit was not a success. Bo was uncomfortable and ill at ease, especially with Cybil. When she was around he withdrew completely, and Kris could not get through to him, however hard he tried. When the boy finally left, he blamed himself for their lack of communication.

"Don't worry," Cybil said comfortingly. "When I was thirteen I didn't even *speak* to my parents. They were like the enemy, y'know?"

"Yeah, but at least they were together. I never get to see Bo. An' that's the way Willow likes it. The only contact she wants me to have with him is to make sure I pay the bleedin' bills."

"Poor baby!" Nineteen-year-old Cybil wrapped her golden curves around him, making him feel a lot better. Cybil was good at that. So was Astrid.

His two blondes . . . Fortunately they didn't know about each other, although he realized it was only a matter of time.

One day he might have to make a choice.

RAFEALLA
1986

★ ☆ ★ ☆ ★

"Mamma! You look marvelous. Oh, and the house is so festive with the Christmas tree still up and the decorations —I remember every single one!"

Anna Le Serre smiled as her beautiful daughter ran around the house, followed by Jon Jon, who at nine was quite the best-looking boy she'd ever seen. "It's a shame you weren't here for Christmas," she scolded. "I don't understand why you couldn't have managed it."

"Mamma," Rafealla explained patiently, "I told you a hundred times, we were working. There was a New Year's Eve booking that was impossible to cancel."

"Yes, dear. However—"

"It's January the fourth," Rafealla interrupted gently but firmly. "And we're here. Let's not have an inquest on why we missed Christmas. We'll celebrate our Christmas now, won't we?" She rushed over to the big leather bag she'd carried on the plane. "Look," she said, pulling out several gift-wrapped packages. "Peace offerings!"

"Yeah, yeah! Presents, Gramma," Jon Jon encouraged. "Shall we all open presents, Gramma?"

"What makes you think you got any, kid?" Rafealla said sternly, ruffling his spiky hair.

"Aw, come on, Mom." He grinned, squirming away from her touch.

"Get lost, small stuff. We'll open presents later. *If* there are any for you. Which I seriously doubt."

"Would you like to explore outside, Jon Jon?" Anna suggested. "We have horses and dogs—"

"Fierce dogs?" he asked hopefully.

"Not exactly fierce," she replied, and then, noting his disappointed face, added matter-of-factly, "They'll kill a burglar, of course. Maul him to death."

Rafealla laughed. "Mamma! What kind of talk is that?"

"Small-boy talk, dear."

One of the stable lads was summoned, and an excited Jon Jon was taken off on a tour of the grounds.

Rafealla embraced her mother. "It is so good to be home," she sighed. "You just don't know."

"Indeed I do," replied Anna. "I've been looking forward to this moment for five years. Do you realize that's how long it is since I've seen you?"

"I know. I plead guilty."

"Well, dear, and what exactly is your excuse?"

"What's *yours?* You could have visited us, you know."

Anna lowered her eyes. "I didn't want to worry you, not until I could tell you face to face."

Rafealla felt panic. "What?" she insisted. "You're not sick, are you? Tell me."

"I will when you give me the chance. Cyrus had a mild stroke shortly after you left. Nothing serious, but the doctors felt he shouldn't make any long journeys."

"Why didn't Rupert tell me?" Rafealla demanded.

"Because when he and Odile came back, I made them promise not to," Anna replied patiently.

"Oh, God, Mamma. Why?"

"He's fine. Really he is," Anna reassured her. "You'll see."

Cyrus, her stepfather, was not as fine as Anna wanted

Rafealla to believe. He had a limp and difficulty with his speech, and he'd aged twenty years.

Rafealla was consumed with guilt, and then anger. She should have been informed. While Cyrus was not her father, and could never have replaced Lucien in her heart, he'd been an excellent and caring stepfather, and she loved him.

Thank God she'd finally come home. It was only for two weeks, but that was better than nothing.

Luiz hadn't come with her. They'd debated for months about whether he should, and in the end they'd both decided it was best for him to stay in Rio, putting the finishing touches to their second album. He wanted to do some remixing and make sure everything was perfect.

It hadn't been an easy year. When Luiz had first blurted out the news he was married, Rafealla felt her safe new world collapse. The one person she loved and depended on had been lying to her all along.

"I didn't lie," he'd stated vehemently.

"Of course you did. We've been *living* a lie."

"No, Rafealla." A Brazilian shrug. "You never asked me."

"Screw *you*, buster." She'd exploded with fury. "What do you think this is? A game? A joke? Well it might be to you, but I don't find it very funny."

She'd taken Jon Jon and two hurriedly packed suitcases and descended on Tinto, Maria, and their seven children.

Tinto was philosophical. "Have you asked him to whom he's married? Have you found out when this took place and why? Does he love the woman? And if so, why is he with you?"

Good questions, every one. And she had a right to know. Storming back, she confronted Luiz.

Calmly he explained things. Being born in the *favela* did not give one much hope for the future. Observing his brothers and sisters, he realized he was caught in a trap, and there was hardly any chance of getting out. At fourteen he was roaming the streets with the rest of his friends, occasionally robbing a rich tourist or stealing from one of the big hotels. At sixteen he was sleeping with the tourists —in the long run it was more lucrative than robbing them.

"One day I met a woman—" he shrugged noncommittally. "An older woman. She offered me an escape."

"And you took it?"

"Yes, I took it." His handsome features darkened. "And so would you if you'd had my life. I was eighteen years old and she was fifty-seven. A Brazilian woman, not rich, not poor. She took me out of the *favela*. She bought me clothes, paid for my music lessons, and made sure I learned English."

Rafealla felt a wave of nausea sweep over her. "Where is she now?"

"In a nursing home. She's been in this place for several years. Now it is my turn to take care of *her*. I won't divorce her, she does not deserve that. She's dying, Rafealla. When she goes I am free. Until then . . ."

There was nothing she could do about it, except try to understand and reluctantly admire his loyalty. With Jon Jon, she moved back in with him, much to Tinto's relief, for their career as a singing duo was really taking off.

When the American soul superstar Bobby Mondella came into town and asked to meet them, Tinto was in heaven. Especially when they all hit it off so well and became friends. Tinto immediately imagined a glowing future in America.

Rafealla loved Bobby. He was like a big brother—the other side of Rupert, who was so very English. Bobby represented the black side of her, and she could listen to his tales of Hollywood and New York and life in the fast lane forever. She sensed he was a troubled man finally coming to peace with himself. His music was sensational, and she was thrilled that he enjoyed performing with her and Luiz.

When the accident happened, she was as shocked as everyone else. She and Luiz rushed to the hospital as soon as they heard, but they were not allowed to see him—nobody was. Armed men guarded his hospital room, and one night he was secretly flown back to America.

The headlines screamed the news:

SUPERSTAR IN DRUNKEN FALL!
BOBBY MONDELLA—BLIND DRUNK!

Rafealla couldn't understand it. Bobby hardly drank anymore, and he rarely went out on his terrace, claiming a bad case of vertigo. She also wondered about the woman he'd said was staying with him. Where was she when it happened?

Combing the newspapers, Rafealla could find no mention of her. The stories merely stated that Bobby was drunk and alone when the accident took place.

Several times she and Luiz tried to contact him in America, but all they received in reply was a form letter: "Bobby Mondella thanks you for your good wishes," etcetera.

Eventually they stopped trying.

"Isn't it odd," Odile said, after an enormous turkey dinner, "that Eddie Mafair has never tried to get in touch with you?" They were sitting on the bed in Rafealla's room, just like old times.

"Why should he?" Rafealla replied defensively. "We *are* divorced, you know."

"Really?" Odile said wryly. "I had no idea."

"Shove it, missy."

"No, *you* shove it, *star*."

Rafealla giggled. "I'm glad you realize I'm famous."

"Sure. In bloody South America," Odile said good-naturedly. "Nobody's heard of you here, so don't start getting bigheaded."

"They will," Rafealla said confidently.

"Yes, and then I bet Eddie Mafair will come running. He'll probably sell his story to the *News of the World*— 'My Life with Rafealla.' What a hoot!"

"You're obsessed with Eddie."

"Merely curious. I know you too well, and there's more to the Eddie Mafair story than you're telling. For instance, how come he's never tried to see Jon Jon? He's his father. It's not normal." She clapped a hand to her mouth. "Holy shit! I've got it! After all this time I've got it!"

"Got what?" Rafealla asked warily.

"You must think I'm the world's biggest idiot!"

"Only some of the time," Rafealla commented dryly, reaching for a cigarette, even though she'd promised Luiz she would give up smoking.

"Eddie," Odile half whispered, "is not Jon Jon's father, is he?"

Rafealla felt a blush suffuse her face. She fixed Odile with a steely glare. "Don't ever say such a thing."

"It's true, isn't it?" Odile persisted. "I know it's true. You don't have to confirm or deny, because I *know*. Your expression gives you away." She shook her head in amazement. "Jon Jon doesn't look at all like Eddie. I can't imagine why I didn't guess before."

"If you say one word of this to another living soul, I will never speak to you again," Rafealla warned fiercely.

Odile's blue eyes were serious for once. She took her friend's hand in hers. "We're almost blood sisters, aren't we?" she asked earnestly. "You can tell me anything and your secret is mine."

In a way it was tremendously therapeutic to confide in Odile. After all those years of holding everything in, she let it all pour out. The hot, sticky night in the back of a limo with Kris Phoenix. Eddie's lies and beatings, and finally her brutal discovery of his homosexuality. For good measure she even told Odile about Luiz's marriage.

Odile listened quietly, and when Rafealla was finished

she hugged her close. "You should have trusted me before," she said. "I might not have been able to do anything, but I could've helped you beat the stuffing out of that bastard Eddie."

"It's not his fault. I forced him into a marriage he didn't want."

"Listen to yourself. You're always making excuses for people. You've got to stop it and toughen up."

"Is that an order?"

"You bet. Now I'm telling you, don't go rushing into anything with this Luiz character."

"He's not a character, Odile," she corrected. "He's a warm and caring man, and I love him very much."

Odile raised a cynical eyebrow. "Don't forget, I've seen his picture on the album cover. He's a good-looking, probably horny as hell, *married* man. So watch out—don't go falling into any more traps."

Rafealla laughed. "You'll have to meet him."

"I intend to. Rupert is getting his orders. No south of France this summer. We're coming back to Rio, I can't wait to see you in action!"

Two weeks with her family was enough for Rafealla. They were wonderful, but smothering. Her mother still treated her as if she were a scatty teenager, and Rupert drove her crazy with his teasing.

She was used to her independence. Besides, she missed Luiz desperately. And at the end of the fortnight, Jon Jon was anxious to get back to his friends.

Leaving her family at Heathrow airport was a wrench. Once she and Jon Jon were on the way, it was easy.

"Marcus Citroen is very interested," Tinto said excitedly, pacing around his office.

"Who?" Rafealla asked coolly, although she knew exactly who Marcus Citroen was. How could she ever forget?

"Marcus Citroen owns Blue Cadillac Records in America," Tinto said, practically jumping with joy. "Blue Cadillac is one of the big fish."

"I thought it was a car," she said disinterestedly.

Luiz glanced at her quizzically.

"He's coming into town for Carnival. He does so every year," Tinto continued.

"How nice," she murmured.

"And he wishes to meet you."

"We'll meet him," Luiz decided. "It is time we began to think of the American market."

Tinto cleared his throat and shifted uncomfortably. "I don't know how to say this, so I will come straight out with it. Rafealla is the one he wishes to meet. Blue Cadillac is not interested in a duo."

"Well, then, I'm not their girl," she said staunchly. "They'll just have to search elsewhere."

"Rafealla—" Tinto began.

"End of story," she said, imperiously tossing back her long hair.

Tinto turned to Luiz for support. Luiz merely shrugged.

"Is that all the business for the day?" she asked briskly. "For if it is, we're going swimming. Want to take the day off and come with us, Tinto?"

The disappointed manager shook his head.

Hand in hand they left his office, strolling along the street to Luiz's red sports car, a present from Rafealla on his recent twenty-sixth birthday.

People turned to scrutinize them; they were local celebrities. To the man and the woman in the street they represented youth and glamour.

A secretary on her lunch break timidly asked Luiz for his autograph, thrusting a magazine at him with his picture inside.

He smiled and requested her name.

Rafealla saw the girl blush and noted the way she gazed

at Luiz as if he were a king. "That female wants your body," she murmured teasingly as they walked away.

"Ah, but it is taken, my Carioca."

"Don't I know it!"

Somehow they didn't go swimming. They went home and spent a lazy afternoon in bed making love. Jon Jon was away for the weekend, so Friday night drifted pleasantly into Saturday morning without any disturbances.

Rafealla awoke early and thought she would surprise him by making breakfast. Cooking was not her forte, but she could manage a delicious concoction of scrambled eggs, tomato, and bacon. Wearing nothing but an oversize T-shirt, her hair braided, she set to work in the kitchen, singing softly to herself.

Luiz slept naked. He walked into the kitchen without benefit of clothes, his body bronzed and hard, his black hair tousled.

"I think I love you," she said, staring pointedly between his legs.

Responding appropriately, he embraced her from behind, his hands exploring under her T-shirt.

Soon the scrambled eggs were history. Who needed food when they had each other?

BOBBY MONDELLA
1986

★ ☆ ★ ☆ ★

"*Mr. Mondella?*"

The voice came from far away.

"Mr. Mondella, are you listening to me?"

What kind of a dumb remark was that? He couldn't do anything else but listen. He was lying in a hospital bed bandaged from head to toe, trussed up like a chicken waiting to be roasted. Even his eyes were covered. They'd given him morphine, but he could still feel the throbbing, unremitting pain.

"Mr. Mondella," the doctor said in a serious voice. "Can you see me?"

"I will when they take the goddamn bandages off," he mumbled.

"They are off," the doctor said. "You can't see me, can you? Can you . . . can you . . . can you . . . can you . . . ?"

He sat up in bed with a jolt, the sweat pouring off him. Recurring nightmare number one. Jesus Christ, he couldn't even sleep without reliving the horror of that fateful night one year ago.

I'm blind, he thought hopelessly. *I'm fucking blind. And nobody gives a damn.*

With a shaking hand he reached for the bottle of bourbon kept beside his bed at all times. The table lamp went flying, crashing to the floor with a dull thud.

"Shit!" he screamed aloud, full of pent-up frustration.

The girl he'd hired a week ago came running into the room. Her name was Sara, and she had a sweet voice. Better than the others he'd employed. There'd been a procession of personal assistants. None of them stayed long and they'd all driven him crazy. Before Sara he'd had a man look after him. A "brother" who'd ripped him off by stealing his clothes and brought women to the house in the middle of the night so he could hear them making love. Sonofabitch.

"Are you all right, Mr. Mondella?" Sara asked anxiously.

"Yeah, I'm fine."

No, baby, I am not fine. My life is totally fucked up and what I really want to do is end the whole fucking ball game. Because, hey—I don't think I can take it much longer.

"Get back to bed," he said roughly.

"No problem. I'm awake," she replied in a soothing voice. "Let me clear up this mess."

He could smell her. A womanly musk mixed with a light scent. The last female assistant he'd had, an ex-nurse, smelled of disinfectant and disdain.

"Don't worry about the mess," he said. "Just get me another bottle."

"It's the middle of the night, Mr. Mondella," she said pointedly.

More frustration burst forth. "So fuckin' what? Do you think it makes any difference to me?"

She held her ground. "I'm sure it doesn't. But a good night's sleep is what you really need."

Christ! Now he had a do-gooder. This one was going to try and get him off the booze and out into the real world. No, thank you very much.

He wondered what she looked like. Juicy. Succulent. He could tell by the way she moved around the room. And young. Twenty-five, she'd told him when he hired her.

Inexplicably he felt horny. It hadn't happened in a long time. The only women he allowed to see him in his current state were paid call girls brought to the house late at night by his driver.

Leave her alone, he warned himself. *Do not ruin a good thing. She works for you.*

It didn't matter. Nothing mattered.

"Sara," he said, warming his tone.

"Yes, Mr. Mondella?" She sounded wary.

"Hey—babe, you can call me Bobby, you mustn't be shy. I don't like things to be too formal."

"Okay."

"Sara?"

"Yes."

"Come sit on the bed. Talk to me. Tell me about yourself."

"I'm not dressed," she said primly.

He laughed bitterly. "Baby, it's not exactly like I can *see* you, is it?"

"Mr. Mondella, it's very late."

"I told you to call me Bobby," he snapped.

"Okay," she said soothingly.

His voice was a command. "Come sit."

"I don't think so."

"What the fuck d'you mean by that?" he exploded.

Taking a deep breath, she said, "I'll get you another bottle of bourbon, Mr. Mondella. I work for you as an assistant. Please let's not forget that."

He heard her leave the room. Bitch! Once she would have been begging on her knees to have a star like Bobby

428

Mondella. Well, screw her. Who did she think she was? Tomorrow he would fire her.

Sara hurried from his bedroom and looked behind the bar in the living room. She was flushed and breathing fast. Cases of bourbon were stacked high; the man was drinking himself into a stupor, and nobody seemed to care. The only people allowed to enter the house were his doctor, his driver, and his business manager. She didn't trust any of them. Why didn't his doctor stop him from drinking? How come the driver was able to sign checks and was probably ripping him off? And why wasn't the business manager advising him properly? All his money was being channeled into a variety of investments, which he didn't even have checked over by a lawyer. For a start, he should get out of the large house he was renting and into a smaller place. The money was going out every week, and nothing was coming in except occasional royalties from his songs.

Sara was shocked at what was going on. She'd only been working there a week, but she could smell a rip-off a mile away.

Sara Johnston was a smart girl. Born and raised in Philadelphia, she'd graduated high school at eighteen and gone straight into a business-management course. From there she'd started work at her father's accountancy firm, specializing in show-business clients. She'd handled the accounts of a lady soul singer, two managers, and a singing trio. The ins and outs of show business intrigued her, and she found the music end of it particularly interesting. Sara would have loved to try a singing career herself. Unfortunately, she had no voice. She had also thought about becoming a model, but she was too short and far too curvy.

Working for her father was merely a stepping-stone to more exciting things. When she heard through business connections that Bobby Mondella was looking for a personal assistant, she flew out to California the next day for an interview. First she saw his business manager, Nils

Holmer, a swarthy white man with shifty eyes. Next she was ushered in to see Bobby. She was shocked by his appearance. He sat in a chair by the window, overweight and unshaven. His hair was too long and in general he looked uncared for. Wraparound dense black sunglasses covered his eyes.

She remembered her first sight of Bobby Mondella in the flesh. Philadelphia, 1979, onstage. She was eighteen years old and she'd thought he was the most gorgeous hunk she'd ever seen in her entire life. Now this angry man sitting next to the window stirred her with a feeling of great compassion.

"Why'd you want this job, girl?" he'd asked harshly.

"Because I need the money," she'd lied.

"Hell, that's a good 'nuff reason to sit around with a blind man. Hire her, Nils."

She'd started work ten days later, and after one week in his company she vowed that she, Sara Johnston, was going to bring this wreck of a man back to life.

"What d'you look like?"

"I beg your pardon?"

"You speak English, girl. It's a simple 'nuff question."

Another week had passed and she was still in his employ, in spite of rejecting his advances that one night.

"Uh, I have shoulder-length black hair."

"Let me feel it."

"I'll make you a bargain."

There was a weary tone to his voice. "What's that, babe?"

"Allow me to arrange for a barber to come to the house and cut *your* hair, and you can feel away."

He laughed cynically. "Cute."

"Is it a deal?"

"Why would I want my hair cut, huh? I don't get to show it to anybody."

"*I* look at you all day."

"You're paid to do it."

"So I am," she said with a faint hint of sarcasm.

This girl pissed him off. She was feisty, not scared of losing her job. Sara with her sweet voice was a tough little cookie.

"Okay, we got ourselves a deal. Come here."

She walked over to him and stood by his chair. He reached up and felt her thick curly hair, breathing deeply as her light scent invaded his nostrils, and oh, no—here came that old familiar feeling. This girl was turning him on again. What *was* it with her?

Before she had a chance to realize what was happening, he dropped his hands to where her breasts should be, and got himself a surprise. This girl was stacked. This lady was more than a handful, she was something else.

"Don't!" Angrily she jerked away.

"Come back here *now*," he commanded.

"No way."

"Hey, baby," he said harshly, "do you want this job or not?"

"Have you ever heard of sexual harassment, Mr. Mondella?"

"Aw, get out. Send my driver in."

His driver had long Rastafarian locks and a permanent sneer. Nothing would give Sara more pleasure than to fire him.

He spent five minutes with Bobby, left, and returned half an hour later accompanied by an ugly black woman in a tight dress that emphasized her huge bosom.

"Hooker time," the driver said with a knowing leer. "An' they don't even havta be pretty."

Sara found it sheer torture to think of Bobby with the whore. She wanted to murder the sleazy driver, but she managed, with difficulty, to keep her cool. "How often does he have them over?" she asked, trying to sound casual.

"Not often," the man replied, picking his teeth with a packet of book matches. "The dude can't get it up no more." A wink. "Not like us *normal* studs."

In the bedroom, Bobby struggled with his feelings of sexual inadequacy. His driver had been right. Bobby Mondella couldn't do it anymore. What was the goddamn point? What was the point of anything? He'd been to the top, and now with some cheap prostitute slobbering all over him he'd hit the bottom.

Bobby Mondella. The star who fell from grace. Literally. Only he hadn't fallen, he'd been thrown from that balcony in Rio. Doused in booze and tossed from the terrace of his tenth-floor apartment. Jesus! They'd intended to murder him, and yet he'd survived to tell the tale—which nobody believed. "You were drunk," everyone, including the police, said. "You were alone," they all agreed. "You fell."

And no amount of argument on his part could convince them otherwise.

Well fuck 'em all. *He* knew it was no accident. If an awning hadn't broken his fall he would have been dead. Someone had tried to have him killed. But he couldn't put a name to the person who had arranged it.

What did it matter? He was finished anyway. They'd achieved their objective.

Nova had apparently vanished from the apartment long before the police arrived, leaving no trace. Bitch. Fucking bitch. He'd heard she was back with Marcus like nothing had happened. She'd certainly never tried to contact him. Not even when he lay in the hospital with nearly every bone in his body broken.

The bones healed. His eyes didn't. He was blind, and nobody could tell him why. It wasn't clinical; psychological, they said.

Psychological, ha! What the fuck did all those fancy-assed doctors know? If he could see, he would. It was as simple as that.

Nichols Kline took care of everything. Guards in the hospital to keep away the press. A private flight to L.A. Nichols even organized the rented house, hired the private nurses and security guards he'd had for the first six months, and arranged for Nils Holmer to have power of attorney and take care of his money.

The money deal wasn't so great. It was all spend, spend, spend, with nothing coming in. He'd never been good at financial matters, always leaving it up to accountants and business managers. Now Nils kept on telling him he was almost broke. And Nichols had vanished from his life forever.

"I don't understand it," he said, when Nils came by with more bad news. "You've gotta know I was one of the biggest-earning stars in the goddamn country. Where the fuck has it all gone?"

"Taxes, expenses, bills, and bad investments. Plus you lived a pretty extravagant life style."

"Jesus Christ! You were supposed to be lookin' after the investments. What happened?"

Nils looked affronted. "I only make 'em. I can't guarantee 'em. It's the financial climate, Bobby. There's no way I can control that."

"Are you tryin' to tell me I've lost everything?"

Nils shrugged. "You've got enough left to get by on. Move out of this house, get a smaller place. I have to leave the country for a while—I'll have someone else in the office take care of things for you."

Bobby knew he was being shafted. So fucking what? There wasn't any place left to go. He was finished. Why prolong the agony?

That night he overdosed. Took every goddamn pill he could lay his hands on.

Sara found him at three o'clock in the morning. He was unconscious on the bathroom floor, spilled bottles of pills all around him.

From that moment on, she took charge. Sara Johnston was a very determined young lady, and she knew, without a doubt, she was going to bring Bobby Mondella right back to the top where he belonged.

KRIS PHOENIX
1987

★ ☆ ★ ☆ ★

"Marcus Citroen would like you to appear at his wife's fund-raiser for Governor Jack Highland in July."

So spoke Hawkins Lamont, resplendent in tennis whites, with his impeccable George Hamilton suntan. The two sat in the garden room of the Polo Lounge eating lunch.

"Screw Marcus Citroen," Kris replied, chewing on a roll.

The Hawk raised a quizzical eyebrow. "What's that supposed to mean?"

Kris stared at his manager. "It means Kris Phoenix don't jump for anyone."

The Hawk waved to an acquaintance across the room, sipped his fresh grapefruit juice, and said, "Has Marcus done something I should know about?"

"The whole bleedin' record industry knows about it," Kris responded sharply.

"In that case," the Hawk replied smoothly, "perhaps you can enlighten *me*."

"Come on, man," Kris said roughly. "Don't give me that you-got-no-idea-what's-goin'-on shit."

"What *is* going on?"

"Sharleen."

435

"Ah." The Hawk shook his head sadly. "A most unfortunate incident."

"Jesus!" Kris exclaimed. "I don't believe you people. A woman kills herself, fuckin' kills herself, an' you call it an *incident*."

"I didn't realize you knew Sharleen," the Hawk said.

"Yes. I knew her. It was a long time ago, but we kept in touch here an' there."

"She was a drug addict."

"She was a poor bitch who got herself fucked over by the record industry, an' especially by your friend Marcus Citroen."

"*My* friend—*your* boss."

The waitress placed a Neil Mcarthy salad in front of Hawkins and a juicy hamburger before Kris.

Kris waited for her to leave before saying, "I don't have a *boss*. I work for myself, an' my record company gets rich off me—just like you do, Hawk."

"We get rich off each other," the Hawk pointed out coldly. Rock stars. Ungrateful, uneducated, unappreciative egomaniacs.

"Anyway," Kris said flatly, "everyone knows she did it because of Marcus. It's not exactly a secret."

"Supposition."

"What?"

"The good old rumor-go-round. As far as I'm aware, Marcus was always very generous to Sharleen. He kept her under contract long after she stopped making hits."

"He sucked the juice out of her. An' when she was dry he cut her loose an' left her with nothing."

"Nonsense."

"Yeah, well, you've got your opinions an' I've got mine, an' there's no way I'm doin' a fund-raiser for him. No bleedin' way."

* * *

"Do you love me?" Cybil demanded, raising her golden head from the task at hand.

He wished she wouldn't ask him that. What was he supposed to say? *Yeah—when I've got a hard-on I love ya t'death. An' when I don't—well—it's only rock 'n roll, ain't it?*

Maybe he wasn't capable of loving anyone. Perhaps catching Willow in bed with that German prick all those years ago had done him in as far as women were concerned. Not to mention ten thousand groupies along the way.

He knew one thing. Women—you couldn't trust 'em.

"Go for it, baby, don't stop," he said, pushing Cybil's glorious mane of hair back into place.

One

Two

Three

JOLT!

Later there was American football on TV and a catered dinner for two from Trader Vic's. Cybil watched the football with him, daintily gnawing on a sparerib as she sat cross-legged on the bed wearing nothing but a man-sized sweatshirt.

At midnight the phone rang. Usually he let the service deal with all calls, but this time he picked it up. The first thing he heard was the faint crackle of long distance, and then a desperate plea. "Kris, Kris, is that you? Uh . . . this is Mikki, remember me? Look, I don't want to bother you, I really don't. But . . . Kris . . . you've got to help Buzz. You've got to help him. *Please.* We're desperate."

British Airways' six o'clock evening flight got him into Heathrow airport at noon the next day. B.A.'s Mike Baverstock met him at the plane and whisked him through passport control and customs with no problem. There had been a time when they always stopped him to search for drugs.

But that was back in the bad old days when The Wild Ones first ran riot and he wasn't considered a respectable elder statesman of rock.

He hadn't warned Astrid of his imminent arrival. Better to surprise her, keep her on edge.

A chauffeured Rolls took him straight to his country mansion. Astrid was out with the dogs. He unpacked his one carry-on bag and made a few calls. Mikki had promised to get Buzz over to the house that evening. He wondered if he'd come. He'd bleedin' better.

"Dinner for four, luv. An' I fancy a roast," he informed Astrid, when she entered the house.

"Kris! What are you doing here?" she shrieked, as his two German shepherds jumped all over him. "God! I bet I look awful."

Astrid's idea of awful was jeans and a sweater with no makeup, her long flaxen hair in a ponytail. She looked pretty good to him, and refreshingly healthy.

"I live here. Remember?"

Throwing her arms around him, she said, "How could I ever forget? Welcome home."

They spent the rest of the afternoon in bed. He felt like a sailor with a wife in every port. Fortunately, however, they weren't wives, and there were only two ports.

Astrid had never met Buzz, and as the evening approached she became more than apprehensive.

"Stay cool," Kris warned. "He's likely to insult you *an'* me. That's his way. The thing is, I don't mind—I just want to see him back on his feet. Understand?"

She'd read plenty about the notorious Buzz Darke. "He's not going to smash up our dining room, is he?" she asked nervously.

"Don't worry. All you gotta do is take Mikki off somewhere after dinner. I want to be alone with him."

"What's Mikki like?"

"Listen, I haven't seen either of them in four years. She

used to be just another rich groupie out on a slumming trip. Get the picture?"

Astrid nodded. She wasn't looking forward to the evening ahead.

"Let's just hope she gets him here," Kris said. "She sounded pretty frantic on the phone. I told her to pretend she bumped into me on the street an' I insisted they come for dinner."

"So," Astrid said, "you flew all the way back here just to help a friend. That's if he even turns up."

"Don't go makin' a big deal out of it. I owe him. We're mates—or at least we were."

She shook her head. "You're unbelievable!"

"Listen, luv, it could've bin me. I was the lucky one. If things were reversed I reckon he'd do the same thing."

Buzz and Mikki arrived two and a half hours late, just when Kris was beginning to give up. They came in a taxi, with no money between the two of them, looking like a couple of tramps. Kris paid.

Buzz walked around the house. "Fuckin' rollin' in it, ain'tcha?" he sneered, adding sardonically, "Can yer spare a few bob while yer at it?"

His appearance was devastating. Whitish-gray skin drawn tightly over bony features. Sunken, dead eyes. Badly dyed black hair curling over the collar of a decrepit leather jacket, and long, skinny legs encased in jeans, with well-worn snakeskin boots completing the ensemble. A joint seemed to have affixed itself permanently to his mouth, and he dragged on it without benefit of hands.

Mikki had turned into a plump, untidy woman with frizzed, yellowish hair. She was not yet thirty, but her lined skin and weary eyes made her seem ten years older. She had on a stained green sweater and baggy khaki pants.

Kris remembered the pretty Mikki he'd once known, and wondered where she'd gone.

Both of them headed straight for the booze. Buzz favored straight vodka, while Mikki settled for red wine, which she immediately spilled down the front of her sweater. It didn't seem to bother her.

"Well," Kris said, pouring himself an Old Kentucky. "It's great to see you two."

"Congratulate us," Buzz said, throwing himself into a chair. "We got married this morning. She's not just fat, y'know, she's pregnant. Fucking stupid cow."

"You're kiddin'?"

Mikki nodded. "It's true, Kris. We suddenly became respectable in our old age."

"Shit! Let's break open the champagne."

"Shit!" Buzz mimicked. "It's not like yer can't afford it."

The evening dragged along, with Buzz making crack after crack about selling out and recording crap and going for commerciality above all else. Halfway through the meal he vanished into the bathroom and didn't come back for twenty minutes.

"You've got to find him a job, Kris," Mikki pleaded while he was gone. "You know how good he can be. He's sensational, and all he can get is backing work on the occasional lousy session. It's criminal. And I'm frightened he's going to do something. . . ." Lowering her red-rimmed eyes, she whispered, "Y'know, like Sharleen."

"Jesus, Mikki. I can't get him shit while he's strung out."

She gulped her wine, talking too fast, pressing out of desperation. "He's coming off dope. Honestly. All he needs is a chance."

Kris had heard that the Orange Dragons, Blue Cadillac's hot new group, were due to do six concerts in England next month and were looking for an opening act. Put Buzz together with a good keyboard player and backing—and if he was on top of it, he'd be perfect for the gig.

"Why don't I see what I can do," he said. "Only you've got to promise me you'll make sure he dries out."

"Oh, yes, Kris. I can promise that. Honestly. You can trust me."

"Someone from Blue Cadillac Records will be in touch. I'm goin' to give you a check—get him in a fucking clinic to clean up, and don't tell him I had anything to do with it. Okay?"

Later, on the phone long distance: "Hawk, I want you to arrange something for me."

"What?"

He told the Hawk exactly what needed doing.

An hour later he got a call back. "It will all be taken care of."

"That's great. I'm pleased."

"One thing, Kris."

"Yeah?"

"Marcus Citroen's fund-raiser. He *can* depend on you, can't he?"

RAFEALLA
1987

★ ★ ★ ☆ ★

Coolly Rafealla stared at the man sitting behind the ornate antique desk. Marcus Citroen. He'd held her future in his hands and he'd delivered. How strangely fate had intertwined their lives over the years.

"Well, my dear," Marcus said triumphantly, "I told you I could do it for you, and now I am delighted to inform you that your single, 'Perfume Nights,' will be number one next week in *six* different countries, including the only two that really matter—England and America."

Standing up, she walked over to the window and gazed out. Marcus Citroen's London office overlooked Hyde Park. It was a crisp February day and the wind was blowing. People were huddled up in overcoats and scarves as they scurried by.

Sometimes on days like this she really missed Rio. But what had she actually given up?

Nothing . . . nothing. . . .

Carnival came and went. Marcus Citroen came and went. Much to Tinto's chagrin, Rafealla refused to meet with him. "You're very foolish," he scolded. "He could make you into a big international star."

"And what about Luiz?" she responded tartly. "We're a team. We do things together or not at all."

"Ah, but Rafealla, maybe you should think of your future."

Stubbornly she stood her ground. "Luiz is my future."

Tinto shrugged. "Perhaps, perhaps not." He didn't know how to tell her that while she was in England, Luiz had been seen out with the very rich Vivienne Riccardo, or, as she was known by her adoring public, "queen of the television soaps."

"You can stuff your negativity," Rafealla said gaily, "and plan on a wedding."

Tinto couldn't conceal his surprise. "When?"

"Soon."

"How soon?"

"You'll be the first to know."

Luiz had been a little quiet since she'd returned from England. She had thought the new album was all finished, but most nights he spent at the studio. "I'll come with you," she suggested.

"You'll be bored," he replied. "It's all technical details."

"I'm bored staying at home," she protested mildly.

Playfully he kissed her. "Ah, my spoiled little English Carioca is bored. Just be patient, my darling. Luiz is working for both of us."

"I am not English. I am not spoiled. And hurry up and get finished with all this work."

She knew the album was important to him. He'd produced it and written four of the songs. Naturally he was concerned about every detail. When it was finally out in the stores he could relax.

She was anxious to ask him about his wife again, the old woman dying in a nursing home somewhere. But it seemed like such a crass thing to do, so she remained silent, wait-

ing until he chose to speak of it. It must be painful enough for him—why should she add to his burden?

One night he failed to come home at all. She reached out upon waking, and he wasn't there. "Luiz?" She called out, got up, and padded around the apartment. Jon Jon had already left for school, and Constanza, their daily maid, was cleaning the kitchen floor.

"Meester no here," said the surly Constanza.

"He must have slept at the studio," Rafealla explained, wondering why she felt the need to make excuses to the maid.

There was no reply when she rang the studio. Feeling foolish, she phoned Tinto at home. "Luiz is missing," she said, half jokingly. "Have you any idea where he might be?"

Tinto wanted to say, "Try Vivienne Riccardo's satin sheets." The whole town was talking about Luiz's blatant affair with the glamorous older actress, and yet no one dared tell Rafealla—including Tinto. He hesitated. "Er . . . I don't know—" he began.

"Give me the telephone," commanded his wife, Maria, snatching the instrument from him. "Rafealla, dear," she said firmly. "We meet today for lunch. We talk. There are things you should know."

Tinto groaned.

Before they could meet, before they could talk, the news hit the airwaves. Luiz Oliveira and Vivienne Riccardo had been secretly married that morning.

"I love London," Rafealla murmured.

Marcus rose from his desk and stood next to her. "Is that all you have to say? I have just told you your record will be number one across the world. Don't you understand what that means?"

Turning to look at him, she said, "Does it mean I'm a star?"

"Yes."

"Famous?"

"Yes."

"Rich?"

"Eventually. With me to guide you."

With me to guide you. It was not the first time he had said those words to her. Not the first time . . .

"I want to meet with Marcus Citroen, Tinto."

"You're too late. He's returned to the United States."

"Call him."

"With all due respect, Raffi, he probably won't even remember his former interest."

She raised an eyebrow and said mockingly, *"What an agent! Such enthusiasm!"*

"I can try."

"Do it."

Marcus Citroen did remember her. He suggested that she fly to New York and cut a demo record. Tinto was ecstatic.

"Forget it," Rafealla said. "Ask him to come back here."

"Don't be silly," Tinto argued. "It is obvious to me you have no idea how important this man is."

"Yes, I do know. Ask him anyway." Instinct told her Marcus Citroen would do as she wished.

A week of silence. Then Phoebe, Mr. Citroen's personal secretary, called to inform Tinto that Mr. Citroen did indeed have further business in Rio, and would be returning in ten days' time.

Rafealla merely nodded when a jubilant Tinto told her. He was full of plans, deciding how to approach the great man, and what strategy they would employ to get the best deal.

"No," Rafealla said evenly. "I want to see him alone."

Tinto shook his head, puzzled. Rafealla was a strange

and wonderful girl—and he didn't understand her at all. When Luiz married Vivienne Riccardo, he, along with Maria and everyone else, had expected her to go to pieces —explode, have hysterics—do something. *No. Not Rafealla. She was calm as could be. A shrug. A philosophical "Luiz must do what he has to do." And that was that.*

She informed Tinto she would never work with Luiz again, and told him to cancel all their bookings.

"But what about the new album?" he asked worriedly. "Surely you will do promotional appearances?"

A flat "No." And then she'd requested the meeting with Marcus Citroen.

Now it was arranged, and she was saying she didn't want Tinto to be there. Peculiar girl. He didn't argue. Rafealla had her own way of doing things.

Marcus Citroen and Rafealla Le Serre met in Citroen's suite at the Copacabana Palace hotel. She was even more exotically beautiful than he remembered. He was even more of a dirty old man than she had thought, with his licentious hooded eyes and dissipated expression.

"Well, my dear, it seems our paths cross again," he said. "You grow more beautiful each time."

She stared straight at him, her brilliant green eyes challenging and direct. She knew exactly what she wanted from Marcus Citroen. She also knew exactly what he wanted from her.

For a moment she thought of Luiz. He could burn in hell for all she cared. He was the last man she would ever allow to hurt her again.

Dear, sweet, wonderful Luiz. Bastard. Basta! He had lied to her from day one. A private detective had found out the whole truth, because she had to know.

Luiz Oliveira. Not his real name. Try Lupe Veira. A child of the favela—*his one true statement. He was thirty-two years old, not twenty-six as he'd claimed.*

Luiz Oliveira alias Lupe Veira. A convicted thief and

*male prostitute. Married twice before the lucky Vivienne
Riccardo.The first time to Juana, the girl who'd worked for
her who he'd claimed was his sister. The second to an old
woman in São Paulo, who'd died after six weeks of marriage, leaving him her fortune. Her grown children immediately contested the will, and after many months of legal
bickering he'd ended up with a paltry payoff settlement. A
month later he'd reentered Rafealla's life.*

By chance? Or had he planned it?

*She didn't know and she didn't care. Men were users.
Now she was going to join their club.*

*"Marcus," she said coolly—"I can call you Marcus,
can't I?"*

*He rubbed his thumb and forefinger together, gazing at
her with lustful dedication. "Certainly, my dear."*

"You know what I think?"

*"What?" Sweat beaded his bald head. This girl had
everything he required. A strong, earthy sexuality, combined with a certain aloofness, and that wonderful olive
skin. In a way, she reminded him of Nova when he'd first
set eyes on her. She had that same exotic quality he
craved.*

*Of course, this girl was different—she already had
breeding and class. And she was talented.*

*Rafealla stared directly at him. "Let's not play games,
Marcus. I'll be very straight with you."*

"Yes?"

*Briefly she thought of Luiz again, and Eddie Mafair. The
two loves of her life. Two phonies. Two lousy sons of
bitches.*

*"Marcus," she said firmly, "I want your power. You
want my body. Why don't we see if we can cut a deal?"*

"So," Marcus said, snaking his arm slowly around her
shoulders, "I kept my part of the bargain. Now, my dear, I
think it is time for you to deliver."

Deftly she moved out of his grasp. "Not yet, Marcus. I have to see it all work."

"You wouldn't try to back out, would you?"

"No."

Rafealla was playing with him. Perhaps she didn't realize she was playing with the greatest game expert of all time. Perversely, Marcus rather enjoyed her independent attitude. It was quite a change to come across a woman who expected him to wait. A true diversion. She obviously had no idea of his real power. He would have to teach her, and he looked forward to the lesson.

"You'll appear at my wife's fund-raiser in July," he decided, with a faint smile. "We'll consummate our relationship then. *And*, my dear, I'm sure you'll find it will be a long and fulfilling one." He paused, adding meaningfully, "For both of us."

BOBBY MONDELLA
1987

★ ☆ ★ ☆ ★

The first time they made love was the most exciting day of Sara Johnston's life. She hadn't come to work for Bobby Mondella with the purpose of climbing into bed with him —but when the opportunity arose, who was she to say no? The man might be blind, but in her book that didn't make him any less of a man. She'd brought him back from the brink. Nurtured him, cared for him. Moved him out of the big, expensive mansion he could no longer afford and into a small, cozy place in Nichols Canyon. She'd got rid of his business manager—slightly too late, as the man had already stolen most of his money. And with enormous pleasure she fired his driver and changed his doctor.

"You're some bossy, woman," Bobby grumbled, as she set about getting him back into shape. "Where you comin' from with all this attitude?"

"Heaven," she replied dryly. "Or hell. Depends which way you look at it."

"Hell!" he complained when she forced him to start swimming and exercising and using his body again.

"Heaven!" he crooned, the first time they made love, and he found everything to be in working order, just as it was before the accident.

What a lover he was! Sara felt weak just thinking about the hours they spent in bed together.

Bobby Mondella. Once she had him in good physical shape, she set about getting his brain in gear. "You planning on sitting around doin' nothing for the rest of your life?" she challenged.

"Yeah," he replied defiantly.

"No way, man."

"You're a pushy little thing."

"An' you love it. Because I'm gonna push you all the way back to the top—whether you wanna go there or not."

"Get lost, woman."

"Don't go givin' me none of your lip, man."

He'd refused to see anyone since the accident. But one day Sara invited some musicians he'd worked with in the past to come to the house. At first he was angry. And then gradually he relaxed when he found no one was being judgmental or treating him as an object of pity. He'd ended up having a good time, and in bed that night he'd showed her his appreciation.

The next day he sat down at the piano and began composing and singing again.

It was a magic moment for Sara. She'd spent months getting him to this point. "You're going to make an album," she told him. "We'll call it *Mondella Alive*, an' it'll be the best thing you've ever done."

He didn't argue. He started writing new songs, arranging them, spending every waking moment on creating something both beautiful and powerful.

When he'd compiled enough rough material, Sara took it around to a few of the big record companies, starting off with Soul On Soul, where Amerika Allen politely said they weren't interested. Reaction after that was not friendly. Doors were closed in her face.

"Bobby Mondella? No way. His time is over."

"Bobby Mondella? I thought he was dead."

"That drunken bum. You must be putting us on!"

One day she got a call from Marcus Citroen, the president of Blue Cadillac Records. "I understand you have new Bobby Mondella material," he said. "Is it good?"

She hesitated. Bobby had told her under no circumstances was she to go to Blue Cadillac. But what the heck —this was their only chance. "It's not just good, Mr. Citroen. It's sensational," she said, with every ounce of enthusiasm she possessed.

"I'd like to hear it."

Within six weeks Bobby was in the recording studio with a fat new contract.

Marcus Citroen was giving him the chance to come back.

"I'm sorry," the specialist said gravely. "There is nothing I can tell you. The cause of Mr. Mondella's sight loss is a complete unknown. There is no physical reason. No deterioration or damage to the optical nerve. The cornea and retina are in perfect condition." The doctor shrugged hopelessly. "This is just one of those medical mysteries one day we hope to be able to solve."

Sara nodded; they'd heard it all before. She took Bobby's arm and they left the office. According to the many doctors and eye specialists they'd visited, Bobby's loss of sight was traumatic, and therefore untreatable. His blindness was unexplainable. They had been told everything from "psychosomatic" to "Perhaps he should see a psychiatrist."

"I'm learnin' to live with it, stay cool," he said, squeezing her hand. "Hey, mamma, I'm workin' again. I feel good. Things aren't that bad."

He never let on to Sara how much it hurt inside to know he would never see again. The pain was his, and he had to bear it in silence, although sometimes in the middle of the night he lay awake for hours just thinking about things.

Why? Why had this happened to him? And who was responsible?

Marcus Citroen was giving him the opportunity to shine again. Was he doing it because of guilt?

Hell, no, that piranha had no conscience.

So maybe Nichols and his band of business associates were responsible.

Shit. He shouldn't even think about it, because it was something he'd never know.

The same week *Mondella Alive* came out, Sharleen committed suicide. She slit her wrists and bled to death in her New York apartment.

Bobby mourned long into the night. He'd loved that woman once, and wished he'd been kinder to her the last time she'd visited him in New York.

Too late now. She'd written him after his tragedy, a sweet note asking if she could come and see him. He'd never replied because he hadn't wanted her to view him as a victim.

Now she was gone. Poor, pretty Sharleen.

A day later he contacted Rocket Fabrizzi—another friend he'd rejected. Rocket was in L.A. making a movie. He came over and they talked the night away, reliving every good old memory.

"I'm glad t'see you're back, man," Rocket said warmly as he left. "Let's stay in touch. You an' I—we'll always remember Sharleen the way she was."

Early reports on the album were excellent. As a favor, Rocket directed a promotional video to help it take off. Sara was by Bobby's side at all times, urging him on.

When Marcus Citroen phoned to say he wanted Bobby Mondella to appear at his wife's fund-raiser, Sara's initial reaction was a short, sharp no. She knew some things about Bobby's affair with Nova—he'd told her bits and pieces, but not the whole story by any means.

When she informed Bobby of Marcus Citroen's request he hesitated for only a moment, and then, to her surprise, said, "Yeah, I'll do it."

Privately he thought it was time he laid some ghosts of the past to rest. And maybe—just maybe—he could find out the real truth about that fateful night in Rio.

"Really?" Sara glared at him disapprovingly.

With a firm nod he said, "Sure. You can tell Marcus Citroen I'll definitely be there."

SATURDAY, JULY 11TH, 1987
THE DINNER

★ ☆ ★ ☆ ★

"Can I see you?" Governor Highland asked in a low voice.

"Huh?" Cybil widened her big blue eyes. "You *are* seeing me."

Leaning closer he murmured, "You know what I mean."

She thought about what Hawkins had said—one day this man might be in the White House. Quite an exhilarating prospect. Then she thought about Kris—he'd been two-timing her with some Danish floozy in London.

"Do you mean lunch?" she asked.

"Dinner," he corrected.

"Okay," she said with a shiver of excitement. "Where and when?"

Governor Highland smiled. He had sharp, pointed teeth. *Attack-dog teeth,* she thought, suppressing a wild giggle.

"I'm married, you know." He was agreeably honest. "Therefore I have to be very discreet."

"That's all right," she replied. "I'm living with someone, I have to be just as careful as you."

"Write down your phone number," he said, surreptitiously handing her a book of matches and a pen. "My aide will contact you."

It was an unfortunate choice of words. Cybil reacted with grim realization—Governor Highland was probably putting it about all over the place; politicians were known to be a randy bunch, especially the married ones. Too risky, as Kris would say.

Quickly she scribbled the wrong number.

More attack-dog teeth as Governor Highland pocketed the information with a true politician's smile.

"Dinner is served." Several maitre d's made the announcement, causing a procession of richly clad and bejeweled guests to begin the walk down toward the dining area. Leading the way was a strip of thick red carpet covering the winding path.

Maxwell Sicily took a wooden toothpick from his pocket and dug it into his gums as he watched them move out. How come his father wasn't among them? The great Carmine Sicily. The great pig. Carmine had tried hard enough to insinuate himself into high society. He'd bought large chunks of a variety of high-profile companies, even gaining controlling interest in a bank. But Maxwell knew the way things were—he was smarter than his old man any day—and the big shots might come to Carmine when they needed a favor, but they would never think of mixing with him socially. To them he was nothing but a rich gangster.

Maxwell had to make sure his life was different. In South America a new identity awaited him. He would have money *and* respect.

Unlike his father, *he* would have everything.

Nova Citroen moved among her guests, assured and in control. She knew Marcus was watching her. Damn him. Let him watch away. There was nothing more he could do to her. He'd taken her to the very depths and then dragged her right up to the top again.

He'd done the same to Bobby Mondella.

455

Ah . . . Bobby. For a moment she thought about her former lover with a feeling of nostalgia. At least he was alive. By all rights he should be dead.

She twisted the huge solitaire diamond ring on her finger. A blood present from her dear husband—and she had accepted it, and kept her silence. After all, deep down, a whore was always a whore.

Memories of Rio returned . . . the nightmare lingered.

Touching her magnificent diamond necklace, she turned to speak to Governor Highland, seated on her right. "I do hope you're enjoying yourself," she said pleasantly.

"Nova, dear, when a man is in your company *everything* is a treat. You are truly the most gracious hostess of all. I cannot begin to tell you how much Mary and I appreciate this evening."

"It's nothing, Jack," she murmured modestly. "I adore entertaining. And doing something for you is always a pleasure."

Gazing into her eyes, he said a very sincere "Thank you, Nova. Thank you so very much. You'll never regret the support you've given us."

Restlessly pacing around her tastefully appointed guest suite, dreading the fact that soon she was going to have to confront Marcus Citroen, Rafealla decided to talk to Bobby, because tonight was the perfect opportunity, and why should she allow him to blank her out of his life? Once they'd been close friends. Was that friendship supposed to end because of his unfortunate accident?

"Trudie," she said, "I'm going to see Bobby Mondella."

"Right now?" Trudie asked unsurely. "Well, I guess if you're dressed and ready to go on, we can stand at the side of the stage."

"I don't mean watch him perform. I want to visit him now."

"That's not a good idea at all," Trudie said firmly, wondering what this was all about. "Bobby is on first, and I'm sure he'll be getting ready even now."

"What room is he in?"

"Uh . . . seriously, Rafealla. The guests are eating dinner. *You* should be getting dressed, and Bobby is probably already on his way down there."

"What room is he in?" she repeated stubbornly.

Trudie shook her head. "I don't know. This isn't a hotel, there are no numbers on the doors. And there's enough doors to house three families!"

"Don't worry about it, I'll be right back."

"Rafealla—" Trudie wailed.

"Five minutes. I promise."

Stepping into the hall, she looked around. Several doors obviously all led into guest suites like hers. She knocked on the first one, and a masculine voice called, "Come in."

Tentatively she did so.

Lounging on a couch, flicking the channels on a large-screen TV, was Kris Phoenix.

A silent moment while their eyes met. Oh, no! She hadn't seen him since that unmemorable night in his limousine ten years ago. Oh, no! For a moment she almost panicked.

"Hi," she mumbled, feeling like a stupid fan.

"Hello, luv," he said, without a flicker of ever having met her before. "Nice of you to come by an' say hello. I like your music, you're doin' all right, girl. Keep it goin'."

"Ooooh, Tom. I thought I'd never find you," Vicki cooed softly, creeping up behind him in the security-control room. "I should've guessed you'd be here."

"Where else would I be?" he asked, a trifle pompously, indicating the bank of TV monitors surrounding him. "I get to see every single thing from this seat."

"So you do," she said in an admiring tone. "What a clever system. Did you set it up?"

"It's all based on my suggestions," he boasted, turning to ogle the cleavage in her partly unbuttoned uniform. She'd been cozying up to him for a while now; it was obvious she couldn't resist him.

He felt Mr. Stiffy stir in his pants. Mavis, his wife of twenty-five years, had named it Mr. Stiffy on their honeymoon. Unfortunately, over the years, it had not exactly lived up to its name, but this red-hot, not-so-little number certainly had its full attention.

"*I* think you're brilliant," she sighed, wondering to herself if she wasn't going just the tiniest bit too far.

"You do?"

"Oooh, sugar-pie, I do!"

He was just about to get up and grab her when the door opened, and one of his guards walked in.

"What is it, Sturgon?" Tom snapped, caught at the pass.

The guard was no idiot. He took one look at Vicki, hovering in the corner, and another look at Tom, red-faced and ready for action, and quickly said, "Just reporting in, boss. No problems. Everybody's in position."

"Good, good," Tom blustered. "Get back to checkpoint one an' stay there."

"Don't you need me to man the screens with you?"

"It's not necessary. I'll contact you later."

Sturgon favored Vicki with a long, lustful leer. He wouldn't mind a crack at her himself. Some people had all the luck. "Okay, boss," he said, with a smart-aleck salute. "I'll see you later."

Tom grunted. He didn't like the way Sturgon eyeballed Vicki. She deserved more respect than that.

Standing at the side of the stage, Bobby smelled money. It was all around him. Along with the light outdoor breeze, there was a subtle mix of heady perfume and expensive aftershave. Above that, the rich aroma of two-hundred-dollar cigars filled the air.

Sara had one hand firmly on his arm. "How do you feel?" she whispered anxiously.

It was the fourth time she'd asked him. "Will you quit?" he muttered angrily. "You're really starting to piss me off. Get lost. Go watch the show someplace else."

"Bobby . . ."

He could hear the hurt in her voice and didn't care. The main thing was to get this show over and done with. Sara by his side would only bug him.

"I said get lost," he repeated harshly. "I need to be left alone right now."

"Sure," she said, hurt and angry at the same time. "I'll go and enjoy the party."

"Do that."

"I will," she replied defiantly. Not that he gave a damn. Since she'd left him alone earlier he'd been in a foul mood. It was confusing being with Bobby. One minute she was his lover, the next merely an employee. What did he *really* feel about her? Did he care at all? Sometimes she doubted it.

One of the musicians had already been elected to escort him onstage, so there was really no reason for her to hang around. Norton St. John had invited her to join the press table and she decided she would. With a firm step she left Bobby standing alone.

Rafealla wanted to laugh. Kris Phoenix had known who she was all right. New hot recording star—Rafealla. And that's all he'd known.

Ha! She *really* must have left a lasting impression that night so long ago in London. He had no idea they'd ever met, let alone made love—if that was the right way to describe their one-time encounter.

It was funny, really—since achieving fame she'd been nervous about running into him, quite sure he would remember the silly little girl he'd taken advantage of, and make fun of her.

No such attitude. Just a friendly grin and words of encouragement.

Wouldn't it blow his mind if he knew the truth!

Backing out of his room, she forgot about visiting Bobby, and hurriedly returned to Trudie, who urged her to get changed, as it was time to make their way down to the performance area. Slowly she put on the simple black dress she'd chosen to wear. It made her crazy to think about Marcus's taking it off her later. Why had she ever agreed to go to bed with such a vile man?

They'd cut a deal, hadn't they? And he'd kept his side of the bargain. He'd made her famous, and after Luiz's betrayal that was all she'd wanted. Fame. Because her one big desire was to get back at Luiz—and fame was the only way to do it. Luiz had always been so ambitious. The U.S. was his dream—he'd talked about it all the time.

Now she had it and he didn't. Too bad. She knew he must be wishing he'd stayed with her.

Smoothing the black dress over her slim body, she decided it was perfect for tonight. Thinking about Luiz still upset her. He'd hurt her badly, devastated her, in fact. But one thing she was sure of. No more love entanglements. Sleeping with Marcus Citroen was better than falling in love any day.

Maxwell Sicily walked away from the kitchen with authority, carrying a full tray.

"Where do you think you're going?" A burly guard stopped him at one of the exit points.

Maxwell indicated his badge and the tray. "A snack for Kris Phoenix. I'm taking it over to the guest house."

"You got authority?"

"Yeah," Maxwell said sarcastically. "The chef stopped

everything and wrote me a note. Jeez! You guys take this crap seriously, don't you?"

With an aggravated wave the guard passed him through.

Security. Forget it. These guys knew nothing. Fortunately for him.

Kris dressed for his appearance in white pants, Reeboks, a black T-shirt and a pink Armani jacket. With his longish hair spiked and streaked, intense ice-blue eyes, athletic body, and deep suntan, he looked exactly like the rock superstar dream.

Okay, so he was thirty-eight years old. Big deal. He still had it. The old bones hadn't given up on him yet. Kris Phoenix was still the hottest.

Norton St. John arrived to escort him to the stage. Kris had sent Cybil off with Hawkins again. Let her enjoy the evening, it was better than having her hanging around driving him nuts.

"Have you seen George Smith anywhere?" Pudgy Chloe grabbed hold of a passing waiter.

"Who?" he asked, balancing a tray of coffee cups.

"George Smith," Chloe repeated impatiently. "He's a waiter, about your height, dark-haired an' good-looking."

"We're all good-lookin'." He smirked.

"Yeah, well, he's *really* handsome," Chloe retorted irritably. "If you see him, tell him I'm looking for him."

The waiter peered at her identification badge: Chloe Bragg—Supervisor—Lilliane's. "Listen," he said, "I'm only temporary. D'you think you can use your influence an' get me on permanent?"

"Find George Smith for me an' we'll see."

He nodded. "I'll keep my eyes open."

"Thanks," she said, stationing herself at the high traffic area between the kitchen and the dining area. Waiters and busboys were buzzing back and forth, but no sign of George Smith, damn him.

Chloe was deeply disappointed.

Much to Speed's disgust, the highway-patrol cop gave him a ticket. Racing along the Pacific Coast Highway, he growled to himself, sounding like a Doberman pinscher. He was late. It didn't matter. He'd make it. He always did.

SATURDAY, JULY 11TH, 1987
THE CONCERT

★ ☆ ★ ☆ ★

And so it began.

Bobby Mondella took the stage with confidence. Fuck it. He wasn't going to let the fact that he couldn't see stand in his way. Once he was out there in position, he went for it, falling into the rhythm of a live performance as if he'd never been away.

The audience was receptive, rising to its feet to welcome him back.

Nova was out there watching him, and for once it didn't matter. He'd faced his past, and that's all she was now—his past.

Maxwell Sicily rode the golf cart to the guest house. There was one black guard roaming around outside, the same guard he'd seen when he'd delivered Bobby Mondella's food earlier.

"Here we go again," Maxwell said with a friendly wave.

"What's happening down there?" the guard asked, wishing he was part of the real action.

"Bobby Mondella is just about to go on."

"Yeah? Really?"

"It's a shame you're missing it."

The guard pulled a disgusted face. "Tell me about it. My wife'll kill me. She thinks I'm gonna come home with a full report."

"Sneak down and take a look," Maxwell encouraged. "Nobody'll miss you."

"I wouldn't mind," the guard said longingly.

"Do it! Who's to know?"

The guard laughed. "Tom. Our chief. He checks us out every twenty minutes."

Maxwell nodded knowingly, hoisted his tray, and said, "I'd love to help you but I've got work to do. I'm supposed to clean this place up while they're performing."

"Good luck."

Maxwell entered the guest house. It was deserted, just as he'd known it would be. The stars and their entourages were all down at the dinner.

Placing the tray in the kitchen, he hurried upstairs. Vicki had told him exactly which guest suite would be unoccupied. He found it, opened the closet, and located his hold-all pushed out of sight in the back. From it he took a rolled black garbage bag, a cache of tools, and a small snub-nosed revolver, just in case.

Prepared, he hurried downstairs and slipped out the kitchen door. Then he sprinted across a vast lawn until he reached the far side of the main house. Entry was no problem; earlier, Vicki had fixed the catch on the sliding glass windows to Marcus Citroen's study.

Letting himself in, he stood quietly for a moment, taking stock. The room was exactly as Vicki had described it, which meant safe number one was located behind the Matisse hanging tastefully in the center of the wall. He would take care of that one on the way out. Right now his mind was on the real money—Nova Citroen's bedroom safe.

* * *

The applause was deafening. It swept over Bobby like sweet nectar as he was led offstage. Performing live had been a challenge hanging over his head. Could he do it?

Yeah, man, he could do it.

For a moment the deadly heat of revenge left him and he was free. "Sara?" he called out, but she wasn't around. He remembered he'd sent her away.

"You were wonderful!" a female voice breathed.

He reached out. "Who's this?"

She took his hand. "Rafaella. Remember me? Your friend from Rio."

"Oh, Jesus! Raffi. This is great!"

"You were great."

They hugged.

"I'm mad at you," she scolded.

"Hey—baby—don't be mad. You gotta understand what happened. Things were out of my control. I—"

"Rafaella." Hands were pulling at her. "You're on."

"Bobby, don't go away," she commanded sternly. "We'll talk. We'll catch up."

I ain't movin' from here, babe. You can depend on that."

Kissing him, she whispered, "Welcome back, superstar. I do love you."

He gave her a little push. "Kill 'em, baby, go give 'em hell!"

Vicki had her timing down pat. She knew exactly when to distract Tom. She knew exactly how. When Vicki Foxe exposed her two greatest assets, grown men crumbled, and Tom was no exception.

She led him to the magic moment carefully. Timing was everything, and if she didn't get it right the first time there was no second chance. Maneuvering him into position, she slowly undid the buttons on her uniform one by one.

"Holy mother!" Tom groaned, bursting at the seams;

he'd never seen anything like her before. This woman was stacked and then some.

"Wanna suck on the candy, big man?" she tempted, giving him no choice as she thrust an upstanding nipple into his mouth.

He was lost in heaven, while behind him, on television monitor five, Maxwell Sicily went to work breaking and entering Nova Citroen's safe.

Rafealla felt great. There was nothing like an audience to give you a buzz, and she was thrilled that Bobby Mondella was standing at the side of the stage waiting for her.

What could Marcus do if she turned up with Bobby? Kill her? Ha! She'd make him wait. She'd make him wait forever.

A wave of relief enveloped her. That's what she'd do—*make him wait forever!* Why hadn't she thought of it before?

Fame was already hers. He couldn't take it away, and if he did—she'd get it back one way or another.

She was a survivor. She'd survived Eddie Mafair, and Luiz and his lies. Now she'd survive Marcus Citroen.

In the long run that was the only thing that really mattered.

"I'm glad t'see you're out an' about," Kris said happily, clapping Bobby on the shoulder as they both waited at the side of the stage. "I've bin meanin' t'get hold of you—I thought it might be a giggle if we recorded somethin' together. Remember? We always threatened we would."

"Yeah, we did, didn't we," Bobby replied, reaching out to touch the brash English singer, whom he'd always liked.

"You do know I tried to call you a few times," Kris said. "After all that shit you went through, I figured you might like to hear a friendly voice."

"Sara told me," Bobby replied. "But, uh, I guess I never felt like talkin' to anyone."

"I can understand that. Only now you're around, let's do it, huh? We gotta make ourselves a record for *us*—y'know —like give all the proceeds to one of them charities. That'd really piss Marcus off. How about it?"

"Hey—anythin' that'd piss Marcus off, you can count me in."

"An' you know somethin'? We'll get *her* to do it, too," Kris said, warming to his theme.

"Who?" Bobby asked.

"Rafealla. She's got an interesting sound. I like her voice, plenty of style. Whadderya think?"

"Sounds good to me. I love that girl."

Rafealla finished her second song, followed by rapturous applause. She ran off the stage elated and glowing.

Winking at her, Kris said, "You were great, darlin', really great."

She smiled at him. God! It was like looking at an older version of Jon Jon. Quite spooky.

"Hang about," he said. "Bobby an' I—we got a proposition for you. The three of us'll split a bottle of champagne up at the house when I'm through. Okay?"

Why not face Marcus with Bobby *and* Kris? Perfect! She nodded. "Terrific."

Blondes were his scene, but this girl was something else. And she could sing. "I'm countin' on it, luv," he said with a crooked grin. Clenching his fist in the air, he yelled, "Okay, let's get this bleedin' show on the road. In and out." And with that, he raced onstage. Mister Energy. Mister Strut. Still full of piss and vinegar and raw, exciting talent.

The sophisticated audience went wild as he launched into "Long-Legged Blondes." Blasé they might be, but they knew a superstar when they saw one.

* * *

The moment Rafealla left the stage, Marcus excused himself from his two dinner partners and slipped away.

Nova saw him leave. Her expression tightened. She didn't care how many whores and starlets he had, but this girl, Rafealla, represented a threat. She was too young and beautiful by far, and Nova didn't like it one little bit.

Maxwell Sicily worked quickly and methodically, well aware that time was at a premium and it was essential he moved fast. The months of planning paid off. Thanks to Vicki, he knew the exact makes and locations of both safes. In prison they'd nicknamed him The Cracker, because it was a well-known fact he could break anything open in record time.

True to his reputation, he had Nova's big safe ajar within seven minutes. With satisfaction he noted it was stocked like the world's most expensive jewelry store.

Without hesitation he began filling the large plastic garbage bag with jewels, tipping them out of their boxes indiscriminately, until the sack was almost half full.

What a cache! More than he'd thought. Enough to set him up for a long, long time. Enough to buy him freedom from the goddamn system.

Shutting the safe, he hurried from her bedroom, careful to duck beneath the laser beam alarm across her door so as not to trip it. Vicki had been most thorough in her description of the alarm system throughout the house.

Outside, two lone guards paraded up and down. Maxwell could make out their shadows through the window. Normally this house was full of staff, but tonight they had gathered on the grassy knolls surrounding the outdoor dining area and the open-air stage to watch the concert. The dogs, usually running wild on the grounds, were locked up because of the influx of people.

He had known this would be the perfect night.

Returning to Marcus's study, he began his work there.
Ten more minutes and he'd be finished.
Ten more minutes and he'd be rich.

"How do I nail him, Hawkie?" Cybil asked, squirming with pleasure as Kris finished his performance to tumultuous applause.

"I beg your pardon?" the Hawk asked, wishing she wouldn't call him Hawkie.

"Well, I know he's got a girlfriend in England," Cybil said matter-of-factly. "And I guess he must like her—a bit. But she's old, you know, almost thirty."

"God forbid!" the Hawk murmured with a sardonic twist. "When's the funeral?"

Cybil giggled. "You know what I mean. I want him to marry me. How can I get him to do that?"

"Force and torture."

Dazzling everyone around her with a wide smile, she said, "You're so *silly*, Hawkie, really you are!"

Tom was at the point of no return. Vicki had him straddled against the circular counter, his back to the bank of television monitors, his pants and undershorts twisted around his ankles. She was on her knees, squashing his erect penis between her magnificent breasts, and every time he felt he was about to climax she sensed it and backed away, cooing, "Be patient, big boy. We've waited so long, let's not rush it."

He was mesmerized by her thrusting, heaving, heavy tits. Nothing else mattered. Nothing in the whole wide world.

As soon as Kris came offstage he took control. He was good at that. After all, he'd been the driving force behind The Wild Ones for all those years; he knew how to get his own way.

"We'll take the golf cart back to the house, just the three of us," he decided, grabbing Bobby by one arm and Rafealla by the other. "Let's have some fun for a change."

"Mr. Phoenix," Norton St. John said anxiously. "I have a table for you all to sit at while the speeches take place. And then there's the auction, and I *know* Mrs. Citroen wishes to introduce you to some of her more important guests. The Governor and his wife certainly want to thank you personally. And there is a French princess who has particularly requested an introduction."

"Must be the same little raver who's bin tryin' to give me one for the last six months," Kris said with a wink. "I think I'll pass. Whaddaya say? Bobby? Raf?"

"I pass," said Bobby solemnly.

"Me too!" Rafealla agreed, enjoying herself for the first time in ages.

"Really—" objected Norton St. John, now surrounded by Trudie and the two matching record executives.

"We're okay," Rafealla assured everyone, helping Kris assist Bobby onto the golf cart. "Go listen to the speeches, we'll see you all later."

"It looks like we're not needed, boys," commented Trudie dryly, wishing she were in Rafealla's position.

"Everyone aboard," yelled Kris. "Let's hit it!"

The electric golf cart jerked into action, while a worried Norton said, "Are you sure you know the way?"

"We'll find it—that's if we don't drive over the cliff first," Kris joked.

Marcus paced around Rafealla's room. He had instructed her to come straight back when she'd finished performing. Where was she? This was not good enough. Rafealla was going too far—she was really testing his patience.

The first thing he would do, he decided, was to teach her a lesson. An unforgettable lesson, as only he knew how.

* * *

A flat tire. No. This couldn't be happening. No freakin' way.

Speed zigzagged the large limousine over to the hard shoulder of the road and climbed out, cursing to himself.

Yes. It was a flat tire all right. What the a-for-ass was going on? Did her majesty, the ditz—his ex-wife—have a doll made up in his image? Was she even now sticking pins in it and chanting little "I'll get you" songs. Je . . . *sus!*

Springing the trunk, he searched for the spare.

There wasn't one.

SATURDAY, JULY 11TH, 1987
THE SCAM

★ ☆ ★ ☆ ★

Maxwell stuffed everything from Marcus Citroen's safe into the bag. There were deeds and letters, photographs and other papers. He decided he would study them at his leisure—it would be interesting to see what he could discover.

There were also a lot of single unset stones—diamonds, sapphires, rubies and emeralds, plus several expensive watches, men's gold jewelry, and wads of cash.

Maxwell licked his lips. His mouth was dry. Glancing quickly at the television camera mounted on the ceiling, he realized how foolish rich people were—they spent fortunes on security, and yet, if the person in charge was busy elsewhere, it all meant nothing.

Vicki was certainly keeping Tom the moron busy. She deserved a bonus.

Quietly shutting the safe, he signaled her, "V for victory," playing directly to camera.

Now she would allow him two minutes to exit the room, and then she was in the clear. A job well done.

The Governor was speaking. Governor Jack Highland. Nova watched him, but she wasn't really listening. She

472

was thinking about Marcus with that little tramp. How dare he pick *her* fund-raiser for *his* tryst. How dare he!

Governor Highland was an attractive man. He had the look. Honest, sincere, boyish—the Kennedy look.

Ah . . . a man like Jack Highland could change the world, and she, Nova Citroen, was helping to put him in position. Great power marked out his future. Everyone who mattered said so.

Watch out, Marcus, she thought, the day may come when I have someone even more influential than you to turn to.

"Jesus H. Didja get a load of all those stuffed shirts?" Kris asked, as the golf cart careened down a twisting path.

"I think we're going in the wrong direction," Rafealla pointed out.

"Hey—they clapped pretty fine," Bobby yelled, gripping the side of the cart for dear life.

"You betcha, baby," Kris shouted gleefully. "I'd clap pretty fine too if I'd paid a hundred thousand big ones for fuck all."

Pretending to be indignant, Rafealla said, "Thanks a lot!"

"Nothin' personal," Kris replied with a grin. "But c'mon, sweetheart, let's face it, it's only rock 'n roll, ain't it? No big deal."

Tom let out an anguished groan. "I can't hold it any longer," he gasped.

Vicki had been doing a slow countdown in her head. Ten more seconds, and she was free and clear. Maxwell was long gone from the TV monitor.

With a little sigh she pulled her left tit out of his mouth, gasping dramatically, "This isn't right, you're a married man. I don't know what came over me."

"Huh?" Tom said stupidly, staring in disbelief as she

struggled into the top half of her dress, covering acres of paradise.

"It's just that deep down I'm a religious girl," she explained.

His erect penis drooped miserably.

Tears brimmed from her eyes. "What we were about to do is a sin. You're married, Tom."

As if he didn't know.

She finished buttoning her dress, gazing at him tearfully. "I'm sorry. I know you must hate me. Oh, I'm so *sorr-reeee, Tom."

Not half as sorry as he was. He had an ache in his groin the like of which he couldn't recall.

"Just suck me off an' we can pretend it never happened," he said hopefully.

She looked at him in horror. "What kind of girl do you think I am?"

"A prick tease," he muttered angrily, full of frustration. "A first-class blue-baller!"

Now came the tricky part. He'd cleaned out the safes, but Maxwell knew that getting the contents and himself off the estate was not going to be easy.

The black plastic sack was heavy as he carried it across the lawn to the comparative safety of the guest house. He slid through the kitchen door and headed straight upstairs to the unoccupied suite.

Just as he was about to enter, a harsh voice called out, "You!"

"Yes?" He turned around slowly, only to face Marcus Citroen. Jesus Christ! Marcus was supposed to be watching the performers and listening to the speeches along with everyone else.

"What are you doing?" Marcus asked.

"Cleaning up, sir," he replied, without missing a beat.

"Cleaning up what?"

"Ashtrays, drinks, food. They want this house spotless before the artists return. Mrs. Citroen's orders." He indicated his badge. "I'm with Lilliane's, sir. George Smith, at your service."

"Okay, okay." Marcus waved him away impatiently, changed his mind, and said, "You can do this room now."

"Certainly, sir."

Maxwell walked into Rafealla's suite, lugging the black sack with him, while Marcus stood back and watched.

Picking up an ashtray, he dropped the contents into the sack. And then he gathered the dirty dishes and glasses, adding them too. With a polite nod he said, "That's all, sir."

Marcus was busy lighting a cigar; he didn't reply.

For the first time Maxwell felt that everything was not going according to plan. He was never supposed to come face to face with Marcus Citroen. What was the man doing in the guest house anyway?

No time to think about it. Into the unoccupied suite. Straight to the closet where Vicki had hidden an expensive Vuitton bag. Working fast, he transferred everything into it, leaving out the dirty dishes. Then he locked it, pocketing the key, and stuffed it into the garbage bag, along with his hold-all.

Now for the next move—if he dared to make it with Marcus Citroen so close by.

Goddamnit. He had no choice.

"So I think the three of us could get together on something really great," Kris said enthusiastically, pulling the golf cart to a jerky halt outside the guest house. "I mean, we're all so different, with such diverse styles. An' I'll get Buzz involved too. Y'know, he's doin' all right now since he came off drugs. Like it'd be a real challenge to blow everyone away. Know what I mean?"

"I'm willin' to try," Bobby said. "In fact, maybe I can write us somethin'."

"If it's for a suitable charity, and considering we're all with Blue Cadillac anyway, I don't see what can stop us," Rafealla joined in.

"*You* can name the charity, luv," Kris said, helping her down, and then taking Bobby's arm. "Starvin' kids. Ethiopia. The homeless. Whatever."

His eyes were just like Jon Jon's, blue and intense. "Let me think," she said, hoping that the tingly feeling she had was just her imagination.

Kris decided she was one of the most beautiful girls he'd ever seen. California blondes paled in comparison. He wondered if she had a steady boyfriend.

Companionably they all walked into the house, the guard nodding them on their way.

"Any of our mob here yet?" Kris asked, as they passed.

"Only a waiter from Lilliane's. Oh, and Mr. Citroen arrived a while ago."

"I can't stand that sonofabitch," Kris muttered. "He treats everyone an' everything like shit." He turned to Bobby and Rafealla. "What's he here for anyway? It's not like Mister Big to come slumming with the talent, is it?"

Rafealla said nothing.

Vicki exited as fast as she could. No good prolonging the old fart's anger. *Put your pecker away and shut up,* she wanted to say.

But she didn't. Instead she hurried out of there, leaving a very unhappy Tom buttoning his fly.

Chloe was seething. George Smith had done a pretty good job of avoiding her, and she didn't like it one bit. Didn't he realize she had clout at Lilliane's? Didn't he realize she could get him fired?

He'd snuck off somewhere to watch the concert without

her, and her feelings were hurt. She'd tried to be friendly, nice, but he'd rejected her, and she was determined to do something about it. Chloe didn't take kindly to being turned down.

"One of my waiters is missing," she informed a uniformed guard standing near the entrance to the dining area. "He's about five foot ten, dark hair, not bad-looking. Perhaps you've seen him. George Smith is his name."

To her surprise the guard responded, "Yeah, I think I know who you mean. Sounds like the one who took a tray over to the guest house an' never came back. I guess they needed him over there."

"The guest house?"

"Yes, ma'am. That's where all the celebs are holed up."

Her mouth tightened. What was George doing at the guest house? "Thank you," she said brusquely.

"A pleasure, ma'am. Any time."

They commandeered the living room—Kris, Rafealla and Bobby, talking and joking—making plans to do something they could enjoy and control for a change.

"I hate bleedin' record bosses, agents, an' managers," Kris said with feeling. "They're just a bunch of untalented wankers on for the ride."

"You got it," agreed Bobby, wishing Sara was with him. "They don't give a shit about quality, only sales."

"Hey, hey, hey—sales ain't bad," admitted Kris, walking to the bar. "I can get off on selling a few million here an' there."

Rafealla laughed. She felt quite carefree, considering Marcus was in the house, and bound to appear at any moment. "Do me a favor," she said quickly.

"Only if it means takin' me clothes off," Kris joked, fixing himself a rum and Coke.

"I don't want to be alone with Marcus."

477

"Nobody wants to be alone with Marcus," Bobby said, fiddling with his dark glasses.

"I mean it," she said urgently. "Promise you won't leave me?"

Kris stared at her. She had the greatest eyes he'd ever seen, and the most incredible smooth olive skin. The rest of her wasn't bad either. Maybe he'd give up blondes forever. It was a thought, because this girl was something else. And in the short period of time they'd been together, he felt connected to her in some strange and special way. It was weird. "Are you married or anything?" he couldn't stop himself from asking, feeling like a right berk.

"Hey," Bobby said lightheartedly. "Stop hittin' on our partner. Don't you answer him, Raf. This old stud considers himself a real lady-killer. I don't want you goin' anywhere near him. Got it?"

Chloe set off toward the guest house with a determined expression. Not only had George Smith let her down but he was slacking off on the job—an even greater crime. If she wanted to get him fired, she could, and unless he gave her good reason not to, that was exactly what she intended to do.

With a snort of anger, Marcus walked from Rafealla's room. He'd waited long enough. She would pay dearly for her behavior.

Along the corridor, Maxwell Sicily hung back, willing Marcus Citroen to get the hell out of his way.

The next part of his plan should go smoothly—but it had to take place while everyone was occupied with the speeches and the auction. He was supposed to leave the guest house, still dressed in his waiter's uniform, carrying the sack of garbage. The guard would wave him on his way, and he would take the golf cart to a prearranged meeting spot near the swimming pool, where Vicki would be waiting with an evening suit for him to change into. Once changed, carrying the Vuitton bag, he would stroll down to the parking area as if he were an early-departing guest, climb casually into his limousine—which Speed would have in the right place at the right time—and take off.

Easy.

If everything went according to plan. And there was no reason why it shouldn't. All he needed was for Marcus Citroen to get the hell out of his way.

SATURDAY, JULY 11TH, 1987
THE CONFRONTATION

★ ☆ ★ ☆ ★

Marcus Citroen threw open the door of the main living room in the guest house and discovered Kris Phoenix, Bobby Mondella, and Rafealla—*his* Rafealla—sitting around enjoying themselves.

His expression registered pure rage as he attempted to keep control.

"How ya doin', Marcus?" Kris asked cockily, raising his glass in salute. "Slummin' tonight, are we?"

Marcus ignored the spiky-haired rock star. He suspected Nova had slept with him, although she denied it. Marcus only tolerated her indiscretions up to a point. It was fortunate for Kris she hadn't become involved—as she had with Bobby Mondella. The black cocksucker was lucky to be alive, and doubly lucky to have been given his career back. Marcus considered himself a fair man. He didn't hold a grudge forever.

"Rafealla," he said sharply, "we had a meeting. Did you forget?"

Kris watched the eye play between them. Rafealla had a trapped look, while Marcus exhibited a malevolent, predatory glare. No wonder she didn't want to be left alone with him—the horny old guy was just about ready to eat her alive.

"Come," Marcus snapped, holding out his arm. "I do not appreciate being kept waiting."

Her voice didn't waver. "I'm busy right now, Marcus."

His mouth tightened into a thin line, while his hooded eyes clouded with anger. "We have business to discuss. Let's go."

"I'm quite happy here," she said bravely.

"Rafealla." His voice was ice. "I want you to come upstairs with me *now*. That's an order."

"An order!" Kris tried to make a joke of it. "I didn't know we were back in bleedin' school!"

Marcus turned to glare at him just as Maxwell Sicily hurried past the open door.

Huffing and puffing, Chloe arrived at the front of the guest house the same time that Maxwell was leaving.

"Oh," she said, quivering with indignation. "This is where you've been hiding, is it?"

She stood between him and the golf cart, a solid lump.

"Mrs. Citroen told me to come here and clean the place up," he said, wishing the fat cow would drop dead.

"Mrs. Citroen told you, did she?" demanded Chloe sharply. "And since when did Mrs. Citroen tell *my* waiters what to do?"

He shrugged, attempting to dodge past her. "We're all working here tonight, aren't we? I was just trying to help out."

Chloe knew plenty about waiters, and the one thing they never did was volunteer their services for nothing. There was something suspicious going on. Chloe knew it—she had a sixth sense about such things. George Smith was a strange one. Handsome, she had to admit, but not honest, and certainly not a gentleman. She didn't like the way he'd treated her at all. Leading her on and then running off and deserting her.

Automatically her eyes dropped to the bulging garbage bag he was carrying. "What's in there?" she asked suspiciously. Some waiters had a very lucrative sideline, removing whole sides of beef, chickens, and the best fillet steaks via the old garbage-sack trick.

No! A voice screamed in his head. The goddamn cunt was going to put him away with her interfering. Why couldn't anything ever go right for him?

Out of the corner of his eye he noticed the guard strolling toward them.

Was this how he got caught?

Fuck! No!

Without saying another word, he shoved past her.

"Stop!" she shouted, and then as if she knew she was on to a sure thing, "Stop, thief!"

At the word "thief," the guard quickened his pace. "What's going on here?"

"This waiter is removing property that's not his," Chloe yelled in a shrill voice. "I demand that you stop him."

Maxwell had one foot on the golf cart. He wasn't going to blow this setup. Winking conspiratorially at the guard, he said, "The old broad's crazy. She's probably on the rag."

"Hold it a sec," the guard said. "Let's clear this up before you go anywhere. Step down."

Outwardly calm, Maxwell did as he was asked. His mind was racing. What he really wanted to do was take out his piece, jam it into the dumb bitch's mouth, and blow the fucking cunt away. That would teach her to stay out of Maxwell Sicily's business.

The guard approached Chloe. "What's the problem, ma'am?"

Flashing her identification badge, she said, "I have reason to believe this man is removing property that does not belong to him."

"Horseshit," Maxwell muttered.

"We can soon clear this up," the guard said, coming to a logical conclusion. The last thing he wanted was any trouble. "Open the sack, make the lady happy."

"I resent this," Maxwell said bitterly. "I resent being falsely accused by this frustrated fucking *bitch!*"

As he spoke he edged back toward the front door.

"Let's not get excited," the guard said, still trying to smooth things over.

"Did you hear what he called me?" screeched Chloe. "Did you *hear* his language? You're fired, George Smith. You are *fired* from Lilliane's right now. Guard! Make him open that sack!"

"Open it," the guard said wearily. How come everyone else got to see a sensational concert? And all he got was a whining restaurant supervisor and a thieving waiter, because, come to think of it, the sack did look kind of bulky.

"All right," Maxwell said, bending down as if to do as he was asked.

Chloe glared. She had him now. They were probably going to discover every ashtray and ornament in the place. She hoped the Citroens would be willing to prosecute, send the petty thief to jail where he belonged. She'd always known there was something strange about George Smith.

With the element of surprise working in his favor, Maxwell swung the heavy sack up in the air, catching the unprepared guard in the stomach and knocking him off balance. Chloe began to yell and scream.

Quickly Maxwell backed into the house, slamming and locking the front door behind him.

Nova fidgeted in her seat. The speeches were finished— a great success—and now the auction was going well, but Marcus had not returned, and she was seething. On tonight of all nights she wished to reap the adulation that came with being one of the most sought after and elegant hostesses in America. She wanted to share this triumph with her husband.

But no, it was not to be. Marcus Citroen was too busy making love to his latest conquest.

Why should she let him get away with it unchallenged? Standing up abruptly, she excused herself. Marcus was going to get a visit from her, whether he liked it or not.

With a roar of frustrated fury Maxwell hurled himself into the living room, waving his gun threateningly in the air. The black garbage sack skittered across the floor ahead of him. "Get your hands up, motherfuckers," he screamed. "This is a hostage situation and you're fucking *it!*"

SATURDAY, JULY 11TH, 1987
THE CONCLUSION

★ ☆ ★ ☆ ★

Four hours had passed. Four of the longest hours of Maxwell Sicily's life.

He'd always tried to be low key, stay away from the spotlight, keep out of other people's business and hope they would afford him the same courtesy.

It wasn't easy being Carmine Sicily's son. No, it wasn't easy at all. In school it was like he'd had a neon sign over his head proclaiming the fact. Decent kids stayed away from him, while the scum couldn't do enough favors.

He grew up confused. Carmine was a larger-than-life figure to have as a role model. Everybody loved Carmine Sicily. Every lowlife who ever breathed.

His mother, Rose, didn't count. She died when he was fourteen, leaving him alone with Carmine and a parade of whores.

He had his first woman the day after his mother's funeral. Carmine forced her onto him, pushing the girl into his room with the words, "She'll cheer you up, an' if she don't, forget about hangin' around *me* with your miserable face."

The girl was twenty-two and experienced. She milked

485

him like a cow, holding his penis in one hand, rubbing between her legs with the other.

He hated it. He hated her. He hated his father.

When he was sixteen, he took a gun from Carmine's closet and robbed a liquor store. The fury of his father knew no bounds. He was beaten every day for a week.

When he was eighteen, he fucked Carmine's nineteen-year-old girlfriend, stole twenty-six thousand dollars in cash from the house, and a black Lincoln, and took off.

Carmine had him tracked down and brought back. This time he was locked in the cellar for three weeks with only bread and water for sustenance.

At twenty-two, he shot and nearly killed a bank guard during the course of a violent robbery.

"I give up," Carmine said. "Let him rot in jail. He's not *my* son."

And so he spent the next seven years in prison without a word from his father.

When he got out he headed for California, and it wasn't long before he decided what his next job would be. Reading a magazine one day, he found out all about Nova and Marcus Citroen and their fabulous wealth. Then he saw the newspaper piece about their forthcoming fund-raiser for Governor Highland. The two articles jelled in his head. It was too good an opportunity to miss.

Now here he was. Fucked.

And outside the house there were police, and people and TV cameras and press.

He was FUCKED.

"Can I please have a drink of water?" Rafealla asked wearily. Like the others she was bound hand and foot, huddled on the floor in the corner.

Maxwell had forced them to tie each other up shortly after he broke in. Wild-eyed, he'd brandished his gun in the air, threatening to shoot every one of them if they didn't comply with his wishes.

He'd sent Rafealla upstairs to fetch sheets. "If you're not back in two minutes, I'll put a bullet through his head," he'd warned, nodding toward Bobby.

Shaking, she raced through the bedrooms, dragging sheets from the beds.

When she brought them downstairs, he made Kris and Marcus tear them into strips and tie Bobby first, then Rafealla. Next, he had Marcus truss Kris up, and finally he'd done the honors to the furious record magnate himself.

Marcus had tried to reason with him. "Be sensible," he'd said. "You'll never get away with this. *Never.* So why don't you be smart and walk away now, before you do something you'll really regret?"

Walk away. That was a joke. He couldn't walk away. He was trapped. All his life he'd been trapped.

Marcus Citroen reminded him of Carmine. A fat cat. A man who thought money could buy him anything.

"How much if I walk?" he'd asked, to see what price Marcus would put on his life.

"Ten thousand dollars. Cash," Marcus had replied with all the confidence of a man able to buy himself out of any situation. "And you have my word. I'll make absolutely certain you're set free."

Sure. And Mother Teresa will get a job in a go-go parlor. Marcus Citroen insulted his intelligence, just like Carmine. Two rich pigs.

Maxwell had laughed in his face, whereupon Marcus Citroen doubled his offer, then tripled it. But by that time Maxwell wasn't listening.

Once his hostages were tied up, he'd felt better. Leaving them for a moment, he'd scanned the house, making sure every window was secured from the inside, and pushing the bolts and chains on the two outside doors.

Soon the police would arrive.

He wasn't wrong.

* * *

All Rafealla could think about was Jon Jon. If anything happened to her, how would her little boy survive? He was ten years old. What would he do without her? Who would teach him about life, and how to treat women, and the difference between right and wrong?

Who would comfort him when he was sad? Laugh with him when he was happy? Scold him when he was naughty?

She was his mother, goddammit, and she was determined to get out of this alive.

Locked into a world of blackness, Bobby struggled with a terrible feeling of inadequacy. There was nothing he could do—he was tied up, helpless, he couldn't even see what was going down.

He, Bobby Mondella, was a prisoner in every way.

Kris, on the other hand, felt pretty damn strong. When Marcus was tying him up he'd managed to loosen the bonds as they were going on. Strips of sheet weren't going to hold *him* back when the moment came to take this psycho out. And the guy *was* a psycho—Kris knew he was right—you only had to look at the creep with his flat, starey eyes and edgy, unsure movements.

Hey—Andy Warhol had said it pretty good—everyone can be famous for fifteen minutes—and that's what this asshole wanted. To hit the headlines, sell his story, have a book written about him, maybe even a miniseries.

Right now he was on the verge. He had three of the biggest recording stars in the world and a billionaire record tycoon wrapped up as hostages. But hey—Kris could figure out what the freak was thinking. If he let them go, what then? One headline, and that was it, he'd fade into obscurity without a trace. The only way he was going to hit it big was if he did something major—like kill them all.

With a shudder, Kris managed to roll toward Rafealla. "You okay?" he whispered.

She nodded.

"Hang in there, kid," he said comfortingly. "Because we're gonna get out of this. An' that's one thing you'll learn about me, I'm never wrong."

Gathered outside the house was a virtual army of people. The police, along with the SWAT team, had cordoned off a large area. Behind them were the TV crews, reporters, and photographers. Most of the important guests had fled the scene, but Governor Highland had remained, giving Nova Citroen comfort and maintaining a suitably heroic image before the press.

Maxwell in his phone negotiations with Police Captain Lynch had insisted the media be allowed onto the estate, figuring he was safer that way. His demands were simple. A helicopter to take him and his hostages to a quiet location, where an unmarked car would be waiting for him to make his getaway. "When I'm certain I'm safe, I'll release the hostages," he promised.

"Sure," Captain Lynch had muttered under his breath.

This conversation had taken place during the second hour of the siege, once the Police Captain took charge, and telephone contact began. "Who are you? What's your name?" was the first question he'd asked.

"George Smith," Maxwell lied.

"No way, pal. We had George Smith checked out. He's only been around for the last couple of months. How about telling us your real name and saving us all a lot of trouble?"

Maxwell felt the frustration build. Just who exactly did they think they were dealing with? Did they imagine he was as stupid as they were?

"If I don't get what I want," he'd said, slowly and precisely, "I will shoot the hostages, one by one. Do we understand each other?"

* * *

Sara's eyes were red-rimmed. She'd tried to stay on top of it, but finally she'd broken. She couldn't bear to think of Bobby and what he must be suffering.

Trudie comforted her. "He's going to be fine," she assured. "They all are."

Sara knew it could go either way. Of course it was possible they'd walk free without a scratch. On the other hand something terrible could happen. She remembered the jewelry store incident on Rodeo Drive in 1986. For many hours the police had insisted the hostages, trapped in Van Cleef & Arpel, were okay. It turned out one was killed within minutes of being taken captive, and more died later in a hail of gunfire.

With a choked-back sob she realized just how much she loved Bobby Mondella. He had become her life, and it wasn't healthy, because if she was truthful with herself, she had to admit he didn't give a damn about her. Sure, he made love to her, and was nice when he felt like it. But he wasn't *in* love with her, and she might as well face up to it.

If he gets out of this I'm going to leave him, she thought. *He's a success again, the man doesn't need me, he'll be a lot happier without me.*

That decided, she said a silent prayer for his safety.

Maxwell held the glass of water to Rafealla's lips.

She sipped it slowly, and asked his name. Somewhere she had read that in a hostage situation it was important to develop a connection with the person holding you prisoner.

"What the fuck has my name got to do with anything?" he said angrily.

"I'd like to be able to call you something," she ventured.

"I know what you can call him," snarled Marcus, unbowed by his captivity. "You can call him a dumb sonofabitch."

This comment incited Maxwell. He turned on Marcus

and said threateningly, "Nobody calls Maxwell Sicily dumb."

"There's your answer," Marcus said with a triumphant snort.

"For Christ's sake, shut up," Kris hissed, flexing his muscles beneath the loose bindings, and trying to decide if he could grab the psycho now. One lunge and it would be all over.

But what if his bindings didn't break? What if the creep had time to turn his gun on him and blow Kris Phoenix away? There was something very unsettling about a gun being pointed in your direction.

Christ! His mum in England must be going crazy. The newspapers had probably called her already. Poor old Avis. She was never short of a bit of excitement with him for a son. And how about Willow and Bo? Willow would somehow make out it was all his fault. And as for Bo—who knew how the kid would react?

Maybe I've been a lousy father, he thought. *If I get out of this I'll try to be better, spend more time with him.*

If I get out . . .

Cybil rested her honey-blond head on Governor Highland's sympathetic shoulder. "I'm so tired," she moaned.

They were sitting in the main house along with Hawkins, Nova, and a slew of other people.

"Maybe you should take a nap," he suggested. "Nova, is there a spare bedroom Cybil can lie down in?"

Nova signaled her assistant. "Norton, take care of it."

Norton St. John escorted Cybil and a concerned Governor Highland upstairs to a spare bedroom.

"Thank you," the Governor said, dismissing Norton with a wave of his hand. "I'll see she settles down."

Cybil sat on the side of the bed, brushing a weary hand through her mane of hair. "This is so awful," she sighed.

"I know," he agreed, sitting down beside her.

"Poor Kris."

"I'm sure he'll be all right."

"I hope so."

"Cybil."

"Yes."

"You're a very lovely young lady."

"Thank you."

Clumsily he began to kiss her. She fell back on the bed, too exhausted to resist. All she could think of was that one day Governor Highland might be President, and wasn't it funny that every man—be he rock star or future President —was exactly the same. Sex-crazy. And who was she to object?

Impatiently Maxwell picked up the phone. "I've waited long enough," he said with cold menace. "If the helicopter isn't here in fifteen minutes, I'm shooting a hostage."

"Come now, let's think about this. Don't be foolish," the Captain reasoned. "It'll be here."

"Don't fuck with me," Maxwell warned, his voice rising. "You've been giving me shit for over an hour. Either it arrives within fifteen minutes or I'm taking one of them out. This is no idle threat. Am I getting through to you, cocksucker?"

"Yes," the Captain replied, humoring him. "I promise you the helicopter is on its way." He wanted to add, "So is your father," because they had discovered "George Smith's" true identity by lifting his fingerprints off his locker at Lilliane's and running them though the main computer.

Some discovery. Maxwell Sicily. Only son and heir of the infamous Carmine Sicily. And Carmine had been tracked down to a suite at the Beverly Wilshire, where he was staying on a business trip.

At first Carmine didn't want to know. "My son? I don't have a son." But when the situation was made clear to him and he found out who was involved, he said, "I'll be there. Don't do anything until I arrive. This can be cleared up in seconds."

Yes, he'd clear it up all right—he'd put a hit out on his own son and get him out of his life forever. The boy was no good, never had been. How dare he embarrass him like this with such important and influential people. Carmine was deeply humiliated. What had he done to deserve a son like Maxwell?

"You still okay, luv?" Kris moved closer to Rafealla, whispering in her ear. "The berk won't do anything. Trust me." They'd all heard Maxwell's furious threats to shoot one of them, and he wanted to reassure her.

Her voice sounded shaky. "I don't know, Kris. This is like a nightmare, and I keep on expecting to wake up."

"I know, babe. But don't worry, the guy's a loser, he's all talk an' no balls—you can see it just by looking at him."

Trying to sound brave, she murmured, "I hope you're right, for all our sakes."

"Hey—Bobby, I'd give you a runnin' commentary," Kris said in a low voice, "but it's boring. We'll be out of here soon."

Bobby grunted.

Maxwell was pacing up and down the room agitatedly, trying to decide what to do next. Everything had been going so smoothly until that cow from the restaurant had gotten in his way. He wished he had her in here with him now. Oh, yes. He'd show her a thing or two. He'd jam his gun in her mouth and blow her head off.

Surprising everyone, Marcus spoke up in a harsh, loud voice, his lingering accent sounding guttural with intensity. "Why don't you shoot the nigger?" he urged. "Shoot the coon and throw him out of here. Then perhaps we can get this charade over and done with."

"You motherfucking sonofabitch," Bobby said, reacting immediately and rolling toward the sound of Marcus's voice.

"Oh, Christ!" groaned Kris, sensing trouble.

"You're filth, Marcus," Rafealla cried out. "You are the lowest slime."

"And what do you think *you* are?" Marcus snarled in return. "You're one of them too. I should have had you thrown over that balcony in Rio along with your friend, you black cunt."

The truth at last. Enraged beyond belief, Bobby kicked out toward the sound of Marcus's voice, feeling the thud of his heel connect with something hard.

He caught Marcus on the side of his jaw. With a snort of agony, Marcus retaliated by lifting his hands, still bound together, and smashing them down like a lethal club on Bobby's head, rendering him unconscious. Meanwhile, Kris was struggling to free himself.

Watching this scene, Maxwell felt like he was losing control. He raised the handgun threateningly and fired a warning shot in the air.

Kris lunged toward him, tripping on the ties that bound his ankles together.

Caught off balance, Maxwell fired wildly, hitting Marcus in the stomach with a stray bullet.

"Oh my God!" Rafealla screamed, watching in horror as blood pumped forth from a gaping hole.

"Help me," moaned Marcus, clutching his stomach in vain. He looked toward Rafealla, then desperately his eyes sought out Kris. "I beg you . . . help me . . . stop the blood. I'll give you anything." His voice began to fade. "All . . . the . . . money . . . you . . . could . . . ever want. Anything. . . ."

At that moment the sound of the helicopter hovering above arrested their attention.

With icy calm, Maxwell said, "We're leaving now. And I don't expect any more trouble."

The noise of the helicopter drowned out the sound of gunfire. Captain Lynch had no idea what had taken place when he next spoke to Maxwell.

"It's time to evacuate," he said. "The helicopter is here."

"Get everyone away from the house," Maxwell instructed. "Just leave one television camera in place. Is that understood?"

"Yes," Captain Lynch replied.

"Do it!" Maxwell insisted. "I'm watching you."

And your daddy is watching you, you little bastard. He's right here, ready to surprise the ass off you. "It'll be done."

"We're coming out in five minutes," Maxwell warned. "And if anything goes wrong—anything at all—I'll shoot them all. Do you understand?"

"You're making yourself very clear."

"Good."

Maxwell turned to confront his hostages, a sorry-looking bunch. Amazing how you could cut the mighty down to size. Walking over to Rafealla, he untied her and said, "Go upstairs and bring down a blanket."

There was blood everywhere, and Marcus was slumped on the floor, ominously silent. "I think he's dead," Rafealla whispered, staring at Marcus in shock.

"So what?" Maxwell said callously. "The same thing can happen to you if you don't follow my instructions. Go upstairs *now,* get a blanket, and come right down. If you don't—he gets it next." He waved his gun at Kris.

"Big fuckin' man with a gun pointed at my head, ain'tcha?" Kris jeered. "I'd like t'see what'd happen if it was just the two of us."

Maxwell ignored him. He wasn't about to be drawn into a confrontation. Kris Phoenix was nothing. They were all nothing. And since he'd killed one of them, he might as well do away with them all. It didn't make any difference.

But not now, not until they'd finished being useful. At this moment they were his only protection.

Captain Lynch had his sharpshooters in place. He also had Carmine Sicily standing in the shadows behind him. The helicopter waited in the middle of the vast lawn at the front of the house. At the controls was a trained member of the SWAT unit.

The press had been cleared away, moved way back on the estate, all except one television camera crew.

Nova Citroen hovered in the background with the Hawk by her side. She'd changed into a warm brown jumpsuit, boots, and a loose mink coat. She was surprisingly calm.

The Hawk said, "When they come out, the Captain is going to tell this Maxwell character to drop his weapon and surrender."

"What makes the Captain think he'll comply?"

"Because at that stage of the game he'll be vulnerable, out in the open. And then his father will step forward and reason with him."

"He can still shoot his hostages."

"No," the Hawk said sharply. "They'll have him under such strict surveillance that if his hand even tightens near the trigger, they'll take him out. One bullet through the head."

"It's dark."

"They have special equipment."

She wondered how Marcus was taking his captivity. Not well. If the police didn't kill his captor, he would certainly see it was taken care of. Marcus Citroen insisted on being in control at all times.

"This is how we're going to do it," Maxwell said. "Listen carefully, because any mistakes can mean the end of

496

your life." Contemptuously he kicked Marcus, rolling him on his side, until the dead man came to rest in a pool of his own blood. "Like him."

Lying on the floor, still bound, Bobby heard the words as he drifted back into consciousness. Opening his eyes, he saw a blurry haze. Gradually the haze sharpened and came into focus.

He blinked once, twice, hardly believing what was happening. He could see! Goddammit, HE COULD SEE!

The doctors had said it could happen, just like that, anytime, anywhere. A conversion reaction could take place, they'd said, brought on by a traumatic situation. Jesus Christ! He could see—but it was best not to tell anyone in view of the danger they were all in. There might be some advantage in not letting anyone know.

"We'll walk outside under the blanket," Maxwell said. "You'll be in front, and I'll be behind with a gun in your backs. The police won't know who is where. Do you get it?"

"Very smart," Kris jeered.

"Yes, very smart," Maxwell agreed. "Because they'll have marksmen out there ready to pick me off, and this way they can't take the risk of making a mistake."

Slowly Bobby looked around, taking in the scene. On the floor, nearby, were his dark glasses. Surreptitiously he groped for them with his hands still tied. He got them on without anyone noticing.

"I'm going to untie your feet," Maxwell announced. "I'm sure I don't have to keep on repeating that what happened to Marcus Citroen can happen to any one of you."

Bobby groaned to let them know he was conscious.

"Are you all right?" Rafealla asked anxiously.

If she only knew! "Yeah," he muttered. "I'm fine."

"Good," said Maxwell sarcastically. "It's nice to know everyone is well."

* * *

"Here they come," said Captain Lynch with a grunt of anticipation as slowly the front door swung open. "Carmine, get ready."

Carmine Sicily stepped up next to the Police Captain. He was ready all right.

Nova Citroen shuddered. She had an ominous feeling of doom.

The Hawk put his arm around her, patting her mink-clad shoulder comfortingly. "It'll soon be over," he said. "Don't worry."

"Jesus Christ!" exclaimed Captain Lynch, as the blanketed group of figures shuffled from the house. *"Shit!"*

"What's the matter?" asked Carmine.

"They're under a fucking blanket. We can't see who's who." Grabbing his walkie-talkie, he barked out a command. "No firing. Hold all gunfire."

Under the blanket it was hot and uncomfortable. Rafealla was positioned in front of Maxwell, his gun jammed into the small of her back. Every step she took, she feared the gun might go off by mistake.

Kris was next to her. Maxwell had tied them together around the waist, making it difficult to walk. Bobby brought up the rear, tethered loosely to Maxwell.

"Any bullets an' you're the ones that get it, my friends," Maxwell boasted. "One false move from any of you, and I'll blow her in half—so don't even think about it."

Slowly they trundled toward the helicopter, every step an ordeal.

The night was silent except for the sounds of nature—waves crashing on the beach way below, crickets chirping, and the sway of the palm trees in the night breeze. There was a bright moon in the sky.

"Maxwell." Suddenly a voice boomed through the bullhorn, breaking the silence. "This is your father, Carmine. I want you to quit what you're doing *now*. Release your hostages an' give yourself up. That's an order."

Maxwell stopped stock-still, frozen in shock. What the fuck was Carmine doing here? What the fuck was that cocksucker interfering for? Wasn't it enough that he'd had to grow up in his shadow, always Carmine Sicily's son, Carmine Sicily's boy? He hated his father with a passion. "What are you doing here?" he screamed hysterically.

Instinctively both Kris and Bobby knew this was their moment, and as if operating on telepathy they acted as one. Kris knocked the gun from Maxwell's hand with a vicious turn of his body, while Bobby kneed him in the back with every bit of force he could muster.

Maxwell fell to the ground, dragging all of them down with him.

"Get the lights on." Captain Lynch yelled the order, as he raced toward the scene, accompanied by several of his officers, guns drawn.

Floodlights lit up the area.

It was over.

EPILOGUE

★ ☆ ★ ☆ ★

At Marcus Citroen's funeral there was a bizarre combination of rock & rollers, high society, the movers and shakers of show business, and the powerful world of real money.

They came from all over to pay their respects, the most popular mode of transport being private plane.

The line of limousines at the burial ground was impressive, and later, at Novaroen, a party atmosphere prevailed.

Nova went through the motions. She made an impressive grieving widow.

Hawkins Lamont—the Hawk—delivered the eulogy. He was going to miss his friend and mentor.

Marcus had remembered him in his will. The Hawk inherited Marcus's prized collection of antique cars, two solid-gold Cartier watches, and an assortment of Tiffany cuff links. The Hawk appreciated the gesture—but above all else he was a dealmaker, and owning a collection of old cars did not appeal to him. He sold them, and with the proceeds bought himself a white Ferrari, a black Maserati, and a weekend apartment in London.

Three months after the funeral he divorced his wife. A few weeks after that, he and Nova Citroen were married in a secret ceremony in Mexico City.

They returned to New York triumphant, the latest

"power" couple. Together they ran Blue Cadillac Records, expanding into television and movies.

Nova Citroen maintained her reputation as one of the most elegant hostesses in America. And the Hawk continued to guide the careers of the cream of the superstars.

Together they made a formidable combination.

By the time Speed fixed the flat tire on the hired limousine and got himself and the car up to the Novaroen estate on that fateful July night, he was too late. The hostage situation was in progress, and everyone was going crazy.

He'd grabbed hold of a parking attendant, demanding hoarsely, "What's going on?"

"There's a guy up there gone wacko. He's grabbin' people, tyin' 'em up, an' demandin' money."

"Who is he?"

"Some waiter from that fancy restaurant. George somethin' or other."

"George Smith?"

"Yeah, that's the dude's name."

Speed had gotten out of there fast. Gunning the limousine, he'd raced back to Hollywood, cleared out of his apartment, dumped the limo outside the rental place, and taken the next plane to Vegas. There, he'd thrown himself upon his ex-wife's mercy, begging her to alibi him lest George Smith pointed the cops in his direction.

She'd obliged. Reluctantly. It had cost him.

He stayed with her for three months. They fought every day, but he'd been forced to admit she had the best pair of bazoombas in captivity. Unfortunately she also had a lethal dose of the clap, contracted from a lounge singer with bad teeth and no talent. Naturally, Speed, with his luck, picked it up too.

He left in a fury, drifting back to Hollywood and his old haunts.

One night he met a man in a bar. There was a big job

going down and this dude had heard he was the best freakin' driver on the West Coast. . . .

Chloe remained at Lilliane's, quite the restaurant celebrity. If it hadn't been for Chloe and her diligent eye, Maxwell Sicily might have got away with the robbery of the year. She reveled in the attention.

It never crossed her mind that if she hadn't interfered, Marcus Citroen would be alive today.

Cybil Wilde and Kris Phoenix broke up, whereupon Cybil embarked on what was supposed to be a top-secret, extremely discreet affair with Governor Highland.

One late summer weekend they played together on a mutual friend's yacht in Acapulco, where, unbeknownst to them, they were photographed by two paparazzi operating with powerful long-distance lenses.

The resultant pictures made headline news, damaging Governor Highland's spotless reputation beyond redemption and catapulting Cybil into a starring role in her first movie.

Vicki Foxe made the best of a bad job. She fled Novaroen during the height of the hostage situation, hitching a ride into town with one of the party guests—an old and shaky lawyer, who believed every word of her hastily made up story about a fight with Mrs. Ivors, the dragon-lady housekeeper.

"Do you need a job, my dear?" he'd asked.

"Yes," Vicki had nodded.

She stayed long enough to share her sexual favors and steal his valuable stamp collection, which she sold to a pawn shop for three thousand dollars. It was worth over a hundred thousand.

Then she ticketed herself to Amarillo, Texas, where she

set herself up in an apartment doling out submission and discipline.

Business was good.

Maxwell Sicily did not fare so well. In prison, awaiting trial for the murder of Marcus Citroen, he mysteriously passed away in his sleep one night. There was no official investigation.

The tentacles of Carmine Sicily's power stretched far and wide.

Sara Johnston and Bobby Mondella planned a quiet wedding ceremony in her home town of Philadelphia. Both of them couldn't be happier.

It had taken him some time to win her over, but he'd done it. After the night at Novaroen, so much had happened. The shock of recovering his sight had sent Bobby into a tailspin. At first he hadn't known how to handle it—everything seemed so strange.

Seeing Sara—a woman he had virtually shared his life with for the last eighteen months—was the biggest shock of all. He'd imagined her to be darker, shorter, plumper, plainer. Instead, she was dazzlingly pretty—reminding him in a way of a young Sharleen.

Before he had a chance to tell her how much she meant to him, she took off, leaving him a short note on which she had written, "You don't need me anymore, so I'll say goodbye. It was great, Bobby, and I'll always love you. But now you've got your life back. Enjoy it. Sara."

It took him two months to find her, and when he did, he told her in no uncertain terms that they would never be apart again.

She acquiesced. After all, she loved him—it was as simple as that.

* * *

Kris Phoenix and Rafealla went their separate ways.

After breaking up with Cybil, Kris returned to England and told Astrid it was over. They'd been together four years—it was long enough. He bought her a house in the country and allowed her to keep the dogs. They parted friends.

Then he sought out Buzz—still off drugs and well on the way to recovery—and suggested they do something together, just the two of them.

"Yeah, I'd like that," Buzz said.

"Yeah, I rather thought you would," Kris replied, adding with a wink, "Ya always fancied workin' with a superstar, didn't you?"

"You're still full of it, you old wanker," Buzz replied, with a wicked grin.

"Yeah, an' you wouldn't have it any other way. Right?"

"Right, mate."

The years disappeared as they broke up laughing, and spontaneously hugged each other.

Rafealla returned to England, collected Jon Jon from her mother, and the two of them settled down in the house she'd bought near Regent's Park.

It was good to be back in England after all the years she'd spent abroad. And it was certainly nice to be an established recording artist without the threat of Marcus Citroen hanging over her head. Sometimes she thought of Marcus and that terrible night at Novaroen. It was an experience she would never forget. But life went on, and she was ready to live it.

Kris Phoenix and Rafealla made the trip to Philadelphia for Bobby Mondella's wedding. They arrived separately, neither aware of the other's presence.

Rocket Fabrizzi was best man, and although Bobby and

Sara had tried to keep the wedding quiet, there was a huge turnout of fans and press.

Rafealla hadn't seen Kris Phoenix since their shared ordeal. She glanced across the aisle, and there he was, cocky as ever, with that ridiculous spiked hair and those intense blue eyes—Jon Jon's eyes.

Tentatively she waved.

He waved back.

She smiled.

He smiled back.

Oh, God! Not again. For the third time in her life she felt that old familiar tingle of anticipation.

She'd struck out twice. That didn't mean she had to stop playing, did it?

Kris was on his feet, heading in her direction. Soon he was beside her.

"Anyone sittin' here?" he asked, indicating the half-empty pew.

"No."

"Mind if I join you?"

"I think I'd like that."

They watched Bobby hurry down the aisle, Rocket beside him.

"He looks nervous," Kris remarked jauntily. "Poor sod."

"He probably is."

"Yeah, well, it's a big step."

"It certainly is."

"Have you ever taken it?"

"Once."

"Me, too. I'm divorced now."

"So am I."

Music began to play, indicating the arrival of the bride. Sara wore white and a big smile.

Bobby turned to look at her as she walked down the aisle. He thought she was the prettiest girl he'd ever seen.

"Romantic, huh?" whispered Kris.

Rafealla nodded. She was frightened to look him in the eye, because once she fell into those two intense pools of blue she might be lost forever.

Maybe she should risk it. What was that old superstition? Third time lucky, or something like that?

"Hey, Raf." He leaned toward her, speaking in a low, intimate voice.

"Yes."

"There's something I've bin meanin' to tell you."

"Yes?" she repeated.

Their eyes met, and it was memorable.

"Uh . . . I just want you to know this."

"What?"

"Did I ever mention that after I met you I gave up blondes forever?"

Gazing at him solemnly, she said, "No. You never told me that."

He winked. "It's true." And with perfect timing he took her hand in his, squeezing it gently. "C'mon, we'd better watch a wedding, see how it's done. It might come in useful one of these days." A cheeky grin. "Right?"

She grinned back. Kris Phoenix was an adventure waiting to be experienced, and this time she was old enough to enjoy it. "Right," she agreed.

"After all—" he began.

Catching his rhythm, she joined in, and together they completed his favorite expression: "It's only rock 'n roll!"